HOUSE

THE
HOUSE HUSBAND

THE HOUSE HUSBAND

Owen Whittaker

LONDON   NEW YORK   SYDNEY   TORONTO

This edition published 1999
by BCA
By arrangement with Orion Books Ltd

CN 7254

Typeset in Great Britain
by Deltatype Ltd, Birkenhead, Merseyside
Printed and bound in Great Britain by
Mackays of Chatham plc, Chatham, Kent

Acknowledgements

Firstly, thanks to the 'Big Feller', Jonathan Lloyd, for having enough faith in me to put his reputation behind the book, and to his assistant Sherif Mehmet for running around organising things on my behalf and not swearing at me when I telephone. Well, not very often. To Susan Lamb for having the taste and discernment to buy *The House Husband* and for responding so quickly and saving my fraying nerves. To Jane Wood, my editor, for all her help and her positive and gentle approach, and to Selina Walker for some very useful notes. To those three and to each and all at Orion Books a big thank you for supporting and working hard for me.

To my mum and dad for the early years. To Don and Janet for letting me Red Star the wife and kids over to them so I could get the damned manuscript finished, and to Caroline Sanderson for being positive about that first draft.

A special and sincere thank you to the good people of Clonakilty, West Cork, for making me feel very welcome, particularly those who tried to keep me sane as I wrote. So cheers to Ken and Kathleen for the rum and Coke, Jane and Mel for the Spanish red, Sarah and Stuart for the Rumptoff, John and Jennifer for the gin, and Jenny Mac for pouring anything alcoholic down my throat that stood still long enough. And *slàinte* to those too numerous to mention for the Murphy's. To Katharine Noren for locking me in the attic of her restaurant with my PC and a potty while I did the rewrites, feeding and watering me periodically and refusing to let me out except in times of crisis. Sometimes mine, sometimes hers.

To our adopted Irish family, the Helens, especially Betty and Doris, for nursing us through traumas with frozen pipes, septic tanks and, astonishingly enough, considering the rain, dry wells.

To the delightful and talented Marian Keyes for refusing to let me believe I would not sell this book, and equal thanks to her husband Tony Baines for all his help. A good lad, for a Watford supporter.

Lastly, the biggest thank you to my wife Lucinda for believing in me and not changing her mind through the leanest of lean years. For ignoring her own writing to look after our gruesome twosome while I scribbled. This meant I could write without my son bursting through the door dressed as Doctor Who and asking me to be a Cyberman, or working with my daughter on my lap, typing snmce9946nfdhwtgk-jahgty on my page and smearing my computer screen with chocolate mousse. And while we're on the subject ...

Finally ... yes, finally, all my love to my beloved children, my young son Harry, and his baby sister Isabella. Thanks for making *me* laugh.

1

'Thank you, New York! You've been a wonderful audience!' I'm announcing this as I leave the stage, having just played my last encore.

A girl has climbed up from amongst the vast crowd and has rushed at me. My minders are closing ranks around me, but it's all right, she's not carrying a gun. And she's still managed to sneak a hand through the crowd of bodies in front of me and grab my crotch.

'I love you!' she's screaming at me.

Someone's taken my guitar for me and I'm being swept past the crowd of well-wishers and liggers and into my dressing room.

Tonight's the night I've finally made it. I look at the sea of well-known faces in front of me, all offering their congratulations. Sir Paul McCartney, Stevie Wonder, Gloria Estefan, Björk, Sporty Spice and others too numerous to mention.

George Martin is whispering something in my ear about wanting to come out of retirement yet again and produce my next album, but I'm not concentrating. In the opposite corner of the room there is someone I've wanted to meet for a long time. She's smiling at me.

I've apologised to George and I'm crossing to her.

'Hi,' I'm saying.

'Hello. Good to meet you at last,' she's replying.

I can't believe it. I'm actually talking to Kate Bush. She looks as sexy and as beautiful as she used to on the poster above my bed.

'Car's ready, guv'nor,' someone's whispering in my ear.

I've grabbed Kate's hand and I'm dragging her behind me as we're ushered out of a back exit and into the rear of a waiting limousine.

'Sorry,' I'm apologising to Kate, 'I suppose this is a bit of a liberty. But I've always been such a fan of yours, I couldn't let you go now that I've met you.'

'That's okay,' she's saying to me, 'I'm glad we're alone.'

I've fantasised about this woman since I was eighteen.

I

She's just leant forward and pulled down the blind that shuts us off from the chauffeur.

I think I'm about to pass out from the excitement. Kate is unbuttoning her dress. She's looking directly into my eyes and she's saying . . .

'UGH! NO! I've just trodden in some poo-poo!'

Actually Kate Bush isn't saying this. My daughter is. She's in the garden somewhere, with her mother. I can't actually see them, they're too far away. But I can bloody hear them, all right! I knew I should have kept that window shut.

Another daydream ruined, a fantasy foiled.

I'm looking out of the window. There are about two acres of land in front of me, most of it consisting of field. Coarse, rough grass of a deep, lush green. Not much in the way of pristine turf, neatly number-one cropped and shaped to a perfect rectangle in this country. Houses built on land where a farmer's livestock used to chomp happily are much more the norm. Definitely ride-on-mower territory here, methinks. Except for us poor buggers who can't afford such luxuries. I'm one of the brave few who wrestle their knotty mass into submission with a knackered old petrol mower that conks out with nervous exhaustion every ten minutes.

Our fields slope downwards towards the road, on the other side of which is, you guessed it, another field. An ancient, ruined boreen nestles in one corner. A large gathering of motherly looking cows chew so lazily that half the grass falls back out of their mouths in soggy clumps, to be skidded in by some welly-booted farmer later in the day.

And at the bottom of that field sits the ocean. A vast, turbulent expanse of the Atlantic. It's late October, nineteen ninety . . . what is it? Ninety-six, and today, miraculously enough, the sun is shining. The ocean looks as blue and enticing as any in the world.

I'm supposed to be trying to write a song, here in my music room, in our house.

Well, that's a lie for a start.

It's the building society's house. We just plummet ever closer to bankruptcy trying to renovate the sodding thing, let alone trying to pay a mortgage, the size of which borders on the criminal.

Still. Cracking view. When the sun is out. Which is about ten times per year. The rest of the time the rain is sheeting down and visibility is restricted to about three feet. I have this horror that, after a massive downpour, the mists will clear and I'll discover I'm really living in the middle of the M1.

Odd that I have a feeling of space, because my music room is little more than a closet. It could only be regarded as spacious if it were a toilet. Once I'd filled it with my guitars, keyboard, amplifiers, desk and sofa-bed, movement became a bit of a problem.

I spend a lot of time looking out of this window, which has nothing to do with the view. Once I have a guitar in my hands, there's no bloody room to face any other way.

So I sit here, a sardine in a generously overfilled tin.

Yet I sense space.

Bit of a paradox, that, really ... Ooh, 'paradox'! That's a clever word. Must see if I can work it into one of my songs, establish a cult following: the thinking man's rock-and-roller.

Better fantasy: thinking woman's rock-and-roller.

I digress.

No, the feeling of space is one of the real bonuses of life since we moved here to West Cork, Ireland, a couple of years ago. It's a bit different from London.

No megastores, no decent bitter and no one rushing to keep appointments. Just small, friendly shops, rivers of stout and someone promising to turn up a week next Thursday, all being well.

Ah, but the space, the countryside, the ocean, all so inspiring! My writing must surely have become more prolific since I moved here. Songs materialising faster than Barbara Cartland novels?

No. Afraid not. Quite the opposite, actually.

But surely the people of West Cork, the population of the local town, are awash with friendliness and character. Each one of them with a fascinating tale to tell, true or otherwise. They must have provided a vaultful of material to write songs about.

I cannot argue. All the above is true.

Trouble is, I spend all my time in the pub getting langers (Cork for falling-over drunk) with them and enjoying their company so much I never seem quite able to drag myself back here to write.

As for the beauty of the place, green fields, blue sea, clean air ... I'm afraid it's seductively soporific. It lulls you into a dangerous and indigenous philosophy, which is ...

Feck it! I'll do it tomorrow.

And you know what they say about tomorrow and coming, don't you?

Out there in the garden, beyond the window, I can see two female figures, their little legs pumping away as they climb the sloping grass back to the house. The bigger of the two, although she does lean on the dwarfish side, is my wife Gina.

Driving, intelligent, independent Gina.

A zest for life that never lets her rest, from my experience. She's gorgeous! Shoulder-length blonde hair, high cheekbones, and a body one step further developed from puberty, even if she is thirty-plus. She has the sort of doleful eyes and petite body that make you want to protect her and shag her senseless at the same time.

Leading the charge is Sophie, our daughter, who's just turned four years old. Big blue eyes like her mother, long, flaxen, curly hair flopping around a face filled with mischief. A two-and-a-half-foot fireball of energy, coupled with an extraordinarily eccentric personality.

Nicola isn't with them. That's our other daughter: three months old and gluttony personified.

She who never sleeps.

In fact, I seem to be the only member of our family who isn't hyperactive. Well, somebody has proudly to wear the badge of sloth, if only to make the rest of the buggers look good.

They're wrestling now, Gina and Sophie, on the grass. They'll take ages to wend their way back. Gina's making the most of it before she returns to work.

Work.

Shit! I don't know.

Maybe I should write a song about mother and daughter, you know, that special bond.

Nah!

I can't write that. It'll come out all sickly and sentimental. Might as well write country-and-western if I'm going to start playing those kind of games.

Trouble is, it's hard to get motivated, because there's no recording contract.

It doesn't exist.

It nearly did.

Once.

4

Actually, two or three times.

But, at present, no one is paying me to write anything.

Don't give me all that artistic vocational bull – the propaganda that says money has nothing to do with the creative process. Whether I believe it or not it won't help me pay to fix the smell of damp that is, as we speak, making my nostrils itch.

You see, the problem is –

'Andy! There's been a disaster! It's desperate. The washing-machine is having a fit, so it is. There's water everywhere. Sorry, did I startle you?'

Perhaps it's the fact I'm clutching my heart that made her form that opinion. She did burst through the door like an SAS soldier who'd forgotten his balaclava and boot polish.

'It's all right, Noreen, I'm coming.'

I'm following her out of the door, through the lounge and into the kitchen.

Noreen.

Nanny.

No, that's a sort of exaggeration. She's in her early twenties and she's been with us for six months or so. Bit of cleaning, bit of cooking, bit of baby-minding.

A little treasure.

I'm paddling into the kitchen now.

'Bloody hell! You weren't kidding, were you?'

'No, I told you, didn't I?'

I'm staring at the washing-machine. 'What shall we do?'

'Why are you after asking me? I don't know,' she's replying nervously.

'What did you do to it, Noreen?'

'Nothing. I swear.'

It's like Niagara Falls. Water is spewing out all over Gina's precious newly laid quarry tiles. They're a disaster, you just can't keep them clean. Oh, well, they're getting a good wash down now, that's for sure.

'What if we turn off the water at the mains, Andy? Will that help?'

'Good thinking, Noreen.'

'Where's your stopcock?'

'What?'

'Your stopcock. The tap to turn the water off.'

'I don't fucking know! What are you asking me for?'

'Sorry, Andy. It's just in our house now, my dad would be the one who knows where it is.'

'Yes, I'm sure he would. I'm certain he tiled your bathroom, re-roofed your house and built a full set of walk-in fucking wardrobes too, but he's not here, is he? I am.'

She's silent, staring down at the paddling-pool with the feature terracotta base.

'Sorry, sorry, Noreen. I'm panicking. Don't take it personally. You know what a useless git I am when it comes to this sort of thing.'

Gina and Sophie have just walked through the back door and into the kitchen.

'Jeeze, what on earth has happened here?'

'Sorry, Gina. The washing-machine is after flooding the kitchen. I wasn't doing anything now, I swear. It just went.'

Gina has just turned off the washing-machine and unplugged it.

Brilliant. Why didn't I think of that?

'Andy. Where's the stopcock?' Gina's asking.

'I don't know! Why's everyone asking me, like it's some secret I've been entrusted with? I haven't got a clue.'

'Well, you should know!'

Oops, she's shouting at me now.

'Look at the water, Daddy. Whee!'

Sophie's kicking it up all up into the air, soaking the kitchen cupboards.

'Don't do that, Sophie. You'll make Mummy cross.'

'Why?'

'Andy.'

'Yes, Gina?'

'Don't just stand there like a wet fish. Phone a plumber.'

'Dad? Er ... Dad?'

'Yes, Sophie?'

'This is good stuff, you know.'

'What is?'

Sophie now has the washing-powder in her hands.

'It's tough on stains,' Sophie's telling me.

'Pardon?'

'And kind to deli*cad*s and colours.'

'Sophie, you're such a sucker for advertising.'

'Andy! Phone a bloody plumber!'

6

'Daddy? Shall we get our swimsuits on and have a splash?'

'Andy. Phone! Now!'

'Yes, yes. I'll use the one in the music room.'

'Dad? If I got my sandbox, we could have our very own beach, couldn't we?'

'Not a good idea, Sophie. Right, phone the plumber.'

Something's just caught my eye as I leave the kitchen: Nicola, my baby daughter. She's in her bouncy chair on top of the kitchen table surrounded by a mini-ocean. Marooned like Robinson Crusoe.

It's a good job Gina turned off the machine when she did. Much more water and Nicola could have floated away, bobbed right out of the fucking door and none of us would have even noticed.

I'm back in the music room. I've climbed over the amp to get to the desk where the phone is.

Quick flick through the *Golden Pages*. They may be yellow in England, but here they are golden.

I'm dialling ... no reply.

'Have you contacted anyone yet, Andy?'

Gina's peering through the door.

'There's no answer.'

'That's just typical. If we were in England we could just call Dyno-Rod. They'd have a squad of receptionists to take the call and someone here within twenty minutes. In Ireland they don't even *answer* the bloody phone for three days.'

'Relax, Gina. What does it matter if it takes a few days?'

'It matters because I've got three linen baskets full of dirty clothes upstairs. Try another number.'

I'm dialling the next one on the page.

'I dread to think what this will cost us,' Gina's saying as she shakes her head.

'Plumbers aren't that expensive, are they?'

'Andy! How can you say that after the amount they've charged us for working on this place?'

'Sorry, sorry. I'd forgotten.'

'Why doesn't that surprise me?' she's replies bitchily. 'I just hope we don't need a new machine. We just can't afford one.'

'We'll have to pick one up, second-hand.'

'Andy! The one we've got *is* second-hand and it's the third time it's gone wrong.'

'Well, how much is a new one?'

'About four hundred pounds.'

'How much? Strewth, that's a lot of money just to wash a few socks, isn't it?'

'Don't be ridiculous, Andy! There are four of us to wash clothes for, one of whom is a new baby. We need a machine we can rely on. Ooh! You're so irritating sometimes. You just don't think, do you?'

'All right, all right.'

She turns to close the door, then stops in afterthought. 'By the way, I've asked Noreen to babysit for us. We're going out tonight.'

'That'd be nice.'

'We need to talk, Andy.'

'Do we?'

'Yes. Now, keep trying until you find a plumber.'

She's gone.

I was wrong.

I don't think it will be nice to go out tonight.

I can't see 'nice' being on the agenda.

I've seen that look before, the one on Gina's face. Brow furrowed, eyes set.

That expression means trouble.

I can sense it.

Suddenly, the feeling of spaciousness has evaporated.

Why are we here?

For what reason?

What exactly is on the agenda for this hastily arranged meeting? And who in their right mind would choose an Irish pub in which to have a private conversation? We'll be lucky if it doesn't turn into a board meeting.

I'm thinking this as Gina stands at the bar. She's buying the drinks. A pint and a glass of Murphy's.

Here, as in all good pubs, the stout is left to stand for a few minutes then topped up, to ensure perfection. Usually, Gina returns to the table and continues our conversation while the Murphy's settles.

But not tonight.

Instead she is standing at the bar until our drinks are ready.

Why?

8

I presume it's basting time. Allowing me to fret. Stew in my own juices of uncertainty and suspicion.

I've suddenly noticed she's wearing sheer stockings. My eyes have wandered down from her bum, looking pert and gorgeous in a tight skirt, and I've realised she's wearing stockings. I should have sensed trouble. Nothing unusual in a woman wearing suspenders you might think, but this is West Cork. Here, apart from on special occasions, it's leggings, trousers, jeans or thick reinforced tights. The sort of hosiery most men feel should carry the word 'support' on their packaging. The point is, the only time I'm treated to a bit of nylon-inspired excitement these days, is when there's trouble afoot.

Then, at the end of the evening, after a massive tear-inducing, glass-breaking, soul-baring argument, there is sometimes a bout of frantic, passionate, over-excited and quick sex.

But only if I've given the right answers. If I fail, the suspender belt is tucked pointedly back in the drawer and we sleep with our backs to one another.

So, Regina, this is serious.

You want to win the day.

My wife's full name is Regina. Pronounced Ree-gee-na. At school, apparently, it was purposely mispronounced to rhyme with vagina.

Regina the Vagina, she was known as.

'I promise you, Andy, my nickname had nothing to do with me being promiscuous.'

Makes you wonder, though, doesn't it?

Andy, that's *my* name. Andy Lawrence.

Actually, it's an abbreviation because my full name is also a bit of an embarrassment. Having said that, I suppose I've half given it away now and, yes, all right, it's Andreas. Hideous.

My parents are not Greek. My mother says her love for things Grecian stems from having been besotted with Anthony Quinn's cinematic portrayal of Zorba. According to my father, it has more to do with a bottom-pinching waiter who became a little over-attentive whilst they were on honeymoon in Athens.

Either way it sucks.

He's a jazz musician, my father, and was probably too pissed or stoned to put up much resistance at the christening. Plus he may have figured that anyone going through life with a name like Andreas just had to be successful.

He was wrong. Well, so far anyway.

The fact that Gina and I had both shortened our Christian names to avoid flak was one of the things that drew us together in the early days.

She's walking back towards me now – Gina, that is, drinks in hand. Her stern face is still fixed in place. It's a professional expression. To help her survive as a journalist. It's the sort of environment in which you need to be able to look after yourself. Basically, confrontation usually makes her cry. Underneath the mask there lurks a complete softie.

We are in O'Leary's. It's an old pub, a muso's pub, slap in the centre of Ballinkilty, which is our nearest town. Instruments hang from the walls. Dusty pots and whiskey jars adorn the shelves. There's a folk club at the back. I play bass guitar there for a local band on Sunday nights. Tonight there's a group playing cover versions of sixties numbers. I can make out the vocals of the Beatles' 'Tell Me Why'. I'm thinking, how sodding appropriate, as Gina puts the drinks on the table.

'Well?' she's saying.

'Well what, sweetheart?'

'Andy. Have you any idea what I want to talk about?'

'No.'

'None at all?'

'No.'

At least I'm honest.

She's chewing her lip. Frustration, I presume.

'You must have some idea.'

'Must I? Why?'

'Come on, think for a change, Andy. This is important.'

Silence.

'Well, say something!'

'What? I'm thinking like you told me to! Look, can't you just tell me, Gina? You're making me a bag of bloody nerves.'

'I've tried raising the subject constantly since Nicola was born. You must have some clue.'

'I haven't.'

'Well, I've mentioned it often enough. You just chose not to listen, as usual.'

In fairness, she is probably right.

'Sorry. I didn't mean to ignore it. Whatever *it* is. But then, we have been married nine years. You are well aware by now that if you wish to make a point to me you do not spend weeks dropping subtle hints. YOU FLASH IT IN FRONT OF MY EYES IN BIG, HUGE FUCKING NEON LIGHTS! Otherwise it skims across the top of my head without penetrating the surface.'

'All right, keep your voice down. This is a private conversation, Andy.'

'I said you were making me nervous. I always shout when I'm tense.'

'Okay.'

She's beginning, pausing to take a sip from her glass.

'I'll tell you. Simply and plainly. Now, Andy darling, you've got to listen. Concentrate. I don't want you looking over my shoulder. I don't want you drifting off into your own space. Understand?'

'You've got me. What's up?'

'How much do you know about our financial situation?'

'Oh, God!'

I'm now diving for my pint. Our finances have a tendency to make me want to do that.

'Don't bring Him into it. He is not our accountant. Do you know the state of our finances or not?'

Shit. She's just produced a notepad from her handbag.

'Enough to know we're skint. That we shouldn't really be here drinking away the money for the phone bill.'

'Anything else?'

'Christmas is probably cancelled this year.'

'But you couldn't tell me facts and figures?'

'You know I couldn't.'

'I see.'

She's taking another sip. I'm taking a ruddy great gulp and signalling 'Same again' to the barman.

'Do you know why we are short of money?'

'Erm, there's the house for a start.'

'What about the house?'

'Gina! What is this? Sodding *Mastermind*? Your specialist subject "The Causes of the Lawrence Family's Poverty, 1987 to 1996"?'

She looks guilty and pained simultaneously.

'I'm not trying to be difficult, Andy, I promise you. I hate talking about this. It's just I need to know how aware you are yourself before I fill in the gaps.'

'Right. Fine.' I'm nodding as I light a cigarette. 'Let's start with the house. We can't afford it. It's like one of those eggs children make at Easter. Pretty on the outside, but its guts have been blown out. The estate agent's details said it needed work. Roughly translated that meant it needed condemning, putting out of its fucking misery. It was a case for euthanasia, Gina, not life support.'

'It was a sound investment at the time, Andy.'

'Was it really? Take our time. Do it slowly. That was the theory, wasn't it? We've done it slowly, all right. Two years, and by my reckoning there are just three rooms completed. Every time we attempt to start a new one we uncover another major problem.'

'Yes,' Gina agrees. 'However, the fact that your DIY skills are limited to putting up the odd shelf at a jaunty angle only for it to collapse three weeks later hasn't helped. I understand that plumbing and electrics are things that should be handled by trained professionals, but we have to pay to get somebody in to change a plug, Andy.'

'You're exaggerating a little, Gina,' I protest, mildly.

'Barely, darling. Come on, Andy, even you must admit you're useless.'

She teases me light-heartedly, trying to make me smile.

I say nothing, but begin my second pint.

'Okay,' she sighs. 'What else?'

Now I'm sighing. Another gulp of stout.

'We overspend. Fail to live within our means. I pop to the pub for too many swifties. You are prone to whipping out your credit card, purely on reflex, when you're within a hundred yards of a clothes shop.'

'What clothes shops? Tell me where they are because I can't find them. I hardly walk down Ballinkilty high street falling into shops stocking Versace, Donna Karan or Ben Di Lisi, do I?' she's snapping at me, defensively.

'True. But the one decent clothes shop in town has to restock after you've been in there. You come home loaded down with bags crying, "It's all right, Andy, I haven't paid for them. I only brought them home to try them on." Then three weeks later when you've worn them a couple of times and spilled red wine all over them we get a thumping great bloody bill . . .'

Gina is blushing. 'All right, accepted, but a woman has to have a new outfit occasionally. Anything else?' she's asking, changing the subject.

'How many more reasons do I have to give before you shout out, "Bingo"?'

Gina is shaking her head in despair. 'You're missing out the biggest single contributory factor, Andy. I'm trying to figure out whether or not you're doing it on purpose. I suspect not. Go on, darling. More.'

This could be a long night.

'Your change of job?'

'Not the factor I'm looking for, but you're right. What about my change of job?'

She's finally finished her first drink. Good. I'm just about to order my third and I had begun to feel like an alcoholic in comparison.

'We came to Ireland because you had the opportunity of a super job editing a new magazine. Ireland's answer to *Tatler*. It went arse up within six months. It didn't so much fold as implode. Unable to find anyone insane enough to buy our house and scarper back to London, you were forced to take the editorship of another magazine here. Infinitely inferior, with a salary drop to match. Ireland's answer to *Just 17*. All photo-stories and teenage angst. Although, this being a good Catholic country, the problem page is somewhat tamer, if not positively limp.'

She's smiling. 'Very accurately summed up.'

'Thank you. Can we talk about something else now?'

'No, we bloody can't!' she says, playfully slapping my arm.

I'm beginning to sulk.

'I'm fed up with this game, Gina. It's not fair. You know the rules and I don't. So can we cut to the chase, please? What *is* the missing link?'

I watch as Gina takes a deep breath, as if to give herself courage. '*You*! Andy Lawrence. *You*'re the missing link!'

'Gina . . .' I'm instinctively fumbling for another cigarette.

'Oh, now, surely I'm not after interrupting a lovers' tiff, am I? You two feckers are far too old for all that, so you are.'

Belly O'Hea.

That's all I need. Belly barging in, completely devoid of tact and sensitivity. An earthquake couldn't shift Belly O'Hea once he's got his backside sat down. Unless he'd a mind to go with the flow himself.

'Now, tell me something, Gina. You live with this feller, so you do. Have yer ever seen him without a drink in his hand, now be honest?'

Brilliant, Belly. Just fucking great.

'How are you, Belly?' she's asking.

'I'm grand altogether, but then when you're as handsome and talented as me, you're always fierce happy, isn't that right, Andy?'

'If you say so, Belly.'

Gina's somehow smiling and gritting her teeth at the same time. Any man in the world, other than Belly O'Hea, could read the words 'Piss Off' stamped all over her face.

He's an old rock-and-roller, is Belly. The wrong side of sixty years old, I would guess.

Big, fat and coarse. Huge fun, in small doses.

Very small doses.

He's the archetypal nearly-made-it man, but without the bitterness. Me, I'd be scared witless and would probably become very twisted indeed if I thought my career . . .

Oh, shit. He's sat down.

I'm torn. On the one hand, he could provide the perfect escape route. Then again, there's every chance Gina will just postpone the conversation and keep us awake talking until dawn.

What shall I do?

Sod it.

'Can I get you a drink, Belly?'

'No, yer fine. Work away yerselves. I've got to be off shortly. A bit of business.'

A glimmer of hope in Gina's eyes.

I wouldn't get excited if I was her. The last time he told me he was in a rush I didn't get rid of him for two hours.

'Now then, Andy. Are yer any nearer to superstardom than when I last gazed upon yer fascinating features?'

'Afraid not.'

'Are yer still playing with that bunch of losers?'

'I am.'

Two ex-members of my band left to form another about six months after I started playing with them. Belly wanted me to leave too. He manages Mix and Match, the breakaway group. I was tempted to leave, but there's not much to choose between the two bands. We're both naff.

'Would there not be any joy with those demo-tapes of yours?'

'Record companies are not exactly beating a path to my door, Belly.'

'You can't just send them into a slush pile, unsolicited. Am I not after telling you that for months?'

'Yes, Belly. You're an old hand at soliciting, are you?'

'What should Andy do, then?' Gina asks, surprisingly.

'He should find a manager with style, sophistication and, above all, contacts. But sure, he wouldn't be after recognising one even if he were sat right under his fecking nose, now would yer, Andy?'

Belly has put his face flush up to mine as he speaks.

'I take your point,' I'm replying, although his face is so close that by moving my mouth I'm in danger of kissing him.

'I tell yer what now, Andy,' he's saying, leaning back in his chair, thank God. 'Why don't yer give me those tapes of yours and I'll see if I can do anything with them?'

'How much is it going to cost me?'

'Ah, now, Andy. Do yer have to introduce so vulgar a subject as money into such an artistic discussion?'

'How much?'

'If you get some sort of deal, I'll take ten per cent. It'll be up to yerself if you decide to keep me on as yer manager or employ someone less gifted with a cockney accent. Fair enough?'

'I haven't got all the tapes. Most are languishing in record executives' wastepaper baskets.'

'How many of the feckers have yer got?'

'A few. Oh, go on, then. I'll drop them in to you over the next day or so.'

He's shaking my hand. 'Right I'm off.' He's spotted someone walking into the bar. 'Yer man's here. Another one of my satisfied clients.'

'With low expectations, Belly.'

It's Michael from Mix and Match.

Belly's gone without saying goodbye.

'Well, that's something, isn't it?' Gina's asking.

'Belly O'Hea? Managing my career? I can't see him playing Colonel Parker to my Elvis, can you?'

'No. I can't. However, he has given us further evidence as to the cause of our financial ruin.'

Oh, well, time to come clean. I confess I've known for some little time where this conversation was heading. I just don't handle guilt particularly well. I've squirmed on the end of Gina's line long enough. She's patiently reeled me in. I may as well hang my head shamefully and wait for the blow to put me out of my misery.

'What do you want me to say?' I ask slowly.

'I don't want you to say anything, Andy. I just want you to recognise it. Own up to the facts.'

Deep breath, Andy.

'Okay. Another reason we're so broke is because I haven't been very ... lucky. With my career, I mean.'

'And ...?'

'I haven't earned any money, really. None worth mentioning, anyway.'

'I'm not blaming you, darling, and I can't tell you how dreadful I feel raising it. But you've earned virtually nothing, Andy, for the nine years we've been married.'

'No. You're right. I haven't.'

Painful things, home truths.

'I go back to work next week. The magazine have been very good letting me have three months' maternity leave, considering the short time I've been there. I don't want to go back, Andy. I have a beautiful three-month-old daughter, whom I adore. Right now, I'd much rather stay at home and look after baby Nicola and Sophie. But I can't. You're unemployed, to all intents and purposes. If I don't work, we starve. That's it. Period.'

'Yes,' I agree, meekly.

She's running her hands through her hair. Tugging at it.

'What did you think would happen when I went back to work?'

'How do you mean?'

'The children. Concentrate on the children.'

'Oh, well ... I sort of presumed ...'

'What?'

It's an awful feeling, being asked a question and knowing you're going to give the wrong answer. Worse still, when you know your answer will make you look selfish, or stupid, or thoughtless.

Or all three.

'... that Noreen would, sort of, you know ... take over. Up her hours or something.'

16

Gina has reached for a cigarette. This must be serious: she only smokes when things are desperate.

'Andy, darling. I don't earn half the salary I used to. When Sophie was born it was different. We could afford help then. On top of which we were in England and my mother was around. Yes, I know that was one of the major reasons you were happy to move to Ireland. But just think how often she took Sophie off our hands for an hour or two. Free babysitting, remember? Andy, I adore you, but we are in serious shit. Noreen has got to go altogether. We have to economise if we're going to survive. Everything that costs money is under review. Including the one pound fifty you slip the young lad at the garage to wash the car, before bringing it home and claiming your back's in pieces from all that graft.'

How did she know about that?

'What will we do without Noreen? You're at work. Who's going to run the house? Look after the kids?'

She's shaking her head.

'Finish your drink, Andy. I'll get you another.'

'But . . .'

'Just finish it, okay.'

I'm doing as instructed.

Empty.

'Well? Who?'

She's staring at me, not speaking.

I'm looking at her and . . .

No!

A horrible thought is penetrating the mist in front of my eyes.

Does she mean . . .? No! It's almost too ludicrous to consider.

Yet . . .

No!

I haven't spoken. I don't have to.

'Yes, Andy, you're right. Who's going to look after our kids and the house while I'm out at work? *You* are.'

She's gone to the bar.

Again she waits for the Murphy's to settle. This time to allow the horror to seep into my 'impractical and totally aesthetic brain cells', as she calls them.

The ramifications are making me dizzy.

I am sitting here in pretty much the identical position she left me in.

17

My face is red, my jaw is dropped widely open and I'm sure my tongue is hanging out of my mouth. If I don't move soon someone will call an ambulance. I must look like I've just suffered a stroke.

Gina's back. She knows I'm in shock because there's a whiskey chaser to go with the Murphy's.

'Well, darling?' she's asking.

'Give us a chance, Gina.'

'A chance to what?'

'Think. You know, mull it over. Study the implications.'

'That's the whole point, Andy. You don't think, you *dream*. You spend your life away with the bloody fairies. Study all you like but I just can't see an alternative,' she says, despairingly.

'There must be some way round it.'

'Must there? I don't think so. Andy, darling, I love you with all my heart. I've been happy to support your dreams all the time I've been in the position to do so. But things have changed. I'm sorry. I just can't do it any more.'

'I'll get a job,' I say, with enough enthusiasm to try to buy me some time.

'Andy, my love, I hate to disillusion you, but even if U2's bass-player died tomorrow they're unlikely to ring you and beg you to replace him. You're not that lucky and we'd need a miracle of that sort of magnitude to make an immediate difference.'

'No,' say I, feigning hurt at being misconstrued, 'I mean a *proper* job.'

'Be serious, Andy. You tried that before, remember? In the early days. Brilliant at the interviews, sacked within three weeks of taking the bloody job. Besides, you're hardly going to be offered an executive job now, are you? You're thirty-seven. Too old to be a young high-flyer. Trust me, if we want to keep our family together this is the best option.'

'But, Gina, it just doesn't seem right somehow.'

As she's stubbing out her cigarette, her eyes are narrowing.

'Right? I'll tell you what's right, you whingeing bastard. There's no money to pay for any other fucker to do this. You have a duty to look after your two beautiful children. That's what's right.'

Anger.

It's been a long time since I last witnessed rage from Gina. Don't get me wrong. She's a forceful woman, for a half-pint, but usually she's controlled. She argues firmly, concisely, intelligently, and it's very effective. I admire her for it.

Gina can make the ridiculous sound perfectly plausible.

Like now.

'Andy, please don't think this is easy for me either. I could spend my days arranging afternoon teas with other stay-at-home mums. Good grief, the only deadline I'd have to worry about was whether I could finish the ironing before the baby woke up. Bliss!'

'Hold on a minute, Gina, you love your job. You've spent your life trying to claw your way to the top. You've always wanted the big career.'

Gina's eyes are beginning to fill with tears.

'I do . . . I mean I did, oh, I don't know. Being a mother . . . changes you. How you feel. I'm older now, not as ambitious as I once was. All I'm saying is we *both* have to make sacrifices here.'

'I suppose you're right.'

'You'll do it?'

'Do I have to wear an apron?'

'You can wear a French maid's outfit, if you like. I've no problem with cross-dressing as long as the kids are fed and the house is tidy.' Her face relaxes and she puts her hand on mine. 'However, I do insist you buy your own knickers. I don't want mine falling round my ankles half-way through an editorial meeting just because you've stretched them.'

Her eyes are kind, warm, as she squeezes my hand.

'We'll see how it goes, then, shall we?'

'Thanks, Andy. I know what I'm asking, but life's been cruel and there is just no other way.'

'Yeah,' I'm muttering, sadly.

'And I do love you very much. I'm so . . . sorry. Look, I'll get another round,' she says, before disappearing back to the bar.

They say when you leap off a tall building or something that your entire life flashes before your eyes in fast-forward. It feels a bit like that, only sort of . . . in reverse.

I see my dreams of EMI recording contracts, Wembley Stadium and under-age groupies fading to black. My chance of recognition as a songwriter of distinction, a bass-player of style and flair slipping through fingers greased with zinc and castor oil.

And into the foreground: sharp, focused, and boweltwitchingly clear, are scenes of domesticity, practicality . . . *femininity*. All played in slow motion, on the longest extended-play tape in the universe.

'Saints preserve us, would yer be after looking at that? Andy ol' son, yer have a face like a smacked arse. Why are yer so fierce feckin' miserable?'

It's Belly O'Hea.

'Don't tell me. That fine woman of yours has finally rejected yer blatant and clearly perverse sexual requests, so she has.'

'Something like that.'

'Well! I'm fecked if I'm going to sit around here trying to cheer you up. Yer clearly a lost cause. Don't forget to drop those tapes off, now.'

'If I have time.'

'Time is it now? Tell me, Andy. What the feck else have yer got to do with yer time?'

Good question.

I'm a bit confused, a bit steam-rollered.

It could be the drink, but I suspect not.

Have I got this wrong?

Would someone please tell me if I have?

Because the fact is, as I see it . . .

I have just agreed to become a House Husband.

2

Our Georgian slum is on the border of a village called Ardfield. Apart from the wildness of the countryside surroundings, the sounds differ from England too. The gentle, peaceful noises of birdsong and breezes playing with the leaves of oak trees are replaced by the never-quite-silent roar of nature's ceaseless battle with the elements. As for the air, it fills your lungs so fast here that it takes several weeks to stop gulping at it and allow it to pass through you at its own pace. A quite breathtakingly lovely area, populated by wonderful people.

Fact.

We live about four miles outside the town of Ballinkilty. You fall over it as you drive down the N71 from Cork City. The N71 is the major road in West Cork, although I use the term 'road' loosely. It's more a cross between a ploughed field and a rollercoaster track.

Ballinkilty is a picturesque town, painted in cheerful Mediterranean pastel colours. It reminds me of the man-made village of Portmeirion in Wales, the place used as the location for the sixties cult series *The Prisoner*. In fact, for the first three weeks I kept looking over my shoulder expecting to be chased down Pearse Street by one of those giant condoms that used to suffocate Patrick McGoohan on a weekly basis.

So Gina and I are back home now. Our home.

I'm in the kitchen, one of the rooms we've actually managed to complete, give or take a few finishing touches.

Like a cooker, for example.

We're saving up, in theory, for the obligatory Aga. In the meantime, we're making do with a microwave and a hob, run off a Calor gas bottle. You know the type. The sort that makes you update your will before lighting it with a match at arm's length.

Gina's in the lounge . . . I call it the lounge, Gina calls it the sitting room.

Tells you quite a bit, that does.

It's the second of the three rooms we have finished. All pinks and yellows and checked curtains. It's been finished less than three months and already the combined efforts of our two children are beginning to make it look seedy.

Deirdre has just entered the kitchen with Gina.

Noreen was too busy to babysit. Deirdre is our only back-up. If she can't do it, it's a takeaway and falling asleep in front of the telly. Deirdre is clearly pissed off that we returned an hour later than we promised. That's why I've stayed in the kitchen while Gina paid her off and apologised profusely.

I'm a coward, on top of all my other faults.

'All well, Deirdre?' Gina's asking.

'Grand,' she replies curtly.

'No trouble, were they?'

'No.'

'Do you want Andy to walk you home?' Gina is asking her.

'No, that won't be necessary at all.'

She lives two minutes away, if that.

'Well, thanks ever so much. We're very grateful, aren't we, Andy?'

'We are.'

'Take care and we'll see you soon,' Gina's shouting after her, as she scuttles out of the door and heads for home.

'Thanks for the back-up, Andy.'

'I was covering your rear.'

'Well, sweetheart,' she nibbles my ear, 'if you want to uncover it, you'd better fix us a nightcap while I check the kids.'

Gina goes upstairs to look at our daughters.

Both the kids were accidents. Holes in one. I confess I felt cheated. Selfishly, the idea of trying for a baby for six months or a year appealed to my libido enormously. I had always fantasised about Gina screaming, 'Now! It has got to be now!' and me unzipping my flies and saying, 'Not again, surely?'

But no, both children were great big 'whoops!', two glorious, adorable, lovable, compulsive boo-boos, the little shysters. Literally, the greatest mistakes of my life.

I've poured us both a Bailey's. Ice in Gina's, none in mine.

Gina has reappeared. She's wearing her towelling robe. I've taken a quick glance underneath. The stockings are still on.

She's taken the Bailey's from me and downed it in one. Then she's given me a big hug.

'I know how hard all this is for you, Andy. If there was any other way . . .'

'I know,' I say, returning her hug.

'You'd better lock up quickly. You don't want me to fall asleep on you, do you?' she's saying, smiling as she heads out of the room.

I've drunk the Bailey's and I'm turning the key in the door.

I don't know.

I feel a bit funny, actually.

As if . . . in some way . . . I just sold out.

It is now five thirty in the morning and I am freezing. Nicola, our baby, is lying on the floor at my feet. She is underneath what I believe is called a baby frame. A cheap, overpriced piece of plastic, from which hangs a mirror and a couple of rubber squeezy toys, in this case Pooh, Piglet and Eeyore.

She keeps screaming noisily. Not in pain or anger but in a I've-just-discovered-the-sound-of-my-own-voice kind of a way.

I'm cold because I'm naked.

I must have said the right things to Gina tonight because, after both of us had checked the sprogs once more, we were thrashing around the king-size with more enthusiasm and invention than I can remember in ages. At least, as far as Gina is concerned. I tend to be consistent in my zest for such matters. Gina is a different matter.

I hate the way sex can become a special treat, dished out for being a good boy. Mind you, better than a choccy drop.

And she kept her makeup on.

Now that *is* a rare privilege.

When we first met, we'd rip each other's clothes off morning, noon and night. Then we got married . . . then we had kids . . . then we ran out of money . . .

For some reason, all this seems to have affected Gina's libido.

I, on the other hand, see it as a reminder of why we put ourselves through all this.

Anyway, the nightmare scenario inevitably clicked in. As I'm thrusting my way towards crescendo, Nicola decides to join in the chorus from her cot in the room next door. Funny how the tiniest of murmurs from one so young can be heard above all the grunts and moans and cries that accompany intercourse. To be fair, I can't have been doing a bad job because Gina was pretending she hadn't heard it as well.

But young Nicola's stirrings began to increase in intensity. Consequently I was forced to double the tempo and race towards orgasm in order to avoid coitus interruptus. Three seconds after a copious climax on both our parts, Gina suddenly decides she can hear little Nicola now and, rather breathlessly, says, 'Baby's awake.' She says this in a way that implies, 'You've had your oats. Now get your arse out of bed and feed the baby for a sodding change.'

I may not exactly have earned the title 'new man', but I have *occasionally* dragged my carcass out of bed at silly hours of the morning with both our kids. So I am perfectly capable of staggering down the stairs, retrieving a bottle of baby milk from the fridge, warming it in the microwave and, nine times out of ten at least, shoving the teat in the right hole. But it's now gone five and I'm hung over, my legs are still jelly-like from the shock and pleasure of a violent climax and I am shivering. I did not have time to slip on a dressing-gown and Nicola, whilst happy to giggle at me as long as I am hovering over her, insists on screaming as if I am pulling out her toe-nails with her mother's tweezers every time I try to sneak up the stairs to grab some protective clothing.

So I'm now debating whether or not to put the heating on.

Trouble is, our system was bought second-hand from a chap called Noah and ripped out from a sort of overgrown houseboat. If I take the brave decision to flick the thermostatic control to ON, this will result in a sort of whirring noise, followed by several loud clunks. After that, as the pipes get used to the oil circulating through them, we get a sort of Shostakovian symphony played on bass pan-pipes and didgeridoos, which continues for about an hour.

I could light a fire, but I'm a lazy son-of-a-bitch who can't be fagged with all that faffing around. Also, my fires flatter to deceive. They flare up dramatically, due to excessive use of firelighters, then disappear into a blanket of black and acrid smoke the minute I wave a few lumps of coal in their general direction.

Speaking of coal, that's another reason not to attack the grate. It's kept outside – the coal, I mean. I would have to venture into the night air to retrieve it, the baby would scream for the welfare department on grounds of desertion and I would have died of frostbite before I'd even begun my new career. Can you die of frostbite? I suppose, if enough bits of you drop off, you can.

There. I said it. Thought it, actually.

My New Career.

Hardly that, more a sort of legalised and politically correct form of castration.

Oh dear. Gina will be awake in a couple of hours and she will want to discuss detail. She likes pinning things down, does Gina. She claims not. She says she has to work her socks off to keep me sharp and give me some sort of focus, because of the blurred, soft-edged, gel-over-the-lens way I look at life, or something.

Gina is a born leader. In the Great War, she would have been the sort of officer to lead from the front, climbing out of the trenches, charging up over the top calling, 'Come on, men, let's sort these buggers out!' whereas I would be ferreting around in the mud trying to find where I'd put my rifle and helmet shouting, 'Two secs, be with you in a minute, loves!'

A marriage of opposites. She needs me to calm her down, stop her burning herself out. I need her to kick my arse into gear.

A couple of hours. Not very long to come up with a strong argument against role-reversal.

Maybe, under the circumstances, there isn't one.

It is now 5.49 a.m. and I'm about to creep up the stairs with a sleeping baby. I watched carefully for the signs. A yawn, a rub of the eyes and I pounced mercilessly. One daughter swept off the floor, one soother slipped into a still vaguely protesting little mouth, then much cradling in arms and tummy-rubbing until Nicola finally decided to give in gracefully.

I can never remember which stairs creak. There's one near the bottom and I think I've avoided that and there's another near the top somewhere . . . Shit! That's the one. Phew! Got away with it. I left the nursery door open wide enough to get through as that creaks as well. One baby flung as gracefully as I can manage into her cot, one toy giraffe placed in little arms, one duvet tucked into sides of cot, one father now exiting as fast as he can before the little swine changes her mind. YES, SUCCESS!

'Good morning, Daddy.'

'ssssSH! Sophie, what are you doing awake? It's the middle of the ruddy night.'

My four-year-old raises her hands, palms up, in a way that almost makes her look middle-aged.

'It feels like morning to me, Daddy,' she says, sighing.

There is no more deflating feeling in the whole world than getting one child off to bed, only to be greeted on the landing by the other.

'Daddy ...'

'Ssssh. I've just got the baby off.'

'Dad ...' she begins, just as loudly as before.

Why do four-year-olds find it physically impossible to whisper, for crying out loud? They can certainly shout and scream loud enough to waken Rip Van Winkle.

'Dad, let's have a cuddle on the sofa and watch cartoons,' Sophie suggests, as she clumps her way down the stairs like a pocket storm-trooper.

I follow her down and switch on the television. For some reason it's stuck on some German-language station, selling the latest rip-off for tightening your abdominal muscles. I flick through the satellite channels until I see the familiar face of Scooby-Doo and sit next to Sophie resignedly.

'We've seen this one dozens of times,' I tell her. 'Shall I see if I can find something else?'

'*No*! It's okay. Dad?'

'Yes, daughter.'

'You used to watch Scooby-Doo when you were a little boy, didn't you?'

'Yes, Sophie.'

'Dad?'

'Yes, Sophie?'

'Was I there?'

'No, of course not.'

'I was, you know,' she says, winking, as if she's just let me in on a secret.

'How could you have been, Sophie? I hadn't even met Mummy yet.'

'Ah, but you see, Dad,' she begins, in a slightly patronising tone, 'I was behind you.'

'Oh, well, that explains it,' I reply, too tired to argue.

'That's why you couldn't see me,' Sophie explains.

'I wondered why.'

'Dad?'

'Yes, daughter?'

'Dad, usually, Dad . . .'

'Yes.'

'You see, Dad, usually, you see, I have my breakfast when Scooby-Doo's on.'

'What? Even if it's lunchtime?' I argue facetiously, trying to stall.

'Don't be silly, Daddy,' Sophie replies seriously.

'Right. Okay, what do you want?'

'Er . . . er . . .'

'Yes?' I wait, as her eyebrows knit together in thought.

'Not Coco-Pops.'

'Right.'

'Not Weetos.'

'Okay.'

'Not water biscuits.'

'Fine.'

'Not fruit.'

'Yes, look, Sophie, we've established what you *don't* want, how about a little clue as to what exactly may tickle your taste buds?'

Damn. I was a little short-tempered there. I didn't mean to be, but I'm tired and cold and there's an African rhythm section playing in my head and . . . oh, I don't know. How does Gina cope with all this? Perhaps, and more poignantly, this will be a compulsory and regular part of my new job spec. If so, how the hell am I going to deal with it?

'Toast.'

'Pardon?'

'Toast, Daddy.'

'Sorry, you lost me there for a minute.'

'TOAST!' she screams.

'Toast, right, yeah, breakfast, I'm with you.'

'Dad?'

'Yes, gotcha, toast. Just as it comes or . . .'

'Er . . . not jam . . .'

'Don't start that again. Do you want anything on it or not?' Short-tempered again.

'Marmite.'

'I see. Well, I'll do my best.'

'Daddy,' Sophie sighs, and raises her hands again, 'it's easy. You just cook the toast and spread the Marmite on it.'

'On top of the butter. Yep, I'm sure I can manage that.'

'*No*! Yuck! No butter.'

'Why?'

'I hate butter,' she states, screwing her face into a ball to emphasise the point.

'You have to have butter, Sophie.'

'Why, Daddy?'

'It's good for you.'

'Yuck!'

'Well, it helps the Marmite stick to the toast.'

'You just put the bread in the toaster thingy and spread the Marmite . . .'

'Well, if you're so clever, little madam, you make the breakfast!'

'Dad.'

'What?'

'It's freezing.'

'I know.'

'Can we have the heating on, Dad?'

'What? Yes, I suppose so. Stop changing the subject.'

'Dad?'

'Yes, Sophie?'

'Why have you got no clothes on?'

'Sorry? Oh! Er . . . Well, you see . . . Crikey, I don't know, ask your mother!'

'Ask me what?'

As if by magic, like the cavalry appearing over the hill, Mummy is there. Resplendent in bright blue towelling robe and red bedsocks.

'You're up early, Gina.'

'I know.' She kisses me. 'I couldn't sleep. I've been thinking.'

Oh, fuck. That spells more trouble.

'Mum?' interrupts first-born.

'Yes, Sophie, darling?'

'Er . . . Mummy?'

'Yes, sweetheart,' Gina replies, with sickening and enviable patience.

'Er . . . Mum, why is Daddy not wearing any clothes?'

'Well, you see, it's all baby Nicola's fault,' Gina replies smoothly.

'That dratted baby,' says Sophie, smiling, shaking her head knowingly, completely satisfied with the flimsiest of explanations.

Brilliant. Why didn't I think of that?

'What time did Baby go back to sleep?' Gina asks me.

'Half an hour ago.'

'Did she have her bottle?'

'Yep.'

'Did you change her nappy?'

'Er . . . no.'

'Oh, Andy Lawrence!' she chides me affectionately.

'Sorry.'

'Why didn't you?'

'I forgot?'

'Try again,' she suggests, folding her arms.

'Gina, you know I've got a weak stomach. I can't help it. I get instantaneously nauseous.'

'Well, you're going to have to get used to it, in the light of our little conversation last night,' she whispers.

Bugger! She hasn't forgotten, then.

She sweeps Sophie off the floor and hugs her. 'What are we having for breakfast then, Sophie?'

'Toast and Marmite, Mummy.'

'Coming right up, angel,' Gina says, putting Sophie down and heading for the kitchen.

'Mum?' Sophie choruses, before Gina can get there.

'Yes, Sophie?'

'Mum . . . Mummy, you said Daddy was going to be looking after me and he can't even make Mummy's Special Toast!'

'Don't worry. Mummy will just have to show Daddy *how* to make it, sweetheart.'

As my wife leaves the room, I'm left feeling outraged that she has discussed this with our four-year-old child before she'd even finished closing the deal on me.

3

10.00 p.m. Sunday night.

I'm in O'Leary's with Connor. He is probably the best friend I have here. He's also my drinking partner.

I've spent the day trailing Gina around the house, like the Sorcerer's Apprentice receiving exact instructions from his master. I never realised what a little miracle-worker Gina is. Well, apparently from now on, the loaves-and-fishes routine is down to me. She's even written things down, compiling them into a sort of House Husband's Manual.

God, I needed a drink.

Connor and I were in the folk club at the back of the pub listening to some has-been, but it was miserable. Four hours of articulate explanation before each song and when he finally sang the bloody thing he mumbled it out of tune so you couldn't hear the words anyway.

We left to move to the front bar and ever since I've been bending Connor's ear about my sorry state of affairs.

He's at the bar getting in a round. He's chatting to some young girl. They all adore our Connor. Women, that is. His wife died in a freak car accident a year or so before Gina and I came to West Cork. He still hasn't recovered from her loss.

Michelle, Gina's best friend here in West Cork, is determined to find him a new woman. She seems to have a production line of no-hopers, which she trots out at her dinner parties at regular intervals. They usually last no longer than a date or two. They exit screaming that they cannot compete with the memory of Connor's dead wife.

Maybe that's what attracts the ladies to him: the air of unavailability. Extremely tall, with Liam Neeson-type looks, all soft blue eyes and rippling muscles. Plus a lilting baritone voice of the liquid honey variety. If his hair wasn't thinning I think I'd be seriously jealous.

'There you have it, Andy,' he's saying, as he places the Murphy's on the table.

'Who was she?'

'Just a friend.'

'Pretty girl.'

'She's very young now, Andy.'

'So?'

'You can't trifle with their affections. She'd start expecting things I'm in no position to be after delivering.'

'You're such a basket case, Connor.'

'How can you say that, when I've spent all night sympathising with you? You're suicidal over the pettiest of problems.'

'Petty! Excuse me, but it's not you who's being emasculated.'

'Calm down now, Andy. You were saying you told Gina you'd get a proper job, but your track record in that department is not good, is that right?'

'To put it mildly,' I confess, as I grasp my pint.

He's shaking his head. 'You really are a useless article, aren't you? What about your musical talent? Is there not some downmarket use to which you could put those skills to earn a punt or two?'

I'm gulping more stout before my next confession.

'I've tried that. I played "mood music" as part of a trio in a hotel bar managed by a closet gay. Drove me up the fucking wall. I mean, how many times can you play "The Girl From Ipanema" without screaming for mercy? I got the sack from there as well.'

'What did you do?'

'I dedicated a tune to the manager on his birthday.'

'What tune was that, exactly now?'

'"Nobody Loves A Fairy When She's Forty".'

He's laughing.

'You're a terrible feller, Andy Lawrence. No wonder you've driven that poor woman of yours to distraction.'

'I know.' I'm sighing in agreement. 'What do I do, Connor?'

'Andy, you're feeling victimised at the moment, but you have to see it from Gina's point of view, now. The poor woman loves you and, if that's not a big enough cross to bear, she's after having to keep you as well. This she has steadfastly done for nine years without complaint. But money, or the lack of it, has reared its ugly head and belts have to be tightened. Be fair now. You have a beautiful wife and she's given

31

you two lovely children. It won't kill you to look after them for a bit until things get better. Give Gina a break, help her out here. She deserves it, doesn't she?'

'I suppose you're right. Listen, speaking of Gina, can you spin her to and from Cork City? We've only the one car and I need it, to chauffeur the kids, apparently.'

'Of course,' he's replying, before draining his pint glass. 'I could do with the company. Anything to keep me from falling asleep behind the wheel.'

I'd like to think he was joking. But he drinks quite a bit, does Connor. Has done ever since the fateful day.

'Thanks. I'm very grateful.'

'Right, I'll buy the poor condemned fecker a large whiskey to go with his pint.'

Connor's back at the bar. The young girl's hands are moving all over him like an airport security guard checking for weapons. And he just looks as if he can't get away from her quickly enough.

Monday, 11.30 p.m. I'm in the kitchen, finishing a ciggie.

Today has been a horrible day. I've always hated Mondays, probably because they herald the beginning of the week and, therefore, you have to let the real world back into your life, no matter how much you try to avoid it.

This has been a particularly crappy Monday by anyone's standards.

We had to fire the staff today. Hark at me sounding like something out of *Upstairs, Downstairs*. What I meant was, today was the day we had to tell Noreen that her services were no longer required.

So, democratically, Gina and I discussed the best way to handle this. Then, scientifically, we tossed a coin to see which poor sod had to do the dirty work.

I lost the toss.

I told you I was unlucky.

Truth is, if it were a decision purely based on Noreen's abilities as a cleaner, neither of us would have minded telling her to sling her proverbial hook. In that department, she is far from thorough. It has never occurred to Noreen, for instance, to go as far as moving the furniture in order to Hoover underneath it. Why bother when you can dance the vacuum gleefully around it? Consequently, when my wife decided to shuffle the furniture around the lounge a bit to ring the changes, we got a nasty shock. All manner of nasties lay in wait. Ageing sticky sweets, Coco-Pops, mouldy squashed banana and enough dust to allow allergy experts a field trip to study the natural habitats of house-dust mites.

But, of course, it's not that simple.

Overall, Noreen is a sweetheart. Kind, helpful, easy-going, eager to please, witty, unimposing, and very, very likeable. More of a friend, really. Both the kids love her too, and she's very good with them.

As I explained the situation to Noreen. I was grateful that Sophie was at playschool.

She started crying on me. Genuine tears of loss and sadness. I explain the reasons for her dismissal truthfully and she nods and says she understands and says she thinks it's very sad but not to worry . . . and I couldn't believe I was doing this. I'm rationally telling Noreen the reasons why I am giving up my dreams and committing professional and social suicide and why this affects her . . . and she's crying and I'm feeling a complete and utter bastard . . . and I'm also looking at this treasure of a girl and I suddenly think I must be well and truly off my fucking rocker!

Why? Why? Why?

Then Gina, who has been listening from behind the other side of the lounge door, finds this is all too much for her and bursts into the kitchen.

So now there are two of them in tears.

I left them opening a bottle of wine while I went to pick up Sophie from playschool, and by the time we got back, that had been drunk and severe headway had been made into a very nice Australian Shiraz I'd been saving for a special occasion.

Sophie wanted to know why everyone was crying, and when we told her it was Noreen's last day . . . you guessed it, she immediately joined the water-works club.

My kitchen resembled the venue for a small-scale wake.

Sophie now definitely sees Noreen's departure as my fault and subsequently made it clear I was not her favourite person for the rest of the day, refusing to speak to me apart from the occasional news bulletin.

Example: 'I'm going up to my room, Daddy, to play by my *own*', or 'Daddy, I need to go for a wee-wee. If Mummy needs me, that's where I am.'

So tomorrow I'm looking after a four-year-old who sees me as the moral equivalent to Stalin.

The rest of the day was spent being brainwashed by Gina in the Dos and Don'ts of House Husbandry.

Every hour on the hour there was another A4 page of notes and instructions, advice and handy hints, descriptions and diagrams, until it began to resemble an unbound car-owner's manual.

It was also about as indecipherable as the aforementioned. It was full of mother-and-baby speak, and as jargon-loaded as any other self-help book, about as clear as the average MFI instruction leaflet.

Apparently, a soother is a dummy is a suckie is a yum-yum. Ruskie-Puskie is not a nickname for a tramp from Moscow, but a type of cereal biscuit, made by Farley's. If I ask my baby daughter if she would like a jig-jig, it is not a reason to send a swat-squad from the social services crashing in through the windows. Apparently I am merely enquiring whether or not she feels inclined to go in her baby-bouncer.

By the end of the day, I was just nodding and smiling. It was all too much. If the theory class was this hard, fuck knows what the practical will be like.

Then, just to round off a perfect day nicely, I came downstairs after reading Sophie a bedtime story to find Gina in floods of tears.

She was curled foetus-like on the sofa. If it wasn't for the fact she was hugging a precariously balanced glass of gin to her bosom, I would have sworn Sophie had sneaked back into the lounge ahead of me.

'What's the matter, Gina?'

'Nothing,' she sobbed, 'I'm fine.'

One of her contradictory little idiosyncrasies. It's like interpreting a foreign language. Roughly translated, 'I'm fine', means, 'I'm a fucking mess'.

'You sure?' I prompt.

'Yes. No!'

More tears and I immediately joined her on the sofa and gave her a cuddle.

'Want to tell me about it?'

'Oh, I don't know, Andy. Maybe we made a horrible mistake coming to Ireland. Let's face it, it's been one long bloody disaster since we arrived here.'

'It's not been all bad,' I countered, genuinely.

'You didn't even want to leave London. I made you leave your career behind, and all because I wanted that stupid, stupid job.'

'Sssh, it's okay. There wasn't much of a career to desert, Gina. Anyway, I like it here. I sort of feel I fit in.'

'That's beside the point. I dragged you here under protest for a stupid job and now ... I DON'T WANT TO WORK!' she screamed, suddenly. 'Even if it was my all-singing, all-dancing, all-prestige old job. I wouldn't want to leave my babies,' she said, as the corners of her mouth slowly turned downwards and the sobs returned once more.

I didn't know what to say, really. I could hardly tell her I didn't want her to go back to work either, so what the fuck was this all about, and how the hell did she think *I* was feeling about this arrangement, could I?

'I'm sorry, Andy. I really wish things were different. I don't want you to have to be a house husband, for pity's sake! I feel so horribly guilty.'

Howls of hysteria.

'No, Gina, no. it's not your fault,' I said, but I'm not sure she heard me. I'm not even sure I meant it. Maybe there is a small, selfish part of me that does blame Gina for my fate. But that's probably because it's too painful to face up to my own shortcomings.

That is why I am still wide awake while Gina snores in the slumber of the emotionally drained.

I am so wound up.

Tense? When I walk you can hear my joints squeaking. My vertebrae have fused from the back of my head to my waist so that when I move I look as if I'm giving a very bad impression of Captain Scarlet.

I need some help to calm down.

Time to raid the tea-pot with the handle missing and switch on the telly.

It is now 12.10 a.m. on Tuesday morning and the highlight of the day is already over. This, of course, is the ten minutes of free, tacky, titillating filth that the Fantasy Channel on the satellite system spews out before they scramble the signal. Little clips of the day's viewing are interspersed by a usually less than attractive girl, almost always with a flat, uninspiring cockney accent telling you what hot, hot, hot action they have, if you'd only get out your credit card and cough up for it.

On one of the other rare occasions I nobly brought Nicola down for a night-time feed, I was fortunate to witness the one occasion when, for some reason, they omitted to scramble the signal.

I say rare, because for the last six months I've been waiting for them to do it again and they haven't.

It was a major disappointment, anyway. Mostly glossy striptease, followed by the occasional shot of two over made-up hags, chewing on each other's nipples.

Mind you, on that one occasion, Nicola went back to bed at ten past one and I had to pretend she'd been a little bugger in order to explain to Gina why I didn't come back to bed until half past four.

Well, I had to see if it got any better.

I'm still staring at the scrambled screen. I can vaguely hear the sounds of faked orgasm through the airwaves but I'm not concentrating properly because I've raided the tea-pot with the missing handle. This does not mean that I have stolen the electricity money, but rather that I have indulged in the traditional vice of musos everywhere.

I've had a little smoke. Not as in Benson and Hedges, as in joint – but not as in roast beef.

I'm much more relaxed now. Much more in touch with who I am.

I'm Andy Lawrence. I'm thirty-seven. I'm tallish, brightish, and while I may not give Jon Bon Jovi sleepless nights, I'm reasonably good-looking. I clean up well. I'm popular enough with the ladies. I must be. You do not land a woman as gorgeous as Gina unless you have something.

Gina. Youthful-looking, slender, are-you-sure-she's-had-two-kids? Gina.

I love her. So very much.

Nobody knows me as well as Gina. No one understands me better. I've never let anyone as close as she.

It bothers me that I may have let her down. I'm useless when it comes to reality. I can't cope with bills, with DIY, with illness, *et al*.

Am I a good father? I ask myself.

Probably. I'm here, for a start. I mean, apart from when I'm rehearsing with the band or gigging, which isn't that often, or in my den writing songs, or down the pub, basically I'm here all the time, really. I'm not disappearing before they get up and coming home ten minutes before they're tucked up in bed. I give them constant attention, total love. Sophie never goes short of a story or a wrestle. Nicola gets regular raspberries blown on her tummy to make her laugh, and silly songs sung to her in front of the mirror to calm her down.

All right, I don't change nappies that often, or feed, or clothe, or bathe or – oh, shit! Now I'm saying this I'm thinking, What the bloody hell *do* you do, you useless great prat? I suppose most of it comes under the heading 'entertainment', instead of 'practical'.

Gina's right.

Financially, we have no choice.

I have no choice.

I love my wife, I worship my kids, it's just, phew, twenty-four hours a day and all that that entails.

Am I up to this?

I honestly don't know.

It's 1.30 a.m. and I can't believe what I'm doing now.

I'm cuddling my bass guitar. Yep, embracing it, like an old, familiar, if somewhat frigid, lover. What a sad bastard I am. Get a grip, Andy. You're not on Death Row, for crying out loud. You love your kids, and all you're being asked to do is look after them.

So why do I keep thinking end-of-an-era type thoughts?

I'm still going to play with my band, aren't I? Will I really metamorphose into another personality just because tomorrow I'm going to cook bangers and mash and wipe my baby's arse?

Why, then, am I lying on my sofa with my arms wrapped around a piece of metal with four strings? Am I touching my instrument for luck? Or am I saying goodbye?

I'd better call it a night before I start making impossible-to-keep pacts with the devil. You know ... like, if you send Mary Poppins floating down on her umbrella tomorrow morning then I'll give up fags, or booze or sex, or my complete collection of Tintin memorabilia.

What happened to our dreams? Not just mine, but Gina's too. We dreamt like men in the desert. We saw our oasis, clear as day. The water blue, the fruit lush and golden. Then, when we reached out to grasp it with our hands, it fizzled and blurred and disappeared.

If we could all see our futures I'm convinced the queue to leap from

Beachy Head would stretch for miles. A little man in a uniform, saying, 'Sorry, guv, no more today, you'll 'ave to come back and chuck yerself orff, tomorrah.'

'But ... but ... but ...' I'd protest.

'No, mate, I'm sorry. Listen, pal, it wouldn't be werf doing today. There's so many bodies over that cliff you'd only fall four foot before you landed on top of 'em.'

How did it all go wrong? What caused the transition from Andy Lawrence, brilliant bass-player, talented vocalist, writer of definitive rock songs and just waiting for that lucky break, to Andy Lawrence, the little woman at home? He who does.

I'm trying to think how it all began ...

4

I first met Gina when her boyfriend – I understate – her *fiancé*, brought her round to my flat at 11.30 p.m. one summer's night.

Must be nine years or so ago.

Her intended was called Max and he was a talent scout, an A&R man for a major record label. I was playing in a band called Don't Ask and we were hot. People were talking deals, and Max was at the head of the queue.

Having said that, I was not expecting him to turn up at my flat with a woman in tow. Consequently, I opened the door wearing my Tintin T-shirt and a pair of Rupert Bear boxer shorts, given to me by a previous girlfriend. This was not the outfit in which I would have chosen to meet the man who held my future in his grubby hands *or* the most beautiful woman I had ever seen. At the very least it lacked maturity, and that's disregarding the fact that the two garments clashed, dramatically.

Gina looked just sensational: wearing a simple (yet obviously designer) white dress, she looked a ringer for a young Mia Farrow. I instantly wanted her to adopt me.

She stood in my doorway smiling and I was transfixed. So much so that I didn't even notice Max was there until he sang out, 'Hi yuh, Andy!'

'Hello, Max.'

'Listen, man. This is a bit awkward, yuh, but is Arnold in?'

'No, he isn't. If it's him you've come to see, you're out of luck. He's spending the next couple of days with his girlfriend.'

'Phew, yuh! That's a relief, isn't it, babe?' he said to Gina, patting her on the buttocks.

I watched her grimace.

'Is it?' I asked.

'Is it what, man?' Max replied.

'A relief?'

'Is what a relief, man?'

'I don't know, Max. You started this conversation. Something about Arnold?'

'Oh, yeah, right. Arnie baby! Right. Listen, Andy, this is a bit . . . uh . . . well, you know, like . . . yuh, yuh . . . listen, Andy, can we come in for a minute?' Max requested.

This was a man who might be about to offer me a recording contract. Of course he could come in.

Just as well I thought that way, as he had walked through me, dragging Gina with him, before I could reply.

'Take a seat, angel face,' he said to Gina, who reclined stylishly on my MFI sofa. 'That's it, babe, mellow out while I put my man here in the picture, in the frame. You take a seat as well, Andy.'

'Thanks,' I replied.

He began to walk backwards and forwards, shakily. Arms extended, he paused occasionally to steady himself, a little fear in his eyes, like a tightrope walker about to sneeze.

The man was very, very pissed. Or stoned. Or tripping. Or all three.

Gina, on the other hand, seemed perfectly sober.

'Right, yuh, now, the thing is right, you know . . . it's like . . . kinda . . . yuh, yuh . . . where was I?'

I looked at Gina and she smiled and shrugged her shoulders.

'Something about "Arnie baby"?' I suggested.

'Right, yeah, right, that's it, good old Arnold, right.'

Long pause.

'What about Arnold, Max?'

'What?'

'Arnold? What about him?'

'Arnold, right. Yuh, bit of a problem there.'

'Is there?'

'Yup, yup, 'fraid so. Sorry and all that, man. But, hey! That's life, man, you know, these things are . . . phew, wow, you know . . . it's just . . . yuh, yuh, yuh . . .'

'Has this got something to do with the recording contract, Max?' I enquired, trying to cut a few corners.

'Right, yuh, absolutely, you've pinned it . . . you know . . . hit that ol' nail . . . got it in one, man.'

Gina was beginning to shift uncomfortably on the sofa. This could have been due to Max's drunken ramblings or the fact that my MFI sofa was so hard. It would turn the average-sized bottom completely numb within fifteen minutes. Either way, it drew attention to her perfect legs, so that even I began to lose concentration.

'Yuh, that's the way the . . . you know, crumbles, an' all that jazz.'

'Max,' I said, tearing my eyeline away from Gina's thighs, 'is there a problem with the contract offer?'

'No, man, it's solid, you know, and I mean, it's a cool offer, it's going to be big. But, you know, speaking of big, it's . . . uh, you see . . . Arnold, no. I mean, like, no way, José. *Comprende*?'

Eventually my brain made a rough, if relatively accurate, translation. 'Are you saying the record company want Arnold out?'

'Uh . . . yuh.'

'Why?'

'Oh, right, well . . . huh, what can I . . . you know how it is, Andy . . . it's, well . . . he's so *pig ugly* man!'

Poor guy.

Hard to picture a rock star called Arnold, I know. Max had a point. His skin was the consistency of a recently deflated balloon and he had a beer belly that prevented him from getting within three feet of the microphone. In short, he had all the sex appeal of a freshly dug whelk. But he could play guitar and his lyrics were sharp and incisive. He was also my friend and my flatmate.

'Fucking hell, Max!'

'I know, man, yuh, yuh, I know. Heavy number. But the contracts can be drawn up next week, you know. And, hey, we know just the guy to replace Arnie. He's playing in a real shit band, you know, but he's got real talent and, man, is he sexy. Whoah! He's a great guy, Andy, we just know you're going to like . . . love him, right?'

I glanced at Gina. Her face was red with embarrassment.

'Max, I don't know about this. Arnold is not a handsome boy, I admit. But he's good. Very good.'

'Yuh, yuh, but I think you should wait until you've met Wayne.'

'Wayne! Wayne, for fuck's sake.'

'Now, Andy . . . chill out, man . . . I mean . . .'

'Wayne! Listen, Max, Arnold's a good friend of mine –'

'Hey! Andy! This is business, right? Now, don't fuck with me, right? We're talking major investment here. You follow me, man?'

I did follow him. Max's eyes had suddenly taken on a look of steel, and I began to see through the slur and appreciate how he earned his money.

'I've got to think about this, Max. I have to talk to the rest of the band. I mean, I don't see how we can just rob Arnold . . .'

'Nope. No time, Andy. I'll give you ten minutes. Red light, green light. I mean, you decide, you know? You're the leader,' he said, flopping down clumsily on to the sofa, his head landing in Gina's lap.

I looked at her again. I could not figure out why she was engaged to marry such an arsehole. Then again, it wasn't the first time that evening I'd had that thought.

The difference was, Gina looked so sad. She did not look comfortable with Max lolloping all over her.

She looked vulnerable.

And stunning.

'I'm waiting, man,' Max yawned.

I stood up and began to pace the room, wondering what to do. Should I phone Arnold? Should I say okay? Should I toss a coin?

The room was suddenly filled with the guttural sound of thunder. Coarse and deep. I looked to the window, waiting for a flash of lightning.

Then a feminine voice said, 'Oh, God! Please, Max, don't do this to me!'

It was not inclement weather. It was the sound of one comatose A&R man, snoring like a geriatric.

'Oh, shit, is he asleep?'

'I think he probably is,' Gina replied, cradling her head in her hands.

My heart melted.

'Look, don't worry . . . er? I'm sorry, I don't think Max introduced us. Unless your name's Babe.'

She smiled.

'My name's Gina,' she said.

'Nice to meet you, Gina. Tell you what, I'll call a cab. I'll ask them to send a strong driver, then we can throw Sleeping Beauty here in the back of the car.'

'You won't shift him. He's very heavy.' She spoke from obvious experience.

Max wasn't the tallest, but he was all muscle. Pocket-battleship territory.

I tried to wake him. I slapped his face, a little harder than necessary. Partly for Arnold, and partly because I couldn't forgive him for having such a gorgeous woman.

'You won't wake him,' Gina said, somehow extricating herself from under his dead weight.

'What do we do, now?' I asked.

She shrugged her shoulders and bit her bottom lip.

'Shall I order *you* a taxi?'

'I live in deepest Surrey. It's a hell of a trek. We were supposed to be staying in a hotel tonight, but I've no idea which one.'

I sighed heavily.

But I wasn't entirely unhappy. Max was deep in the Land of Nod and I was free to admire his woman to my heart's content.

Gina looked so forlorn, rather like a child who had lost her mother in a large supermarket. I somehow resisted the temptation to throw my arms round her and hug her. I had the strangest feeling that we'd known each other for much longer than the past fifteen minutes.

'Tell you what?'

'What?' she asked, a trifle nervously.

'Let's do what Brits do in times of crisis and have a cup of tea. Give Rip Van Winkle a chance to wake up.'

'Okay.' She nodded and followed me into my shamefully filthy kitchen.

Moving a couple of pairs of Arnold's underpants, a bra, which certainly wasn't Arnold's, and a pile of newspapers from a black vinyl-covered chair, I shifted it back from the table and Gina sat down gingerly.

I thought how out of place she looked. Sort of Cinderella in reverse.

I switched the kettle on and set about disposing of the mould growing in seemingly every mug in the kitchen.

'I've seen you play, you know,' Gina volunteered. 'I thought you were very good.'

'Thanks.'

'Max is really excited about the band.'

'Minus Arnold, of course.' I sighed.

'That's show-business.' She smiled.

'I suppose. Sugar and milk?'

I was praying she was on the usual female calorie count, as the bag of sugar had turned into a solid rock that would need an ice-pick to gouge out a spoonful.

'Just milk, thanks.' Gina leant her elbows on the table as I brought the mugs across and sat down. 'Max is a pretentious prat, isn't he?'

I nearly choked on my cuppa. This was the woman who was just about to sign a contract to spend the rest of her life with him, have his babies and drive a suitably trendy wife-of-an-A&R-man car.

'I . . .'

'Come on, Andy. Just because he's going to offer you possible megabucks and fame and fortune, it doesn't mean you have to like him.'

'I think you're wrong there,' I said, with feeling. 'I could learn to like Colonel Gadaffi if he was offering me similar. I mean, it's not as if I have to sleep with him or anyth—'

The words fell out of my mouth before I could stop them.

'Sorry,' I muttered, blushing.

Gina blushed too. 'It's okay. You're right, of course.' She sighed, deep and long. 'I'm getting married in six weeks' time. Three hundred guests and a huge reception at a hotel in Surrey and . . . and . . .' her eyes filled with tears '. . . I don't like him, let alone love him. Sorry, I'm sorry. I shouldn't be telling you all this. It's just that I looked at him, passed out on your sofa, and finally knew that I'm about to make the biggest mistake of my life.'

'Here.' I tore off a piece of grubby kitchen paper and handed it to her. She blew her nose hard, and gulped, trying to swallow back the tears.

'You see, the thing is he's just not right for me. Max needs a woman who is prepared to live in his nice big house in Kent, issue the cleaning lady with instructions and tolerate his revolting habits for the sake of financial security, a wardrobe full of designer clothes and a holiday in the Bahamas twice a year.'

I gazed at her in silence, wondering whether I could facilitate an immediate sex-change and become his fiancée as soon as the post had been vacated.

'I thought I could do it. I mean, Max is most girls' dream man. And my mother thought . . . *thinks* he's wonderful. She's thrilled I'm going to marry him. But . . . oh, Andy, I can't, I just can't!'

She sobbed some more. I placed an arm ineffectually around her shoulder.

'You see, I have a job too. I know Max decries it, because it's not as high-flying as his own, but I like it. I enjoy being a working woman, earning my own way, making my own decisions.'

'What do you do?'

'I'm a journalist. I work for a female glossy, test face-creams, compare penis sizes, you know the kind of thing.' She smiled at me through her tears.

I didn't, actually. *Melody Maker* and the *Guardian* were more my scene but, to be sure, I was going to pick up a glossy the next time I stepped into a newsagent. After all, even though I'd never had a female actually complain, it would be interesting to compare . . .

'Of course, my mother, bless her, put me through a good private education and university for the sake of my future, then the minute Max came through the door, I could have been Elizabeth Bennett from *Pride and Prejudice*.' She shrugged. 'I guess I'm still yearning for my Mr Darcy and I know now I can't settle for anything less. The bottom line is that I'm not cut out to be a bimbo, however hard I try.'

'Mmnn,' I said, profoundly. 'I see what you're saying.'

'Max never bothers to ask my opinion. He even orders my food for me in restaurants! God! Now I think about it, I've been such a fool!' The anger in Gina's eyes made her even sexier. 'Do you know, Andy, that I got a first in English from Exeter? Max, on the other hand, was kicked out of Harrow for smoking pot and ended up in one of those ghastly crammer schools for the no-hoper children of aristos and celebs. He's never done a day's hard graft in his life. He's only got where he has 'cos his uncle owns the bloody label! He wouldn't know musical talent if it bit him on the bum . . .' It was Gina's turn to look sheepish. 'Present company excepted, of course.'

I lit a cigarette.

'Can I have one?' Gina reached for a cigarette and lit it. 'The point is, intellectually, I can beat him hands down, but he's not interested in my brain, oh, no.' She shook her head violently. 'His initial chat-up line was, "Hi, babe. I'm a talent scout for a bi–ii–ig label, yuh, and I spotted your talent from the other side of the club, you know." Christ!'

Gina's impression of Max's retro sixties-speak was so spot on, I threw back my head and laughed.

This was no beauty with a sexy mouth, shapely legs and pert breasts. Well . . . actually, yes, it was, come to think of it, but on top of that this girl had intelligence, opinions, articulate conversation, a sense of humour *and* tight buttocks. She was . . . *everything* I'd ever dreamt of.

'I mean, have you ever met such an arsehole in all your born days?'

Now Gina's eyes were twinkling.

'Er, possibly not.'

'There! I've got you to admit it! Thank God! I thought I was the only one.' Gina stubbed out the cigarette thoughtfully. 'I first knew I was in trouble when we tried to compile our wedding list. I wanted nice, normal things like a good dinner service and some Waterford crystal. Max insisted on adding a leopardskin bedspread, a ceiling mirror and a remote-control camcorder!'

I giggled, and this time so did she.

It was *great*.

'God knows what my mother will say, but I have to do something before it's too late. Tell her and Max how I feel. It's partly my fault. But it was almost like Max and my mother conspired to waltz me down the aisle and I just got taken along with them. The point is, Andy, I wouldn't be doing it for me, I'd be doing it for *her*.'

I was just boiling the kettle for another couple of mugs of tea and further revelations when a figure appeared at the door of the kitchen.

'Hey, babe! What's goin' down, huh? Can I join in?'

Gina's expression changed immediately. 'We were just talking, Max, while you took a nap.'

'Yeah, uh, right. Well, time to go, yuh.'

'Of course, Max.' Gina stood up and moved towards him. She went through the door and Max slapped her bum again.

I could have killed him. Honest.

I followed them to the front door and opened it.

'Right, uh, well, Andy. Thanks.'

'Any time. I'll have a think about the business we discussed earlier.'

Max stared at me. 'What business was that?'

'Arnold,' I prompted.

'Oh, yeah, Arnold. Right, yeah, uh, you do that. 'Bye.'

''Bye, Andy.' Gina reached forward and kissed my cheek. 'And thanks.'

''Bye, Gina.'

The door had closed behind them and I stood there forlornly, knowing I was In Love.

I had just met My Perfect Woman.

But there wasn't a hope in hell of it ever progressing. Even if Gina *did* cancel the wedding, which I still thought unlikely, she was hardly the type of girl who'd settle for a penniless musician, even if he did hate leopardskin bedspreads with the same passion as she.

I went to bed that night, my hormones making it impossible for me to settle. I even stole a half-smoked roach from Arnold ... poor, fat, ugly Arnold's squalid bedroom.

Two weeks later, having attempted to claim back my emotions and my brain from a misty, faraway, rose-coloured land that I had never previously visited, I received a letter.

From Gina.

To tell me that the wedding was off. That if it hadn't been for me she'd soon be viewing her backside in a mirror and on celluloid and 'thank you for being so sweet and understanding'. Could she take me out to dinner to repay me?

Well.

It seemed churlish to refuse!

A man who had spent the past two weeks thinking of nothing else? Had even forgotten to video *A Hard Day's Night* when it appeared on BBC2?

I left it an appropriate amount of time – three minutes – before I called her at her glossy magazine. And we arranged to meet at a restaurant in Belsize Park.

And the rest ...

The rest is history.

Max took it very well, considering, leaving aside the recording contract, which he took great pleasure in tearing into tiny pieces in front of my wonky, bleeding nose.

Marrying Gina did not do a lot for my career ...

On reflection, the omens were ominous.

5

Tuesday.

Today is the big day. In my head I can hear an American voice saying sincerely, 'And remember, today is the foist day of the rest of your life. Be positive. And *smile*.'

As it *is* my first day I have been allowed the luxury of a shit, shave and shower. I have been assured that this will not usually be the case and I will have to work these things into my new routine when I can.

What do I do exactly? Do I lay Nicola on the bottom of the bath while I shower above her? Do I shave whilst doing an impression of Santa Claus with my white foam beard, while Sophie and Nicola play with my spare razor-blades to keep them quiet?

Do I sit on the loo, bouncing Nicola up and down on my lap singing 'Here Comes The Galloping Major', hoping that this distraction will cure my constipation?

I'm pointing this out to Gina now I'm back in the kitchen and she says, 'I think you'll find the baby-bouncer an invaluable ally on such occasions.'

'I can't have Nicola suspended from the door-frame watching me go to war with my bowels. And what about Sophie?'

'She's a little large for the bouncer,' Gina replies giggling.

'Maybe I should tie her to the bidet for ten minutes.'

'Andy, you are the only person I know who spends half an hour on the loo anyway. What do you do up there?'

'If a job's worth doing, Gina. Anyway, what do you mean, what do I do?' I hope I'm sounding indignant. 'Same as everyone else, I presume.'

'Andy, if you start getting up a bit earlier, you'll have plenty of time to go to the loo. I suggest you shower and shave after you've taken Sophie to playschool. The baby will be perfectly happy to swing about in her bouncer while you have a quick, and I did say quick, shower and shave. *Think*, Andy. I know it's coming as a shock to those lateral-functioning little grey cells of yours, but apply a tiny bit of logic and you'll do just fine. Honest.'

Sophie comes into the kitchen already dressed, fed and watered, and I shudder at the thought that tomorrow I'll be responsible for this as well.

She still hasn't forgiven me for Noreen's departure, so I'm hoping a morning at playschool will help her forget what a ruthless pig her father is.

Nicola is in the lounge playing under her baby frame and watching the cartoon channel left blaring away by her big sister. She's being PB, Perfect Baby, but the day is still frighteningly young.

'So, what's the first thing you have to do when Sophie and I leave?' asks Gina. Oh, God, yesterday was the lesson, today she's asking questions.

'Sob, panic, phone Rent-A-Nanny and throw myself at their mercy?'

'No. Come on now, you can remember.'

'Er . . . breakfast.'

'Very good,' Gina says, a tad patronisingly. 'Now,' she continues, 'I've left the box of baby porridge and written instructions by the kettle for you. Just do what it says and you can't go wrong. Okay?'

I nod. I didn't like to tell her I'd been thinking about my own stomach. You know, more bacon and eggs than prepacked slop.

'Right, then. I'm taking Sophie to playschool. Remember, today she's staying to lunch there, along with Michelle's little Richard.'

'Oh, what are they eating? Tutti-Frutti?'

'Pardon?'

'You know, is Long Tall Sally joining them?' I try again.

'Who's she?' Gina asks me.

I shrug in despair. 'No one. Muso's gag.'

'Concentrate, Andy! You'll need to cook her a spot of tea at –'

'About five o'clock,' I interrupt as I follow her across the kitchen. 'You see, I have retained some information from yesterday's barrage.'

She's continuing as if she didn't hear me.

'You'll have to cook her a proper meal for her tea. Bangers and mash, or something equally simple.'

Bangers and mash are not something 'simple' to me. Bangers and mash are grey, watery spuds, grill on fire, belated cremations of bits of pig, to me.

'Michelle will bring Sophie home when she picks up Richard, so you don't have to worry about that today.'

Gina has crossed to Nicola, who is slumped and looking suitably bemused in her bouncy chair, and given her a big hug.

'Bye-bye, my angel,' she says, as she kisses her and then hugs her until the poor baby begins to turn slightly blue. 'Mummy's going to miss you,' she tells her, before turning away, tears in her eyes.

'Now, kiss Daddy goodbye, Sophie,' Gina says, snivelling as she leads the way out of the house towards the car.

I'm offered a cheek by my daughter. I suppose, the way she feels about me today, I'm lucky it's the one on her face.

'Bub-bye. I'll see you later. Have a good morning, Stinks.'

That's my nickname for Sophie. It's a hangover from the first few weeks of her life. She didn't seem to be here for five minutes before she permeated the flat with noxious smells.

'Of course I will, Daddy,' she says, as she climbs into her car chair and Gina fastens the safety-belt.

Gina has just thrown her arms around me and given me the sort of kiss she hasn't often blessed me with in the morning since our courting days. 'Take care,' she whispers in my ear. 'Look after them for me, won't you? Have a good day and thanks a million. You'll be just brilliant, I know you will. I love you.'

With that, she clambers in behind the steering-wheel, waves to me, starts the engine and drives off.

I've just closed the door. This very second. Simultaneously Nicola starts crying at full volume.

I've swooped her up in my arms, but it's no use. She's at full throttle. I've been alone with her for three minutes and already the sheer intensity of her screaming has frayed my nerves into a thousand tiny fragments.

Breakfast.

I'm jigging her around with her back to me and we're looking at each other in the mirror. Finally I get a smile. I tell her she's beautiful in one of those silly voices you automatically adopt when you're a parent and, yes ... the smile develops into a chuckle. So now I'm milking the silly voice for all it's worth and okay, I admit it, there's nothing like the sight and sound of your baby laughing to make you feel good. A combination of a sense of victory combined with an ahh-I-made-this-little-thing kind of smugness.

That's enough of the gooey stuff. Back to business. She'll be going red in the face with anger again if I don't feed her soon. I'll say this much for Nicola: she enjoys her grub. Eats for Ireland, this one.

So, I'm putting her in her high chair with cushions stuffed down the side to stop her leaning like the Tower of Pisa. I place a few toys on the tray to keep her amused. A rattle, a transparent ball with water and a plastic fish inside it, a spoon and one of Sophie's socks. I boil the kettle and read my instructions. According to Gina, I need to mix some pure fruit in with the mush to make it more appetising, and there's a jar in the fridge. So there is. Right, pour flakes in ... add water ... mix ... make a paste ... more water ... more flakes ... too runny ... add more flakes ... right consistency ... add fruit ... test ... add more fruit ... not too hot ... shove in baby's gob. Right, super.

Except it's not. I've been left a complete set of idiot-proof instructions for something that, in principle, isn't difficult.

Given this, why does my baby's porridge look like the sort of gruel they fed Oliver in the workhouse, with half a dozen suet balls thrown into the middle for good measure?

She's complaining of hunger so there's no time to make some more. It'll have to do.

Nicola is getting overexcited, as she always does at the sight of a teaspoon full of food approaching her mouth.

That's it, open wide and ...

Aren't babies' faces expressive? It's extraordinary that they don't seem to need a vocabulary to convey their basic feelings and obtain their needs.

A smile tells you she's having a good time and to continue. A widening of the eyes and tensing of the limbs say you're frightening her. A rubbing of the eyes and a yawn tell you she's tired. And a screwing up of the face, gagging and the clenching of teeth to avoid a second spoonful tell you you're a shit cook.

Okay, no need to panic. A quick trip to the fridge reveals some fromage frais. All right, this was supposed to be lunch but we can worry about that later.

There is a sense of sheer relief from Nicola as she recovers from the trauma of having her mouth prised open with a spoon to discover the taste of something she enjoys.

She'd better get used to this. Nicola could be eating bucketfuls of *fromage frais* in the not-too-distant future, as even I couldn't balls this up.

Disaster. I forgot to remove the porridge, such as it was, from the tray on the high chair. Nicola may not have been prepared to eat it, but she had positively no objection to wearing it as makeup and body lotion. She looks as if a drunk has vomited wantonly all over her. I've whipped her into the lounge, laid her on her changing mat and set about her with baby wipes, scraping her clean, or sort of. She's still a mite sticky.

She's just turned very red in the face. Probably because she held her breath. Or she could be practising for a spot of snorkelling in the bath tonight, but I suspect not. She objects to my lifting her legs in the air and sniffing at her posterior. I can't blame her, perhaps she thinks it lacks dignity.

Oh, Lordy.

It's here. The moment I've been dreading. She's done a packet. A steamer by the smell of it. How come babies' doings are so pungent? The pong permeates the room for ages after you've incinerated the nappy, or encased it in a bin-bag and driven it to the nearest dump.

I peel off her Babygro and vest as, according to my manual for house husbands with a brain the size of a pomegranate seed, it's time to get her dressed. I've unfolded a new nappy, on which I congratulate myself for being quite forward-thinking. I'm undoing the dirty nappy, whilst holding my breath.

Hellfire and bloody flame! It's everywhere. It smells revolting and glows at me in luminous green. I'm setting to work with the wipes, dumping them in the old nappy.

I now have a dilemma. It would have been different if I had produced a son. I would have no hesitation in wiping off any residual waste that had become glued to his little testicles. I could have said, 'Sorry about this, son,' and could have heard him reply in my head, 'Hey, Dad, no problem, it's gotta be done.'

But with a girl it's different. I mean, these sort of organs are more what you might call . . . internal. We're talking invasion here. I'm sure this is a major reason for my reluctance in nappy-changing . . . Well, hey, this is the nineties and people can lock up whole villages for going into this kind of area. I'm looking at her little . . . *folds*, shall we say? And I'm thinking, Am I out of my jurisdiction here? On the other

52

hand, to have any orifice clogged up with poo can't be that healthy, can it?

I take an executive decision and wipe it away, apologising to her profusely as I do so.

I'm taking my time to line up the new nappy under her bum, gumming it in place with the sticky tabs.

I've just realised I'm still holding my breath as I do this and I let it go.

Oh, yuck! That's disgusting. While I was distracted, Nicola has located the old nappy, which I foolishly left open, and is now using her left foot to paddle in her own poo!

The shame of it. I have brought a Philistine into the world.

More wipes.

It's now time to find the girl some clothes.

Back to the manual for house husbands with the imagination of a professional potato peeler. Sure enough, I find a page or two on clothes. Which items, which drawers to find them in, which colours go with what, and, for day one, the exact dress she is to wear.

Fine, so I'm up the stairs rummaging about in the nursery, clean vest, top, tights . . . Where is the sodding frock? Nope, nothing even remotely resembling the description. I know, airing cupboard, or hot-press as they call them over here. Bingo! There she blows. Back down the stairs. Talk to Baby as I put on her vest, top, tights. Shite, these things are tricky. Doesn't Gina screw the legs of the tights up before putting them on? Okay.

Nicola is not playing ball. Every time I get one foot in, she wriggles out of it before I can put the other in place. Try both at the same time. That's the kiddie, now I'm hoisting them up, lifting her bum off the floor, much to her annoyance.

The thing is, as a man, you spend most of your adult life trying to pull tights down, not up, so I'm having to think in reverse here. Probably just as well you don't have to put tights on before sex, I think even I would have lost interest by the time I'd got the gusset into position.

Now the frock. Oh, Gina, you git! Look at all these buttons! They're the tiny fiddly things with little material eyes to thread them through. There's about forty-seven of the ruddy things as well. I could grow a beard before I get this frock on her.

There. I've succeeded. Oh, and that's a yawn. My manual for house husbands who can barely dress themselves, let alone a child, says it may be time for sleepy.

So bottle and cuddle in front of MTV, methinks.

Nicola is in her cot, asleep.

For how long? I don't know, and the manual fails to give an exact time-span. I can't settle. I keep running up and down the stairs listening at the nursery door.

It wouldn't surprise me if the next time I do this a small voice says, 'Can't you piss off and do something useful, Daddy? I'm trying to get some shut-eye.'

Something useful?

I know, I'll go and peel the spuds for Sophie's mash. Wah-ho-ho! Forward thinking again.

I may just prove better at this than I thought.

Cancel that last statement. The rest of the day has been a bloody catastrophe.

The trouble with babies, even bright ones like my Nicola, is their attention span is rather short.

Today I have sung every children's song I could trawl from my memory. I have pulled more funny faces than Jerry Lewis. I have played with every toy Nicola possesses and some of Sophie's. Yet that deafening wail bounced off the walls every time I turned my back or tried to sneak out for a crafty cigarette.

I've used the baby-bouncer, the automatic baby-rocker, even my wife's lap-top computer to keep her amused. And still she grumbled and groaned her way through the day.

The first thing that went wrong was that, having taken the trouble to peel the potatoes early, they happened to catch my eye as I was waltzing Nicola around the kitchen whilst singing 'Edelweiss'. (If any of my muso friends discover I was singing 'Edelweiss', I'm dead.)

So the potatoes catch my eye and they've turned brown. Why? I consult the house husband manual for the culinarily challenged and there it is. Remember to put the potatoes in water if you peel them early, otherwise they will turn a funny colour.

I don't find brown particularly humorous.

But it was there, in the manual. I really hate a smart-arse.

So I have to peel a whole new bunch while doing a sort of cross between tap-dancing and, I don't know, Dutch clog-clicking to stop Nicola from protesting.

Bloody nightmare.

The one moment of light relief was when Michelle, Gina's friend, brought Sophie home from school.

I like Michelle. She's English, like me, a year or so older than I am. She's tall and athletically built, not like Gina, busty, definitely not like Gina, and quite a live wire. Jet black hair, cut in a bob. Very toned body. Quite fanciable, actually.

We have a good rapport, consisting of mock-flirtatious banter, largely based on sexual innuendo. I can't remember how that started but I've kept it up, if you'll pardon the expression, because she has such a wonderfully dirty laugh. It's infectious.

She's also one of those people who never seems down or depressed. Must be sometimes. She may go home and weep suicidally on her husband's shoulders every night for all I know, but the rest of the world never sees it.

Norman, that's her husband's name. Norman. Solicitor. Successful. Very.

Man, oh, man, what a boring bastard he is.

Anyway, she's a good mate, Michelle. I get on well with her and she's been an extremely good friend to Gina since we moved here.

Nicola had felt the need for a more physical protest at my lack of talent in the cookery field. So I was clearing banana and milk from the floor when she walked in with Sophie.

'My God, Andy! You're going to make someone a beautiful wife one day.'

'Fuck off, Michelle.'

'Daddy, don't swear,' my four-year-old reprimands me.

'You're quite right, poppet. How's my bestest girl?'

'Fine.'

'How was playschool?'

'Fine.'

'What did you do today?'

Big sigh. 'You know, Dad, I just can't remember. Can I watch cartoons?'

'Yes, of course you can. Go on, I'll ask you about your day later.'

'Cup of coffee?' I ask Michelle, desperate for an adult interlude of some kind.

'I'd love to stay and talk to you but I can't. I've got to take Richard to the doctor's.'

'Nothing serious, I hope?'

'No, just the usual West Cork runny nose and hacking cough. It's the damp, you know. Speaking of damp, how's the nappy-changing going?'

'Great. Three stonkers today and I haven't thrown up once.'

'You're such a hero. Listen, Andy, if you're thinking of taking this role-reversal business seriously, I've got a lovely little off-the-shoulder number you could borrow if Gina fancies treating you to a night out.'

'Sod off, Michelle.'

'I'm going, I'm going.' She smiles. 'I'll call in at the end of the week to see how you're getting on. I'll bring a bottle of wine, sit on your knee and mop your furrowed brow while you tell me how unappreciated you are.'

'I'll look forward to that.'

The rest of the day has been kids, kids, kids.

Sophie's tea was a flop. The sausages were well tanned, to say the least, and the mashed potato was 'lumpy, dumpy', apparently.

It's now six o'clock and Sophie's still watching television. I feel bad about that. I love Sophie to bits. She's my best friend. But this ruddy baby, who is also gorgeous, just won't let me do anything else, for pity's sake. I haven't even been able to go for a pee for the last three hours. I want to wrestle with Sophie. I want to pretend to be Fireman Sam, or Big Ears, or whoever. But Nicola won't let me go.

Funny thing is, Sophie hasn't asked. Normally she's after my attention every five minutes. Wanting Daddy to play. But today, not a single request. Odd. Maybe she knows I'm struggling to cope.

I find myself a little disturbed by this. I must try to make amends tomorrow.

If I haven't shot myself by then.

Ten past six and Gina has just walked through the door.

Do I hug her? Ask how her first day back at work has been?

Do I bugger!

I pass Nicola to her at the sort of speed one might pass a grenade that has just had the pin pulled.

56

'Hello, Sweetums, Mummy missed you, yes, she did.'

'I think she missed you too,' I inform her.

'Really? Did you, Mummy's girl?' she says, giving Nicola a big hug.

'At least, I think that's what she was complaining about.'

'Well, then, Baby, how did Daddy get on?'

Am I invisible? 'Fine, fine, fine.'

Okay. I'm lying.

'Daddy could have tidied the kitchen a bit now, couldn't he, little one?' She's still speaking to Nicola as she sits down at the kitchen table.

'Give us a break, Gina.' I groan.

'Why is Mummy's darling's dress on back to front?'

She'd get a shock if Nicola answered, wouldn't she?

'Is it?' I ask, between clenched teeth.

'Yes. Daddy didn't realise the buttons go at the back, did he, darling?'

I'm glad I was ignorant of this fact. Otherwise I'd have had to undo the bloody thing and start again.

'And where's Mummy's other girl?' Gina asks, still talking to me through Nicola, as if the baby is some kind of interpreter.

'In the lounge. Watching cartoons.'

'You've not been letting her do that since she got home, have you?' Gina's enquiring, deciding she can talk directly to me now.

'Well, I've been a bit busy,' I tell her, trying to keep my temper.

'You'll have to play with Sophie as well. You can't let this little madam take up *all* of your time.'

'Oh, don't worry. Tomorrow I'll put on my clown costume and throw a few custard pies. Then I'll make some interesting and amusing animals by folding a few balloons together.'

'My, my, Daddy is a little testy, isn't he?' Gina observes, while bouncing Nicola on her knee. 'What's for dinner, Daddy?'

'Sorry? Dinner? That's part of my job spec as well, is it? I'm supposed to turn into Keith bloody Floyd now, too, am I?'

'Well, you can drink like him. Let's see if you can cook like him,' Gina says bitchily, as she stands and walks with Nicola into the lounge.

'I'll peel some potatoes. I've had plenty of ruddy practice,' I'm screaming after her as she exits.

*

It's now half eleven at night. Gina and I are sat at opposite ends of the sofa, blearing at some dreadful action picture on the movie channel.

We haven't spoken. I haven't forgiven her for not congratulating me on my efforts and she hasn't forgiven me for making her feel guilty for asking me to be a house husband in the first place.

So we don't talk.

I want to. I'd like to admit to not doing a very good job today. I'd like to confess to large moments of panic. I'd even go as far as to own up to shovelling four gallons of *fromage frais* down Nicola's gullet as she wouldn't eat anything else.

But I don't.

I'd like to talk about why I made such a mess of things. But I guess it would just sound like a series of excuses. After all, she's been doing it for years.

So I say nothing.

Neither does she.

It's now 12.15 a.m. Wednesday morning and I'm watching Gina undress for bed. I'll say one thing for her: she certainly has the kind of body that makes you want to forgive her very quickly.

1.30 a.m.

Same morning and we are lying in bed with our backs to each other.

As I saw it, I may have had an error-strewn day, but I made a heroic bloody effort. An effort worthy of some reward in the way of rumpty-tumpty.

Gina, though, was having none of it.

She turned over without even the offer of a congratulatory blow-job.

Mind you, on reflection, I probably don't deserve it.

So here I am with my back to my wife, sulking.

And I can't sleep because I've got the car tomorrow. Connor's giving Gina a spin to work. I'm worrying about how I'm going to get the baby fed, and Sophie to playschool and wash and shave with Nicola in tow and give Sophie more attention and . . .

How do I feel at the end of my first day?

Don't know.

Not sure.

Except, and this is worrying as it's only been one day . . .
I'm not sure I feel like *me* . . . really.

6

Wednesday morning, 4.30 a.m.

I'm having a cup of tea as I can't get back to sleep.

I've been having some funny dreams. All about my past. I've obviously reached the age when nostalgia is more attractive than reality. Some of it was quite nice. Apart from the scenes when Sylvia, Gina's mother, or my father appeared. That was sodding nightmare territory.

If Gina was love-at-first-sight, then meeting Sylvia was the exact opposite.

It was mutual hate-at-first-sight from the first moment I met her on the doorstep of her mock-Tudor house in Esher.

I had the slight handicap of arriving as Gina's penniless muso fiancé two months after she'd ditched rich A&R man Max.

On the train down to Surrey, Gina had told me a little more about her childhood.

Her father had been Irish and had apparently left home when Gina was eight, insisting it was the only way he could guarantee not murdering his wife. Gina never saw him again. Apparently he moved to Canada where he slowly drank himself to death.

Sylvia divorced and remarried, purely for money.

Now, I call that mercenary. Sylvia calls it common sense. Why have nothing but love to keep you warm, when you can have a centrally heated, seven-bedroom house and a wardrobe full of furs?

She drove her second husband so hard that the poor man died of nervous exhaustion.

As we'd walked up the drive, Gina had suddenly stopped and grabbed my arm. 'Just remember, I love you, darling.'

A sentence delivered with passion, and all the urgency of a woman whose lover was about to go off to the battle of Ypres.

As it transpired, Ypres was not a bad analogy.

My first impression of Sylvia was that she looked very young.

Apparently Gina was conceived in the first few passionate clinches on the honeymoon bed. At least, that's Sylvia's story and she's sticking to it.

I also noticed how immaculate she looked: pristine, bordering on the clinical, actually. Not a hair out of place. Her clothes were so crease-free you would think they were sewn on, like a second skin. She sat on the very edge of her sofa, her posture rigid, as if she had a steel rod running from the top of her spine down to her anus.

But, admittedly, she was very attractive.

Gina did not look unlike her. It's the only thing I've ever been grateful to Sylvia for; that she passed on her pretty face and slim figure to her daughter and kept her sour personality to herself.

'Mother, this is Andy.'

'Pleasure to meet you, Mrs Wilson.'

'I wish I could say the same about you, dear,' Sylvia replied, before sitting down on the Chesterfield, leaving my outstretched hand clutching at thin air. 'Well! You're the loser my daughter has thrown everything out of the window for, are you?'

I'll say one thing for her, there was no attempt at diplomacy. Open hostility, right from the start.

'Erm . . . yes . . .' I responded feebly, looking to Gina for guidance.

'Mother, please, give him a chance.'

'Chance? He's just taken the best chance for happiness my daughter will ever have away from her.'

'Now hang on . . .' I tried to intervene.

'I understand you're a musician?' Sylvia continued.

'Yes that's –'

'What kind?'

'Well, I write songs, play the guitar, sing and play bass in a band.'

'What band?'

'Don't Ask.'

'But I am asking, you impertinent little twerp.'

'No, I mean that's the name of the band.'

'Should I have heard of them?'

'Well, that depends . . .'

'Exactly as I thought. I'll tell you what type of a musician you are. You're a poor one.'

'But talented,' I suggested, by way of an excuse.

'Mother, for goodness' sake! This isn't helping anything. I love

61

Andy. And we're going to get married, whatever you say. So you might as well get used to the idea.'

'Love, yes, of course,' Sylvia mused, slowly, 'You're quite right, Gina dear. I was forgetting. Why don't you make us all a cup of tea? You know where everything is. Give Andy and me a chance to start again.'

Gina looked at her mother in a way that warned her to behave.

I looked at Gina in a way I hoped conveyed, 'Don't leave me alone with this witch,' but I must have failed dismally in the subtle-exchange-of-glances stakes, because Gina headed off to the kitchen.

'Credit where credit is due, Andy. You've clearly made quite an impression on my daughter.'

'And she on me, Mrs Wilson.'

'Yes, of course she has,' she barked at me. 'Love . . .' she began, before pausing, dramatically. '. . . I married for love once. It was the biggest fucking disaster of my life.'

It is the only time I have heard Sylvia swear in all the years I have had to put up with her.

'So I've heard.'

'Love? Don't be pathetic. You've only known each other for a couple of months. Just because you've pushed the right buttons between the sheets, my dear, it does not mean you've discovered the secret of marital bliss. Believe me, I know. Gina was just weeks from a lifetime of security and you come along and ruin it all.'

'It really wasn't like that, Mrs Wilson. You see –'

'Well, Andy, I will not sit back and let you destroy my daughter's future happiness. She deserves better. I will do everything in my power to ensure that this . . . fling, is as short-lived as it deserves to be.'

I was speechless. I just gawped at her like a goldfish with lockjaw.

'*Mother*!'

'Gina?'

She had appeared from nowhere, like the rabbit out of the hat.

'Gina, I thought –'

'– I was brewing a pot of tea while you made small talk with Andy? I knew what you'd try to do, I just knew it!'

'Gina, darling, it's you I'm thinking of.'

'No, it isn't, it's you! What *you* think is right, what makes *you* happy, not me. I don't want a cold marriage with pots of money and no love.

I've had a good, hard look at that kind of life, Mother, and I'm not interested. I don't care how many houses or cars or trinkets Max could have bought me because I don't want to be bought by *any* man. I want to get those things on my own, don't you understand? I want to be successful by myself, *for* myself.'

'I see,' Sylvia responded, with tight lips.

Silence.

Gina finally broke it. 'I'm going back home with Andy now. Think about what I've said.'

With that, Gina headed for the door.

'Right, then, looks like we're off,' I said, rather feebly, and followed.

It actually took ten minutes into the train journey back to London before I could speak again.

'Gina . . .'

'I want to thank you, Andy.' Gina interjected cleverly. 'That's the first time I've stood up to my mother since I was a brattish four-year-old.'

'I don't think she liked me very much,' I stuttered, as always, the master of understatement.

'Oh, she's just scared for me. Scared that I might have to live how she did when she was married to my father. She'll calm down. I'll call her tomorrow, maybe pop back and see her next weekend.'

'Well, I'd rather you than me,' I confessed. 'I'd sooner get in the ring with Mike Tyson. At least I could "take a dive" and collect a large cheque. When your mother takes a bite she doesn't let go, does she?'

'Don't be too hard on her. When my father left he cleaned out their bank account. We had some dreadful years before she remarried. It's left her very bitter.'

Gina reached for my hand and tucked it into hers. 'Anyway, I couldn't give a fuck what she thinks. I love you and that's all that matters.'

'Are you sure?'

'Absolutely.'

So I held her close.

I've never really wanted to let go ever since.

In retrospect, I've realised that, in the early days, Sylvia's opposition drew Gina and me closer together. It always does. There's nothing

63

like a bit of parental disapproval to make someone infinitely more attractive. I must try to remember that when my two horrors reach fourteen. If they haven't finished me off by then.

Apart from embarrassing Christian names, Gina and I had something else in common. My father left home during my relatively formative years as well. The difference is that mine kept coming back. Periodically. A jazz musician of moderate success, he'd just piss off on tour at the drop of a hat, leaving my mother and me to fend for ourselves. Which, by and large, we did very well, as my mother earned quite a nice salary as a PA to some bigwig industrialist. She was good at organising things, was Mother. My father's tours just got longer and longer. One lasted three years, the whole time I was at university. He came back to find he was divorced and my mother was affianced to an Australian heart surgeon from Sydney. So he just buggered off on the road again for another six months. My mother married and emigrated, and I graduated and moved into a flat in Balham.

So the only time Gina ever met my mother was at our wedding. Which was the only time I ever met the Australian heart surgeon. He was about to retire, which was just as well as his hands shook as if he was a First World War veteran suffering from shell-shock. If he was ferreting about with your heart, I'm convinced he would have flipped it into the air like a pancake, leaving a team of nurses, doctors and anaesthetists diving to catch it in the slips, to a rousing cry of ''Ow's that!' from the successful fielder.

In my entire life my father has only given me two things of any worth. Well, maybe three, if you include having a bit of a squirt into my mother's nether regions after a successful gig in Dudley.

One: taught me how to play the guitar. Two: turned up unexpectedly at the register office for my wedding, accompanied by a small troupe of fellow musicians to play at his son's meagre reception.

Nice touch.

That was our wedding, then. My mother cried, Sylvia sulked and my father got stoned, played guitar brilliantly and sang fucking appallingly.

Having said all that, for the next few years Gina and I were blissfully happy. Gina was rising steadily up the ranks in the world of problem pages and articles about the G-spot, and I had formed another band that was beginning to do noticeably well. With a bit of juggling of figures we got a mortgage and bought a small flat in Crouch End. I'd never seen Gina so happy. At work she was ambitious and forceful and dynamic. At home she was kind and loving and sexy.

Then one cosily drunken night, Gina got her dates confused and I showed that, for a musician, I have a lousy sense of rhythm.

One year after Gina reached the dizzy heights of assistant editor we stood speechless, staring at the glowingly cerise pink of 'Positive'.

Sophie was on her way.

Wednesday morning, 8.20 a.m.

Gina has gone to work. Connor has taken her.

The baby is half dressed. She's had her breakfast. She actually ate some of it today. Possibly because I drowned the porridge in a tin of Pure Fruit to disguise its rather dubious texture.

Sophie has had a bowl of Coco-Pops. According to the manual for house husbands who are brain-dead, she should also have had a chopped apple and sliced banana. But I didn't have the energy for the fight this morning.

I've abandoned dressing Nicola halfway through because I've panicked. I have to get Sophie's clothes on her ready for playschool and I'm running out of time. If I have to take Nicola up the road with her backside hanging out, then so be it.

I've prioritised.

The reason I have done this is because I know from bitter experience that trying to get Sophie dressed is a harrowing ordeal. For some inexplicable reason, a five-minute job is expanded, due to the eccentricity of my daughter, to anything up to three-quarters of an hour. Between each article of clothing, she has either to run around the room, or stand on your thighs and pinch your face, or throw herself over the back of the sofa. You start off with the simple task of getting your daughter dressed and by the time you've finished you're tempted to refer her to a child psychologist. On an average day, when the world is drifting on around you, and somebody else, namely Gina, is in charge of the task, this can be endearing, even amusing. When it's day two and you're in a big hurry, it drives you up the effing wall.

Currently, she is lying on the floor next to Nicola.

'Sophie! Will you keep your legs still? I can't get your knickers on if you keep wriggling about.'

'Ooh, Daddy,' she screams, for no apparent reason.

'Come on, get on your feet. No, Sophie, don't stand on my thighs. Ouch! Sophie, don't pull my hair. It hurts Daddy.'

'Yer Jessie!' she shouts disrespectfully, if entirely accurately.

Okay, vest on. Back to front, but who gives a toss? Shirt on and I lay her down for the dungarees. I hate these things. Especially crossed-straps-at-the-back-style dungarees. Why does Gina keep leaving out clothes that are like the mental puzzles on the *Krypton Factor*?

'Ugh! Ugh! Daddy! Daddy!' says Sophie, suddenly agitated.

Mini-panic.

'What is it, darling, did Daddy hurt you?'

'No, no, no. It's Nicola.'

'What's wrong with her?'

Major panic.

'Oh, Daddy, she's done a poo!'

She's right. Unquestionably.

'You're not wrong, Sophie.'

'Oh, Daddy, Daddy, I can't stand it, I can't stand it,' Sophie declares dramatically, and is off chasing around the room again.

'Sophie, don't you think you're overreacting just a tinge?'

'The smell makes me feel sick.'

'A touch hypocritical too. I hate to be the one to tell you this, Sophie, but yours does not exactly have the scent of Calvin Klein's Obsession either.'

'Ooh, Daddy, *ooh, Daddy!*'

'Sophie, come here and get your dungarees on.'

'No, Daddy, no. *Change the baby first!*'

'SOPHIE, COME HERE!'

This is getting bloody ridiculous. I'm now chasing my daughter around the sofa, up and down the lounge, in and out of doors, like a scene reminiscent of a silent movie.

Caught her. Tickled her. Wrestled on the dungarees. Left-hand strap twisted. Sod it, it'll do.

Change Nicola's bum.

Dress her.

Put baby in all-in-one snowsuit, which makes her look like she's been swallowed down the throat of a polar bear with stunted growth, and time to load them into the car.

It's a miserable sodding day. There's a mist so damp it makes your clothes feel soggy.

At this time of year, the rain beats down so hard on the ground, you would swear it was trying to drill for oil. The angry, aggressive wind batters buildings and people alike into submission.

Yet perhaps the worst kind of weather here is the 'grey-sky' day. There are a lot of those. The sort of mornings when you throw open the bedroom curtains and the mere lack of brightness in the heavens makes you instantly depressed.

It is the briefest of drives to the playschool, along a winding country road, which moves slightly inland, until you reach the middle of Ardfield. Then the countryside is interrupted by a few houses and bungalows until you turn off once more. Then another, even narrower country road that after a few more twists and turns leads to the tiny building that houses Sophie's playschool. An idyllic setting in which to learn.

No gridlock here. The only type of jam in which you're likely to find yourself consists of cows, not cars. Cattle being moved across the road from field to field. You're unlikely to be involved in a pile-up, but if Daisy decides to have a bit of a chew on your wing mirror, it can be equally expensive.

Cows have a tendency to be uninsured.

I'm locking the car, because Nicola's asleep, and dragging poor Sophie back up the hill towards playschool so fast her little legs keep leaving the ground.

Inside the door and pleasantries exchanged with the teacher, I'm getting flustered as Sophie insists I take off her shoes and put on the obligatory slippers for her. She's perfectly capable of doing this for herself, but has decided this is part of the routine.

Objective achieved, Sophie is giving me a big hug goodbye.

I should be pushing her away and running back to Nicola, but I'm not.

This hug tells me I'm forgiven for Noreen's dismissal.

I'm running back down the hill now and, sure enough, Nicola is awake and howling blue bloody murder.

I'm now panicking as I see a woman leaning into the window of my car. That would look good, wouldn't it? My baby snatched on the second day I'm in charge of her.

It's okay. It's only Michelle.

'Sorry, Michelle. I should have taken her with me. Where's the bloody soother?'

'Surely you don't need that, Andy? I would have thought a man of your experience knew lots more interesting ways to help a girl relax,' she says, winking.

'I do. I just need them to be a little older and preferably not a blood relative.'

I'm diving into the back of the car to search frantically for the ejected soother, dummy, suckie, yum-yum.

'How's the legal eagle?' I'm referring to Norman, her husband.

'Oh, you know. Busying about with his briefs.'

'Really? Didn't he give that up when he discovered girls?'

She's laughing, huskily. 'All I know is, the last time Norman ferreted around in my briefs they were still navy blue with a school monogram sewn on the front.'

'What was the school motto?'

'Roughly translated it said, "Be honest, true and *open* to your fellow men."'

'It never said that,' I'm saying, as I chuckle.

'Oh, yes, it did! Anyway, Andy, must dash. I'll pop in later with that bottle of wine.'

'Do, and make it a fucking big one, will you?'

'Bye.'

Now where is that soother? Nicola's still bawling.

It's a recent discovery this. Not only can she take the soother out of her mouth with her hand, but she can now spit it over great distances. When she's older and it's time to play Let's Lean Out of a High Window and Flob on the People Below, Nicola is going to win high praise from her peers for her power and accuracy.

I've found it. The soother. It was on the floor and now it's covered in fur and dust and bits of what look like hundreds and thousands, though heaven knows how they got in the car. Can't use this. Mental note to take a spare next time. She'll just have to scream until she falls asleep or I crash the car.

Whichever comes first.

How do you keep two children amused at the same time? Particularly children of different age ranges.

I am finding this desperately difficult. At the moment we are all three on the bed. Mummy and Daddy's big bed. We are playing spaceships.

Sophie is Captain Sophie, naturally. Sophie always casts herself in the big parts, demoting me to special guest star, at the very best. Nicola is First Officer Nicola and I am Chief Engineer Andy, in a game I fully confess draws its inspiration from *Star Trek, The Next Generation*. Rather apt, considering who I'm playing with.

I, needless to say, am also in charge of sound-effects, bouncing the mattress during take-off and ensuring Nicola isn't sprung off the bed by an over-exuberant Sophie.

Number one daughter is enjoying herself immensely. I'm happy about this. I'm trying my best to include Nicola in this game, but it's very difficult. I keep saying things like, 'Check the scanner, First Officer Nicola,' and 'Give me a diagnostic of the planet's surface. Are there any signs of life-forms, First Officer Nicola?'

She just looks at me with those wide saucer-shaped eyes, the rabbit caught in the headlights' stare, which say, 'What the fuck is going on, Dad?' A mixture of confusion and a little fear.

Maybe if we made her a Vulcan it would liven it up a bit for her.

If it wasn't for Sophie diving periodically under the duvet to make Nicola laugh, I'd think she'd be in floods of tears by now.

Oh, balls, what did I tell you? The floodgates have opened. Time to get the baby-bouncer.

4.00 p.m.

A moment or two of sanctuary.

Nicola's asleep, though probably not for much longer.

Michelle's here, which means Sophie's playing with Richard in the lounge while we consume a large bottle of particularly acidic Cabernet Sauvignon in the kitchen.

'You're far too tense, Andy Lawrence. You must relax. Put the kids to bed tonight, open yet another bottle of wine and get Gina to help you . . . unwind,' she says, in a loaded manner.

'There's wishful thinking.'

'Oh dear. Gina not fulfilling her conjugal duties, then?'

'It's not her fault, Michelle. She was knackered after her first day back at work. Mind you, if it keeps on like this I'm going to hand her a pipe and slippers as she walks through the door.'

'Ooh! Cross-dressing. Now there's a game I'd like to try.'

'Norman objects to putting on a bra and French knickers, does he?'

She's giggling. 'I'm afraid Norman is a jump-on-jump-off, straight-up-and-down man.'

'Should you be telling me this?' I ask.

'I'm surprised Gina hasn't already. We do discuss our husbands, you know. Apparently,' she looks up at me from under hooded eyes, 'you're a bit of an animal in the sack.'

'Oh, really? Which one?'

'A stud horse, according to your better half. I must admit, when I heard that, I asked if I could hire you for a bit of siring.' She cackles wickedly into her wine-glass.

'Was that for you, or for Norman?'

'Daddy, the baby's screaming,' Sophie tells me, as she and Richard fall through the kitchen door.

Michelle is draining her glass. 'I must be off, anyway. Tell Gina I'll phone her later, okay?'

'I will. Can you see yourself out?'

'Sure. Come on, Richard, we're going. Andy,' she calls, as I'm heading into the lounge.

'Yes?'

'I really enjoyed today.'

'Thanks. So did I,' I'm replying, for want of something better to say.

'See you soon, then. 'Bye!'

''Bye.'

Shit, Nicola's probably turned purple with rage by now.

5.54 p.m.

Before Gina's imminent return, I tried making a game of dusting with Sophie and Nicola. I wasn't going to be accused of not keeping the house tidy again. Big mistake. I smashed a piece of Lladro china. A blue and white girl holding a large hat and looking winsome. I've never liked it, personally. I've sworn Sophie to secrecy, explaining that it would only upset Mummy if she knew and, after all, we were only trying to help.

To make matters worse, Sophie spilt a glass of Coke over the sofa. I attacked it vigorously with a damp cloth and a bit of washing-up liquid, which is what I think I've watched Gina do. There's still a dark ring, though, and the Fairy Liquid is twice as hard to get off the cushion as the ruddy Coke was.

Still. I tried.

Gina has just arrived home. I didn't hear her coming because Connor dropped her at the end of the drive.

So here I stand. Fag in mouth, gin and tonic in hand and not a child in sight.

Bollocks, bollocks, bollocks!

So unfair. It's creating such a false impression.

'Hello, sweetheart.'

'Hi, Andy.' She kisses me. 'Where are the kids?'

Fuck, I knew that would be the first thing she said.

'In the lounge. Nicola's under her baby frame and Sophie's chatting to her for five minutes.'

'And what, might I ask, are you doing?' Gina takes the gin and the fag and has a slug of both.

'Celebrating.'

'What?'

'Surviving day two,' I say, rather weakly.

'Join the club. Cheers.'

She sits down and drains the remainder of my gin from the glass.

'What a day,' she moans. 'There must be an easier way of not making a living.'

Sophie comes rushing in from the lounge and Gina guiltily stubs out the cigarette.

'Hello, my little darling, Mummy missed you.'

Sophie climbs on to Gina's knee.

'Mummy, Mummy, Daddy smashed the Lladro! Daddy smashed the Lladro!'

The little shit! Snitch! Grass! Tale-teller! After all the bloody attention I gave her today. Cow!

'It was an accident. We were dusting,' I tell Gina, with the emphasis on the *we*.

'Never mind now. I'm sure Daddy tried to do his best. Did Daddy Hoover as well, Sophie?'

I'm invisible again. I'm biting my tongue.

'No. *Daddy* didn't. *Daddy* tried, didn't he, Sophie? But the Hoover wouldn't work.'

'Er, Mum, Daddy says he . . .'

'Yes, I heard, Sophie. What in the devil's name was wrong with it?'

71

'Search me. It wouldn't suck. It just sort of went . . . phut.'

'Did Daddy try emptying it, we wonder?' Gina has just winked at Sophie conspiratorially

'Yes,' I spit.

I'm lying again.

'But *Daddy* couldn't find the Hoover bags, could he, Sophie?'

'Mum, Daddy says he –'

'Blind as a bat, your daddy. Try under the sink next time, Andy.'

'Sorry, it wasn't in the manual,' I say pointedly. 'Anyway, how come it's my job to Hoover as well?'

Gina sighs. 'How come it was Mummy's job for the last God knows how many years, eh, Sophie?'

'Er, Dad, Mummy says, how come –'

'Yes, thanks, Sophie. I can't do all your jobs, Gina. It's not fair. Unless it's a complete swap. Are you going to start mowing the lawn and washing the bloody car?'

'Mum, Daddy says are you going to wash the bloody –'

'Language, Sophie!'

'But Daddy –'

'Sophie! Anyway, we'll discuss this later, shall we?' Gina's suggesting, shooting me a not-in-front-of-the-children type of glare.

So I'm exiting into the lounge, where Nicola is playing happily under the baby frame, looking as if butter wouldn't melt.

It's really pissing me off, that Gina walks through the door and, instead of saying well done, nitpicks on the things I haven't managed to get to.

Baby's poo-ed. Right, Mummy can have this one.

Midnight.

I'm writing myself a list of things I've got to do tomorrow. I've found looking after children erodes your memory.

I bathed the kids and put them to bed, and when I came down I discovered Gina had cooked us both a nice meal.

Over pudding, Gina glanced at me. 'Why exactly are you sulking, Andy?'

I shrugged.

'I suppose I just feel my efforts are a little unappreciated, that's all.'

Gina went off into peals of laughter.

'It's not funny.' I pouted unattractively.

'But it is. A couple of days as a house husband and you're muttering the war cry of stay-at-home women everywhere. Honestly, Andy.'

'I'm doing my best, you know, but it's impossible to look after two kids, cook, wash, tidy, all at the same time.'

'Don't I know it.' Gina rolled her eyes.

'The point is,' I whinged, 'I'd like some encouragement.'

'Well, you don't inspire me to drag my arse into Cork every day. You haven't once said, "Did you have a nice day at the office, dear?"'

'Well, no, but –'

'Shall I tell you how I spent my day?' she asked rhetorically.

I did not try to interrupt.

'The first thing I discover is that a commissioned article has still failed to materialise, ten days past its deadline. I ring the guilty party and discover, according to her mother, that she is in hospital having an ovarian cyst removed. So when her mother has finished giving me the gory details of her daughter's medical condition, I put down the phone and proceed to ghost-write a two-thousand-word article on a subject about which I know nothing.'

'Which was?' I asked.

'"Is the reason teenagers are no longer becoming nuns, because the modern Irish girl refuses to give up her love life?"'

'I can see the title now: "When Giving Up Sex Becomes a Bad Habit!"'

'Don't be flippant, I'm not in the mood,' she rebuked me. 'Then I discover our one remaining staff photographer has broken his wrist, due to someone striking it with a hurling stick.'

'Ouch! I always said it was a dangerous-looking sport.'

'He wasn't playing at the time. He was in a pub, but that's beside the point. The problem is he can't take pictures.'

'Oh dear.'

'So,' she continued, 'I ring the powers that be to ask them to sanction a temporary replacement and I'm told no-can-do. I am also informed that my staff budget is to be cut. On top of which, I have to sack one of my junior reporters, and do you know why?'

'Tell me.'

'Because she is pregnant. That's why. My staff budget is cut and we do not have the money to pay her maternity leave. Can you imagine how that made me feel, especially as I was given maternity leave when I'd only been at the place five minutes? To make matters worse, it is illegal to fire someone because they are with child. Which means I have to pretend I am sacking her for incompetence. So, Mr Lawrence, you're not the only one who's had it tough,' she said, slamming her wine-glass down on the table.

Long pause.

'You had a bad day, then?' I enquired, smiling.

Gina hurled a bread roll at me.

I took her hands across the table.

'I'm sorry, I had no idea. It must have been awful for you.'

Gina sighed and drank the last dregs of her wine. 'No, I'm sorry too. I'm finding it harder to adjust this time, compared to when I returned after Sophie. But if I still want to feed my kids I'm going to have work like a Trojan. The circulation figures have plummeted dramatically since I was away.'

'Hold on a minute, Gina. I've just realised. You've turned this around. I'm not supposed to start feeling sorry for you. This is my whinge. I bagsy it. I started first.'

She chuckled. 'Let's call it quits. Come on, Andy, we'll take our coffee into the sitting room and I'll smooth your furrowed brow.'

We snuggled on the sofa and indulged in a passionate kiss. Then, just as things looked as if they were going to become excitingly rude, Gina complained of a soggy bum. Consequently, she discovered the spillage on the sofa.

She was not best pleased.

7

It's Friday. Nearly 9.30 a.m. The end of the first week.

How do I feel? I don't know, really.

I feel a bit like a machine. An automaton. Pre-programmed to feed children, dress children, wash children, do housework, go to bed, sleep, then get up and do it all over again the next sodding day.

Lost in a world of domestic routine, duties replacing thoughts and feelings, I haven't had time to think what clothes to dress myself in, let alone ponder any wider issues. Which is ironical, really, when you consider how well informed on current affairs I am.

The reason for this?

Repetition.

Sky News repeats the same twenty-minute bulletins twenty-four hours a day. Over and over and over. It makes you realise how little is actually going on in the world. From morning to dusk, the same twenty-minute bulletin.

Why am I such an expert?

Didn't I tell you?

I've taken over all the night shifts with naughty Nicola, that's why.

Nicola has decided she hates MTV. She screams at it. Not in a Oasis groupie way. More a Dad-all-these-weird-videos-are-doing-my-head-in style.

It's a conspiracy. She's in league with my wife to keep me as far away from my dream of rock stardom as possible.

It'll be Sophie next. Gina will be encouraging her to use my Beatles CD collection as Frisbees.

We've just arrived at playschool. Let's unload number one daughter and see if I can make it back before number two reaches enough decibels to send for the Noise Abatement Society.

'Come on, Sophie, pick those feet up.'

'I can't. I'd fall over, Daddy,' she replies, in a rather literal manner.

'It's an expression.'

'No, silly, this is an expression.' And she pokes her tongue out and screws up her eyes.

'Very funny, Sophie. No, by expression I mean –'

'Hi, Andy, how's the happy homestead running? Like clockwork, I presume?'

It's Michelle.

'Of course. I'm taking Nicola into town for a coffee to celebrate surviving the first week. Fancy joining us?'

'Sorry, Andy. I'd love a date with you, but no-can-do.'

'Oh, you're always standing me up.'

'I really want to come . . .' she's pausing, smiling '. . . but it can't be helped. Sorcha's got an appointment with her gynaecologist.'

'Who's Sorcha?'

'Fionnuala's mother.'

'Oh, right.' I'm none the wiser. 'So you've got to hold her hand while Doctor gropes around in her naughty bits, have you?'

'Don't be disgusting. Her husband's doing that.'

'What? Groping around in her?'

'No, holding her hand while she's examined. I'm looking after Fionnuala for an hour or two.'

'Nice for you.'

'Anyway. I didn't think husbands did grope around with their wives any more, only their mistresses,' Michelle informs me, adopting a French accent.

'That's sad,' I observe.

'Not if you're the mistress, it isn't,' she says, looking directly into my eyes.

'Daddy,' Sophie interjects, perhaps not before time, 'Dad, what's a gyna-ger-opa-miss?' she asks.

'Er, it's a type of doctor, darling.'

'Like a vet, Daddy?'

'Very similar, Sophie. They go in up to their elbows on occasions as well.'

This joke has brought Michelle's rude laugh to the fore.

'Listen, sorry about coffee, but you and Gina must come to dinner tomorrow night.'

'Love to. If we can get a babysitter.'

'Oh, bring the kids with you if you can't. You deserve a good night out. Tell you what, I'll give Connor a ring. I've found him a new woman, did I tell you?'

'No, I don't think you did.'

'She's a friend of Norman's, actually.'

'Oh dear,' I say, before thinking.

'Now, don't be like that. Norman met her at some fund-raising event or other. Then Connor had to pop round to see Norman on some legal matter or other and Elisa just happened to pop in too.'

'Really? Now isn't that a coincidence, Michelle.'

'Andy! You make it sound like I planned the whole thing. Anyway, I think Connor saw her a couple of times last week. I'll try to persuade him to bring her with him.'

'What's she like?' I ask, tentatively.

'She's . . . interesting.'

'Blimey, she must be ugly if she's . . . interesting.'

'Oh, Andy, you're an awful man,' she tells me, giggling. 'I'll get Gina to call you. Come on, Sophie, let's get you into school.'

'Is it like one of those doctors what fixes your teeth, Daddy?'

'What, darling?'

'You know, one of them like what you said . . .'

I've just come out of the playschool and I'm making a mental note to stop sexual-innuendo jokes with Michelle as they're getting a bit out of hand.

Actually, Michelle is still here. Her legs are dangling out the driver's door of her Mercedes and she's flicking her shoe on and off her heel. I wonder if women know men find that sexy? I must ask Gina. Come to think of it, I wonder if *Michelle* knows men find that sexy?

'You waiting for someone?'

'Yes, I'm waiting for you. You've been ages.'

'Sophie insists I put on her slippers and we can never find the bloody things.'

'What a lucky girl to have a mummy like you. I just shove poor Richard through the door and do a runner.'

'He looks well enough on it to me.'

'Getting to the point, Andy, how would you like me to take Nicola off your hands for an hour or two this afternoon?'

Would I!

'You serious?'

'Yes. I've got a houseful and one more won't make any difference.'

'In that case, how about taking Sophie as well?'

'Don't push your luck. Bring a goodie bag to playschool at lunchtime. Nappies, wipes, bum cream, baby-food, bottles, that kind of thing. Then you can pick her up at, say . . . three o'clock. I'll have a large gin poured to toast your successful week,' she tells me, as she swings her legs back into the car.

'Great.'

'Go down the pub, Andy. The boys are beginning to wonder whether you're still alive.'

'Well, they haven't exactly been ringing every day to find out where I am.'

'They know where you are.'

'Do they?'

'Yeah, pop in and see them. Take Sophie and buy her a Coke and some crisps.'

Today is my lucky day.

It's 10.05 a.m. and I'm feeling alive. Yes, indeedy!

I have a baby on my knee whom I'm bouncing up and down whilst singing the William Tell Overture.

She's laughing, she's happy.

I'm laughing and I am frigging delirious.

FREEDOM!

Escape from Alcatraz. Hello, Murphy's! Here I come. The world is a beautiful place again. Praise be. Hallelujah!

Listen to me! Am I not bloody pathetic?

I'm going down the pub and I sound like a pubescent schoolboy getting excited about having a fag behind the bike sheds. I used to be down the pub three out of every four lunch-times. Putting the world to rights. Having a crack. Planning my career. Downing a few beers with the boys in the band, sorting out which gigs we were going to play. Now, less than a week into my new regime, I'm like a vicar's son who's been allowed to skip evensong. Unshackled. Released. I'm slap-happy at the thought of doing something I'd been doing for bloody years. That can't be right, can it? Is this what it's all about? Is it all designed just to make you feel grateful for what you used to have?

'Sorry, darling.'

78

Nicola's complaining because the William Tell Overture bumpy ride seems to have ground to a halt.

Never mind. Two hours to pub time.

It's 12.35 p.m. and I've already handed Nicola over to Michelle. I noticed she'd changed her dress. Bit flimsy, I thought, for this kind of weather.

I must admit it felt very weird passing over my child, a bit like handing over a spy in the Cold War.

Still, Nicola knows Michelle and goes quite happily to her which, for some reason, really pisses me off.

'Where's Nicola, Daddy?' Sophie's asking as I'm driving down the hill.

'Michelle's looking after her for a bit while you and I pop out.'

'Just you and me, Dad?' she says, smiling.

'Yep.'

'Where are we going?'

'Pub.'

'Naaghh!' she screams in protest.

'You don't want Coke and chippies for lunch?'

'Chippies! Yummy!'

That's one little battle won. I must try bribery again. 'Just don't tell your mother,' I say.

But I know she will.

Right. Car parked, miles from the pub, needless to say, child's hood placed on head to ward off the typhoon that's presently falling from the heavens, car locked, off we go.

It's turned into a filthy day. When it rains here it really doesn't fuck about. The clouds discharge their copious quantities of water with uncanny accuracy. You can feel it pouring down the back of your shirt, and filling your boots.

I can taste that pint of Murphy's already. I'm running Sophie down the street, then pushing her through the pub door to get her out of the rain and me to my pint.

It's O'Leary's. The same pub where Gina bullied me into submission, the one with the folk club at the back. It's slap-bang in the middle of town. All the local bands play here and most of them drink in it as well.

My daughter and I enter the pub drenched, like the survivors of a shipwreck.

What's that noise?

Oh, shit.

That noise is three blokes standing at the bar singing to me. 'MAMMY, HOW I LOVE YER, HOW I LOVE YER, MY DEAR OLD MAMMY!'

All waving their hands like Al Jolson. I'm surprised they haven't blacked up.

Michelle said they knew where I'd been.

I think this big mammy is going to have the urine extracted from him pretty heavily this lunchtime.

Fifteen minutes of flak, at least.

'Hey, Andy, how's the breastfeeding going?'

'I saw a lovely set of saucepans for sale in Cork the other day and I immediately thought of you.'

'Don't you just get pissed off when you've slaved away looking after the kids and your husband walks through the door and demands sex?'

Still, they let me off reasonably lightly, I suppose.

Let me explain who *they* are. The *they* in question are the Blow-ins. That's the name of the band I fart-arse around with while I'm waiting for the Beatles to re-form and ask me to replace John Lennon.

We do cover versions, and I'm allowed occasionally to slip in the latest song I have penned.

We're called the Blow-ins, because that's what we are.

Blow-ins is the expression used in West Cork to describe us immigrants.

Is it a term of affection or a derogatory insult?

Bit of both, depending on which Blow-in is being discussed at any given time. It's fair enough. This is someone else's country and we are privileged to live here.

Hold on, no bullshit, it's true. I've never been for living in another country and setting up little Englands. If you live on someone else's patch, you have to expect a certain amount of stick for it.

Back to the group.

Matt: American, thirty-three, talented guitar-player, decent singer (we share lead vocals), loud, brash, tactless, married to a very weird girl, who gives classes in homoeopathy and reflexology.

Johan: Dutch, forty-two, drummer. Been there, seen it, done it and failed at it in just about every other country in Europe, so it was time to give Ireland a try.

Fozzie: nickname, obviously. Fozzie, as in Bear. No need for a physical description, then. Rhythm-guitar. Harmonises well, but voice a little thin for lead vocals. Married, four kids, English, nice guy.

Andy: the sex symbol of the group. Not difficult if you see the others. Not an Adonis but in reasonable shape, best songwriter, great bass-player. I also play accoustic guitar. The reason I play bass is because no other fucker wants to do it. Name me another high profile, glamorous bass-player apart from Sting and Paul McCartney.

Exactly.

So there you are. Ladies and gentleman, I give you . . . the Blow-ins.

Well, here I am, halfway down my second pint of Murphy's, my reputation as one of the last great bohemian eccentrics in tatters and my four-year-old running riot around the bar.

If her mother could see her, rolling on the pub floor, annoying other customers, eating chips, she'd form a one-woman firing squad with yours truly as the target.

'Andy, what are we going to do about Thursday afternoon rehearsals? Is the game still on, or are we busy changing diapers instead of key signatures?' Matt's asking me.

Bit of friction between Matt and I. We're the ambitious ones. We both think we're too good for this group.

'Change it to Thursday nights.'

'No-can-do, I'm afraid, boiz. Luf to, but Thursday nights I haf to wurk at the restaurant. You know this, Andy, I'm not just being awkward.' Johan is apologising, again. It's what he does best.

'Saturday afternoons, then,' I suggest.

'Not a good idea,' says Fozzie. 'We have families as well,' referring to him and Matt. 'It's difficult enough gigging at weekends. Can't see the little woman being happy about rehearsal creeping into shopping time, know what I mean?'

I do, sadly.

'I don't know, guys. Christ, does it matter? I mean, all we do is run through the same bloody numbers we play every week. We do that on Tuesday nights anyway. Do we need Thursday afternoons too? We can play those tunes in our sleep now. Maybe it might be worthwhile if we were going to throw in a few more originals.'

I'm pitching for my own material now. I can't resist it. I do it on a daily basis. At least I used to, when I saw these guys on a daily basis.

''Scuse me, buddy boy, but I hardly feel you're in a position to blackmail your songs into the act any more,' replies Matt, the jealous bastard.

'What do you mean, blackmail? Look, guys, if you're trying to tell me you want to replace me just because I'm going to find it difficult to rehearse on Thursday afternoons . . .'

'No, no, nobody's saying that. We have to work around each other. We all accept that.' Fozzie, the peace-maker.

The other two are conspicuously silent.

'Listen. All I'm saying is we could probably get away with practising once a week. Unless we want to add some new songs to the repertoire. Then we could arrange rehearsals as and when necessary. To suit everybody.'

Silence.

'Daddy, that little boy over there says I'm beautiful.'

This is more than I can cope with. While I'm arguing the toss with the band, my daughter's pulling blokes in pubs.

I take a good look at her. She has tomato ketchup around her mouth, her dress is black from romping on the floor, and her hair looks like a backcombed wig. I have respect for the young man in question. If he thinks this is beautiful, it must be love.

'Look at the state of you, Sophie. Your mother's going to kill me. Come on, let's pick up Nicola and get the two of you home.'

To tell the truth, I'm happy for the excuse to get out of the pub. I'm feeling uncomfortable. I don't normally feel this way with these guys. But today is different, for some reason.

Sophie is ignoring me. There are none so deaf as children if they do not like the gist of what they are supposed to be hearing.

'Sophie, come on, now, we've got to go.'

'*Nahh*! I don't want to go, Daddy.'

'Neither do I, Stinks. I could quite happily down another Murphy's. But we have to collect your baby sister.'

I hate being ignored, it always makes me tense and short-tempered.

'SOPHIE!'

'No, I won't.'

'You'll do as you're told, young lady. Now, come and put your coat on.'

She's sat down on the floor. Slap in the middle of the pub.

People are having to step over her.

'Sophie, you're getting in people's way.'

'Don't care.'

That's it. I've snapped.

'SOPHIE! GET OFF YOUR BACKSIDE THIS INSTANT. COME AND PUT YOUR COAT ON BEFORE I REALLY LOSE MY TEMPER WITH YOU!'

'Go away, Daddy.'

'I'll give you go away, young lady. Just wait till I get my hands on you.'

I've leapt out of my seat and I'm bearing down on her.

'You bad Daddy,' she's spat at me, through gritted teeth, stabbing her finger at me as if it were a lethal weapon.

'We're going, right now.'

'Nahhhh!'

Tears to match the temper. She's pushing all her body weight into the ground and beating her fists on the floor. I can't lift her up.

I'm sliding my child across the pub floor like a human mop. I look like a lion dragging an unsuccessful kill back to my lair.

'NAHHH! Bad Daddy, bad Daddy!'

It's show-time for the entire bar.

Mixed responses on the faces around me, some trying to conceal their laughter at my lack of control, others clearly ready to recommend that Sophie should be taken into care and myself incarcerated for cruelty.

The band are exchanging unnerving glances between them.

I want to die.

I want to be swallowed whole.

I want to be beamed back up to the mother ship.

'NAHH! I WANT MUMMY! I WANT MUMMY!'

'I don't think Mummy would want you if she saw how you were behaving,' I tell her, as I throw her across my lap and force her arms into her coat.

'Wahh!'

'Stop crying, Sophie. You're embarrassing Daddy in front of all these people. They don't want to hear you. They want to have a nice quiet drink. Any more of this and you can spend the rest of the day in your room.'

'Okay, okay. I'll cheer up, I'll cheer up,' she's saying, whilst changing down an emotional gear and sobbing pitifully.

A real vote-winner, that. If you polled the pub now, Sophie would be just a little overtired and I would be an insensitive bastard.

'Listen,' I'm saying to the band, 'I'll see you Sunday for the gig, unless I hear otherwise, okay?'

There's a variety of mutterings to this, at varying levels of enthusiasm.

'Bye-bye, pumpkin.' Matt's bidding farewell to Sophie. Ever the charmer. He enjoyed the floor-show. I'm certain of that.

'Do you know, Matt? Daddy's my new mummy. He's not very good.'

I'm stunned. Why did she just say that? I swear I'll kill her when I get her home.

Hiatus isn't the word.

'Well, you take care until the next time we see you, okay, sugar?' Matt oozes.

'Okay,' replies Sophie, snivelling to maximum effect, and we're out of that door as fast as I can get us there.

I'm driving to Michelle's to collect Nicola and I'm seething.

I'm not sure which makes me more angry, the shame of Sophie's outburst or the Blow-ins' intolerant attitude.

I actually think they might want to kick me out of their little tinpot band because I can't rehearse on Thursday afternoons.

I wasn't trying to blackmail anyone. We *can* play our set in our sleep, and my songs *are* bloody good and nobody makes it big by singing other people's material unless you look like Take That.

We look more sort of Keep It Away From Me.

But what's really bugging me is that *I*'m the pro. I shout, 'Amateur,' when one of the others can't make a practice session. Now *I*'m the one saying I have other priorities. Or should I say responsibilities? The shoe's on the other foot and I don't like it.

Frankly, I can't really complain if they take their pound of flesh, now they've got the chance.

As Sophie would say, her new mummy is too busy looking after *her* to come out to play.

Damn! Why did she call me that? On top of her tantrum.

She's next to me in the front seat now, listening to a spoken-book tape of *The Lion, the Witch and the Wardrobe*.

We're not speaking.

Do I say anything to her, discuss things rationally with her? Can I explain to her that I'm not Mummy, just Daddy doing some of the jobs Mummy and Noreen used to do? Would that be true? Can I explain the concept of the New Man to her? Do I understand it myself? Or am I making too much of a cheeky comment made by a four-year-old on the back of childish temper?

Perhaps I should talk to Gina about it and take it from there.

We've arrived in Glandore. A village about four miles or so from our house.

This is *the* place to live if you have a bit of cash. Having said that, you have to be into boats and sailing as well.

It's a small harbour as beautiful as the Bay of Naples. When the sun shines, that is. The place is empty in the winter, heaving in the summer.

Norman and Michelle live on top of a hill with a panoramic view of the bay.

Am I jealous? I'm luminous ruddy green.

Maybe this is an uncool feeling for a wannabe rock star. I should be all left-wing youth culture and balls to the establishment.

Tosh!

It is the true and right path for every successful rock-and-roller to move from social anarchist to rich, Tory-voting capitalist in as short a space of time as is humanly possible.

Name me a rock icon who doesn't own at least four houses.

I rest my case, as Norman would say.

I pull into the long drive of Michelle's house. A small, pale-yellow mansion would be an accurate description.

Time to collect my baby.

'You stay in the car, Sophie. I won't be long,' I bark at her, in a way that tells her not to argue.

I knock on the back door, basically because front-door bells are a rarity here. In fact, not that many people bother to knock, they just stroll into your house.

*

Michelle opens the door. 'Come in, Andy. Richard's playing and Nicola is having a little sleep.'

'Oh, Gawd! She'll keep me up all night, now.'

'Your kind of woman, eh, Andy?'

She laughs suggestively.

'Come through to the sitting room. I've got a fire going and a bottle of wine open.'

'I'd better not. I've just come from the pub, thanks to your kindness, and I'd better be careful. Anyway, it's a fair drive to my house from yours and if I don't get a move on I'll be all behind schedule.'

'Oh. I was looking forward to a chat, you know.'

'Another time.'

'You disappoint me, Andy. You sure I can't persuade you to stay for a bit?' Michelle's asking, her eyes twinkling with mischief.

'No. Sorry.' She's sighing.

'Oh, okay. I'll fetch Nicola.'

I follow her into the hall and watch her ascend the opulent staircase. I'm trying not to look up her skirt.

I feel a bit uncomfortable, somehow.

'There's your daddy,' Michelle is saying, as she comes back down the stairs and hands Nicola to me.

'Strewth! You're a lump, baby,' I say, as I give her a kiss.

'You load her in the car, Andy, and I'll bring her kit-bag.'

I've bimbled across to my battered Ford Sierra and I'm placing Nicola in her car chair.

'Dad . . .'

'I'm not speaking to you, Sophie.'

Her bottom lip is quivering. I hate that.

'Here we are,' Michelle's saying, as she hands me Nicola's bag. 'Cheerio, then.'

She's thrown her arms around my shoulders and is giving me a big hug. I was right, that dress is flimsy. No Wonderbra there. I can feel . . . Put it this way: it must be colder than I thought.

'Bye, then. See you tomorrow night and thanks,' I say, as she releases her grip and walks back towards her house.

I do feel unnerved, for some reason. Must be the pressure of looking after the kids. Psychiatrist's couch within a month, I reckon.

*

It's 6.15 p.m. and Gina's on the phone. I didn't hear her come in as I have the CD on full blast. The phone must have rung and she picked it up just as she walked through the door.

I've got Nicola in my arms. We've been dancing round the lounge to Kate Bush's 'Rubber Band Girl'. It's Sophie's favourite song and she's shaking her bum in time with the rhythm.

We've forgiven each other, Sophie and I.

When we arrived home she said to me, 'Dad? I'm sorry about that, Dad. I probably just need some Oasis.'

'Some what?' I enquired, perplexed.

'Oasis, Dad. You know, the drink. It gets you back to your old self.'

She watches far too much telly. Particularly commercials.

But I had to laugh.

I know. As a disciplinarian, I suck.

I spent most of the afternoon reading her a Tintin book. I've brainwashed her into being a fan. Awful that, isn't it? The way you can't resist nostalgically reliving your youth through your kids.

Gina has just walked into the room, her eyebrows tied at the centre in a reef knot. I recognise a scowl of disapproval when I see one.

She's turned off the CD.

'Oh, Mum!' Sophie's complaining.

'Everything okay?' I ask.

'Fine.'

Liar.

'Connor's popped in for a sundowner. Do you want to fix us all a drink?' she says, taking Nicola from me.

'Yeah, okay. Back in a minute, Stinks,' I tell Sophie.

'Okay, Dad. I'll just finish Tintin,' she says, jumping back on to the sofa.

I'm following Gina into the kitchen. What's eating her? Maybe she's afraid Connor's presence will lead to a bit of a session. A few drinks too many. Which it generally does.

'Hi, Connor. Come to raid my booze cabinet again, have you?'

'Now, don't be like that. Am I after mentioning a word about the vast fortune in petrol I'm spending taking your wife to her place of employment? You wouldn't begrudge me a small gin now, would you?'

'Probably cheaper to pay for the petrol,' I tell him.

'Not at all. Gin is cheaper than petrol.'

'Not the amount you drink, it isn't.'

Gina is pacing back and forth with the baby slung under her arm. Faffing. She's rattled about something.

'Who was that on the phone?' I'm asking Gina as I fix the drinks.

'Michelle. I hear she took Nicola for a couple of hours this afternoon while you went for a pint.'

'Yes, she did. That's all right, isn't it?'

'Oh, yuh.'

It isn't, obviously.

'You don't mind Michelle looking after Nicola from time to time, do you? She's done it for you on a fair few occasions, hasn't she?'

'She has,' she's replying, moodily.

'So that's all right, then.'

'Well, it's just . . .'

'What?'

'Nothing, nothing.'

Wait for it.

'It's just . . .'

Here it comes.

'Well, you know. I left the kids with you. I'm happy to do that . . .'

I bet she is.

'. . . I trust you. But I feel a bit . . . funny about you dumping them on somebody else while you swan off down the pub.'

Connor looks embarrassed. We don't usually air our dirty linen in public. Especially not Gina.

'I didn't *dump* them. I took Sophie with me for a start.'

'Well, that's worse.'

'Is it? Why? She comes to the pub with you and me, Gina. We were only there for an hour. As far as Nicola's concerned I didn't just walk up to someone in the street and say, "Excuse me, can I leave my baby with you while I go and hurl a few pints down my throat?" I left her with Michelle. Your best friend. You know, the one *you* leave Nicola with in emergencies, like when you just have to go shopping for a new pair of shoes.'

'I know it's . . . oh, you're probably right. Listen, I'm going to get the kids in the bath. Excuse me, Connor, but if I don't do it now we'll get all behind.'

'That's fine, Gina. You work away, now.'

She's gone. I can hear Sophie complaining about bath-time from the lounge. She must think it's hairwashing night again.

'Honestly, Connor, what is it with that woman? I can't do a bloody thing right, these days.' I sigh as I pour us both a stiff Cork Dry Gin, and ferret around in the cupboards for tonic water that still has some fizz.

'Don't take it so seriously, Andy. Look at it from your Gina's point of view. She's relinquished the care of her beloved babies to you. She's their mother. It's bound now to make her feel a little insecure. Mothers like to be in control of their children. It's only natural. She's bound to worry.'

'But it's not as if I'm letting them play hide-and-seek on the main road while I'm tripping on acid, is it?'

'Andy, you're doing a grand job. I know that. I'm certain Gina knows that. She loves you, Andy, but you'll never stop a mother worrying about her children unless they're right under her nose.'

'I suppose. She's just so . . . defensive, lately.'

'Well, now, perhaps that's because she feels unhappy . . . perhaps even a little guilty about not being here herself. Women don't have a good deal, these days. Sure they're expected to have a career and look after their children. Can't be easy now, Andy. Think about it.'

Another reason for his attraction to the opposite sex. He sees their point of view so clearly. I look at Connor now. He's got it all in some ways. He's good-looking, wealthy. Yet he's lonely. I suspect he'd give it all up if it would bring his wife back. I still have Gina and the kids. So far. Maybe I'm luckier than I think.

'Yes, you're right.' I nod balefully. 'I'd better go and apologise.'

'There's something more important you have to do first.'

'Oh, is there?'

'Yes. Will you finish fixing my gin? I mean, come on, a man is hardly likely to die of alcoholic poisoning in this house, is he?'

I'm reaching for the tonic bottle, laughing.

'Speaking of alcohol, I saw Michelle today. She's inviting us around for a drunken dinner party tomorrow. Says I just *have* to meet your latest paramour.' I smile at him.

'So you do, Andy,'

'What's she like, then?' I ask, as I pour the tonic water.

'I'll let you judge for yourself,' he's saying, sighing heavily.

'Funny, that's what Michelle said. Right, there's your gin, I'll go and grovel to Gina. Back in a mo.'

'Daddy!'

Sophie's just run into the kitchen dripping and thrown her arms around my waist.

That's the first time since our new arrangement began that she hasn't disappeared up her mother's skirt for the entire evening.

So, ironically, I must have got something right today.

8

7.30 p.m.

We're off to dinner at Norman and Michelle's tonight. Gina has taken an eternity to decide what to wear before going back to the first dress she tried on, of course, so I have five minutes to make myself look presentable.

I've been thinking about Gina and her tetchy behaviour. Trying to figure it out. It got me into nostalgia again. I've got to stop this. I'll start buying *Doctor Who* videos soon or trying to get my hands on early-edition Filofaxes.

Things became difficult for Gina with the birth of Sophie. Not physically, although our first-born literally tore her way out of Gina's body the same way she tears enthusiastically at the wrapping paper on her birthday presents.

I remember Sophie's birth so clearly.

It was agony!

Not just for Gina. It went on for hours. I rubbed her back, I held her upright and I supported her weight as she squatted like a constipated Chinaman in a paddy field. She squeezed my hands so hard it was weeks before I could pick up a guitar again.

Gina was so brave and so strong. Sixteen hours and not one painkiller. No pethidine, no epidural and not so much as a whiff of gas and air. I, on the other hand, gulped at the latter with visible relish every time the midwife popped out for a pee.

All worth it, though. Every cliché in the book is absolutely true. From that day forth, your life is never your own. You never sleep properly again, your sex life is ruined, routines are destroyed, you spend the rest of your life worrying about them . . . and yet, when they smile their first smile, take their first step, speak their first words . . . there's not a better feeling in the world.

However, in many ways, this was the moment our fortunes began to turn for the worse. Understandably Gina became confused. Part of her wanted to pursue the career she had worked so hard to build, and part of her wanted to do nothing more than stay home and look after the baby.

To make matters worse, my second group disbanded, just as we were getting close to cracking open the golden egg. Artistic differences, which is a euphemism for the fact that we hated each other's fucking guts.

Money became even tighter, so Gina had to go back to work soon after Sophie's birth and any pitiful amount I earned, from failed proper jobs and solo gigs, went on paying someone to help with Sophie.

To solve this in part, Sylvia moved to Highgate to give a hand which, needless to say, put more strain on our marriage than all the rest put together.

That's when Gina started to become unhappy, frustrated.

I worked in sales, shops, bars, and my father started to blame Gina for 'ruining my career'. Sylvia blamed me for ruining Gina's life. This went on for two and a half years, until one day my spouse walked through the door with a smile on her face and announced she'd been offered a job in Ireland and how did I feel about it?

Good question. How did I feel about it?

I wasn't exactly what you might call . . . keen.

London is where it's at. It's the only place to be if you want to be 'discovered'. No use living in Doncaster or Exeter or Minehead if you want a career in rock and roll. Ireland seemed like professional suicide.

Yet, living in the capital, my luck had begun to seem genuinely poxed. And Gina . . . well, Gina wanted to move *so* badly. For the job, to live in her father's homeland, to get away from her mother.

I still occasionally miss the pace, the action, the anything-could-happen-tomorrowness of London.

But the compensations are fantastic. Especially for my children.

To replace the grime and claustrophobia of the big city for clean air and open space and, above all, safety. Reported instances of children being abducted are minimal. Although there is some crime here. Recently a tourist was mugged in Cork City and it made front-page news. The victim was apologised to and given the freedom of the city, for heaven's sake!

I also enjoy the fact that the area is devoid of huge, headache-inducing shopping malls, and supermarkets so big you need an Indian scout and a compass to navigate your way around them. I like the fact that when I buy my loaf of bread, I am greeted with a smile and a 'How are yer now, Andy? Any news?' instead of the customary glare and barked 'faw'ee pee' of London.

There you are, you see. It's a dodgy thing to say, in this neck of the woods, but I'm a convert.

10.30 p.m., or thereabouts, then, on a Saturday night. We're sat around Norman and Michelle's dining table, having recently devoured something green and spicy and distinctly vegetarian.

There's a lot of veggies around West Cork. Not the indigenous locals – at least, not for the most part. I hadn't realised the trend had spread to Glandore, of all places. Maybe it's in deference to the latest girlfriend Michelle has drummed up for Connor. Boy, is she a doozy. She's English. Terribly. She has large, come-to-bed eyes and full lips, and I suspect she's hiding a decent body under her I'm-a-feminist costume, but her face, hairstyle, demeanour ... everything about her screams, 'Save the sodding whale.'

At least Norman and Michelle are not into saving the planet and embracing alternative medicine as well. As far as I'm aware. I can tolerate a fixation with any one of these subjects, but not all three. When you're sitting around a meal table with alternative vegetarian ecologists, who're telling you they're curing their thrush by using grapefruit extract, I draw the line. I tend to get drunk and play the carnivorous, aerosol-spraying, pill-popping devil incarnate, just to stop myself dying of fucking boredom.

Speaking of boredom, Norman is on top form tonight.

It's partly Gina's fault. She made the mistake of asking him how things were at work. You'd have thought she'd have learnt by now.

You see, as I may have mentioned, Norman is a solicitor in West Cork. He deals with conveyancing and land disputes and insurance claims.

He is not Rumpole of the Bailey.

So, we've had a riveting half-hour of courtroom drama about the exact positioning of somebody's fence-posts.

Not exactly edge-of-the-seat stuff.

But, you see, Norman thinks it is. He can't believe that it isn't as fascinating to the world at large as it is to him. He waffles on in monotones while rigor mortis is visibly setting in on all who surround

93

him, blissfully unaware that everyone else's brain switched off two sentences into his speech.

What does an attractive woman like Michelle see in Norman? Dollar signs? Can it be as simple as that? Is he hung like a bazooka? Is Michelle an incurable insomniac and Norman the answer to a sick woman's prayers? I don't know.

Talking of Michelle, she's opposite me in a little black number so tight you can hear it rustle when she breathes. She's had a bit to drink. So have I, mind. She's made several lewd comments. She's winked at me so many times tonight I'd begun to think she had a nervous tic.

I wonder if anyone else has noticed.

'Tell me, Norman ...' Elisa is saying – that's Mrs Greenpeace, Connor's woman.

She's very taken with Norman. Good luck to her.

'. . . if you were to win the lottery tomorrow, what would you spend the money on?'

Why ask Norman? He could build a sizeable bonfire using his pocket money as tinder. What does he need to dream of lottery jackpots for?

'Now, Elisa. That's a very tricky question.'

Oh, please! Methinks it's time to top up the old wine-glass.

'What would you use it for, Elisa?'

Make a good politician, Norman. He follows the maxim 'Answer a question with another question.'

'Well, let's say I won two million. Obviously, I'd keep, say, a couple of hundred thousand for myself and my family. I'm only human, after all.'

I wouldn't put it to a referendum, missus.

'And the rest?' Norman enquires.

Here we go. Refugees in former Yugoslavia? Elephants in India? Pollution in inner cities?

'I think I'd reforest Ireland. I mean, there are no trees any more. It's changed dramatically from when I arrived here fifteen years ago. Ecologically, it's a disaster.'

Oh, for fuck's sake!

More wine.

'Yes ...' Norman is oozing sincerity. 'Yes, I see what you mean. Yes, it would be hard to think of a more worthwhile use for such a windfall. Yes, I might be tempted to agree with you there, Elisa. What about you, Andy?'

'Me?'

'That's right now, Andy,' Connor has chipped in. 'What about you?'

'Well, if you two are reforesting Ireland, I think I'll build a paper-mill.'

Connor is forced to spit his wine back into his glass or choke with laughter.

'*Andy*!'

Gina is rebuking me. Under the table she is clattering my shin with her heel.

'Sorry, only joking. What about you, Connor?' I'm asking, sloshed enough to stir the shit a little.

'Ah, now, you see, Andy, I'm a convert. I've seen the light.'

'Oh, really? So all the dyes used on those "Ye Olde Celtic Design" sweatshirts your factory churns out are environmentally friendly, are they?' I ask, innocently.

'They are,' he replies, confidently.

'And all the testing for any nasty allergy the dye may cause to skin, that's all done on computer, I suppose. No poor little bunny rabbits with their paws shaved bare and their eyes watering? No mutant mice dyed a nice shade of purple, then?'

'Perish the thought, now. I'm proud of our record, so I am. My wife, when she was alive, was determined that our track record on all such matters would be spotlessly clean.'

'Yes, of course. Sorry I was forgetting,' I say, and I feel instantaneously like a complete shit.

'You needn't worry, Andy. I interviewed Connor before I agreed to go out with him,' Elisa tells me. 'I couldn't possibly have entered into a relationship with someone who wasn't ecologically sound.'

She said that in a way that informs me I would have been struck off her list of potential sexual partners after a two-second glance at my curriculum vitae.

'He has a letter from Anita Roddick. I've seen it,' says Elisa, beaming.

'I'm impressed, Connor.'

So that's why she thinks he's Mr Wonderful.

He's grinning at me as he raises his glass.

'Andy?'

'Yes, Norman?'

'Enough about mine and Connor's work . . .'

Thank God.

'How's *your* new . . . employment going?'

Here we bloody go. I'm surprised it's taken this long. He smirks as well. Another slug of wine, Andy. I think you're going to need it.

'I'm adjusting.'

'Adjusting,' Norman repeats, thoughtfully. 'Adjusting, yes, good choice of word.'

What? Wanker!

'I mean . . .'

'Yes, go on, Norman.'

'You know . . . adjusting . . . I mean to not being the traditional bread-winner.'

'Gina's always been the bread-winner, I've just never been the bread-*maker* before.'

'Yes,' says Norman, in a way that tells me he hasn't understood what I've just said.

'Well, I think it's fantastic, what Andy is doing,' Michelle has suddenly put in.

'Is it?'

'Yes. I think it's about time men and women cut out all the crap about what society tells them they should and shouldn't do. I think he's been very brave,' she's saying, licking her lips.

'Well said, now, Michelle,' Connor adds, 'and Gina is doing wonders holding that magazine together. They're a fine partnership.'

Oh, shit, Andy old son, this is going from bad to worse.

'Look, I've just gone from guitar strings to apron strings, simple as that. No big deal.'

'It's fantastic that you can do it,' Michelle continues her praise, 'that Gina trusts you enough to do it. You're brilliant with your kids, Andy. I could even grow to love you for it. You're doing amazingly well. I mean, Norman would be useless.'

I can believe that.

'I've only been doing it for a week. I think we should leave it a bit longer before we start dishing out medals.'

Did I hear the word *love* mentioned?

'You see . . .'

Oops, Norman's woken up again.

'. . . I'm afraid I was raised to believe that the wife stayed at home and the man went out and earned the money.'

'On the other hand there is something very sexy about a big strong man with a baby in his arms.' Michelle is eyeing me, dipping her finger in her wine then putting it in her mouth.

I've just caught Connor's face out of the corner of my eye.

He's raising a suspicious eyebrow at me.

'Now, some may say that's old-fashioned of me,' continues Norman.

Lord! This man is insensitive. Has he listened to a bloody word I've said? More wine, Andy, definitely more wine.

'Norman, you're not with me here. Supposing, perish the thought, in a few years' time your practice decided to make you redundant in favour of a younger man.'

'But I'm a partner, Andy.'

'Yes, bear with me, Norman, I'm talking hypothetically here. Let's say when this happens, because of your age, you can't get another job. But Michelle can get decent employment . . . I don't know – running an escort agency or something.'

Shit! Why did I say that?

'Thanks, Andy. You can be my first customer.'

'That's okay, Michelle. Now, Norman, under those circumstances, would you be happy to stay at home and look after young Richard?'

'He'd be old enough to look after himself by then.'

'Artistic licence. Let's pretend he's drunk from the fountain of youth.'

'Michelle is very talented. She'd probably earn enough for us to pay for a nanny.'

Should I bang my head on the table now or save it for the finale?

'Norman, play the bloody game!'

'Yes . . . I suppose, given all the hypotheses . . . yes, I would.'

'Ah. But what if you thought you were the greatest solicitor that ever lived . . .'

Because I know he does.

'. . . how would you feel about it then?'

'But that's what makes it all so silly. I am a great solicitor.'

Jeeze! That's it, I've lost it.

'You sanctimonious bastard, Norman. You sit there, completely fucking oblivious to real life, smugly thinking nothing can ever go wrong in your little world, and do you know what really pisses me off? You're probably right.'

Norman's face has frozen solid. He may even have stopped breathing.

You're up to your neck in trouble now, Andy.

'It's like this, Norman. Andy is doing a difficult job in tricky circumstances, and he's doing it very well. Because, you see, it's not as easy as most men think.'

That from Gina. High praise indeed. Unexpected. I'm quite touched.

'Well, I'd marry you tomorrow, if you were free,' says Connor. 'What do you say now, Andy? Will you have me?'

'I *have* had you, Connor, and you were rubbish.'

General laughter.

He knew what he was doing. Connor, I mean.

Bailed me out there. Someone remind me to thank him.

It's 1.30 a.m. on Sunday morning and Michelle is saying goodnight at the door. Norman's inside, recovering, and helping Elisa on with her backpack, for all I know.

Gina's just kissed Michelle goodbye and is walking over to Connor's car to say goodnight.

I'd better apologise.

'Goodnight, Michelle, and listen, sorry . . .'

'Forget it, Andy. You're right. He is a sanctimonious bastard.'

She's kissing me lightly on the mouth.

Either I'm very drunk or I just felt the faintest sliver of tongue slide between my lips.

'Night-night,' she says, as she closes the door.

Alarm bells are ringing like fucking Notre Dame in my head.

Gina always says I have no idea when a woman is flirting with me. Well, even I can't have got this one wrong, surely?

Gina has just given Connor a goodnight kiss as he stands in front of his passenger door.

As I approach she turns and walks towards our own little rust-bucket.

'Good night, Connor,' I say, as I reach him. 'Was I a little rude to Elisa?'

'Not at all. To tell you the truth,' he's whispering to me, 'I don't think it's a match made in heaven. She's fanatical. Nobody should be made to eat tofu! Knit with it, maybe, but not digest it, for heaven's sake.'

'Drive carefully, now,' I suggest.

'Andy,' he continues whispering.

'Yes,' I reply.

'Watch yourself with young Michelle, now. She's lusting after you, I swear.'

'Oh, behave yourself.'

'I'm serious. Come on, Andy. Yer may be out of touch with the way the game's played, but you must have noticed the way she was behaving tonight?'

'She was just a bit langers, that's all. She won't remember in the morning.'

'Have it your own way, but I'm telling you she's dangerous while she feels like this. You be careful. You have a lovely wife, and her best friend behaving like this just isn't on, now.'

'You're beginning to sound like a priest.'

'I'm only trying to warn you.'

'Thanks. I hear what you're saying.'

'Good man. Listen, your wife is a vision of loveliness tonight, so she is. Take her home and look after her, if you know what I mean,' he tells me, accompanied by a suggestive wink.

'Nice idea, but I think I might have blotted my copybook a little too much for that to happen.'

He's laughing as Elisa clomps across the drive, struggling to keep her feet encased in her wooden mules.

I'd better join Gina in our car. She's driving.

I'm getting in, bracing myself for thirty-nine lashes.

'Before you say anything, I know. I was out of order, Gina. I'm sorry.'

'No. It's okay. I understand.'

She's starting the engine.

I have the feeling that's all she's going to say.

Why?

Did she notice Michelle's behaviour?

Should I mention it?

Silence still.

It's something about the look on her face that's worrying me.

Sunday. 8.00 p.m.
I've enjoyed today. It's been . . . more normal. Gina's been around and she's taken charge of the kids. It's clear, to be fair, that she misses them like crazy when she's working. I look at Gina and I feel guilty that my music hasn't taken off and given her the choice.

Anyway, today has been fun. I had my customary wrestles with Sophie and cuddles with Nicola. We popped to the pub, all four of us, then came home, lit a fire and had tea and cakes in front of it.

Both children behaved perfectly. Maybe they just liked having things back to their old routine. Maybe Gina and I enjoyed having things as they were too. Maybe everyone relaxes when the responsibility is shared.

And now I'm going out to do what I do best. Make music.

Gina can't come tonight. No babysitter. We'd be pushing the boat out a bit to pay for a sitter twice in one weekend anyway.

I've tucked Nicola up in bed. She fell asleep in my arms after her ruskie-puskies.

Sophie has had a further riveting episode of Tintin read to her.

Gina seems happy as there is a soppy film she can curl up in front of on Sky Movies.

A toot of a horn means my spin is here. I'll load my stuff into the van, kiss Gina goodbye and be off.

I've just had a nasty shock.

I opened the door to the back of the van in order to load my gear into it and there, buried amongst the drum kit, is Belly O'Hea.

'What the bloody hell are you doing there?'

'What a lovely man yer are, Andy. Sure now, you're awash with English charm.'

'Sorry, but you gave me a fright.'

'Am I that gruesome a sight, now?'

'You don't really want me to answer that, do you?'

'Maybe not.'

'So what *are* you doing in there?' I'm asking again, as I begin heaving my equipment into the van.

'Well, I was after thinking, if Mohammed won't go to the

mountain, then the mountain will have to get off his arse and go chase up the lazy little prophet.'

'Very good, Belly. Very cryptic. Don't know what it means, but it sounds impressive.'

'I've come to collect the tapes. The demo-tapes. You know, the ones you were promising to spin round to me a couple of decades ago.'

'Oh, shit! Yes. Hang on, I'll go and get them,' I say to him, as I slide my bass guitar between a set of cymbals and Belly's left leg.

'Will it be taking long now? Only yer wouldn't believe the angles and directions I've had to stretch my fine figure of a body into in order to fit in the back of this feckin' van. You may not believe it to look at me, but I was not born a natural contortionist.'

'No, no. Two secs. Don't move.'

'I can't feckin' move, yer idjit. That's what I'm telling yer.'

'Oh, good. Captive audience. I'll play you some of my new songs when I've loaded up.'

'Go and get the feckin' tapes!'

'On my way.'

Poor Belly.

It's a pointless exercise giving him my demos.

But at least he's enthusiastic. Which is more than anyone else is. Including me, these days.

It's now ten forty-five and the band is taking a break. Wow! I'm on a real buzz. I'm flying tonight and it's got nothing to do with what I smoked before the gig. More like I've been let out of the madhouse and allowed to behave exactly as I want.

I think I understand what a hit Clark Kent must have got when he took off his glasses, ripped off his clothes and started leaping tall buildings in a single bound again.

Amazing.

Even Matt, ballsing around with his riffs and making snide comments, can't bring me down. I'm cooking tonight. This is my show and he knows it.

People keep coming up to me and telling me what a great gig it is. Women mostly. I feel sexy again. It's ruddy hard to feel attractive when you're spending your days wiping your baby's vomit from off your shirt, or shoving frozen lasagne in the oven for your wife's tea, or crawling around on all fours pretending to be Baloo the Bear for your daughter.

But tonight I've got my dick back.

I'll have them dancing on the tables before the night's out, you see if I don't.

'Hi, Andy!'

'Michelle! What are you doing here?'

She's sidled up to me and put her arm through mine.

'We came to watch you play. This is Laura – she's a friend from Dublin. She's staying for a few days.'

She's introducing me to a plumpish girl, dressed sensibly in a tweed twin-set. Schoolteacher, definitely.

'Nice to meet you,' she says, shaking my hand.

'I've told Laura all about you. Join us when you've finished playing. I'll have a pint waiting for you,' she says, planting a kiss on my cheek.

'Sorry, Michelle, no-can-do. I've got to discuss future gigs with the boys, I'm afraid.'

The smile is fading from Michelle's face.

'Never mind. Some other time,' says the schoolteacher, as Michelle turns away and heads for the bar.

Oh dear.

1.35 a.m. Monday morning. I'm in the back of the Transit van being driven home, which is just as well as I'm a bit drunk. I spent the money I earned tonight on booze, trying to make the performance high last longer.

So I'm skint again. As bloody usual. I can feel a big downer lurking in the back of my mind.

You see, however enjoyable tonight was, it doesn't matter whether friends, loved ones, the public, any of them think you're great. What matters is that *they* do. The people with POWER. The big guns who tell you if you can have a career or not. Official, professional recognition of talent. Without it, no matter how good you are, it's just a matter of hot air. Just as light, fleeting, intangible.

Oh, feck it! Who cares?

I was on top form.

I'm even tempted to see if I can make Gina feel a bit frisky.

9

December 7.

Ding dong merrily on bleeding high. Yippee, it's Christmas. Well, not quite, it's the second week of December. I've been lying low for a bit. I'm like that. Silent, introvert, anti-social when I'm unhappy.

We've got the tree up. Decorations festoon the house. Sophie is like Road-Runner on speed, completely on fast-forward, she's so excited. Nicola thinks she's off her trolley, but you can't expect a baby to understand.

I like Christmas, usually. Gina adores it. But not so much this year. Mr and Mrs Festive we ain't.

But, then, money is tight and Gina and I . . . well, you know how it can be. Can't be sparks and fireworks all the time. I'm not expecting catherine wheels, but the odd banger would be nice.

Ho, ho, ho, eh?

It's two o'clock on a Wednesday afternoon and Sophie has just bowled me a googly.

The nativity play. She's an angel. Open to debate admittedly, not exactly type-casting but, nevertheless, it's a fact.

What's the problem? Costume. Lack of. Apparently it's a DIY job.

Why the air of desperation? I should have been informed of this three weeks ago. There's a deadline, you see. I'm not good at deadlines. That's more Gina's field, she's used to them.

Yes, that's right, there is a dress rehearsal . . . tomorrow.

Apparently the teacher wants them to get used to their costumes as early as possible.

How can I phrase this? Well, I have never been the type of person who would have stood a cat-in-hell's chance of passing a *Blue Peter* audition.

'Sophie! Why didn't you tell me sooner?'

'I just forgot.' Hands raised heavenwards again.

'How did you forget? You must be practising for it every day.'

'Yes, but I'm practising in my own clothes, silly.'

I'm not sure what a child makes of an adult holding his head in his hands.

At least the baby's having a nap. Let's hope it's a long one. I need as much time as I can muster.

'Right. Angel.'

Okay, I have an array of goodies strewn on the floor before us and I have my model ready and waiting.

Where to begin?

Sheet.

'Daddy?'

'Yes, Sophie.'

'That sheet's not white, is it, Daddy?'

'Isn't it? It is ... sort of. It's cream, ivory or something.'

'Angels dress in white, don't they, Daddy?'

'That's stereotyping.'

'They do, don't they, Daddy? They dress in white, don't they?'

'How do you know? Have you ever seen one?'

'I've seen the pictures.'

'Artists' impressions.'

She's pointing to the sheet.

'It's not white, though, is it, Daddy?'

'No. Look, maybe this angel isn't as good as she should be. Maybe she's let her halo slip a bit. I don't know, Sophie. You're playing her, invent a bit of background. Come on, it could be worse, at least it's not black.'

I hate it when she looks at me like that.

'Sophie, darling, don't worry, it'll look white under the lights.'

'Ooh, are we having lights at playschool, Daddy?'

'I'm sure you are, and dry ice as well, now ...'

She's gone quiet. She's thinking. It unnerves me.

'Daddy?'

'Yes.'

'What are you doing, Daddy?'

'I'm cutting a hole in the sheet for your head.'

'Daddy?'

'Yes, Sophie.' I do wish she'd shut up and let me concentrate.

'Daddy? Mummy's not going to like this, is she, Daddy?'

'Probably not.'

'That's one of Mummy's best sheets, isn't it, Daddy?'

'Yes.'

'Ooh, Daddy!'

'"Ooh, Daddy" what? Unless you wanted to be dressed in pink, or be purple-patterned from top to toe, I don't see what choice we have. Try this.'

It fits over her head all right, but she now has a train behind her roughly three times the length of the *Flying Scotsman*.

Bit more chopping to be done, methinks.

Now my daughter will be the first angel in history to wear a mini-dress.

'Right, that's that, then. Now for the halo.'

'What's that, Dad?'

'It's the bright shiny thing that floats above their heads.'

'But will it make me glow, Daddy?'

'Sophie, don't expect miracles.'

'I know, Daddy. We could use a battery.'

'We could use a solar panel, Sophie. But we won't. Now, halo. I know, this will do.'

It's now 6.10 p.m., same Wednesday, and we're done. It took a little longer than I thought, but it wasn't helped by interruptions from Baby Nicola and all that entails.

Sophie is modelling before us.

'Turn round, Sophie, let's get a good look.'

She's spinning like a top.

'What do you think?' I'm asking Nicola, who is in my arms and staring at me blankly.

I'd thought I'd cracked it when I finally got the halo to stay in place.

Then Sophie reminded me that angels have wings. Of course they do!

So my daughter, the angel, stands before me. Her dress barely covers her knickers. The halo is a pair of Deely Boppers. I've cut the antennae off them and attached one of Gina's Alice bands to the top. This I have covered in white tissue paper. It doesn't look too disastrous from the front, but when she turns round, the gap in the

Alice band left for the head makes it look as if this angel bought it second-hand, as seen and tested.

The wings are made by attaching two coat-hangers together, then glueing them to bits of sheet I had already cut trying to make the dress.

Waste not want not, as they say.

She looks ... hideous. She looks like a tacky monster from a particularly low-budget episode of *Doctor Who*.

Horrifying.

If this angel descended from on high to bring peace on earth, the shepherds would not so much be sore afraid as shitting fucking bricks.

Gina has just walked into the lounge.

'Mummy, Mummy, I'm an angel, I'm an angel. Daddy made it, Daddy made it!'

Gina's pausing.

'Well, that's lovely, Mummy's girl. You look altogether wonderful. In fact, you look *so lovely*, Mummy's going to get the camera and take a picture.'

There's something in Gina's eyes, but I can't recognise what.

I'm following her into the kitchen and closing the door behind me.

The sheet! That's what it'll be, the flipping sheet.

I'm a dead man.

Gina's bent over, rummaging through the drawers of the Welsh dresser – looking for the camera, I presume.

She's crying, I think. Her shoulders are visibly shaking. She's stood up now and I see tears are streaming down her cheeks. She's putting a finger to her lips and gesturing to the lounge with the other hand.

'It's not that bad, is it?' I'm whispering.

She's waving a hand at me, unable to speak.

'Well, you see if you can do better then,' I challenge, but I'm giggling too, now.

Blimey! If Gina keeps on like this she'll have a seizure.

Good to see, though.

That's what it was I didn't recognise in her eyes: laughter.

Thursday afternoon. Ballinkilty. 2.43 p.m., to be precise.

I hate shopping. Granted, shopping for food isn't as bad as shopping for clothes, or cookers, or houses, but it's still shopping and I hate it.

Loathsome. Especially when it's food-shopping for Christmas, with two kids in tow.

I didn't do it when Sophie was in playschool rehearsing for her starring role because Michelle popped in.

I used to enjoy our chats. You know, adult conversation. Saves your sanity.

Just.

I even began to see the attraction of mother-and-toddler groups and coffee mornings.

Now it's different.

This morning when Michelle popped in she gave me a Christmas present and told me to open it then and there. It was a pair of black silk boxer-shorts. 'I hope they're big enough,' she said. 'Why don't you try them on, Andy?'

After that I just kept moving around the house pretending to tidy the rooms and Michelle followed. She stuck closer than a central defender marking a star striker. I became so tense she asked if she was making me nervous.

I made some excuse about having to pick up a prescription for Gina, before collecting Sophie, and ushered her out of the house as quickly as I could.

I dumped the boxer-shorts in a hedgerow *en route*. Don't want to have to start explaining *those* away to Gina.

Anyway, that's the reason why I'm shopping in Ballinkilty now. There's hordes of manic consumers, swarming up and down the aisles of the supermarket, devouring shelves full of goods that cost twice as much this week because someone's glued a festive label on the packaging.

My immediate problem is this: I have one of those special baby trolleys. These are like standard trolleys, only a bit smaller. At the front they have a large baby seat attached at the top, complete with straps, except Nicola is too fat for them to fit around her.

Because Nicola is riding in the trolley, Sophie has to ride in the trolley too. In the main compartment, as it were. The part where the food should go is now chock full of four-year-old. So where am I supposed to put the bloody shopping?

I have a list, longer than the Gettysburg Address, so I have had to take a second trolley. In a feat that would test your average pentathlete, I'm wheeling these buggers in a straight line up and down the aisles, cornering included.

I am also facing a sea of daggerish expressions each time I near the till end of the store, because it's Christmas and the queue for people waiting to use these vehicles is a mile deep.

'Daddy, I want a bread roll.'

'You can't have one, Sophie.'

'But I want one.'

'I want to be stranded on a desert island with Jill Dando, but it's not going to happen, is it?'

'But I *always* have one when Mummy wheels me round the supermarket.'

'No, Sophie.'

'Daddy! It is Christmas.'

She's got me there. Cute little bugger. Accuse someone of Scrooge-like tendencies at Christmas and it nails them every time.

Dickens has a lot to answer for.

So Sophie has her bread roll; Nicola, remarkably, still has her soother *in situ* and I think I've got an ulcer from fighting my way to the shelves, and trying to find space in the trolley either side of my daughter to fit in all this shopping that we can't afford.

'Having fun there, Andy?'

It's Connor.

'Hello, there. What are you doing here?'

'Sure, the same as you, Andy. Suffering.'

'No, I mean, why so early?'

'I took a half day off,' Connor replies.

'What for?'

'To come and join this mania.'

'Why didn't you do it in the city?'

'I did. I liked it so much I thought I'd come out to Ballinkilty and do it all again, so I did.'

'Pardon?'

'Finishing off, Andy. The bits I was after forgetting.'

'What about Gina?'

'I tried to persuade her to join me in this romantic little adventure, but she said she'd rather be getting off home to you.'

'She's at home? Now?'

'Dropped her there meself.'

'How come she got out early?'

'Because her spin was leaving early.'

'Oh, right. Shit. I wish I'd known. She could have joined me.'

Connor's sighing. He's taken the list out of my hand and torn it in half.

'There. I can't stand to see a grown man despair. You work away on that half of the list, I'll take this trolley and sort the other. Last one to the checkout is a pillock.'

Good man, Connor.

4.40 p.m. Home at last. Bundling Sophie through the door, handing Nicola, who is wrapped up so that only her eyes are visible, to her mother.

Sophie heads straight for the lounge, taking off her coat and shoes as she goes, leaving them spread across the kitchen floor for others to tidy up,

'Hi!' Gina appears to have been diligently wrapping presents at the kitchen table. 'And where have you been?'

'Shopping.'

'All this time?'

'You should have seen it. It was heaving. Chaos, absolute chaos.'

I've neglected to mention the quick detour to the pub with Connor. I paid. I was last to the checkout.

'I got home early,' Gina says, putting Nicola in her high chair.

'I know. Connor just told me.'

'Oh, you've seen Connor? That's why you're late. You've been to the pub.'

Rumbled.

'Well, he did collect half the shopping for me. I couldn't really refuse, could I?' I ask rhetorically, as Gina heads for the washing-machine.

'Did you put on a wash today?'

'Yes. Oh, damn! I forgot to take it out.'

I'm remembering this as Gina is pulling it out of the machine, dripping.

'Oh, for crying out loud, Andy! What did you put in it?'

'How do you mean? Whatever was in the pile you left me. Same as usual.'

'This wasn't in the pile.'

She is holding up a blue sweater.

'It must have been.'

'*I* would never have put this in the pile because it's hand wash only.'

'Oh. Does it matter?'

'Well, I hope you like the colour blue, Andy Lawrence, because thanks to you, that's the only colour any bugger in this house is going to be wearing for the rest of the month.'

Oops.

'Oh, no, Jeeze!' Gina has clapped her hand to her mouth in horror.

'What is it?' I say, nervously.

'Sophie's angel dress was in there.'

'What was that doing in the pile?'

'I'd hoped it might shrink it down a bit, Instead of it hanging off both her shoulders. You must have noticed that if she stands with her legs together, she looks like a milk-flavoured ice lolly,' Gina remarks, a little unkindly.

'Is it . . .?'

'Blue? Oh, yes,' she tells me, firmly. 'It's ruined, Andy. What are we going to do? We could bleach it, I suppose.'

'That's a good idea,' I say, though I've really no idea what difference it'll make.

'You try it tomorrow. When she's not here to see or there'll be hell to play.'

'Okay, leave it with me. Right, I'll get the shopping in from the car, shall I?'

'Why not?' she's replying lovingly, I don't think.

I look at the vast array of shopping bags in the boot of the car. At least we'll be able to eat and drink ourselves into oblivion this Christmas.

There are worse ways to go.

Then again, I can think of better.

12.30 a.m. Friday morning.

Backs to each other again.

We're not exactly running the full gamut of the *Kama Sutra* from A to Z, these days. In fact, we haven't got as far as finding out what B stands for.

There's a cruel irony here. On the one hand, I'm certain I have a woman waiting for the slightest encouragement from me before tossing her knickers gleefully in my direction, while my wife, the woman I love, is treating me like a sexual fucking leper.

It has to be said that having financial pressures isn't conducive to nice, relaxed nookie.

But it's more than that.

I've always found it more difficult to be as assertive, sexually, with Gina as I have with my previous lovers.

This is partly because she has been More Successful than me and earned More Money. It seems difficult to ask for certain things, or take charge, when your partner is holding the purse strings.

It breeds gratitude.

Gratitude from a woman may mean you can go at it like a rabbit without complaint.

Gratitude from a man means you feel guilty about hassling your old lady for sex.

Add *this* to the equation: *you* are now the little woman indoors. Not only are you financially inferior to your wife, but you have now swapped roles totally to complete your emasculation. What chance have you, then, of bending your loved one around the bed the way you've fantasised about for years, eh?

Sexual frustration, without visible end, is a disease.

I can't talk it through with her because I'm a man and that's all we're interested in, right?

This is bad shit. I don't need this.

Fuck it, I'll get up and make a cup of tea.

Saturday morning.

There are certain phrases, expressions and clichés in the English language which should never be used. They are a curse.

Example 1: 'Things can only get better.'

Example 2: 'It can't get any worse.'

Example 3: 'At least it's all uphill from here on in.'

Only this morning I used the phrase, 'Things might be difficult, but we can still have a good time,' in reference to Christmas.

Prat. You'd think I'd know better.

I nipped down to the shops with Nicola this morning to buy a newspaper, and when I returned Gina gave me a big hug. She expressed concern that I was looking so tired. She suggested I have a bath and then offered to run it for me. Two minutes after I climbed into the hot water, she fetched me a gin and tonic to 'help me relax'. By this time I was suspicious. It was only a quarter past eleven in the morning. Usually, if I reach for alcohol before lunch-time, Gina shoots me a glare of disapproval, often accompanied by a guttural growl. Now here she was, thrusting a stonking great stiff gin into my hands, with enough ice to sink the *Titanic* all over again.

Just as she reached the door – no, correction, as she was half-way out of the door, her hand poised to close it behind her, she said, 'Oh, by the way, I forgot to mention, Mother's coming for Christmas. The children will be thrilled.'

Then she was gone. Vanished. I could hear her running down the stairs as fast as she could safely manage. No doubt she had her fingers in her ears to protect her from the howl of anguish she knew would follow that little bombshell.

So here I lie. Nuked. The gin has disappeared down my throat in one desperate gulp.

Sylvia is coming for Christmas.

Does the expression 'I need this like a fucking hole in the head' ring any bells at all?

Today I watched Sophie in her nativity play.

Gina couldn't make it. She was devastated, but it wasn't her fault. The trouble with being an editor of a magazine considerably less glamorous than the publications you have worked on before is that you discover they expect considerably more for the pittance they pay you.

So I filmed every precious second with the camcorder.

Sophie was just gorgeous.

Come on, let's hear it for the proud parent!

Seriously, I would never have believed that Sophie could be that angelic.

We are all watching the video, including Nicola, thirty seconds after poor Mummy has walked through the door. Just as impressive the second time around, from my point of view.

The costume by the way, barely resembles its original design. It fell apart when I bleached it, so Gina stayed up into the small hours and started from scratch.

She's preening, is Sophie. She's a star and she knows it.

'You were just the best, Sophie.'

'Was I, Daddy?' she says, with the casual air of a film star.

'Yes. Mummy and Daddy are so proud of their girl,' Gina's adding.

Sophie's chest is swelling so much she's in danger of reaching puberty early.

We've all laughed and Gina's just hugged me in a way she's neglected to do for some time. A sort of we-made-her-that-little-girl kind of hug. Through our love, and all that jazz.

It's twelve forty-five and we've just made love. Sort of.

I don't know why it happened tonight after so long.

It could be that the video of Sophie brought out the romantics in us. Reminded us of the love that made her. And the passion.

Tonight could easily have been a result of our children pulling us together instead of driving us apart, sexually, which is usually the case. From a technical point of view.

Or it could be that Gina knew she couldn't get away with it for much longer. She's very good at that. Coming up with the goods in the nick of time.

Wasn't perfect. Very tense. Very by numbers. Like two strangers, actually. All nerves, apologies and clumsiness.

Upsetting in many ways.

But better than nothing.

It's the Saturday before Christmas, lunch-time, and my father's just turned up. He does that. Out of the blue. No prior warning. Just appears.

No need to panic as he's not stopping. Passing through, as usual, on the way to some gig or other. Jazz musician, I think I told you.

He wants me to go for a drink in town, which has not pleased Gina.

But then, the sight of my father generally doesn't. Please Gina, I mean.

A shrug of the shoulders and I'm gone. He's my father, what can I do?

I'll suffer the consequences later.

4.00 p.m., and I'm still here. In the pub, with my dad. Not one of the usual pubs I prop up. And there are a few of those. There's something like forty-plus bars in this town which, for its size, is remarkable. I've done my best to help keep them afloat, especially in the winter when the tourist trade drops off. But I don't take my father to one of my favourites. He's too . . . unpredictable.

He plonks another round on the table. This is the third drink I have refused, only to find it slapped down in front of me.

He keeps going to the loo then buying another drink for both of us as he's passing.

He knows his son. Not as well as he thinks, but enough to guarantee that if it's put in front of me I'll drink it.

'What exactly are you up to these days, son?'

'Not a lot.'

'Still gigging with those wasters?'

'Yep. Busy this Christmas. Though not as much as usual.'

'Anything else in the pipeline?'

'Few demo-tapes on a few desks, but I'm not holding my breath.'

'Why don't you come and play jazz with me?'

'Because I fucking hate jazz. No melody, naff lyrics, the front man is always someone whose mother told them they could sing and, worse still, it's played by old farts with silly little beards, like you.'

'Pays a few bills, though.'

'Just. Anyway, I can't go dragging my carcass around Europe with you, I've a wife and family to think about.'

'So?'

'So not everyone can just bugger off and leave their emotional ties behind them, the way you did.'

He shrugs, unaffected by my criticism. 'So get a proper job, then, if you're settling down.'

'I've got one.'

'Oh? What?'

'Housewife.'

His eyes are narrowing as he stares at me. 'Come again?'

'You heard me. I'm looking after the kids while Gina works.'

'Eh?'

'I'm a house husband. The "other half". I'm a "new man".'

'You're a fucking poof!'

'What?'

'House husband! What sort of shit is that for a son of mine to come out with?'

'It's the truth. I know that's a concept you find difficult to grasp, but there we have it.'

'My son. *My* son, looking after the kids, doing the shopping, washing the nappies?'

'You don't wash nappies any more, they're disposable.'

'Oh, well, that's all right then, as long as the bleedin' nappies are disposable. Is this Andy I'm hearing? What's happened to you, boy? The best bass-player to emerge in the last twenty years or more, the man whose mission it was to change the face of popular music with his compositions. He's washing dishes and sterilising dummies? What put out the fire in your belly, boy?'

'Life, Dad, life.'

'Don't give me that. It's that woman of yours. You've been soft ever since she first let you take her knickers down. Don't let her do this to you, Andy. Have some pride! She's strangled the life out of you. Swallowed your ambition along with your cock.'

'That's not true, Dad,' I'm arguing, but without much conviction.

'Isn't it? Look how well you were doing until she came on the scene. Everyone was after you, everyone. You were going places, Andy lad.'

'But they were blind alleys, all of them. I don't want end-of-the-pier stuff, Dad, never did. I want big-time or nothing. It hasn't happened. Maybe now's the time to accept that it never will. I don't want to be over sixty and scrubbing around doing sad little gigs, talking about the old days and how I *nearly* made it. Still half believing I'm going to be discovered like some sad, pathetic . . .'

'Like me, son.'

'Yes, Dad. Like you.'

He's standing up, gathering his things together.

'I'll be off, now.'

'Where you heading?'

'Schull.'

'I'll give you a lift as far as Skibbereen, if you like.'

'No thanks, son. I'll hitch. Merry Christmas.'

'Yeah. You too, Dad.'

And he's walking out of the door.

Again.

It's always been like this, all through my life. He arrives, stirs the shit, then leaves.

Funny, I just found myself arguing the house husband's corner. Justifying decisions.

But he's just walked out of the door, backpack and guitar, and part of me is jealous. Envious.

And he fucking knows it.

10

December 22. 11.30 p.m.

I've just got back from the pub to find Lucretia Borgia sitting at our kitchen table. 'Good evening, Andy. I was about to put the kettle on. You look as if you could use a coffee, dear.'

It's started already. Fifteen-love to Sylvia.

'Sylvia, dearest, merry Christmas, and what a spectacularly decorative frock you're wearing. Now I know how the Baby Jesus must have felt when the three kings stuck their heads around the barn door.'

'Thank you, Andy. I'll take that as a compliment, coming from one with such exemplary dress sense as yourself.'

'I take it you come bearing gifts. Gold, frankincense and the usual set of villages-of-England place mats. Always a winner that. Surprises us every year.'

Gina has entered the kitchen. 'Hi, Andy. How was Connor?'

'Fine. I've invited him for Christmas Day as usual. No point in him being by himself.'

'No, of course not,' says Gina, looking a little awkward. She generally does feel uncomfortable when her mother and I are in the same room.

Sylvia stands up. 'Well, if you'll excuse me for a moment, I'll just get ready for bed. Finish making the coffee, would you, Andy? There's a good boy.'

I resist the temptation to bark and wag my tail.

'Please refrain from wearing the baby-doll nightie, Sylvia. I don't think my poor, deprived little body could stand it.'

'Very funny, dear,' she says, as she heads for the door.

'What do you take in your coffee these days, Sylvia? Milk? Sugar? Strychnine?' I add, when she's out of earshot.

'*Andy!*' Gina reprimands me.

'I'm sorry, but she started bitching at me two minutes after I came through the door.'

'Oh, Andy. Promise me you'll try to get along with her this Christmas. If not for my sake, then for the children's. You know how easily they pick up on atmospheres.'

'I'll try.'

'Thanks, darling, it is appreciated,' she assures me, and gives me a hug.

'Listen,' I change the subject swiftly, 'you didn't mind me inviting Connor, did you?'

'No. It's just I thought we might have enough on our plates with my mother here, that's all.'

'Frankly,' I confess, 'I could use the moral support.'

'That's better,' Sylvia says, as she re-enters the kitchen. 'Oh, Andy, you haven't finished making the coffee.'

She is resplendent in red velvet dressing-gown with matching hood. I bite my lip to prevent myself from telling her that she has left her beard and sack back in Lapland. For Gina's sake.

There's a knock at the back door.

'I'll get it,' Sylvia insists, taking over as usual.

She has opened the door and somebody has fallen through it, landing right on top of her. Sylvia is pinned to the ground.

The intruder has lifted up his head.

'Hello, son. My gigs got cancelled. So I thought I'd spend Christmas with my favourite boy.'

He's suddenly noticed that Sylvia is underneath him.

'Ironically enough, it looks like I've finally landed on my feet, so to speak,' my father says, grinning. 'Hello, sweetheart, what might your name be?'

'Dad . . .'

Sylvia is making little snivelling noises.

'Can't remember? It's all right, love, I've had a couple of drinks as well. Who cares? Give us a kiss.'

He's started to grind his hips as he swoops his lips down to meet hers.

'*Gina*!'

Sylvia is screaming, as Gina and I grip each other's hands in sheer horror.

It's Christmas Eve, 7.10 p.m. and I've just walked through the door.

Gina is seated at the kitchen table with her mother. I can hear my father playing with Nicola in the lounge. Which is ironic as I have no recollection of him playing with me – or my sister, for that matter.

I'm soaking wet, I'm tired, cold and I've just driven half-way round West Cork.

But I'm happy.

Why? Because I've got Texas Tessie!

It's not a porn video, it's a toy. Correction it's *the* toy, at least as far as this Yuletide is concerned.

Who remembers Buzz Lightyear now? That's how it is in the toy world. Fickle. It makes success in the pop industry seem eternal by comparison.

No store in Ireland had Texas Tessie. No stores in England. You couldn't get them from the manufacturer's. I know, I rang all these places. My phone bill will be roughly five times the cost of the sodding toy. No shops, no supermarkets, no toy warehouses, nobody had them.

Except a little feller called Sean, who lives in a village the other side of Cork, who had a few that had toppled off the back of a lorry. As fast as he ran he just couldn't catch the truck up. So, in the light of this, he was willing to sell me one at roughly two and a half times the manufacturer's recommended retail price.

I didn't care. I tracked Sean down, I tracked down Texas Tessie.

Tomorrow, when my little girl rips off the wrapping paper and sees the doll of the year in her sweaty little paws, I'll be there.

Then she'll think of all the bullshit I fed her about Santa falling on hard times and having to lay off half his workforce of elves and just not having enough Texas Tessies to go round, and she'll smile. Then she'll say, 'You was only joking me, weren't you, Daddy?' and I'll grin and say, 'Course I was. And you believed me!'

I've got the toy hidden in my coat as Sophie's in the kitchen, sitting on the floor, drawing another picture of Santa.

Gina's looking at me as if to say, 'Did you get it?'

I'm winking and giving a little nod.

She's smiling at me and I'm smiling back.

It's the first joy we've shared since the gruesome twosome arrived to stir the hornets' nest.

Christmas Eve. 10.00 p.m.

The rest of the evening has resembled peace negotiations in the Middle East: tense, with war likely to resume at any moment. Were it not for the festive season and little ears flapping, I'm sure hostilities would have broken out in full by now.

Speaking of little ears, I'm only just putting a very overexcited Sophie to bed.

'Dad?'

'Yes, Sophie.'

'How does Father Christmas manage to fit down the chimney?'

'With great difficulty, I should imagine.'

'Cos he's quite fat, Dad, isn't he?'

'I suppose so. But he's also magic. Now get to sleep.'

'Dad? How come he doesn't crash into all those aeroplanes when he's flying around in his sleigh?'

'Rudolph's nose. You can see it coming from miles away. Bit like your granny's.'

Sophie's giggling.

'You're very naughty, Daddy. D'you know, Dad? I don't think Granny Sylvia and Grandpa Eddie like each other very much, do you?'

'I think you might be on to something there, Sophie.'

'They should try harder to be nice to each other. It is Christmas and that's what you're supposed to do, you know.'

'I'll remind them. Now, will you go to sleep? Santa's on his way and he won't stop here if you're still awake.'

'Okay, Dad. Goodnight. Merry Christmas.'

'Merry Christmas. Sweet dreams, Daddy's girl.'

'Dad?' a little voice sings out as I reach the bedroom door.

'Yes, Sophie.'

'Is Father Christmas really on his way?'

'Of course he is.'

'Then d'you think it would be a good idea to put the fire out? We don't want him to go to hospital with three-degreeve burns, do we, Dad?'

'The word's degree, Sophie. Don't worry, I'll get right on to it,' I'm saying as I exit, laughing.

11.37 p.m.

We're all a bit drunk, even Sylvia, and a bit desperate, so we're playing the obligatory game of charades. We've stuck to television programmes, as Sylvia was too stupid to remember all the signs for theatre, stage and film. She just kept flapping her arms about stiffly. So much so that I thought I'd better simplify things before she guided a small light aircraft to taxi around my lounge.

I've had my turn. Nice and simple. I just walked into the centre of the room and raised my beer glass.

'*Cheers!*'

Yes! Thank you very much. Now I can sit back and watch other people make fools of themselves.

Sylvia is on the green at the moment and fuck knows what she's trying to do.

'Are you sure this is a television programme?' my father enquires.

'Yes, Edward,' Sylvia replies.

Dad hates being called Edward and she knows it.

'Though it isn't part of children's BBC so it may be a bit out of your cultural range.' Sylvia smirks.

'That's odd. Because you're looking more like a Teenage Mutant Ninja Turtle by the minute.'

'Eddie!' Gina warns.

'Well, maybe not teenage ... more old age ...'

'Dad!' My turn to reprimand.

'Why are you all being so stupid?' asks Sylvia, in a fit of pique. 'It's so obvious. I couldn't have given you more clues.'

'How many words is it?' asks Gina.

'Three, dear, three.'

'Which one are you miming?' I chip in.

'I'm doing the whole thing.'

'Well, what are you doing? *War and* bloody *Peace*?' my father asks in anger.

'I'm doing *The South Bank Show*, you ignorant little man!'

Stunned silence, which I break. 'You were doing the *whole* of *The South Bank Show*?'

'Of course. Any idiot could have guessed it. I did a bit of music, a bit of painting, sculpting, acting, dancing. I even pinched my nose and mimed talking through it. If that didn't give the game away, I don't know what would.'

'*The South Bank Show*, and you expected us to guess?' my father says, shaking his head. 'Oh, for fuck's sake!'

'It's not my fault, Edward, if the closest you've come to adult programming is *Blind Date*.'

'I'm a musician. Of course I watch *The South Bank Show* from time to time. But you should have seen the faces you were pulling. It was more like *Some Mothers Do 'Ave 'Em.'*

'And so do some fathers,' Sylvia replied, bitchily.

'What do you mean by that?' My father is leaping to his feet. Sylvia joins him and they stand toe to toe, their noses almost touching.

'I mean, what sort of a man would let his wife work all the hours in the day while he loafs around writing songs that nobody will buy?'

Well done, Sylvia. Great. Here we fucking go.

'The same sort of man who will let a woman destroy a promising career just because she has a nice arse,' my father retaliates.

'*Mother!*'

'*Dad!*'

'Well, what else has she got going for her?'

'Oh, thanks very much,' says Gina, clearly offended.

'She has a damn sight more than your son ever had, Edward Lawrence,' Sylvia responds.

'My son had it all laid out for him, until your daughter laid him. She scrambled his brains along with his dick. Now she's cutting his balls off and turning him into a bloody housewife.'

'You always were a crude man, Edward.'

'At least I'm still a real man, which is more than can be said for my son.'

'Thanks, Dad.' Now it's my turn to be offended.

'Well, look at yourself, boy,' my father shouts at me.

'I agree, he's pathetic,' naturally enough, Sylvia couldn't resist snapping at that bait, 'but you cannot blame Gina for that. He was a loser when she married him. She gave up wealth and security just so your son could become a kept man.'

'Well, that's something in your daughter's favour, I suppose. Unlike her mother, at least she doesn't check the size of a man's bank account before she lies on her back and opens her legs.'

Sylvia has just let out an ear-piercing scream and has run up the stairs towards the bedrooms. If that doesn't wake the kids, then even I'll believe in Father Christmas.

Gina has followed her mother, needless to say.

I'm turning to my father. 'Dad, you're such a – such – such a wanker!'

I've stormed into the kitchen in search of another beer and he's trotted behind me.

'I'm sorry son, but I just can't stand by and see you . . . emasculated like this.'

'Then do what you always do. Sod off.'

'Now, that's not fair.'

'Isn't it?'

'I was working –'

'That's just an excuse. You were never there for me, Dad. Never. I can't tell you how bloody hard that made life. Now, having ruined your wife's life and screwed up your kids, you have the bare-faced cheek to encourage me to do the same to my family. Well, it's just not on.' I slam the fridge door to emphasise the point.

'It wasn't like that, son.'

'Oh, please!' I take a healthy slug from my beer can.

'All right, I admit, in the end, before the divorce, I mean, I'd have done anything to keep out of your mother's way. I couldn't stand to hear her tell me what a mistake she'd made in marrying me. Listening to her go on about the life she might have had. How much she'd sacrificed because she loved me. To be reminded that her love had turned to bitterness and resentment and, yes, hate. What a selfish bastard I was to still be chasing rainbows at my age. An impossible dream, she said.'

Dad sighs.

'She was right, of course. I've never been a better than average musician, but you, son, you're different. You have real talent, real potential, and am I supposed to stand by and let you piss it away in the back of beyond?'

'Oh, fuck, I don't know, Dad. I'm all confused.'

There's a brief silence, during which I sink into one of the kitchen chairs.

'In the beginning I wanted success for myself. Then for your mother and then for my children. I wanted to be someone you would look up to, someone you could respect and it drove me on. I knew I was never going to be president of ICI, so I chased what I was good at. It's the same for you, son. You have to use your talent, it's your only chance. Make your kids respect you. They'll never be proud of a father dressed in an apron.'

'Will they, Dad? Will they respect me if I disappear, promising to come back when I've made my fortune? Can they respect someone they never see?'

He's not answering. Just staring at me. Eventually he says, 'It's gone awfully quiet upstairs, Andy. Maybe you'd better tiptoe on up there and see if things have calmed down.'

'Yeah, I suppose I'd better,' I say, putting down my beer and standing up.

'You could apologise to Sylvia for me, while you're there.'

'Oh, no, Dad, you can do your own dirty work. I'm not bailing you out of this one.'

'Okay,' he replies, as I leave the kitchen and head for the stairs.

I'm hovering on the landing, just outside our bedroom door. I've stopped because I can hear Gina and Sylvia talking. I should go in and interrupt. But I want to hear.

Or do I?

'Believe me, Gina, I know what it costs to love a man like Andy. He reminds me of your father. I think that's what probably attracts you to him. But it's not enough! How long can you keep him? Pay the bills, organise your finances, wipe his backside along with your children's.'

'Mother, Andy is doing a wonderful job . . .'

'. . . looking after the children, I know. Meantime they're growing up, changing, developing, and you're missing it all. They'll be teenagers before you know it, and you won't have been there to see all those wonderful moments a mother should. Don't you want to be there, dear? Don't you want to see little Nicola take her first steps? Hear her string together her first sentence? Take Sophie for her first day at big school? Hug her as she comes rushing out of the school gates?'

'Of course I do.'

'Then find yourself a man who can support you and your children.'

'They're Andy's children too, Mother.'

'He can still see them.'

'You don't understand. It's different for women these days.'

'You rushed into a second-rate job because Andy doesn't earn a penny. Not exactly a career move, was it? He's even denied you that.'

'Andy hasn't intentionally denied me anything. It just hasn't worked out for him. I can't just walk out on him.'

'So it's all just bad luck now, is it? If he had any sense of decency he'd forget about becoming a pop star, or whatever he wants to be, and get himself a proper job. One that pays a decent wage. Look after his wife and children.'

There was an unnerving silence for a while. Then Gina: 'In so many ways Andy is the perfect husband. He's a kind man, he's funny, intelligent, a good father. That's the man I love.'

'But you don't love the man who daydreams and never earns a penny, do you, Gina?'

The pause is agonising from where I'm standing.

'No . . . yes . . . I don't know, Mother. It's all so difficult.'

'Leave Andy now, Gina. Before you lose all respect for him. Before you begin to resent him. Before you make the children resent him.'

I've heard enough. I'm going in.

I'm staring at the two of them. My wife and her mother. I find I don't know what to say. Perhaps I'm as embarrassed as they both look.

'My father wants to apologise to you, Sylvia.'

'Thank you, Andy,' she replies, calmly. 'I'll be down in a minute.'

I've come downstairs to the kitchen and rescued my beer. The house feels suddenly cold. I've noticed the back door is ajar. I've found the note on the table.

CATCH YOU SOMETIME.
HAPPY NEW YEAR TO YOU ALL.

Seems he's run out at the first sign of trouble once again.

11

January 27, 1997. 11.30 p.m.

Christmas passed in a flash, to be replaced by the soggy grey realities of a West Cork winter. It just hasn't stopped pouring down. Worse still, for the children and me, the rain has become our jailer. Due to the lack of wetsuits and oxygen tanks, we just haven't been able to get out of the house. We're going stir-crazy. And children make the most hysterical of cellmates when trapped in a confined space, believe me.

Texas Tessie has been buried alive at the bottom of Sophie's toy box. Crushed to death by talking computers, Barbie's Four-Track, and her moth-eaten collection of My Little Ponies. Gina and I are left with a terrifying overdraft and a collection of letters from credit-card companies threatening public execution.

Christmas Day was rescued by Connor. He stepped into the breach, all charm, wit and diplomacy, the bastard. Can't think why I'm so fond of the bloke.

Sylvia loved him, of course. Healthy bank balance, own business and sensitive Irish sex appeal. He's everything she wanted for herself and her daughter, I suppose.

The month has been miserable. Nappies, washing disasters, broken nights, shopping, pissing rain, money worries, back-to-back sleeping, runny noses, etc.

Oh, and returned demo-tapes with complimentary rejection letters, just to add to the general gaiety.

I'm in the pub. Not O'Leary's. The next one along. Sophie's in playschool. I'm here with Nicola, who is sleeping peacefully in her buggy.

So I'm having a pint with Norman.

Why? That's what I'm wondering. I just bumped into him in the street. That's odd in itself. Norman's not the sort of person you just bump into. Especially not in the daytime. He's usually in court on some life-or-death matter. Like an argument over land boundaries.

He suggested we went for a swift one, Norman did. It was his idea. He's teetering across the pub floor towards me now, spilling the drinks as he walks. By the time he gets here my pint will be a half.

'There you are, my friend.'

My friend!

'We haven't had a chat, just the two of us, you know, for ages. Man to man, as it were.'

Man to man? What is he thinking of doing? Telling me the facts of life?

'No,' I'm replying sceptically, 'I don't think we have.'

'No,' he says, taking a sip from his beer-glass, like someone who would really prefer a glass of sherry. 'No,' he repeats.

Bit of a hiatus now.

A minute, and we've run out of conversation.

He's not saying anything. He's just sat opposite me smiling. Falsely. Down to me, then.

'So . . . Norm, what exactly did you want to talk to me about . . . man to man?'

'Ah, yes, I'm glad you brought that up . . .'

Thank fuck one of us did or we could have been here all day.

'. . . because it's a bit delicate, actually. A bit tricky.' Oh, Gawd, is it?

'In what way, exactly, Norman?'

'Well . . . well . . . well . . .'

He's coughing nervously between each 'well'.

'Just give me the general drift, Norman.'

'Sex, Andy.'

If there was one word I never thought I'd hear Norman say it was 'sex'.

'I see. Er . . . having trouble with the construction business, are you?' I ask, tactfully, I thought.

'Pardon?'

'Struggling to erect the old scaffold?'

'No!' he replies, looking wounded. 'Well, not exactly. It's not me, you see.'

Oh, he's not going to try and pull that one, is he?

'Don't tell me, Norman, it's a friend of yours, is it?'

'No, no, no. Actually, it's Michelle.'

Oh, bugger.

'Michelle?'

'Yes.'

I'm beginning to feel very uncomfortable about this.

'She's all right, isn't she?'

'Yes, yes, she's fine. The trouble is . . . the trouble is . . .'

The suspense is killing me.

'Is what, Norman?'

'It's just that she's always had a healthy appetite in the bedroom department, as it were. But lately, she's . . . she's . . .'

'Gone on a strict diet?' I suggest.

'Pardon?'

'Gone off it?' I clarify.

'No! No, quite the opposite. She's uncontrollable! Can't seem to think about anything else. She won't let me work, she won't let me sleep. It's intolerable. Really, I mean it,' he adds, probably in response to a half-grin I failed to suppress.

'She's stripping off at the drop of a hat. I come home from work, she's lying naked on the sitting-room sofa. I try to work, she's crawling under my study table and fiddling with my flies. Bed-time brings forth the most extraordinary parade of erotic underwear you could possibly imagine. I just don't know what to do.'

'Have you tried giving her one?'

'*I beg your pardon?*'

'Sorry, Norman. That was crude of me. I mean, have you tried satisfying her demands?'

'No, I can't. I mean I could, there's nothing wrong . . . technically. It's just that it's rather . . . putting me off. I mean, it's a little bit threatening. Aggressive. I feel I *have* to . . . I mean, I half expect her to give me marks out of ten at the end or something. It's just not what I'm used to, you see.'

'Yes, quite,' I say, half envious that Gina isn't crawling under my study table and grappling with my 501s. If I had a study table. Or a pair of 501s, come to that.

'The thing is, Andy, and this is where I think you may be able to help, there has to be some reason for this increase in desire. Something must have turned her on, as they say.'

Alarm bells are ringing again.

He's leaning across the table now, lowering his voice.

'I've heard somewhere that sex actually increases at home if your partner is playing away. I mean, do you think Michelle is having an affair?'

Oh, shit, shit, *shit*!

'Surely that's just an old wives' tale, isn't it?'

'Is it?' he asks.

'Yes,' I reply, trying to defuse the situation. 'It's right up there with . . . say . . . you can't get pregnant if you do it standing up, or – gin and a hot bath being mother's ruin, or oysters are an aphrodisiac, or all public-school boys have had a homosexual experience.'

Naughty of me, but I couldn't resist it.

Norm is blushing.

'No, no, no. I don't think that's true at all. Anyway, I'm certain I'm right. If a partner is having . . .'

'Sex,' I help out.

'. . . an affair, then they often up the rations at home. Sort of all part of the deception, if you understand me. Stop hubby getting suspicious.'

'If you say so, Norman. But we're talking about Michelle here. She loves you.'

'Yes, I know that. Still . . .'

'Honestly, Norman, I don't think you need to worry on that score. She's always telling me how . . . exciting she finds you.'

What else can I say? 'Well, actually, Norman, I can't say for certain she's shagging someone else, but I have a sneaking suspicion she's set her heart on a length or two of my dick. Now you come to mention it . . . Norm, baby.'

'Is she? Of course, that could be part of the pretence as well.'

Damn. This is not working. Maybe I should tell him the truth. I mean, I haven't done anything.

'You see, Andy, if she is, you know, having another man, then I feel I should take steps to find out who it is. I mean, my reputation is at stake here. If I find out who it is, perhaps I should do something violent. I don't know – shoot the swine, or something.'

On the other hand, I think I'll put the truth on hold and stick to the bullshit. Truth is open to misinterpretation.

'Isn't murder a bit out of order for a solicitor? Won't they strike you off or something?'

'Mmmm. Well, it's academic at the moment. I mean, I've no idea who the man might be. Tell me, Andy, you know Michelle as well as any of our friends. If she was going to stray, who do you think she would choose as a lover?'

Aghhh! Does he know? Is this a warning? Know what, for fuck's sake? Nothing's happened.

'For example . . .'

Here it comes.

'. . . what about Connor?'

Phew! 'Connor? God, no, he's still in love with his dear departed. Even if he was over it all, I can't see him taking another man's wife.'

'No, you're probably right. Who, then?'

'Norman, aren't you rushing ahead of yourself here? You could end up punching someone on the nose, then finding out they're perfectly innocent. Impetuosity could ruin a marvellous career,' I argue, not without self-interest

'I see what you mean.' Norman nods slowly.

'You're a legal man. Have you discovered any other evidence to support this prosecution? Any love letters? Diary entries? Condoms blocking up your U-bends?'

'She's sterilised.'

'Pardon?'

'Michelle. After giving birth to Richard. Said she wasn't going to go through that pain again for all the tea in China.'

'Really? Never mind, you're missing the point. Maybe she just fancies the socks off you and is frustrated because work takes up so much of your time.'

'Possibly,' he acknowledges, without much conviction.

'Why don't you try giving in gracefully occasionally?'

'Because – because she's an animal, Andy. It just turns me off.'

'Well, then . . .' I'm searching frantically for the right key here '. . . then fantasise. Who have you secretly thought about having it off with? Claudia Schiffer? Elizabeth Hurley?' Wait a minute, this is Norman. 'Delia Smith? Angela Rippon? Clare Short? There must be somebody.'

He's grinning ruefully.

'There is someone, actually.'

'I knew it. Well, close your eyes and imagine it's . . . whoever it is, lying there gagging for it.'

'Do you think it will help?'

'I'm convinced.'

'Yes, yes.' Norman's nodding in agreement. 'Gosh, look at the time. Must dash. Client to see. That's why I'm not in the office.'

He's got what he came for, in other words.

'Thank you, Andy,' he says, standing and shaking my hand. 'You're a real friend.'

'Any time. Glad to help,' I say, as he heads for the pub door.

Nicola is awake in her buggy. She's silent. Just looking up at me, staring.

If I didn't know better, I'd swear that look said: 'You hypocritical old basket, Dad.'

February 3, 1.45 p.m., or thereabouts.

My nerves are a bit too frayed to be accurate.

I'm driving home through puddles so deep that in England they'd be called reservoirs. Nicola is asleep in the back of the car. Sophie is in her car chair next to me. She's unusually quiet and I'm not surprised.

I've just had an awful shock.

I arrived at playschool this lunch-time to find Sophie was nowhere to be seen.

'Sophie just left. Michelle said that that was the arrangement. That was all right, wasn't it, Andy?' the teacher asked.

'Yes, sure, no problem. Must have slipped my mind,' I said, for some obscure reason.

I hot-footed it immediately to Michelle's house, to be greeted by incredulity at my fear.

'I'm not trying to kidnap your children, Andy. Gina asked me to collect Sophie. Something about you taking Nicola off somewhere?'

'The doctor's, but that's tomorrow and, anyway, that's in the morning while Sophie's still in playschool.'

'Maybe I got it wrong, then. Sorry. Anyway, no harm done. Sophie's playing quite happily upstairs with Richard. You look tired, Andy. Has Nicola been keeping you up at nights?'

'Yes, yes, she has.'

I admit I was thrown off track by this show of concern.

'Hasn't Gina taken over a couple of shifts?'

'Of course. Weekends, if she's not too shagged. Michelle . . .'

She tutted. 'They catch up with you. I know, I speak from

experience. Norman never did any nights.' She appraised me again. 'You look stick-thin.'

'Excuse me?'

'You're obviously not eating properly.'

'I am.'

'No, you're not. Gina's not cooking for you any more, is she? Andy, I'm worried about you.'

'Really, I'm fine, Michelle.'

'Anyway come through into the dining room. I've fixed us a light lunch.'

She headed off, obliging me to follow.

The dining-room table was fully set. A bottle of white wine stood in a bucket of ice. Two candles stood burning in a silver centrepiece.

'It's nothing fancy. Just some soup, with fish to follow.'

It was then that I took time to notice what she was wearing. It was a black blouse of see-through chiffon. A matching lace bra was visible underneath. Her long skirt was slit to the thigh.

It looked wonderful, but not the sort of thing one wears for a casual lunch with an old mate.

'Michelle, look, you really shouldn't have gone to all this trouble.'

'It's no trouble, Andy. You're working so hard looking after your children, and who's looking after you?'

'Well, Gina –'

'Nobody,' she interrupted me, firmly. 'No one is looking after your . . . needs.'

She crossed her legs as she said this.

I felt very . . . threatened.

'Sit yourself down, Andy. We haven't chatted for ages. I was beginning to think you were avoiding me,' she said, as she took the wine from the bucket and filled two glasses.

At this point, Sophie came down the stairs and ran into the dining room. She must have heard my voice. Clearly she was not playing happily with Richard.

There were tears in her eyes. 'Daddy, you didn't tell me you weren't picking me up today.'

Sobs. Floods of tears.

I cuddled her. 'I'm sorry, Stinks. There must have been some misunderstanding. Daddy didn't mean to frighten you.'

'Can – we – go – home, now?'

'Yes of course we can.'

I could have kissed her.

'Sorry, Michelle. What can I say?'

'Nothing,' she replied, brusquely. 'It doesn't matter. I mean, it's not important. I just thought it would be nice, that's all,' she clarified.

So that was that. I made a hasty exit, apologising as I went.

I hadn't taken the sleeping Nicola out of the car.

I'd had a suspicion we would need to make a fast exit.

11.15 p.m. Same night.

I just casually asked Gina if she had asked Michelle to pick Sophie up from school today.

'No. Why?' she replied.

'Oh, there was a bit of confusion. Sophie got a bit upset.'

'Well, I didn't ask her. Did you?'

'No. She must have got the wrong end of the stick. Anyway, all sorted. No harm done.'

I don't like this.

Not one little bit.

February 4, 10.00 a.m.

I'm in Rosscarbery. I like Rosscarbery. It's a beautiful village, like so many others here in West Cork. You approach it via a causeway, overlooking a beautiful estuary filled with all manner of birdlife. Swans, herons, oystercatchers. A tractor ploughs its way across the sand twice a day to collect nets full of oysters. In the summer, I sometimes drive to the end of the pier and look out at the magnificent view over the Atlantic, just to remind myself how bloody lucky I am to have this on my doorstep. The village itself is full of nice pubs and restaurants and cheerful people.

But I do not want to come to Rosscarbery today. That's because our doctor also resides here, and the reason I am a bit twitchy is because it's injection time.

Not for me, no, I could deal with that. The days when I fainted at the head of the queue for TB jabs at school are long behind me. Even if I do still occasionally dream of the shame of it all.

No. It's vaccination time for Nicola.

We debated at great length, Gina and I, whether or not to have Nicola immunised. We had Sophie inoculated without a second thought, but there has been some adverse publicity about health risks from one or more of the serums since then and naturally it caused a bit of doubt.

Plus we seem to be surrounded by the alternative-health brigade here in West Cork. It's the *big* thing.

Gina's been indoctrinated now, too. She's all homoeopathy, reflexology, aromatherapy, and she even periodically bathes in disgustingly smelly seaweed.

We finally decided to go ahead with the vaccines for one reason: fear. If Nicola didn't have the jabs and a year or so on caught something related, neither of us could forgive ourselves.

That's why I'm sitting outside the surgery, ready to take the poor little mite in to be tortured.

I'm looking at Nicola now. She's asleep in the car chair next to me.

I can't do this. I shouldn't have to do this. She trusts me. What is she going to think when I goo and gah at her and cuddle her and introduce her to the nice nursey and nice doctor man, and two seconds later they're shoving ruddy great knitting needles up her jacksie?

She'll never forgive me.

No, I won't do it. I can't. This is out of my remit. I'm going to call the house-husbands' union and demand they take action on this.

Start the car, get out of here.

Oh, Andy, turn the engine off.

It's me, isn't it? It's Andy I'm thinking of. I just don't want to see it all. I don't want to be there if it's going to hurt her.

Perfect timing. She's woken up.

'Hiya! Did you have a nice sleepsie? Oh, yes, big stretch for the little girl. Don't pull your hat down over your eyes like that, you twit. Nicola? Where's my Nicola gone? There she is! Oh, baby! Look, we're going to go and see the nice doctor man now. He may do some things that you won't like, but it's for your own good, I swear. You must promise Daddy that you won't hate me when we come out, okay?'

She's smiling at me. A big, gummy smile.

Oh, well, here goes.

So far, so good. Nicola's lying on the bed in the surgery. She's playing with my car keys. I've had to strip her down to her vest and take her nappy off. She's been weighed. She's suitably fat for her age, even though my earliest culinary attempts forced her into a starvation diet.

The nurse is going to take her temperature and then we'll see the doctor.

For some reason, Nursey can't find a thermometer.

Doesn't exactly inspire confidence, does it?

Here she comes.

'Right, Daddy. If you can amuse Baby for me for a second.'

'Eh, Daddy's girl. You're going to have your temperature taken. Who's a big brave girlie, then? Now open wide for the nice nursey.'

'Don't be silly, Daddy. We can't expect Baby to hold a thermometer in her mouth, now, can we?'

'What do you mean?'

OH, JEEZE, SHIT, BUGGER, FUCKING HELLFIRE AND FLAME!

She's just shoved the thermometer up Nicola's bum.

'Is that really necessary?'

'Trust us, Daddy, it's the best way. It's no trouble.'

Maybe not to you, I'm thinking, But what about poor Nicola? How would Nursey like someone to shove something solid up her anus five minutes after meeting them? Though by the look of her . . .

'It's all right, darling, Daddy's here.'

I'm looking at Nicola . . . and she's not bothered. She hasn't even flinched. A slight look in the eyes that says, 'That's a bit kinky, Dad,' but no more than that. If she carries on like this, she could become a very popular girl in time to come and I'm going to spend her teenage years worried sick.

'All done, Daddy. Temperature's fine. Doctor will be with you in a moment.'

'Can I put a nappy on her now?'

'Yes, I'm sure that will be fine.'

I'm putting a Pampers Premium protectively around her little botty. Before she comes here again, I think I'll have a miniature-size suit of armour made especially for her.

We're back in the car now. I've blown raspberries on her neck and spun her round and talked in silly voices and she's laughing again. She's fine. She's okay.

It was awful. It went from bad to worse. A pipette full of heaven-knows-what squirted down her throat, one needle jammed in her leg, another in her arm.

She screamed. Floods of tears. I felt such a bastard. I wanted to punch the doctor for hurting my girl.

I'll take her home and give her a Nice biscuit. She likes those. That'll cheer her up. Gina can take a sodding day off work next time. If there is a next time.

I AM NEVER DOING THAT AGAIN!

3.10 a.m., the next morning.

It never rains but it pours, isn't that what they say?

Well, here it hurricanes, tornados and monsoons. Indoors and out. We're all up. Gina, Sophie, Nicola and yours truly.

Sophie started the ball rolling. A cry from the bedroom, a sprint to answer her call of distress in time to watch her puke majestically on to her mattress.

Why do four-year-olds never stand still when they're being ill? Mine doesn't, anyway. Sophie insists on wandering around the room, chucking up wherever she happens to be standing at the time.

Twenty minutes after she began, her room looks as if it were the venue for a rave. You would never believe it was all the work of one small child.

Gina did the clearing up. I was thankful for that. I might have been barfing next to Sophie if I'd had to do it.

'What have you been feeding her?' was Gina's one line of criticism.

'Nothing,' I replied, defensively, and there's an element of truth in that. She's been off her food lately. Not because of my cooking. I'm actually quite good now, proper grown-up things too. I can follow a recipe as well as the next man. But it's been a bit of a war of attrition, trying to get Sophie to eat something of late. Maybe this has been coming on for some time. I mentioned this to Gina and she looked horrified.

'Why haven't you mentioned this to me before?'

'I didn't want you to worry.'

'Well, I'm twice as bloody worried now!'

'I'm sorry, Gina. Look, she hasn't been *ill* as such, until tonight. I just thought it was a . . . phase or something.'

'Just tell me next time, okay?'

'I will, I promise.'

'Then we can discuss it and decide between us if she needs to see a doctor or not.'

'Okay.'

At this point, Nicola woke up screaming due to the noise the rest of us were making. She's a bit off as well. It could be teething or it could be a reaction to the injections.

Gina is seeing to her.

I'm cuddling Sophie on the sofa. Reading a bit more Tintin.

She doesn't seem to have a temperature so no need for immediate panic.

Aghhh! Kids!

4.02 a.m.

Nicola's back in her cot and Gina's back in Mummy and Daddy's big bed. I insisted she went. She looked exhausted, not to mention fraught, and she has a very heavy day at work tomorrow. I'm in the single bed with Sophie.

This is more uncomfortable than it sounds. There may not be much of her, but when she gets into bed she sort of . . . swells to ten times her size and spreads herself across the entire mattress. I'm left balancing precariously on about two inches like a Russian gymnast on the beam. But without the grace.

I set the rules as I climbed in with her. No fidgeting, no snoring, no apple-tarting. She giggled, snuggled in to me, and has finally drifted off, leaving me wide awake and hovering over her like a mother hen.

Is Sophie ill because I haven't looked after her properly? Maybe I should have kept a closer eye on her.

Nicola is easier to monitor because she never lets you leave her alone long enough for something to sneak up on you, but Sophie . . . she plays her cards close to her chest. Always has done.

Anyway, she's sleeping now. With a bit of luck her stomach's shifted the last of the poison.

I hope so, otherwise I'm right slap-bang in the firing line, matey. What a dreadful, dreadful day.

12

February 14. Valentine's Day.

Embarrassing when the most you can afford to show how much you love your spouse is a pathetically small bunch of flowers.

Equally depressing is that you cannot afford to go out to a nice restaurant, just the two of you, even if you'd remembered to book it before the rush. Nope, the coffers won't stretch to it, and besides, the babysitters are all out indulging in a little furtive groping with their own beaux. So, in order to make the effort, you have to have friends round to dinner.

This is particularly morale-shattering, when one of those friends has to be Norman.

I subtly found a quiet moment to ask if he'd sorted out his little problem, *re* Michelle. He looked momentarily flustered, and said, 'Yes, yes, everything's fine,' and went back to being his irritating self.

So, no more man-to-man chats with his big pal Andy, then.

Tonight he's enthralling us with a tale of bitterness and revenge, envy and despair.

Apparently a friend looks after her neighbour's toucan while they're away on holiday. Needless to say dear old Beaky croaks while neighbour is swanning around the Seychelles. This was not a particularly youthful creature.

'So what happened then?' Gina's asking.

'Well, the poor friend was mortified,' Norman's informing us in deadly earnest, 'so she purchased another toucan at great expense and gave it to her neighbour with a sincere apology. The neighbour accepted the toucan and told her friend to drop dead.'

I've just felt a stockinged foot creeping up the inside of my leg. I've looked across the table at Gina who is smiling.

Things are looking up.

'How ungrateful,' Michelle is saying to her husband. 'What did the poor friend do?'

The stockinged foot has just reached my crotch and my old chap is responding in the traditional manner. I'm winking at Gina and she's smiling back.

Yes! Yes! Yes!

Not hassling her sexually may finally be about to pay off.

'Well,' Norman drivels on, 'she was so hurt and affronted by this, she used the unreturned front-door key to her neighbour's house, entered, wrung the toucan's neck and attempted to flush it down the toilet in the *en suite* bedroom. Allegedly.'

'Who are you representing, Norman?' Gina asks, her foot continuing to tease me mercilessly under the table.

'I'm defending the friend, of course.'

'Pity nobody defended the toucan, really,' I jest, and only Michelle finds it funny.

Gina has started to gather dishes.

'It's okay, I'll do that,' I'm saying, giving her a suggestive wink.

'No need,' she says, still smiling and, sadly, removing her foot. But I'm helping anyway. Don't want to lose Brownie points now. This has embarrassed our guests into mucking in as well, so we all troop into the kitchen.

I've just noticed.

Gina isn't wearing stockings or tights but . . . socks. Yes, *socks*! She's wearing trousers and socks. You know, the sort that used to be the prerogative of men until Top Shop or some such decided they were trendy for women to wear, thus killing off foreplay up and down the country.

Socks.

Gina isn't wearing stockings.

But Michelle is.

Now I'm the one being winked at suggestively.

Michelle has achieved something I would not have believed possible. She's actually made me feel sorry for Norman.

I mean her bloody husband was sitting next to her while she . . .

Shit! Shit! Shit!

This is getting out of hand.

I'd better have a word with Michelle as soon as possible.

I feel a disaster looming.

3.17 a.m. and I've just been refused sex.

Again.

What was all that smiling about? Don't tell me she found Norman's story funny?

I mean, it's Valentine's Day for heaven's sake! A time for lovers. Maybe she just doesn't fancy me any more.

Perhaps I should fuck Michelle. At least she wants me.

February 16.

My birthday. I'm thirty-eight.

Ugh!

We've no money, so celebrations have been somewhat muted. A Marks and Spencer chicken tikka masala Gina brought back from Cork, and a bottle of sparkling vinegar. Moët de Sarsons.

A few cheap, though admittedly thoughtful, gifts, and I was let off the washing-up.

No birthday treats in the bedroom department either, surprise, surprise.

I don't care.

I've no desire to be reminded that I'm too old to rock and roll.

Middle of March.

I haven't spoken to Michelle since Valentine's Day. Norman whisked her off to Sri Lanka or somewhere. Came back without her. Apparently she decided to stay on. With a bit of luck she's taking out her sexual frustration on some poor unsuspecting native.

It's a Tuesday night, the Blow-ins have finished rehearsing and Matt and I are opposite each other in O'Leary's.

For some reason, the others didn't come with us for the customary pint. I didn't hear the excuses, or if I did they were forgettable.

Matt's just bought some drinks, which is a bit of a rarity. He usually finds an excuse to leave just before his round, but seeing as there are only two of us tonight I suppose he was snookered.

'Listen up, boy, because have I got some news for you, my friend,' he's just drawled at me.

'Oh?'

'Yup. I sure hope you think it's good news. We've been offered a tour.'

'A tour?'

'Yes, sir. You know, where you travel around playing lots of different venues. Like, a tour, man.'

'Who has?'

'Who has, what?'

'Been offered a tour, Matt.'

'The band. The Blow-ins.'

'Really? Where do we play? Limerick? Galway? Dublin?'

'No, sirree. Frankfurt, Hamburg, Essen, Cologne, and one or two other places I can't pronounce,' he quips at me.

'Correct me if I'm wrong, but that's Germany, isn't it?'

'Woah! Way to go, Andy. Top marks for geography.'

'How the hell did we get offered a tour of Germany?'

'Connections,' he's saying smugly.

I've just remembered. Matt's wife's father is German or something.

'And there's more. We get a chance to cut a record too.'

'You're pulling my plonker.'

'Swear to God. We may even be able to lay down some of those dipso tunes of yours you call songs.'

My head is spinning.

'Why would they want us to record?'

'It works like this: we record the CD at the start and sell it at the gigs. The people play the CD, then a few months later we go back and do the same tour again, hopefully with a bigger following.'

He's buzzing. I've never seen him so animated.

'A second tour?' I'm asking, trying to grasp all this.

'That's what I said. So. Are you in or not?' he's asking, slugging back his lager while he awaits my answer.

'Pardon?'

'The tour. The boys have asked me to find out if you're up for this or not.'

'The boys, Matt? You mean, Fozzie and Johan. You've already discussed it with them, have you?'

'Yes, sir. They're 'bout as keen as mustard. How about you?'

I'm nodding cagily. Don't want to seem too eager at this stage. Though the adrenaline is pumping round my body.

'It sounds fun. Money?'

'What about it?'

'That's sodding ominous. Wages, Matt, wages. What's the money like?'

'So-so. Two fifty a week. But listen, man, wowee, the venues! We're not playing little Bavarian village pubs here. No, sir. Well, not for the most part. These are big cities, loaded with possibilities. This is real positive. Hey, Andy, Hamburg! A chance to walk the streets that made the Beatles famous, eh? You following me here? Wonder if the Star Club's still there? This time it could be you they're all shouting, "Mak music," at, eh, boy? Course if you've got other priorities now ...'

I'm placing my pint down on the table and I'm staring at him.

'What's that supposed to mean?'

'Don't fuck with me, Andy. You know what I'm getting at, man. Since you took over the family bra, you haven't shown the same commitment and you know it.'

I'm furious. 'Bullshit!'

'No, it's not, Andy. You've started missing rehearsals, turning up late for gigs. You're not as ... professional as you once were.'

'Professional? Don't make me laugh! What about all the occasions you've pissed off back to America and I've covered your back? What about when we've played without a drummer because Johan can't get a night off from waiting at tables? What about when Fozzie disappears up-country to try and flog his wood-burning stoves? What happens to professionalism then?'

'It's not the same, Andy.'

'Bollocks!'

He's shaking his head. 'No, it isn't. The difference is you're here, and yet you're not here, man. If you catch my drift. Physically you're amongst us, but mentally, man, wow! I don't know where your head's been.'

I'm sighing heavily. 'When is this tour?'

'Ten days.'

'*What?*'

'Ten days. We hit the road in ten days.'

'Jeeze!'

'So the boys are kinda anxious. Are you in or out? 'Cos if you're out, man, we have to move real fast to replace you or cover our arses some way or another.'

He doesn't want me in.

Odd. Ballinkilty, West Cork. Such a beautiful, seductive little town. Full of peace and tranquillity. Yet even here treachery can rear its ugly little head.

'What does Fozzie's wife have to say about all this?' I'm asking, looking for another weak link.

'She's cool. That marriage is on the rocks anyway.'

'Johan's employer?'

'He's quitting.'

'You're joking! What about your – er – good lady?'

'She's coming with us. So are the kids.'

'How cosy.'

'What about you, Andy? You coming?'

'Look, you'll have to give me a couple of days.'

'Andy, we don't *have* a couple of days.'

'Fuck you, Matt! I've worked hard for this band and I've covered everyone else's back countless times. *I want two fucking days!* You owe me that much at least.'

'All right, Andy, you got it. Two days, but no longer.' He's shaking his head and looking sheepish. 'Shit, Andy, it isn't as if we don't want you to come on the tour, boy.'

'Yeah, right.'

'Let me buy you another drink.'

He must be feeling guilty. Catholicism must be catching.

'No, thanks. Better get home. Things to discuss. I'll ring you Saturday night.'

'Sure, Andy. Take real care now.'

'Yeah, right. Leave it with me.'

'Okay. Do your best, you hear?'

I've driven home. I'm sat inside the car, just outside the house. It's raining so hard I swear it's going to break through the windscreen and drown me any minute.

Strewth, what a mess.

Forty-eight hours.

I've got to mention it tonight. I haven't the time to wait.

I'm rehearsing. I'm so scared about Gina's reaction I'm actually sitting here practising what I'm going to say.

A glimmer of hope at last. A flicker. They're few and far between, these days.

Come on, Andy, be sensible. This isn't the big break. A few gigs and a badly recorded CD. You shouldn't even be considering it.

I am, though. Considering it.

How the mighty have fallen, eh?

Matt's such a shit. He sits there telling me he's taking his entire brood. That's because of his private means, his wife's money. Come on, why else do you think he's hitched to someone who should have been committed to the funny-farm donkey's years ago? So he has no conception of how family ties can pull you in another direction.

You see, the thing is, they're playing some big cities and I could probably argue for using more of my new material, which will probably be recorded and . . . well . . . I'm running out of last chances.

This is the biggest opportunity to present itself to me in years.

So it's got to be tonight. Have to set the cat amongst the pigeons. Let the fur and feathers fly, in the hope that things can be looked at rationally when it's all landed.

Here goes.

Gina is standing in the kitchen.

I've closed the door behind me.

'Hiya, Andy. Good rehearsal?'

'Yes. Gina?'

Bugger! She's walked into the lounge. Freshly made cup of tea in hand. Just as I'd screwed my courage to the sticky place, or however the quote goes.

I've taken off my waxed jacket, compulsory attire for weather like this, and now I've joined Gina on the sofa.

She looks odd. Something's wrong.

'You okay, Gina?'

'Fine.'

'Sure?'

'I said, didn't I?' she replies irritably.

'Sorry, sorry.'

'It's just . . .'

'Yes?'

'I'm late.'

'What for?'

She's sighing. Usually a sign that I'm being thick.

'Guess.'

'You're late?'

'*Yes!*'

'All right, all right. So, what for? A deadline?'

'No.'

'An appointment?'

'No.'

'A very important date?'

'*No!*'

'WHAT THEN?'

'My period.'

'What?'

'My cycle. My monthlies. I haven't been visited by the little red devil.' She's angrily slurping at her tea. 'Jeeze, Andy, you're so stupid tonight. I've not come on, boy. Must I draw you a frigging diagram? I haven't bled.'

'Therefore . . .?'

'You got there, well done. I might be pregnant, yes.'

'I see.'

Outwardly, I'm nodding calmly.

Inwardly, I'm screaming in blind panic.

'You need to go to the chemist for me tomorrow. Pick up a home pregnancy test.'

'Right. Leave it with me.'

'*Oh, Andy!*'

She's thrown her arms around me.

Gina is holding me in a grip that would not embarrass a champion of the World Wrestling Federation.

'We can't have another baby now, we can't. It's wrong, wrong, wrong. We can't afford it for a start. I can't get maternity leave – the magazine's struggling as it is. If I left, I wouldn't have a job to go back to. And you've got your hands full enough. What are we going to do?'

Good question.

Pity I can't find a worthy answer.

I can't even remember having sex. Maybe we did, once. Must have, under the circumstances.

Oh, Christ! Not another hole in one.

Gina is physically shaking.

Maybe tonight is not the right time to mention the tour.

Following evening. 6.30 p.m.

I don't know what day it is. I don't know whether I'm on my head or my arse at present. I've been climbing walls waiting for Gina to come home and do the test. I still haven't mentioned the tour. I can't.

She's just read the instructions and apparently I purchased one of the few kits you have to use first thing in the morning. It was cheaper than the others.

Fucking marvellous news.

Just what I wanted to hear.

I'm running out of time if I'm going to get on that tour.

What am I going to do?

To say the atmosphere in the house is a little tense would be a complete mastery of understatement.

6.00 a.m. The following morning.

Gina's just emerged from the bathroom and the test is negative – after all that.

Apparently it means nothing. The home kit said negative last time, and a few months later out pops Nicola.

Gina's too distraught for me to begin to mention anything else.

I have to let Matt know tomorrow. I'm looking at the future and I see my career disappearing on that plane while I'm condemned to a life of Bonjela and Calpol and Cow and fucking Gate and I'm scared.

Both children are picking up on our stress levels and misbehaving accordingly.

It was a two-test packet. We'll double check tomorrow.

6.30 a.m., next day.

Negative again. Yet still no sign of blood.

So that means she's pregnant, doesn't it? Plum duff, up the spout, bun-in-the-oven, one-on-the-way, pregnant.

Shit! This can't be happening. We've no money, no time, no life as it is. We can't have another baby.

It's all very well Gina freaking over this, but it's me that will have to look after the sodding thing.

I can't cope!

I'm up all hours of the bloody night with Nicola as it is.

Then there's Sophie. I mean, what am I going to do if I've got a new baby to look after? It's too much. Three's too much, I can't hack it, I'm flat out with two, another one is going to push me right over the fucking edge. I promise you. I will crack.

Fuck it! I'm past caring. I won't be trapped. I'm just going to pick up my bass guitar and get on that bloody plane to Hamburg.

Ten days later. Back end of March, I think. I'm not sure.

It's morning. I know that much because Sophie's at playschool. I'm walking round the lounge with Nicola in my arms.

This morning was surreal. Weird.

Blood.

Gina doing cartwheels of joy around the lounge, screaming, 'Yes! Yes! Yes!'

We had to try to explain to Sophie why Mummy was so hyper, which was awkward.

Sophie was upset. She wanted a baby.

We celebrated the fact that we weren't going to have another child by eating a cooked breakfast. Appetites returning now our stomachs have stopped churning.

Ten days. Ten long days of mental torture.

It's eleven thirty in the morning.

The plane is taking off for Hamburg and I'm not on it.

I didn't discuss the tour with Gina.

Like the baby, the timing wasn't right.

I'm crying.

Here, now.

I am crying because we're not going to have another nipper and I'm actually happy about that.

Elated.

Or am I weeping because I'm not on that bloody plane?

Do I feel I've not so much missed the plane as the boat?

Is that it?

Who knows how long I'll have to wait for another opportunity?

If there will be another.

So I'll calm Gina down and I'll comfort Nicola and I'll play with Sophie because she's been neglected.

Perhaps as I hold the baby I'll realise I would have been miserable away from her, and my family.

All I know is I'm holding my baby daughter close. Hugging her.

I'm holding a baby and I'm crying like one.

All I know is . . .

I'm fucked up.

13

It's Easter. Well, just after. The last day of Sophie's school holidays and, for a change, the sun is out.

Gina's at home with Nicola. She took Easter week off to give me a hand with the children.

So I've brought Sophie to the beach.

There's a surprisingly large amount of people here. Mums and dads with their kids, retired people taking walks, and young lovers. The first sunny day and the residents come out of hibernation.

There are lots of beautiful beaches around here. We've come to Inchydoney today, the biggest in the area. It's the kind of picture-perfect bay everyone seems to remember from their childhood. The sand is soft and comforting under your feet and the beach seems as long as it is wide. The cliffs decorate its edges like giant sculptures and the sea air is intoxicating. We're waiting for the waves to sweep towards us and then we're rushing towards them, trying to jump up out of their way at the last minute. I wore swimming trunks under my trousers. When I take my daughter to the beach, we end up getting wet, whatever the weather, believe me. So, I'm getting my gonads tickled by freezing cold water and Sophie's getting drowned from head to foot and adoring every second of it.

I love seeing her like this. It makes up for all the days when she's a complete pain to look after. All those times when she's awkward, difficult, demanding and obtuse. It's all forgotten. We've made sandcastles. Dug up half the beach and had an ice-cream.

I'd better take her home now. Otherwise she's going to catch her death of cold. She's shivering, but she doesn't care.

In a minute, she's going to have a massive tantrum and spoil it all when I tell her it's time to go home.

That's children for you.

There's a tug on my arm.

'Daddy?'

'Yes, Sophie?'

'Daddy. Can I whisper?'

'Of course.'

I'm bending down so she can reach my ear.

'Can I have a secret wee-wee?'

'No, Sophie, not now.'

'But, Dad, I'm desperate.'

'You'll have to hold on till we get home.'

'Dad?'

'What?'

'Dad?'

'Yes, Sophie?'

'I don't think I can make it, you know.'

'Why have you left it so late?'

'It just crept up on me, Daddy.'

'Go on, then. Be discreet.'

I can't believe it. She's just flung down her knickers, opened her legs and piddled where she's stood. In full view of everyone.

Howls of laughter, hysterical cackling from the dozen or so people close enough to witness the show.

What an exhibitionist!

She's looking up at me now. Smiling.

'Daddy?'

'Yes, Sophie?'

'What's discreet?'

Time to go, I think.

11.10 a.m. Following morning.

I'm shaking. I'm physically quivering. I can't seem to stop. I've been like this for the last ten minutes.

Thank goodness Nicola's in bed otherwise she'd probably think her daddy had shell-shock. Which he has, sort of.

It's Sophie's first day back at playschool and Gina's back at work. Anyway, I dropped Sophie off at school; nothing unusual in that. I drove home, gave Nicola a bottle and she nodded off to sleep. Again, as per usual.

Just an ordinary day in the life of a house husband. Just a bog-standard day. Nothing to give me the slightest clue what was about to unfold.

Literally.

About half an hour after I've put Nicola in her cot, Michelle turns up. So I try not to panic. I'm an adult. A rational human being. This is a little awkward, nothing more, I tell myself. I've been waiting for an opportunity to let Michelle know it's no-go and here it is.

I make a couple of cups of Gold Blend and we go into the lounge.

That *was* a bit different actually. Usually we stay in the kitchen, but today she walked into the lounge and I followed her.

My mind was whirring as I tried to think exactly what to say. How to phrase it so we can both walk away with our dignity and remain friends.

Michelle sat on the sofa and I sat on the chair opposite.

'So how was Sri Lanka?' I asked, stalling for time while I tried to give my courage a good plucking.

'Wonderful! I rediscovered the joy of painting.'

'Oh, really? What did you paint?'

'Nudes mostly,' she said, smiling. 'It's amazing how uninhibited those waiters can be in exchange for a modest fee.'

'Is that a fact?' I asked, trying not to sound shocked.

'I'm joking, Andy! Where's your sense of humour? I painted the surrounding scenery. I found it helped me relax,' she informed me, as she slipped her high heels off her feet. 'How have things been for you?'

'Oh, you know. Same as ever, really.'

'Mmmm, for me too, since I came home. Isn't it dull?'

'Is it?'

'Don't you think so? It gets so repetitive, routine. There's no . . . excitement.'

She kept moving about as she said this. Fidgeting. Tucking her legs up under her bum then stretching them out again. She was wearing a very short dress and I kept getting a flash of her knickers.

I admit I looked. I didn't particularly mean to, but it was difficult to ignore.

'Yes. I see what you mean.'

'Don't you ever wish for something amazing to happen, Andy? Something *memorable*.'

'Yes, if I'm honest. I suppose I do. Little fantasies, you know.'

'Ooh, Andy, tell me more.'

First mistake.

'No, not that sort of fantasy. I'm talking about record deals, telephone calls from the Gallagher twins, that sort of thing.'

'Shall I tell you something?'

'Go on, then.' I knew she would anyway.

'I have those sort of fantasies.'

'What? You dream of getting a record deal as well, do you?'

I knew what she meant. I was just desperately trying to defuse the situation with a feeble attempt at humour.

'No, sexual fantasies. Well, Norman and I haven't had it for months and that makes a girl's mind wander.'

'I'm sure it does.'

'Sometimes I fantasise about someone from the telly or a film star. Then again it might be the postman or the delivery-boy. But my favourite is when I fantasise about a friend. Someone I know, really quite well.'

I tell you, by this time my heart was beating a drum solo.

I couldn't speak. I just stared at her.

'Do you like my tan?' she asked suddenly, changing the subject.

'Yes, you look wonderful,' I said, and immediately wished I hadn't. But, in fairness, she did look good. The time spent on a foreign beach had not been wasted. It suited her. Made her look like a Continental. Spanish, perhaps.

'I usually sunbathe topless, but I didn't this time.'

'Really?' I managed to splutter, my voice breaking like a choirboy's.

'No. If you ask me nicely, I'll let you see my white bits.'

How did she know about that? It's a personal kink of mine. In the days before children and when Gina and I could afford holidays I wouldn't allow her to sunbathe topless. Gina thought I was being prudish, but I find all those vital areas highlighted, glowing white against the brown, a real turn-on.

She must have spoken to Gina.

Shit! That's devious.

'Would you like to see them, Andy? Be honest with yourself, now.'

'Listen ... Michelle ... before we go ... any further ... I ...'

At that moment she missed the edge of the coffee table with her cup and spilled its contents down the bottom half of her dress.

It was timed to perfection. Almost rehearsed. It looked like an accident.

I didn't wait to find out. It gave me a chance to get out of the room and I fucking leapt at it.

'I'll get a cloth,' I said, and I ran into the kitchen.

I fished a clean J-cloth out from under the sink and soaked it in cold water. Then I rubbed it all over my flushed face. After that I wet it again and walked back into the lounge.

And there she stood.

Naked.

She held her dress in her hands and was scrubbing it with a baby wipe she must have retrieved from her handbag.

'Sorry, Andy, I was soaked through,' she explained, and I could see the milky coffee running down her thighs before she attacked them with a fresh wipe.

'Bloody marvellous things these Wet Ones. So versatile.'

I stood frozen to the spot with fear, I swear. I said nothing, I couldn't speak.

'Oh, well, I'll just have to wait for them to dry,' she said, as she placed her dress and knickers on the nearest available radiator.

I still didn't move.

She turned to me and smiled.

'So, Andy. Was I right to keep my bikini on?'

I didn't reply. I just stood there, still holding out the J-cloth I had brought for her to use.

'Which bit of me are you going to dab first?' she asked, laughing, before crossing to the chair behind her.

She sat down, arching her back slightly to accentuate her breasts, which stood full and beckoning before me. Then she threw a leg over each arm of the chair.

'You can fuck me if you like, Andy. Here, now. No strings, no emotions, no ramifications, no repercussions. Just sex.'

'I ... I ... I ...'

In the days when I was young, free, single and gigging in London, I'd have leapt upon Michelle with all the enthusiasm of a lapsed hunger-striker at a running buffet. But now, with Gina and the kids ...

'Norman need never know. Gina need never know. Nobody will. It will be our little secret.'

'Michelle, this isn't ...'

'I know Gina hasn't been looking after you. She told me. We do talk, you know. Girls do.'

'Michelle.'

'You're a healthy man with a healthy appetite. You can't deny your needs.'

'No! Michelle –'

'I know you want me,' she said, standing up from the chair and crossing towards me.

'I can see you do,' she said, as she stroked my erection through my jeans.

Okay, I admit it. It doesn't matter what signals of panic or alarm bells my brain was sending down to my groin, *he* wasn't listening.

At this point I was tempted.

'Gina and I, we haven't . . . we don't . . . Well, she doesn't seem to want to . . .' and here was Michelle, naked, falling to her knees, undoing my trousers and pulling my cock free.

'What have we here?' she said, as she moved her mouth towards – STOP!

Finally I came to my senses, or not, depending on your point of view.

'*No!*'

I stepped away from her. As I did this I tripped over my jeans, which by this time were residing around my ankles, and went arse over tit, landing my full body weight on my swollen member. I let out a scream of bloody agony.

'*Ahhhhrg!*'

She towered over me as I lay, foetus-like, nursing my damaged tackle.

'I'm sorry, but I love Gina,' I panted out, amidst whimpers of pain.

'BASTARD!' Michelle screamed, before sweeping her clothes off the radiator and heading in the direction of the downstairs loo.

By the time she came back into the lounge we were both dressed, the coffee stain on her white dress still visible in the form of a dark ring.

'I'm sorry, Andy.' Her eyes were red, but she spoke softly and appeared to have calmed down.

'No, I am. I'm sorry. I didn't mean to offend –'

'It's just,' she interrupted, 'I need to feel attractive.'

'You are, Michelle. Just because –'

'Norman ignores me. I wear stockings, I dance naked, I sit on his bloody face, for fuck's sake, and there's no response. The man's dead from the neck down.'

That I can believe.

'It never used to be that way. Before Richard was born we never stopped making love. Now? I know I'm not as young as I was. Maybe I'm just a saggy, stretch-marked old hag . . .'

'Nonsense. You're a very beautiful woman, with a lovely body and –'

'How can you say that? I just stripped naked and opened my legs for you and you turned me down.'

'Not because you're not sexy. But because I love Gina and –'

'Oh, God! Please don't tell Gina, Andy. She's my best friend,' she said, a touch hypocritically.

'I can't promise, Michelle. I don't know what to do about that. You see Gina and I have the sort of relationship whereby –'

'OH, ANDY! YOU'RE SUCH A SAP! You fucking deserve to get hurt.'

And with that she stormed out.

On an insult.

Fucking charming.

So that's why I'm here drinking a huge Scotch, hoping Nicola doesn't start screaming for me before I've steadied my nerves. Cleared my thoughts.

I've ballsed up here. We were good mates, Michelle and I.

True, we've become closer since I started looking after the house and the children. We may have joked a bit about sex but, then, we always have.

Did I encourage this? Maybe I should have nipped it in the bud sooner, but it was awkward. She is my wife's best friend. Maybe I just enjoyed the attention. I must admit, since Gina and I have stopped making love so frequently I have been more . . . aware of other women.

Fucking hell! Is this my fault?

I still can't believe it was offered to me on a plate and I refused the meal.

Did you want to, though, Andy? Did you want to?

Ironical, isn't it? I'm gagging for Gina. Aching for her. Then along comes a very good-looking woman, with a lovely body, and says yes, please, and I freeze with fear.

I wouldn't. I *couldn't.*

So much for the rock-and-roller in you, eh, Andy?

I don't think I'm going to tell Gina. I can't.

I need advice.

I'll ring Connor.

I'm on the phone and I've just given Connor chapter and verse.

'Fucking hellfire! Oh, Andy, didn't I warn you this would be after happening?'

'I know, I know.'

'Then why didn't you do something to defuse the situation sooner?'

'Connor, short of bursting out of the nearest available closet and seducing Norman, I don't think anything would have put her off. She's a very determined woman, you know.'

'I was afraid she might be.'

'I suppose you think I should tell Gina?'

'NO!' He's screaming down the phone at me.

'Funny, I thought you would.'

'Under normal circumstances, I probably would have. But this is complicated. You've let it go too far now.'

'But part of me feels I should tell Gina, Connor.'

'Are you barking fecking mad? You tell *any* female that another of her sex threw off her clothes and begged you for it, there's not a woman in the world would believe you didn't grasp the opportunity. Not even your Gina.'

'But I *didn't.*'

'It's beside the point. Most other men would have taken full advantage. Just lay it to rest now, why don't you? It's for the best, I'm telling you. If you say something now you'll only cause unnecessary pain. Worse still, she might never trust you again.'

'What if Michelle says something to Gina?'

'She won't. She'll start off being too busy to see Gina until she's gathered her nerves then she'll act like nothing's happened.'

'You think so?'

'I know so.'

'Well, if you're sure.'

'I am.'

'Oh, God, Connor! It's such a bloody mess. How did I ever let it get to this stage?'

'Ah, come on now, Andy. Don't be too hard on yourself. Listen, if it makes you feel any better you're not the only man in the world who's recently made a mistake with a woman.'

'What's-her-name giving you trouble, is she? You know, Mrs Save the World and Eat Vegetarian?'

'Elisa?'

'That's her.'

'Correct. Sadly she is no more.'

'Oh. What happened?'

'She ditched me after catching me kicking the cat's backside.'

'You're joking!'

'No. It was dragging a piece of chicken I thought was safely hidden across the kitchen floor at the time, so I sort of double-faulted really.'

He's a good lad, is Connor. Always cheers me up, just in time.

'Listen, now, I have to be getting some work done. Go away and just be thankful the women still fancy an old git like you, okay?'

'Okay.'

Decision taken. I pray it's the right one.

I don't tell Gina.

14

12.30 p.m. Middle of June.

Things have been calmer of late. A lull after the storm.

A bit of peace. Well, what passes as peace when you have children.

Nicola is in her high chair, finally sated after a large bowl of baby rice and Pure Fruit, two *fromage frais*, three Nice biscuits, topped off with a half-bottle of milk. She's saying, 'Mama!' and 'Dada!' in turn. Still can't get her to eat much in the way of savoury. She has a sweet tooth. Sophie is at the table eating frankfurters, mashed potatoes and carrots, under sufferance.

She's so eccentric. All these things have to be served to her on different dishes. Why? It's all going in the same gob, isn't it? All ending up in the same stomach?

Sophie broke up from school last Friday, so this is the first day of an agonisingly long summer holiday, during which I have to look after *both* the fruit of my loins from the crack of dawn onwards.

Gina was off work both at Christmas and Easter.

Fortunately, we're actually having a heat-wave. I have to keep pinching myself to remember I'm not in Greece or Turkey.

It should make an enormous difference. The garden will become accessible, the kids and I can take a picnic to the beach, and Sophie can burn off as much steam as she needs to in the wide open spaces.

Ballinkilty has never looked more beautiful. The houses and shop-fronts have all had their Mediterranean pastel paintwork renewed, and hanging baskets in glorious bloom line the narrow streets like soldiers of colour.

One festival after another is taking place. Summer festivals, old-time festivals, country-and-western festivals, all featuring locals dressed in authentic-looking costumes.

The drawback to all this, of course, is that the town is crammed full of tourists. These days, if you do not have an ancestral Irish background to look up, you're just not hip. British, American,

German, French, you name them, they're here. You can't get parked, and every time you open the door to your local, some pissed Scandinavian falls on top of you, reeking of Murphy's.

Anyway, I have had my two little darlings for less than a day and I am already screaming, 'SUBMIT,' at the top of my voice. They have been tortuous this morning. I never realised how much energy Sophie must work off at playschool until now.

Today she's been trying to re-create her morning session at home. That's meant we have had to read stories, polish the brass, sing songs, dress up and paint pictures.

Actually the last statement is not quite true. She's painted the kitchen table, the walls, the floor, the front of the fridge, the portable telly and, oh . . . Nicola.

I've spent half the morning clearing up after her. I've shouted, 'SOPHIE, NO!' so many times I'm thinking of using it as a refrain for one of my songs.

Nicola is clearly pissed off that Sophie has encroached on her quality time with Daddy. It's just not on, according to her. So she has cried and whinged and screamed and shouted, 'Dada!' all morning. Which is clever, because as soon as I hear her call, 'Dada!' I go all soppy and give her my attention.

She may be young, but she's learning fast.

'Daddy?'

'Yes, Sophie?'

'I don't want this.'

'Really? That's sad because you've got to eat it.'

Big sigh.

'Ugh! Daddy!'

'You don't want another tummy bug, do you? You've had too many of them recently. A girl can't live by sweets, crisps and Mini-Rolls alone. Now eat.'

'Wish Mummy was here.'

Whispered.

'What did you say?'

'Nothing,' she replies, as she pounds her mashed potatoes with a teaspoon.

'I wish Mummy was here as well. I could use the help. But she'd tell you exactly the same, Sophie.'

Spoonful going in mouth to defuse situation.

'Dada!'

'Yes, darling, what is it?'

I'm turning to demanding daughter number two.

'Maybe Nicola would like some frankfurter?'

'No, Sophie. Nicola isn't going to bail you out either.'

'I'll just try her and see.'

'Sophie. SOPHIE! Get back in your chair and eat. Now come on, don't mess your poor daddy around like this.'

I'm clock-watching. I do generally. But not every three minutes. I'm ageing. Fast.

It's 6.15 p.m. and I'm knackered.

Part of my list of written duties was to take Sophie for a haircut today.

Disaster.

Sophie was hysterical. Howling, uncontrollable. Writhing round the floor, screaming, 'Please, Daddy, no, Daddy!', and I couldn't reason with her. She just went off like a rocket again the minute I suggested she sat in the chair and let poor Frankie, the hairdresser, so much as brush her hair.

The whole salon was staring and I know everyone was thinking I couldn't control my child and they were sodding well right.

Frankie did his best, but was obviously worried about his customers and passing trade. If someone walks by a hairdresser's and the screams emanating from within are louder than those from the average dentist's, they're likely to go elsewhere.

So, consequently, Sophie's hair is not a millimetre shorter than when we left.

Mine is. Quite considerably.

I sat in the chair and let nice Frankie run riot with full creative freedom in order to show my darling daughter that it didn't hurt.

What a bozo!

Consequently I look like a Latin American rent-boy. I can't remember anyone achieving success in the wonderful world of rock-and-roll music with a haircut like this. My career has been set back some weeks, as if it wasn't already set so far back as to be left behind.

To add insult to injury, Sophie now wants to play hairdressers.

I'm lying on the grass in the garden and blowing raspberries at Nicola. I'm also making 'snip-snip' noises to Sophie at the same time.

When she's not jumping on my back and nearly falling on the baby, that is.

Gina has just walked into the garden.

I'm rolling Sophie off my stomach, taking my hair from Nicola's clenched little fist, and now I'm kicking my legs in the air and shouting, '*I surrender*,' at the top of my voice.

Gina is laughing at me.

'Nice haircut,' she says.

11.30 p.m.

It's about a week later, so what's that? Last week of June? Who cares.

I am a broken man. Physically wrecked.

A week flying solo with my two demolition-derby experts and anyone would need a month at a health farm, coupled with intensive psychiatric treatment. I don't know how much longer I can keep this up. I really don't.

I've got to have some help. It's not on, this, it really isn't. I'm stretching myself too far. I don't go out, I don't write songs any more, I rarely eat. I just flop in front of the television like an old man.

Help.

12.15 a.m. Just three-quarters of an hour later.

Pin back your ears for this one. Listen up, now. This is news. This defies belief. It's an I-never-thought-I'd-see-the-day story, is this.

I have just refused sex.

That's right.

Shall I say it again?

Well! You see, Gina, yes, *Gina*, came in a bit frisky. I don't know if it's the new haircut, which is quite good now it's had time to settle down a bit, or the hot weather, or what, but she was definitely in the mood.

And I . . . wasn't.

I'm too tired. My kids have already left me feeling completely fucked. She didn't believe me. Thought I was playing hard to get. Something she's often asked me to do, but I've never had the patience to try. No amount of pulling or licking of the old chap could change my mind.

I just wasn't going to get it up tonight.

It's happened once or twice before over the years. Either due to excessive over-emotion or, more likely, excessive booze.

But he, like I, wasn't interested.

Gina has taken it personally. How do you like that? After years of telling *me* not to every time she's rejected my advances, which is a fair bloody few, I promise you.

Tonight, she is positively sulking.

Isn't life ironical?

Next night. About the same time.

It's all right. I haven't become impotent. It still works.

Gina rose to the challenge.

She has a body that, under normal circumstances, I find hard to resist. When she puts on the stockings and saucy underwear I'll agree to anything in order to have her. She hasn't actually asked me for anything yet. Although she's lying with her head in my lap at the moment. Definitely a potential position from which to barter.

'We don't do this often enough, Andy.'

'You're telling me, girl!'

'Not just sex,' she says, playfully slapping my thigh, 'I mean, spend time together. Alone, free from the kids.'

'You're right. I can't remember the last time you and I were by ourselves,' I confess.

'Maybe we should get a babysitter. Pay her for an entire day. Go off to Kinsale or somewhere, just you and me.'

'They're not easy to find. Especially during a heatwave.'

'I could always ask Michelle.'

'I don't think that's a good idea,' I've blurted out, before engaging my brain.

'Oh? Why not?'

'I think Sophie's gone off her a bit. You know, since that time when Michelle picked her up by mistake.'

'She's not said anything to me.'

'Hasn't she? Maybe I'm wrong.'

'It's just I think we need to make more of an effort with each other. Be a bit more understanding. The past few months have been difficult for us both. We've changed, somehow.'

'That was bound to happen, I suppose,' I say.

'We seem to be growing apart, Andy.'

At least she recognises this too.

'And I don't think I want that to happen. Not to us.'

She doesn't *think* she wants that to happen?

'I do still love you, you know,' she says, snaking out her tongue.

'Do you?'

'Yes,' she replies, before closing her mouth around me.

Twenty minutes later and my wife is asleep in my arms.

There is not a more beautiful woman or a more sexy body in the whole world. Trust me.

It's not just me that thinks this. Men are always trying to hit on Gina. Not just behind my back but right under my bloody nose, most of the time. I don't like it, but it's the price you pay when you're married to someone so special.

Bright, intelligent, funny, kind and physically perfect!

Now I know why I couldn't take Michelle.

You see, the point is, I'm lost. Have been from the moment I set eyes on her, really. I fell so hard I haven't been able to get up since and I don't think I ever will. At least my harrowing experience with Michelle taught me that. So I stay here, on my knees. For better or worse.

I love Gina.

I just wish I could more often.

It's the middle of August.

The sun's shining, but for once I'm not on the beach with my brood, I'm in town.

I've just put Nicola in the pram-stroke-buggy thingy, and I can tell you that is no mean feat in itself.

They're like an overgrown jigsaw puzzle. Worse than car chairs. 'Push this, step on that, slot this in there, clip this on here,' etc. The amount of times I've said, 'Sod it!' and ended up carrying her, which is always a mistake.

She's bloody heavy.

She's almost a year old and she's crawling, like a human dodgem car, colliding with everything. Unlike Sophie, for whom a firm *no* was enough, you have to have eyes in the back of your head to stop Nicola getting into grief. She's really into cupboards, attacking the fireguard, sticking her fingers into plug sockets and mutilating rubber plants.

Anyway, car's parked, pram's up, baby's loaded, Sophie's holding on to said pram and we're off to do bit of shopping.

'Look, Daddy! Look, it's Fozzie.'

So it is. I can't steer the pram around him, I haven't the room to turn around, due to excessive overcrowding of streets by tourists, so, short of mowing him down, I suppose I'd better have a word.

'Hello, Fozzie, how was Germany?'

'Oh, hi, Andy, good to see you. Yeah, yeah, it was really good, you know, really great, really . . . successful.'

Embarrassed or what?

'How long have you been back?'

'Er, about a week or so, now. Yeah, about that long,' he's informing me, his slightly nasal voice and Essex accent somehow exaggerated by nerves.

Now, Ballinkilty is a small town. Everyone knows everything. Put a step out of line and news travels at twice the speed of the Internet. I know full well the band has been back for at least a fortnight.

'Oh? Only nobody's rung me.'

'Sorry about that, Andy. Meant to give you a bell. Got a bit sidetracked. You know how it is.'

I wasn't sure, but I'm beginning to get the picture.

'Uncle Fozzie's funny, isn't he, Daddy?' Sophie says giggling.

'Hysterical. So, Fozzie . . .' I'm not letting him off the hook. I sort of know already, but I just want to hear it. '. . . what's happening about the Sunday-night gigs?'

'Well, we don't start for another week. Look the thing is, Andy, it's like this. Gerry came in . . .'

'Gerry?'

'A Dubliner. Moved down here just before Christmas last. Plays with the Farmer's Boys.'

Crap band.

'Oh, I know, go on.'

He's wriggling, restless. So is Nicola, but Sophie, bless her, is keeping her sister amused by pulling stupid faces.

'Well,' Fozzie's continuing, 'like I say, Gerry did well on the tour and the lads all like him and that. He writes as well and we put down a few tracks of his on the CD. So . . . the thing is, Andy, it went really well. Germany, I mean. We're going back. Cutting another little record. There's talk of a residency in an amazing venue. Good money this time. But they want the same line-up, you see. It's important to them or something . . .'

This isn't Fozzie talking. It's Matt.

'. . . and Gerry, well, he's no ties anyway. No wife, no job, so he's ready to roll any time.'

'Fozzie.'

'Yeah?'

'Cut to the chase, will you?'

'Yeah, well, right. Look, Matt was supposed to do all this.'

'I bet he was.'

'The thing is, Andy. You're out, man. Sorry, it's just circumstantial. Nothing personal. But . . . there it is. Look, I'm really sorry, Andy. I mean, we go back a long way and I know it's not fair. I mean, think of the Beatles and Pete Best. These things happen, Andy. I didn't like the idea . . .'

'Fozzie?'

'Yeah?'

'It doesn't matter. Don't upset yourself. It really doesn't matter.'

But it does.

'Yeah. Well, I'd best be off. Catch you around. I'll give you a bell and we'll go out for a beer.'

'Course you will, Fozzie.'

'Eh?'

'Nothing. Go on, bugger off.'

I never knew he could move so fast. You would have thought there was a man with a stopwatch at the top of the street recording his time.

'Aren't you going to be in the group no more, Daddy?'

Ears like radar, Sophie. Even when you think she's not listening.

'No.'

'Ooh, Daddy! What are you going to do?' she's asking, raising her shoulders.

It's a good question. Punch Matt? Go to the next gig and heckle? Cry?

I have to do something. It's all slipping away. It's just children, housework, children, washing, children, gardening, children.

'I'll tell you what I'm going to do, Sophie. I'm going to buy you a Coke and a packet of crisps and Daddy a pint of Murphy's with a whiskey chaser.'

'But, Daddy, what about Nicola?'

She's grizzling, trying to climb out of her buggy.

'I'll slip a brandy in her bottle. She might nod off then and give you and me a few minutes' peace.'

'Daddy . . .'

She's looking at me earnestly. It unnerves me when she does this.

'. . . I don't think that's very . . . erm? What's the word, Daddy?'

'I shudder to think.'

'Responsible. That's the one, Daddy. It's not very responsible, is it?' she's announcing to me, looking very pleased with herself.

'Oh, really?'

Now my daughter's a critic. That's all I need.

'I might have to phone that woman and tell her.'

'Might you? What woman?'

'Esther.'

'Esther who, for pity's sake?'

'The one from Childline, silly.'

'Childline! Childline, for fuck's sake! Where did you hear about Childline?'

'I'd better have a word with her about your swearing too, Daddy,' she's sighing at me.

'I'll give you Childline, you little horror! Come on.'

'Where are we going, Daddy?'

'I told you. To the pub. We're going to find a pay-phone and I'm going to ring Esther, then I'm going to beat the crap out of you and hand you the phone so you can complain live on air.'

I'm pretending to strangle her now and she's giggling.

Boy, do I need a drink.

It's about 5.00 a.m.

Nicola's crawling under her baby frame. I'm perched on the edge of the sofa looking at her.

'Yes, you're a saucy girl. Yes, you are. What are you doing looking so lively at this time in the morning, eh, pickle? You're murdering your poor daddy. Yes, you are, yes, you are. Don't laugh at me, it's true.'

She has a lovely chuckle. So natural. Babies don't look for laughter, search for it frantically, the way an adult does. They don't have to. Joy just comes to them. Little, daft, simple things give them such pleasure.

We lose that, us grown-ups.

Sometimes we pretend we haven't lost it. We cite the fact we can enjoy a country walk or pleasant conversation or just being with someone we love, but it's not the same. It's forced. I'm not saying we take no pleasure from simple things, just that it's not the same pleasure. Because somewhere, secretly, in the back of our minds, maybe, we're searching for something more. Something bigger. That's because we know it's there.

A baby doesn't.

For them it's all so wonderfully uncluttered.

6.15 a.m.

Nicola's nodded off so I've put her back in her cot.

I should go back to bed, really. I could get another hour maybe before Sophie comes bounding down the stairs.

No point. I wouldn't sleep, so I'm smoking a joint.

I know. It is shameless behaviour at this time of the morning, but I don't get much chance to be shameless any more. To feel special, dangerous, anarchistic, artistic . . . different . . . *alive*.

My job now is to be respectable, sensible, the voice of authority and reason for my children. My job. There's the nub of the matter. I scream but no one hears. And until the right person does, I'm destined to be seen as someone who plays at being an artist and no more. Now my last dabblings have disappeared with my sacking from the Blowins. It hurts. Maybe it shouldn't, but it does. I feel desolate.

Like Pete Best, as Fozzie said so pointedly. The Beatle they left behind just as they made it big.

A chance gone. Probably my last.

I'm toying with the idea of setting fire to my guitar. What use is it now? What's the point of letting it sit there gathering dust?

I look at Nicola, and I think, Yes, she loves me now because I'm funny and I feed her and I love her and look after her. But what happens when she's in the playground and everybody's comparing their daddies' jobs?

'What does your daddy do, then, Nicola?'

What will she say? What *can* she say? Will she be proud of Daddy then? Will Daddy be as easy to love, without pity entering in to her emotions?

Sophie could face that pretty soon.

I feel so depressed. Time has all but run out.

You could count the grains in the top half of the hour-glass on one tiny hand.

15

11.15 a.m. Saturday, back end of August.

Nicola's in bed, Gina's in the bath and Sophie is in the kitchen with me. She's doing a spot of painting up at the table.

I'm on the phone to my number-one fan. Gina's mother. Oh, joy, oh, rapture.

'Sylvia! How nice to speak to you again.'

I lie.

'You too, Andy.'

We both lie.

I'm winking at Sophie and pulling a face behind Granny's back, as it were. She's grinning at me. Now she's jumping off her chair and running over to me.

Oh! Big hug.

'I love you, Daddy,' she's saying, in a loud voice.

'I love you too, poppet,' I say twice as loudly, because I know it will annoy Sylvia, who hates the fact that my children and I are close.

'Daddy's girl at the moment, is she?' Sylvia snarls down the line.

'Well, we're spending a lot of time together.'

'Yes, of course, I keep forgetting your . . . how should we say . . .?'

We say?!

'. . . new position . . . in the family, as it were.'

Yes, I bet she does.

'Tell me Andy, don't you find it a little . . .?'

'A little what?'

'Nothing. I'm probably being a tad old-fashioned.'

'A hip chick like you, Sylvia? Surely not. I tell you what, I'll tell Gina you called and get her to call you back. How's that?' I say, before my temper completely takes over.

'Make it later this evening. I'm going out now. And don't forget to tell her, will you, Andy?'

'As if I would, Sylvia, 'bye!'

Bitch.

3.00 p.m.

I'm changing Nicola's scutty bottom on the floor in the lounge. Gina is sat on the sofa, hovering over me, nit-picking.

The attempt at being more understanding and rekindling our love lasted for about a day. Then it was back to sniping at each other.

We never got to Kinsale.

'Shouldn't you put her on a changing mat or something, Andy?'

'No, it's all right.'

'It's not very hygienic.'

'After all the things this carpet's had spilt on it, I don't think a bit of baby-poo will make much difference.'

'I meant unhygienic for little Nicola. Oh, Andy, look at her little bottom. It's red-raw. Have you been changing her regularly?'

'Like clockwork, Gina. She's teething. You know she gets a little sore when she's teething.'

'What's that you're using on her little cheeks?'

'It's Kamillosan.'

'I told you to use the Weleda cream on her botty.'

Well, I've used Vaseline and KY Jelly on your botty, Gina, in days of yore, but that's another story.

I think this. Obviously I do not speak.

'That nappy rash will never dry up if you don't let her run around without a nappy for a bit. Get some air to it.'

She says this in a you-don't-have-a-clue-how-to-look-after-a-baby-like-I-do way.

She's thinking this. Needless to say, she does not say it.

'Couldn't you be a little gentler putting on her little tights?'

I'm biting my lip.

'Wouldn't it be easier to slip that little suit over her head than hauling it up over her hips like that, Andy?'

'She hates having her face covered. It's best to avoid it where possible.'

'She's never going to learn that way. She won't be able to pull all her clothes on over her hips when she gets older, will she?'

I'm gritting my teeth.

'Aren't you going to put a cardigan on her, Andy? We don't want her getting a little chill, do we?'

'Well, you fucking dress her, then! Do something constructive instead of sitting on your arse criticising.'

'Sorry, Andy, I didn't mean –'

'Didn't you? It's the weekend. I spend all week doing this. Why don't you take over for a change?'

'I will. Happily. I am her mother, after all.'

'Oh, really? There was me thinking I was.'

'That's not fair. If you earned any bloody money then I'd be happy to stay home and look after my children.'

'I haven't noticed you barging me out of the way, nappy in hand. You haven't moved from in front of your bloody computer all day except to have a nice relaxing bath.'

'I can't help it. I've got work to do.'

'Why have you? Shit! You spend enough hours working overtime to publish *six* bloody magazines.'

'Because it's struggling, and if I don't pull it round it'll go under, just like the first one. Then we're really fucked, Andy.'

'Really fucked? Interesting choice of phrase. I can't remember what it feels like to be *really fucked*.'

'Oh, that's just typical. Why do you have to talk about sex every time we argue?'

'Because it's the only type of oral sex I get to indulge in, these days.'

'You're just like all men. Led by the fucking dick.'

'That's crap. If I let my cock do the thinking, I wouldn't still be in this marriage.'

'And if you had a bloody job, earning decent money, I might not be working myself to death and I could find the energy for sex.'

'Well, I work my arse off all day and I still –'

Silence.

I think we both realised, simultaneously.

Sophie is standing in the doorway.

How long has she been there?

Gina's gone to her.

'Mummy? What's all the noise about?'

'Nothing, darling, nothing at all.'

'But I heard you shouting. It was *very* loud.'

'Oh, that was just Daddy getting carried away.'

Thanks, Gina.

'Yes. Just silly Daddy, Sophie. I was telling Mummy about the goal my footie team scored the other night and I got a bit excited. I'm a twit, aren't I?'

I hate lying to my kids. It makes me uncomfortable even if the lie is Persil white.

Sophie looks calmer for the explanation.

'You are a twit, Daddy. Football's boring, isn't it, Mummy?'

'Yes, darling, it is. Now, how about some tea and biscuits?' she's saying, as she steers Sophie back into the kitchen, pausing to shoot me a concerned look over her shoulder.

Damn! I wonder how much she heard?

It's 11.00 p.m. I'm in bed. Alone.

Gina is downstairs talking to her mother on the telephone.

I know what's being said. Within a little.

Sylvia's slagging me off.

Much as Gina says she loves me, the brainwashing usually takes its toll, especially in the current Cold War climate of our relationship.

Only one thing can stop it. Success. I need my music to bring success. Then, man-oh-man, could I have a good time ramming that success down a few people's throats. Except, of course, I won't. Because they won't matter then. As it stands, they act as an added incentive, which is not a bad thing.

I have to find some time for me. So I can do something for us. Otherwise all this time spent being the little woman at home, trying to keep the marriage together, will have been academic.

Because I'll lose them all anyway.

Gina, Sophie, Nicola.

I know I will.

I can feel it.

Not much longer now.

6.00 p.m., the following Tuesday.

Gina's just telephoned. She's got to work late again.

It's such a pisser!

This is becoming a regular occurrence. That bloody magazine is completely understaffed and they're too tight-fisted to cough up for some extra help. This is the second night on the trot.

The thing is, I'm knackered.

Now I've got to get everyone's supper, bathe the little buggers all by myself, make bottles, pyjama Sophie, Babygro Nicola, put them to bed, read stories . . .

God, this is bringing me down.

It's 11.20 p.m.

Gina's just got home.

At least they're paying for a taxi for her, though you could argue for what it's costing them they could hire another member of staff.

I'm in bed.

I was too bloody shagged to wait up any longer.

It's Wednesday. 7.30 a.m.

Nicola's recently back in her cot.

Sophie is still asleep.

Gina's up, though. She's just brought us a couple of mugs of tea into the lounge. She looks pale and stressed.

'So what exactly did you have to do last night?' I'm asking as she hands me a mug and sits on the sofa next to me.

'Eileen was sick. I had to stand in. I was interviewing a girl who's just had her first book published at the age of sixteen.'

'Couldn't someone else have done it?'

'Wouldn't you think I'd have got someone else to do it if I could?'

'I suppose so. It just seems to be happening rather a lot lately.'

'You're telling me! I know this, Andy. I'm the one who is having to do three hundred jobs at once to make sure there is actually a publication to put on the shelves.'

'But it's ludicrous!'

'I know.'

'Can't you do something?'

'No. I can't. My hands are tied. Frankly I'd like to tell the tossers where they could stick their magazine. I'm just so depressed. Do you know, Andy? I'd give anything to be you for a day. Stay at home, be my own boss, take things easy, no *real* work to worry about and –'

'I beg your pardon! If a man were to suggest that a housewife didn't actually do any *real* work, he would be publicly lynched by a group of militant feminists. You, Gina, would be the first person to chant that he deserved everything he got.'

'Okay, you're right. I'm sorry. It's just I'm under so much pressure. A day at home looks incredibly appealing.'

'Gina! When we first met, you wanted to work. You wanted a career. It was important to you. Let's not lose sight of that. Independence. Wasn't that what you used to say? You never wanted to have to rely financially on a man. Wasn't that how the tune used to go? No man was going to be able to control you just because he held the purse strings. Your very words, as I remember.'

Gina's running her hand through her hair again, tensely.

'Yes, Andy, but don't you understand? Sometimes it all gets too much. I still believe those things. Just now and again the responsibility of having to provide the resources to keep us ticking over with a basic lifestyle becomes almost unbearable. I'm only human, Andy. I can't help it if I want someone to look after me for a change, occasionally.'

'And I don't look after you, is that it?'

She's placed her head in her hands.

'No, I don't mean that, exactly. We're both miserable, Andy. Neither of us is happy with our lot. I feel guilty and depressed because I'm not looking after my kids, and you feel terrible because you're not the one earning the money.'

'That's true, Gina. I fully admit that. It makes me feel a complete shit. But this whole idea was your suggestion and –'

'What choice was there? You think I'm enjoying this, Andy? You think I like working in a shit job? Am I supposed to be relishing desperately holding together a magazine that has a smaller circulation than your average church pamphlet? Have you ever considered how demeaning it is for me to have to arse-lick the bunch of amateurs who own that rag of a publication, just so I can provide this family with a living wage?'

'That's all it is now, isn't it? Work, kids and money worries,' I say, shaking my head in frustration.

She crosses to me and takes my hand.

'I want my old Andy back. The proud, funny, talented, unique man I married.'

'I don't know where he is. If you find him, let me know.'

'Andy, darling. I didn't mean –'

'You take the piss sometimes, Gina.'

I feel my head exploding with sudden, uncontrollable rage.

'Andy, please don't –'

'You, my dear, have emasculated your husband, in more ways than bloody one.'

'What do you mean?'

'You know what I mean.'

'Oh, Andy, please, not sex again.'

'Again! Again? Do you know when we last made love, Gina?'

'I'm sorry, but you have to understand, Andy –'

'Of course I do. It's always me who has to bloody understand!'

'That's not fair,' she's saying, the tears starting to gather weight in her eyes.

'Let me tell you what I *understand*, Gina. You have control over every single area of our lives. You are the boss. And that includes our sex-life. You're a complete control freak! You decide everything. Where we are going to live, how we're going to spend our money, what we can or cannot eat, just bloody everything. And it's got nothing to do with the fact I don't earn any money, or that I'm too impractical. It's about you, charging at things like a bull in a china shop, without thinking things through, and being so convinced you're always in the sodding right that you never listen to a single word any other fucker says!'

'Stop it! This isn't like you. It's not my Andy speaking –'

'Here we go again. "Not my Andy." "Where's my good old Andy, I want him back." Well, Gina, of course I've changed. I mean, look at me. The old Andy was not a man in a vinyl bloody pinny. He was not the little man at home. He was a musician, and a bloody good one at that. He had hopes and dreams and ambition and . . . and I'll tell you something else. The old Andy would not have sat around staring at bits of bloody litmus paper waiting to see if they turned pink. He would have been on that plane with the rest of his band grasping probably the last chance he'll ever get to salvage some fucking pride!'

She looks confused.

'I don't understand.'

'Don't you?' I snap.

'You mean the tour?'

'Yes, of course I mean the tour.'

'But you told me the rest of the band didn't want you to go. You said they never gave you the choice.'

'Yeah, well, I lied. They kicked me out when I turned the tour down. I put you and the kids first, Gina. It's what I do. Only you seem to have conveniently forgotten that.'

She's sobbing uncontrollably now.

Gina is sobbing and I feel like a total and utter bastard.

'Mummy, Daddy, what's everyone making all this racket for?'

We've both turned round to face Sophie.

At this moment, it would be hard to say which of us feels the most guilty.

'Sorry, Sophie. Daddy's sorry.' I'm crossing to her. I've picked her up in my arms.

'You weren't telling Mummy about the football again, were you, Daddy?'

I can tell by the way she's looking at me that she won't accept a flimsy excuse this time.

'No, Sophie. Mummy and Daddy were having a bit of an argument over something very silly.'

'Why, Daddy?'

I wish she wasn't looking at me with such concern in her young eyes.

'Because everybody disagrees with one another about something. Even Mummy and Daddy occasionally.'

There's something in her eyes I don't like.

What is it? Confusion? Distress? Fear?

She's witnessing too many of these arguments lately.

'Well you're both very naughty. You can't have any sweets today, okay?'

'Fair enough.'

Gina is wiping her eyes harshly.

'What would Mummy's girl like for breakfast this morning?'

'Toast and Marmite.'

'Mummy will make it for you.'

'But, Mummy, you'll be late for work, silly.'

'I know.'

'Won't they be cross with you?'

'Well, they'll just have to be. I want to make my little girl's breakfast,' she's telling Sophie, as she takes her out of my arms and into her own.

'Mummy?'

'Yes, Sophie?'

'Daddy's crap at making Marmite and toast, isn't he?'

'Yes, darling. Now, I'll put a cartoon on for you and find you some socks. Your feet are freezing, Sophie.'

She's right. Daddy is crap at making Marmite on toast.

Daddy's crap at a lot of things.

Why didn't I keep my big mouth shut about the tour? I should never have mentioned it. I shouldn't have said any of those things. It's not as if they were untrue, but I was way out of line.

Why did I do it? It's so unlike me. I'm not usually so bloody caustic, so . . . bitter.

Anyway, I'm not important.

The fact is, I've hurt her.

And I've never wanted to do that.

Oh, Lord!

It's all getting out of hand. The signs say . . . Danger! Proceed with caution.

16

Sunny September.

We're three-quarters of the way through the month at least, and so far we're talking Indian summer here. Often the case in this neck of the woods, according to local legend. The minute the kids go back to school you can guarantee the sun will shine. I've started a petition suggesting we send the little buggers back on 1st August.

It's about 10.30 a.m. Sophie started back at playschool today and I can almost hear the sigh of relief from my weary body.

We're having a cup of coffee in the little tea-shop that's attached to the local supermarket. Well, obviously Nicola isn't having a cup of coffee. She is, however, getting into an extraordinary mess with a chocolate éclair I bought for her. I probably shouldn't have, but she lunged forward from my arms and grabbed it off the plate on the top of the counter. Once she had her grubby paws on it I felt obliged to pay for the ruddy thing.

Actually, I'm completely overexcited.

Stanley Larke is coming to Ballinkilty. I couldn't believe it when I saw the poster, but it's true.

He is going to grace the very same stage in the same folk club that another talented bass-player used to grace – before the losers he used to gig with decided they couldn't bear being made to look inferior any more so they fired him.

I can't believe he's actually coming to Ballinkilty.

I mentioned this to Connor last night and he said, 'Who the fuck is Stanley Larke?'

Dear, dear, dear, what gaps we have in our education today.

Stanley Larke is recognised as one of the greatest bass-guitar players in the world. Who's he played with? Shit, who hasn't he bloody played with? I'm tingling with anticipation.

I keep looking at Nicola, burying her face in the cream and saying, 'Ooh, Nicola, can you believe Stanley Wanley Larke is coming to

Westie Corkie? Yes, he is, yes, he is, little one. Isn't it exciting? Are you excited, Daddy's girl? Are you? Are you?'

She's clearly not heard of him either. I'd bet she'd be wetting herself if I said Barney was gigging here.

Connor also said, 'So, Andy, if he's the bee's bollocks, like you say he is, what's he doing playing a folk club in Ballinkilty, now?'

A fair question. A favour, I would guess. Someone has pulled a few strings, called in a few markers. Unless he's on one of those hey-I-want-to-get-back-to-basics-get-in-touch-with-my-musical-roots-play-to-small-audiences-to-get-back-on-track kind of trips. They do that, don't they? Successful musicians. I won't. When I get there it'll be Shea Stadium or you can sod off. I'm tired of playing to a few appreciative fans. I want to be a pinprick in the distance to someone who's forked out a week's wages just to see me play live.

So. There you have it.

Trouble is, he's playing tonight. One night only.

That means, when Gina walks through the door, moaning and groaning and bitching on about how tired she is, I'm going to have some serious grovelling to do.

'Yes, I am, Daddy's little monster. Yes, I am.'

6.30 p.m. I've been in a state of exuberance all day.

Neither Sophie nor Nicola can understand the sunny-natured man that has taken care of them. Sophie even went as far as asking, 'Are you all right, Daddy?' Makes you wonder if I'm that awful on a normal day, doesn't it?

One problem: no sign of Gina.

I wish Connor would put his toe down and get her home. I'm running out of time to be charming, understanding and helpful before appealing to her generous nature.

I just hope she comes back soon.

7.20 p.m.
Nicola's in bed, Sophie's in her pyjamas and still no sign of Mummy. I've checked the answering-machine, just in case I was in the bathroom or bringing the coal in or something when the phone rang.

Nothing.

I don't know what to do.

Phone's ringing. I have a bad feeling about this.

'Hello. It's me here. Who's that?'

Sophie's answered the phone in the kitchen.

'Oh! It's Mummy, Daddy.'

I'm hovering over her, desperate to find out what's happening. I'll have to wait. If I rush Sophie off the telephone now, she'll have a major tantrum.

'Yes, yes. Fine. That's okay, Mummy. Yes, 'bye!'

She's just blown her mother a kiss and put the bloody receiver down.

'Sophie! What are you doing?'

'It's okay, Daddy. I've finished speaking to Mummy now.'

'Well, I'm very happy for you, but I wanted a word.'

'SORRY!' she's screaming at me, as she shoots off into the lounge.

'What did she say, Sophie?'

It's ringing again.

7.54 p.m.

It's not fair. There's no sodding justice in the world. Tonight of all nights.

The telephone conversation went like this:

'Hello?'

'Andy. It's me. What happened?'

'Sophie hung up.'

'Little devil.'

'Why aren't you home?'

'I've got to work late again.'

'Oh, shit, *no*!'

'I'm sorry, I'm sorry. It's not my fault.'

'You can't. Not tonight, Gina.'

'I've no choice, Andy.'

'But, Gina, you see there's this gig –'

'Take the photos across to the opera house. They've asked for approval before we can print. They're not that chuffed at a photo-story being shot in their hallowed bloody building –'

'*What*? Gina, what are you going on about?'

'Sorry, darling. I wasn't talking to you.'

'Well, could you talk to me, please? I'm trying to tell you something.'

'What's that, then? No, *now*, Katrina. You've got to take them

179

straight away. We can't print without appro. So it has to be this very second.'

'Gina!'

'Sorry, Andy. You were saying?'

'Look, there's this bass-player –'

'Katrina! I don't care if the woman has probably gone home by now. Just find someone who can okay it and make sure you get it in writing.'

'Gina, Stanley Larke is –'

'Who?'

'Strewth! Am I the only one in the world ever to hear of this guy or what?'

'Katrina, don't go without taking this!'

'Gina. Stanley Larke is playing in Ballinkilty tonight. It's a gig. A one-off –'

'I'm sorry, Andy, there's nothing I can do.'

'But, Gina, just this once –'

'Katrina, why am I still staring at your droopy face? Listen, Andy, I've got to go. I'm really busy.'

'Gina. You don't understand. I may never get the chance to see him again.'

'Katrina! Shift!'

'Oh, fuck it! I'll see you later.'

Then I followed my daughter's example and I hung up.

It's just not bloody fair.

I tried ringing Deirdre to babysit, but she's studying for mock exams. I gave Noreen a call, as I figured Sophie's over the trauma and would probably enjoy seeing her again. Apparently she's in Limerick visiting her aunt. I even gave Connor a buzz. Well, the kids know him and he's not too overpowering. I would have put Sophie to bed and he wouldn't have had to do much. Just sit on his arse and watch the telly while drinking his way through my whiskey. That, and pop up the stairs occasionally to check the kids were okay. Any problems, he could have rung the pub and I would have come home.

No answer – wouldn't you have guessed?

So. What to do?

I really want to see this gig.

I'm in charge, am I not?

Fuck it!

'Sophie. How do you fancy coming out to listen to some live music with your old daddy?'

'But what about the baby, Daddy?' she's asking, palms upwards.

'We'll take her with us.'

'But I'm in my PJs, Daddy.'

'I'll pull some clothes on over the top.'

'Erm . . . okay.'

That's settled it, then.

9.00 p.m.

I think I may be responsible for causing something of a stir.

I've just walked into the pub with a four-year-old hanging on to my shirt-tails and my arms full of baby.

To add to the equation, I have a Pooh Bear changing-bag full of bottles, nappies, bum-cream and squeaky toys slung over my shoulder like a badly chosen accessory.

It is perfectly common, in a child-orientated society, such as the one we have in West Cork, for parents to take their children into the boozer at lunchtime. Ditto early evening. It is not exactly unheard-of for those same children still to be trying to drag their mater and pater away from the bar at nine o'clock at night. It is a little unusual, however, for someone to *arrive* at the pub with sprogs in tow at this hour.

The landlord is giving me black looks.

Tough. I've worked hard entertaining his punters for peanuts whilst his bar takings doubled once too often for him to go as far as lodging a complaint.

I'm moving through to the folk club. I've just commandeered a couple of seats at the back.

People can be very obliging when they see a man struggling with his children.

Matt and Fozzie are in the front row, I see. I thought they were in Germany. Must be next week.

Johan's not here. He must be waiting on tables to get a bit of spending money together for the tour.

Unless they've given him the boot as well.

11.30 p.m.

I'm trying to make a fast exit. Two reasons. First, now the gig's

181

over, I'm in a real rush to get home to Gina. When you're on Death Row with no hope of a reprieve, you want them to break the gas pellet as fast as possible. You do not want to dwell on how horrible a death it may be a minute longer than you have to. Second, my children are an embarrassment. They have no social graces whatsoever.

Maybe it's my fault. Partly, at least. After all, it's my job to teach them things. Basically, they're a couple of oiks. Reprobates. The sort of people who are likely to keep Club 18–30 holidays in existence well into the next century.

I'll begin with Nicola.

The first number began and Nicola shot up. Bolt upright.

Boy, did she fucking scream!

This is a tiny venue, full of noisy drinkers, a four-piece band a few feet away, drums, electric guitars blasting through amplifiers and PAs far too powerful for a space that size and you could still hear Nicola bawling her head off above the lot.

First number and I had to take her out.

I asked a young, spotty pseudo-hippie to keep an eye on Sophie for me and I took Nicola out into the main bar.

Then I'm panicking because I've left Sophie in there and I have visions of her howling because Daddy's abandoned her or, worse still, of her being kidnapped or something.

I calm Nicola down by walking round the bar singing 'Bare Necessities' to her, much to the amusement of everyone who can hear. I take her back in and Sophie is fine. Not only oblivious to my absence, but she's standing on the chair, shaking her bum in time with the music. This, much to the annoyance of the punters behind her who can't see a thing but Sophie's *derrière*.

I persuade her to sit and just as things seemed to have settled down, Nicola decided she had another trick up her sleeve.

Or, should I say, up her nappy?

She never does that. She just *doesn't* drop her load after she goes to bed at night. It's not part of her little routine. I clearly disturbed that by bringing her out.

I was cradling her in my arms listening to a great bass riff when Nicola decided to play one of her own. I felt a tremor on my hand as she blew the tubes clear ready for action. Moments later, people all over the place were sniffing disgustedly and looking for the feckin' dog in order to give it a good kicking.

I could have died.

Others, I'm sure, were swearing something already had.

She began complaining bitterly about this, so I begged assistance from the pseudo-hippie once more and ran out with my Pooh Bear clutch-bag to change her.

The pub is not exactly packed with facilities for such things. Consequently, I had to change her on my lap in the gents, while my own posterior rested on the only toilet.

Murphy's law said somebody would bang on the door, urgently requiring somewhere to lodge his deposit, and sure enough, they did.

The technicalities of changing a bum whilst sitting on the loo are difficult enough. If someone is banging on the door enquiring what is going on, suggesting scenarios as diverse as masturbation to a *ménage à trois*, the pressure is frightening. Fingers and thumbs cease to function properly.

Therefore, by the time I staggered past the aggressor, apologising profusely, Nicola may have been clean, but I was certainly not. A fair smattering of the contents of her nappy still lingered, in heaven knows what quantities, aromatically on my jeans.

The pong may have lessened, but it had certainly not disappeared. Upon our return, even the hippie had the gall to move his chair a few significant inches away from my own.

Arriving back in my seat in time to listen to the great man Larke introducing the next item, my baby then decided to chant, 'Dada, Dada, *Dada*, DADA!' at the top of her voice.

I have never before slammed a teat-capped bottle of milk between her lips so quickly in all her young life.

And that was just number two daughter's contribution.

Here are a few edited highlights, from my first-born:

'Daddy, I can't understand what they're saying.'

'Daddy, why does that man pull such funny faces when he's singing?'

'Daddy, why does that man think he's famous?'

'Daddy, why does that man tell boring stories between all them songs?'

And, the most cringe-making of all:

'DADDY. THAT MAN'S BLACK, ISN'T HE, DADDY?'

OH, GOD!

'He is, though, isn't he, Daddy? HE'S A BLACK MAN, ISN'T HE?'

Now let's get one thing straight. Neither Gina nor I have a single racist bone in our bodies. The simple truth is, West Cork has extremely few people of African or Asian descent, who have chosen to make this their home.

As Sophie pointed out, in an incredibly booming voice for one so young, 'YOU DON'T SEE MANY OF THEM ROUND HERE, DO YOU, DADDY?'

So there you have it. In one evening my children have destroyed any respect, reputation, admiration and love I may have enjoyed in Ballinkilty. In one of the fellest of swoops.

'Daddy, can we go home, now?' Sophie's asking me, unsteady on her feet through sheer exhaustion.

'Of course we can, Stinks. Right away.'

11.40 p.m.

We're in the car-park. The large one at the back of one of Ballinkilty's hotels. It's chock full in the day-time and completely empty by this time of night. Most people prefer to park in the main street. Not so far to stagger at closing time.

I'm holding Nicola under one arm and dragging poor Sophie to our car with the other hand.

'Daddy?'

'Yes, Stinks?'

'Daddy, why is the car next to ours moving up and down like that?'

She's right. It's a Nissan of some kind. Sickly green colour. I half recognise it from somewhere. It's bouncing up and down as though it were epileptic.

'I don't know.'

Yes, I do. My memory is flashing me a mental picture of a car or two of mine rocking and rolling like that. Surely not! Not in Ballinkilty.

'Daddy, there's people in there. What are they doing, Daddy?' Sophie's asking, as she heads for the green Nissan.

No! I don't want her to see this.

'Never mind, Sophie. We're in a rush.'

'But, Dad, I want to see.'

'You'll have to use your imagination,' I say, as I bundle her into her car chair, then strap Nicola in the back.

I'm walking round to the driver's door and I can't resist taking a closer look.

They're using the back seat. The woman is crumpled up against the door closest to me. His legs are hanging out of the opposite door, which he's obviously left open to give him enough room to thrust.

Blimey! He's giving it some stick! If he's not careful –

OH, LORDY! What did I tell you? The door nearest me has opened and the woman's tumbled backwards. She's stopped herself falling, putting her hands on the ground, her very impressive breasts tumbling towards her chin.

'Sorry, don't mind me,' I'm saying, stifling a laugh.

Shit. I recognise those breasts. Even with her face upside down I can now see who it is.

'Michelle.'

'Hello, Andy,' she's replying, her whole body seeming to blush.

'Wait there,' she's instructed me, as she disengages herself from the man, pulls down her top and clambers out of the car.

The man has not moved. I can now see his face.

I thought I recognised the car.

'Johan?'

'Oh, fok! Hello, Andy. Sorry about this. Luffly to see you again.'

No wonder he wasn't at the bloody gig.

'I suppose you'll tell Norman,' Michelle snaps at me.

'No, I won't. But you have to admit it's not very fair to him. I mean, in a car park in Ballinkilty! It's not very discreet, is it? You know what this town's like for gossip.'

'Bit hypocritical, aren't you, Andy? You've always hated Norman.'

'I think hate's a bit strong.'

'So if I'd been discreet, like some others I could mention, that would have been all right, would it?'

'I didn't say that.'

'Oh, piss off, you moralistic bastard!'

'Michelle!'

'And don't look so bloody smug. I'm not the only wife fucking another man behind her husband's back, dear!'

'What do you mean by that?!'

'Daddy. I can see Johan's bum!'

Shit! Sophie.

Where is she? Damn! She's round the other side of Johan's car, having escaped from her car chair.

'Come away, Sophie.'

Michelle's face has changed. The aggression has gone. What's replaced it? Is that shame?

'I'm sorry, Andy,' she's saying, as she gets into Johan's car.

'But, Dad?' Sophie's saying as she reaches me. 'Why *is* Johan's bum hanging out of his trousers?'

'I don't know, Sophie,' I'm saying, as I load her into the car, strapping her in this time.

'Don't they fit properly, Dad?'

'Erm . . .'

'Is he very poor?'

'Probably, I suppose . . .'

'Is that why,' she's saying, stifling a yawn, 'he's got his bottom out? Because he can't afford trousers that fit, Dad?'

'Maybe,' I reply, getting into the car.

'Perhaps a bee stung him on his botty,' she says, giggling, 'and Michelle had to suck the poison out. Yuck!'

'That's exactly right,' I'm agreeing. 'How clever of you to guess.'

'I am clever, aren't I, Daddy?' she says, yawning again.

'Yes, you are, daughter,' I'm telling her, as I start the car.

I'm racing home. Both daughters have passed out, thankfully.

'I'm not the only wife fucking another man behind her husband's back.'

That's what Michelle just said, wasn't it?

What did she say on the day I rejected her advances? Before she left? She insulted me.

'You deserve to get hurt.'

Something like that, wasn't it? Am I putting two and two together and making five?

My mind is racing, searching for clues.

Is Gina . . .?

I must get home. I've got to find out.

12.10 a.m.

I've just driven down our lane, having rather unusually passed a car coming the other way. The glare of his full-beamed headlights nearly bloody blinded me. I half thought, for the second time this evening, that I recognised the car. For one daft minute I thought Johan had sprinted home ahead of me on his rounds, servicing the frustrated wives of . . .

But that's just me being paranoid.

Isn't it?

It was probably Gina's taxi. In other words, she's only just arrived home too. Therefore, she will not have read the note explaining our absence yet.

Of course I left a note! I'm not a totally self-centred son of a bitch, you know.

Suppose I'd better pop my head around the door and hope it stays on my shoulders long enough to come back and get the children out of the car.

Besides, I've a question or two of my own to ask.

12.25 a.m.

I've just unwrapped Nicola and put her to bed. Gina is currently doing the same with Sophie. I've made Gina a hot-water bottle out of habit. Gina always goes to bed with a hot-water bottle, whatever the weather. She's just walked through the kitchen door and she's taken the hot-water bottle from my hands.

'Thanks. I'm going to bed.'

She's walking to the door.

'Gina, don't go . . .'

'I just want to say that I can't believe you did that, Andy. You selfish, selfish cunt.'

'Yeah, that's me all over, Gina. Mr Selfish.'

'Can you describe tonight any other way?'

'Yes, if you'll listen. Tonight I had the opportunity to see one of my idols live in action.'

'That is no excuse.'

'It wasn't meant to be an excuse.'

'You can't justify this! It's outrageous.'

'Tosh! Overreaction. The children came to no harm. They were well looked-after. Sophie had a good time.'

'This wasn't about Sophie having a good time. It was about Andy Lawrence doing what he wanted to do.'

'And where the fuck were you, Gina? Tell me that?'

'I was – no, hold on a minute. You're not turning this one around and making me feel guilty.'

'Look, I've spent the last ten months doing nothing but putting the kids' needs before my own. This was *one* night, Gina. I tried to tell you. I tried to get help, but everybody was the same as you. Too fucking busy. So I took the decision to take them with me. They're fine. Unharmed. So where's the fire?'

She's sighing. 'I'm not going to argue with you, Andy. There's no point. Whatever you say, you'll never convince me you weren't way out of fucking line tonight.'

Door slammed.

End of conversation.

I've just been completely sidetracked.

Perhaps that's not a bad thing. I mean, what if I'm wrong? Michelle could just be making mischief. If that's the case I could open up a whole set of wounds we just don't need right now.

1.25 a.m.

I'm sat up in bed.

It's been a backs-to-each-other night, you'll not be surprised to hear.

That's not why I am now sat upright.

I've just realised something.

The car.

Not mine, but the one that brought Gina home.

That wasn't a taxi. I recognised that motor.

It was Connor's.

It was Connor's car that brought Gina home, after midnight, tonight.

17

I have to ask.

I've been awake all night thinking about it, my imagination running riot. Is my nasty suspicious mind warping the perfectly innocent?

Gina's stood in the kitchen. She's at the half-ready stage. Makeup on, underwear and tights worn under towelling robe.

The irony is Gina always looks extraordinarily beautiful at this stage of a working morning. I'm never more in love with her than at this time. I fantasise about peeling off her robe and making love to her . . . here in the kitchen.

Tried it once. Major knock-back. Bad timing again.

I have a strong feeling that I am on dangerous territory. I may hear things I do not wish to.

Well, here goes:

'Gina?'

'I don't think I want to talk to you this morning, Andy Lawrence.'

'I understand that.'

Her robe falls open and I want her. To pretend I never doubted. But it can't stop the part of me that needs to know, the voice that will worry me to death if I don't open my mouth to speak.

'I want to ask you something.'

'If it's a favour, Andy, I'd advise you not to.'

'No, it isn't.'

'Go on, then, out with it,' she's urging me, as she puts her cup down on the work-surface.

'How come Connor brought you home last night?'

'What makes you think he did?'

'Are you saying he didn't?'

She looks a little flushed.

'No. He called me to say he was going out for a drink after work and couldn't take me home. I told him I was working late anyway. So he said he'd swing by the office when he'd finished partying and see if I was still there.'

'And?'

'And I was. I told him I had a taxi booked, but you know how insistent he is. I've never been so petrified in all my life. He's not the safest driver *before* he's had a few. We were all over the road. That's why I was so tense when I arrived home last night, if I'm honest.'

But she's not being honest. I know this woman very well.

She blushes when she's lying. Same as Sophie. Whatever the lie. Small or large, white, or – as in this case – the blackest of black.

'Will you?'

'Will I what, Andy?'

'Be honest.'

'What are you talking about?'

'I know you're lying to me, Gina. You're having an affair with Connor, aren't you?'

Time has slowed down. I seem to be waiting hours for Gina to reply, yet I know by the time she speaks only seconds will have passed.

I hear the clock ticking, the fridge-freezer whirring, the heating clanking. But these are silent compared to the sound of my own blood, rushing around my veins and gathering weight in my temples.

I look at her. There are the beginnings of tears in her eyes.

Perhaps I'd rather not have hit this particular nail on the head. I think I would happily have missed and struck myself across the wrist. Shattered the bones. The pain would have been considerably easier to live with.

'I . . .' She's wringing her hands. 'Andy. It's not quite as bad as it seems . . .'

Howling from the bedroom above.

'Baby's awake,' Gina's saying, wiping her eyes with the back of her hand.

I'm nodding. I can't quite speak, yet.

Gina turns to me.

'You get her up. I'll make a couple of fast calls and we'll go somewhere and talk. Away from the kids.'

I'm standing in the nursery and cradling Nicola in my arms.

I don't want to let go. I'm kissing her head and nuzzling her tummy.

It suddenly struck me that I'm not sure how much longer I'll be doing this. Not here anyway.

Struck me.

That's a very accurate description.

I'm back in the lounge with Baby, and Sophie has crept down the stairs while I dallied in the nursery.

She's cuddling Gina.

'Mummy's been crying, Daddy.'

'Has she? That's not very nice for Mummy. She must be very upset.'

'She banged her toe. But it's all right now 'cos I kissed it better.'

'Thank you, Sophie. Good girl.'

Gina's stroking Sophie's hair.

'I know what will cheer you up, Mummy.'

'What's that, darling?' Gina's asking.

'Daddy and I can tell you all about the concert we watched last night. It was dead good, wasn't it, Daddy?'

'It was.'

'Yes, Mummy. It was real, live music. Not like on the telly where they're not really there, you see.'

'Is that right?' Gina asks, her eyes red.

'Yes, Mummy. You could see them sweating and everything, couldn't you, Dad?'

'You could, Sophie.'

'And one time, right, the man couldn't remember the words and he started swearing and things. Just like Daddy does sometimes, didn't he, Daddy?'

'He did.'

'Thing is, though, they didn't play any tunes I knew, did they, Dad? The men didn't play no Boyzone or Spice Girls or Smurfs or anything. So, you see, that bit wasn't so good.'

Arms raised, yet again.

'Well, still sounds fantastic. Mummy's sorry she missed it.'

'Yeah. Bit of a pity that, Mummy, wasn't it?'

'Yes, darling.'

'And then, when we got to the car park . . .'

'Sophie! You can tell Mummy the rest later.'

'But, Dad –'

'Listen, Sophie,' Gina interrupts her, 'Mummy has a surprise for you.'

'A SURPRISE!'

'Calm down! It's not that exciting. An old friend is coming round to see you in an hour or so.'

'But who, Mummy?'

'Noreen.'

'Noreen? My old Noreen?'

'I don't think she'd be too happy to hear you call her that, but yes.'

'Why is she coming?'

'To see you.'

'Is she going to look after me again?'

A painful exchange of glances between Gina and me.

'I don't know about that, she's just going to play with you for a few hours while Daddy and I pop into Ballinkilty to have a chat.'

'Why go all the way to Ballinkilty to chat? Can't you just chat to Daddy here? Silly.'

'Well, we've a bit of business to sort out. We won't be long. Then I'll come home and play with you, darling. I've taken the day off.'

'Oh. Okay.'

A bit of business to sort out.

Yes indeed.

Must be a bit after nine o'clock. Approximately.

Duneen beach.

Just a stone's throw or so from our house, really. Well, a stone's throw by Jean-Claude Van Damme maybe, but you get the picture. It's close.

The beach is empty, almost. By the end of September the main bulk of the tourist season is over.

So it's just Gina and I, and a man throwing a stick into the sea for a black Labrador to retrieve, its coat heavy with water as it gallops clumsily back to its master.

It's a cove, Duneen. Not a massive beach, but big enough. Very beautiful and, when virtually empty as it is now, very serene and peaceful.

Gina and I are sat next to each other on my coat, retrieved from the boot of the car where it's spent the summer in hibernation.

We're at the back of the beach, probably because one man and his dog are at the front. This is not the sort of conversation you want overheard, nor observed.

We haven't spoken yet.

Gina has lit two cigarettes and passed one to me and we've smoked in silence. I don't know which question to ask first.

I thought I'd have to know every gory detail if this day ever arrived. Now I'm not so sure.

'How long have you known?' she's asking me.

'I didn't know. I just suspected. Then we bumped into Michelle last night. We caught her humping Johan in the back of his car –'

'WHAT?'

'I know. It seems infidelity is catching, doesn't it? That's what Sophie was about to tell you this morning.' I'm pausing as I stub out my cigarette on the rock. 'Michelle made a pass at me, you know. Your best friend.'

'I know.'

'Oh? How do – Connor! He told you? Said I shagged her, did he? Used it as a lever to get you into bed?'

'No, he didn't. He told me you sent her packing. That's why I never mentioned it.'

'In her embarrassment yesterday, your friend hinted she was not alone in seeking satisfaction elsewhere.'

'Bitch!'

'Yes. You can't trust anyone these days, can you?' I say pointedly. 'Even then I was tempted to dismiss it as shit-stirring. Then on the drive home I began to think. Little nigglings: the way Connor continually told me how beautiful and wonderful you were, the fact he always saw your side of the argument, not mine. Then I've rung him a few times when you've been working late, just to see if he fancied popping round for a chat or to watch a football match. He's never been there, of course. And when I suddenly realised it was his car . . . when I saw him drop you off last night . . . I knew then, really. All those nights working late. I know why now.'

'Do you?'

'Don't play games with me, Gina. Don't fuck with me now. It's time to stop all that.'

She's silent.

'It's not necessarily as bad as you think.'

'Yes, it is.'

'No. Look, it's over. I finished it last night.'

'Oh, now, there's a coincidence. I'm expected to believe that, am I?'

Gina's picked up a stone and tossed it ineffectually towards the sea.

'It's true.'

'What does it matter? The damage is done. You fucked him, didn't you?'

'Andy, please . . .'

'Didn't you?'

'Yes, all right. I admit it. I fucked Connor. There. Happy now?'

This hurts, it really fucking hurts! There can be no greater physical pain. No disease can rampage through you like this.

'How many times?'

'Shit, Andy. I wasn't keeping count. What difference does it make? It's not important.'

'It is to me. Because I'm humiliated, Gina. All those times you've found it so easy to say no to me, all those nights of sexual rejection. All those years of completely controlling our sex-life and then Mr Sensitive comes along and your knickers hit the ground faster than a dropped crystal glass. So I want to know. I want all the gory details. When did it begin? Where were you when you did it the first time? Did he go down on you? Did you suck his cock, Gina? Is it bigger than mine? Is he a better screw than me? Is that why you let him have you?'

'STOP! STOP! STOP!'

She's crying.

'You don't really want to know all that, do you?'

I'm shaking. As if I have a fever. Can't seem to stop it.

'I don't know. Part of me does. For whatever reason. Perhaps to help me believe it. Help me face it. Maybe so I don't hear it from someone else. I don't want someone stopping me in the street and telling me they saw you bending over in a shop doorway, somewhere.'

'Oh, Jesus, Andy.'

'Then again, part of me never wants to hear. Because I know how much it will hurt.'

'I'm sorry, Andy. I really am.'

'That's it, is it? I'm supposed to peck you on the cheek and say, "Never mind, all's well that ends well", am I?'

'No, of course not.'

'Gina, there is not a worse scenario than your wife and one of your best friends. It's such a sodding cliché. Like one of those photo-stories in that tacky little magazine you edit.'

I know. I can't help being vicious. Not now. I want to hurt her. I want revenge for the way she's making me feel.

'It's a standard, isn't it? The boss and the secretary. The teacher and the pupil. The bored housewife and the television-repair man. I know, I'll go home and give Noreen a seeing-to, and we can have the husband and the nanny as well.'

She's tugging nervously at her hair.

'Look, Andy, I have had an affair with Connor. I've admitted it.'

'Because you got caught, Gina.'

'Yes, okay. But what's more important is why I did it and what *we* are going to do now?'

'So why did you, Gina? Why did you cheat on me? Why did you find Connor so irresistible? You tell me.'

She's lighting another cigarette. Now she's running her hand nervously through her hair. She looks tired, suddenly. Weary.

'Because he's so capable! So . . . in control. It's difficult to explain. I suppose what's happened is . . . Well, it goes back a long way, really. You're not the man I married now, Andy. I'm not blaming you. I'm not accusing you, I'm not even criticising you. It's just . . . you've been unlucky. Things just haven't happened for you. I don't know why. I think you're incredibly talented and different and I'm a big fan of your work. I always have been. But, for whatever reason, it's just not coming off and now . . .'

'Do go on.'

'You've changed, Andy. You're not fun any more. You've lost your . . . charisma. The man who could hold a room spellbound two seconds after he walked into it has just disappeared. When you spoke, everybody listened. Everyone was interested in what you had to say, because it was worth hearing. It was enlightening, or funny or challenging. You just don't do that any more. You've become bitter, Andy. Depressed. Maybe looking after the children . . . maybe it's taken you even lower.'

'You were the one who chained a man to the kitchen sink, Gina.'

'Be fair. Circumstances did that.'

'So that's why you slept with Connor?'

'Yes, in a way. Because Connor is what you *used* to be. He's a poorer version, but he's witty and charming and bright and attentive and –'

'And rich and successful and powerful –'

'That's not fair, Andy. You know I'm not turned on by those things. That's simply you being bitter.'

'Yes, you *are* turned on by those things, Gina.'

'Oh,' she shrugs, 'maybe.'

I'm lighting another cigarette. I'm feeling empty, drained.

Gina continues. 'I love you, Andy –'

'Oh, that's fucking obvious.'

'– and I know you love me –'

'Do you, now?'

'– but I'm not sure if we're *in* love with each other any more.'

Slam!

My guts are torn.

'There's not much left to say then, is there?'

She's looking directly into my eyes.

'Aren't you going to fight for me, Andy?'

She's looking at me questioningly, with her blue eyes.

'Should I fight for a wife who's been unfaithful?'

'No, I suppose not.'

People are starting to arrive on the beach.

We stay quiet until the last of them are out of earshot.

'Maybe we both need a bit of space. Some time to think,' she's saying. 'It's probably easier to see things clearly if we're apart. Maybe you should think about going back to London? Ireland hasn't done you any favours . . .'

'Oh, that would be sodding convenient for you, wouldn't it? Get old Andy out of the way then Connor can safely park his boots under my fucking bed!'

'*No*! I didn't mean that. Maybe I should go back to England then.'

'It doesn't matter, Gina. It's irrelevant. Problems do not disappear just because you move house. They travel on the van with you, along with the fridge, and the telly, and the bathroom bloody mirror. You open a tea-chest and out they flood. Just as big and ugly and painful as before.'

'I know, I know,' she says, tugging at her hair, 'but I still think we need thinking-time apart. I'll move out,' she's announcing, 'take the kids.'

'Wait a minute, hold on just a fucking second, girl. Those are my children too!'

'I know, I know, Andy.'

She's speaking in a low voice. I raised mine. It embarrassed her.

'I promise you, I don't ever want to take your children away from you.'

'You can't take them away from the house, Gina. It's their home. Look, I accept we need some time to sort out this mess. So maybe I'm the one who should go. We'll have to talk some more tonight. This could have a huge impact on the children. Especially Sophie. I mean, what the hell are we going to say to her?'

'I can't even begin to think,' she says, shaking her head.

'Let's get out of here. I can't talk any more.'

I've stood up and I'm making my way back to the car, leaving Gina to follow me . . . at least, I presume she's following me.

I'm not stopping to check.

I'm parked just around the corner from my house.

I've dropped Gina off.

She promised she'd play with Sophie this afternoon.

I couldn't go in. I couldn't.

I just can't face my children. Not just yet.

I won't let them see me cry and I am crying.

Sobbing, like the big woman I've become.

If they see me crying now it will frighten them. Unsettle them. Make them ask questions and I . . .

My world has just folded.

I have nothing left now.

Except . . .

There's somebody I want to visit.

My wrist hurts.

I've practically broken it hammering on Connor's door.

He's not in. Unless he's cowering in a corner somewhere.

It's a nice house. A big fuck-you house right on the water at Rosscarbery. No leaking roofs or dodgy heating systems here.

Maybe he's at work.

He didn't call for Gina before we left for the beach and he would have done normally. She must have phoned him to warn him.

No point in hanging around outside. I'll go back to the car.

'Is it Connor you're after?'

A man in wellies clutching a pair of hedge-clippers has appeared from goodness knows where.

'It is.'

'You'll have a bit of a wait, I'm thinking.'

'Oh?'

'Sure, he's off abroad. Business. He'll be gone a couple of months or more.'

'I see.'

'You a friend of his?'

I thought I was.

'My wife is. He gives her a lift into the city. I was just bringing him a message.'

'Wasn't he after telling her he was off?'

'Probably. Must have got the dates mixed up.'

'Ah, well, now, these things happen.'

'You're right there Thanks anyway.'

'No problem. Take care now.'

'I will.'

Out of the country. How bloody convenient.

It's Friday. It's been two days now since I found out.

I've become a recluse. I can't face anyone. Least of all my children. I can't trust myself. I'm over-emotional with them. When I'm not crying, I'm bear-hugging them, clinging to them.

We've talked a little, Gina and I, but I keep walking out in the middle of the conversations. I get upset, or angry, or frightened.

I can't quite accept it. I'm finding it difficult to think of a life without . . .

Oh, well, early days.

It's Saturday.

Three days since the earth was pulled from under my feet.

I'm sort of numb. Shock, possibly. I'm still scratching around trying to find something to get a foothold on.

We're in a pub garden having a drink. One of the few pub gardens in Ballinkilty. Gina's idea. It's lunch-time and she's inside getting another round.

The sun is still shining. Nicola is in her buggy, parked in the shade.

She's chuckling and waving her arms whilst watching the chaos Sophie and half a dozen new-found friends are making, desperate to join in.

They're playing on the boards still in place after the last céili. Sophie's attempts at Irish dancing have to be seen to be believed. Doesn't stop her bowing stupendously. She's such an actress.

Gina's returning with the drinks.

'Sophie, your Coke and crisps are here.'

'But, Mum, I'm busy!'

'Okay, whenever you're ready.'

Gina's just handed me my pint.

'Thanks.'

'Andy, I know you find it hard to talk about, but we have to come to a decision. I think we definitely need some time apart.'

'Yes, I know. I've said already. I'll go.'

'Have you thought what you'll do for money?'

'No. Get a job. Sign on.'

'We'd probably have to legally separate straight away, without thinking-time, in order for you to receive enough benefit to live on.'

I hadn't thought of that. Shit! The ramifications just go on and on.

'I could let you have a little if it —'

'No. Thank you.'

She's pausing, thinking, before she continues.

'I spoke to Noreen last night, Andy.'

'Oh? Where was I?'

'In your music room, I presume.'

'What did she have to say?'

'She's got another job. Good money too. More than I could afford to pay her to look after the kids.'

'Dad? Sing the music. I'm dancing, can't you see?'

So now I'm trying to have a serious conversation about separation from my spouse whilst attempting to both compose and sing an Irish reel at the same time.

'De diddle de diddle de diddle de diddly, diddle de diddle . . . So what will you do, look for someone else? . . . de diddle de diddle de . . .'

'I suppose so. Unless?'

'. . . de diddle de diddle de diddly . . . unless what? . . . de diddle de diddly de dye, dye . . .'

'I've had a thought. You're going to need somewhere to live right?'

'De diddle de diddle de . . . Yes?'

'And you're going to have to find a way to pay for that. It could get awkward. There's not much employment in this town. You'd have to go to the city and you don't have transport.'

'De diddle, de diddle, de diddly, diddly, de de!'

She's right. This just gets worse and worse.

'Dad!'

'Yes, sorry, Sophie. I'm trying to talk to Mummy.'

'But the *music*, Daddy.'

'It's over, sweetheart. Didn't you notice my applause-winning crescendo?'

'What?'

'Don't say "what", say "pardon". Big finish, my big finish.'

'Has it finished, Dad?'

'That's what I just said!'

'Well, if it's finished then the dance is finished. So why aren't you clapping, Daddy?'

'I'm sorry, you're quite correct. And thunderous applause.'

I'm clapping till my hands hurt for the old trooper.

'Thank you. The next show will start in two minutes'.'

I can't wait.

'Can I run an idea past you, Andy? Just to see how it sounds?' Gina's asking me, as Nicola's patience runs out and I lift her out of the buggy.

'Go on, then.'

'What if you carried on looking after the children?'

'What? Where?'

'In our house. You find a flat or something in Ballinkilty and I'll pay you a wage to look after the kids.'

'I can't take money for looking after my own children!'

'I know, but if you don't carry on looking after them I'm still going to have to pay somebody else to do the job. And you know what Sophie's like. Nicola too. I mean she's used to you now, Andy. She's settled. She loves her daddy. It's going to be hard for her to deal with someone else.'

Nicola is standing on the edge of the céili board, holding on to my fingers for balance. She is smiling at me.

'You're emotionally blackmailing me, Gina.'

'I don't mean to. But you must see the sense of it? The money I give you will pay for the flat and your keep, just about. Then we wouldn't have to involve anyone else. Not yet. Not until we're certain what we're going to do. At least it will give me time to see if I can find another treasure like Noreen. Say yes, Andy. Please. Not for me. For the kids.'

She's steam-rollering me again. She's good at that. Gina can make anything, even the most outrageous idea, seem perfectly plausible.

'Daddy! Music, Daddy, music!'

'Sorry, Sophie. Bam, bam, bam. Ba-bam bam bam.'

'What's that Daddy?'

'Daddy's singing "The Stripper", Sophie.'

'What?'

'Just Daddy's silly joke, Stinks. DE! DE! ... diddle, de diddle, de diddle, de diddly ... Yes ... de diddle, de diddle, de diddle, de ...'

'Pardon?' Gina's asking.

'... de diddle de diddly ... I said I'll do it ... de diddle, de diddle ... de diddle ...'

What choice do I have? If you look at the cold, hard facts.

'Daddy! Look, Daddy! Look at Nicola!'

Panic.

I'm looking at Nicola and she's walking ... teetering towards her older sister.

Her first steps.

I hadn't even realised she'd let go of my fingers.

I'm turning to Gina.

And she's crying as she watches.

I've just sent Gina on ahead. She's heading back to the car with Nicola.

Sophie is with me.

'Where are we going, Daddy?'

'You're coming with me.'

'I know that, Daddy. But where?'

'I'm going to see a man about a dog.'

'Ooh, Daddy! That's a good idea, Daddy. A very good idea. Can we have a Labrador? Julie's got a Labrador. It's ever so big.'

'I don't mean a real dog. We're not going to buy a real dog.'

'But you said ...'

'It's just an expression, Sophie.'

'But, Dad! I want a doggie.'

'You'll have to settle for a packet of peanuts and a Cidona then.'

'Is that as big as a Labrador, Daddy?'

'It's not a dog. It's that fizzy apple drink you like.'

'But, Daddy! I want –'

'A doggie. I get the message, Sophie. Put it on your Christmas list this year. Maybe Santa's a pet lover.'

Sophie can still make me laugh. Even at a time like this. Trouble is, I sort of want to cry at the same time, if you understand what I mean. At least, if Gina's suggestion works, I've not lost her altogether.

Not yet.

3.15 p.m.

Back at the house.

Not sure if it's even *my* house any more.

In front of the children it's as if Gina and I were in a play. We pretend to be the perfect couple, behaving as if everything was just fine. Then when the kids have gone to bed it's like living in a library.

Silence. Afraid to speak in case it breaks the rules.

I'm supposed to be sleeping in the spare room. But I spend most nights pacing about . . . thinking.

Today, however, I've thrown myself a lifeline. Just a thin one. But a little ray of hope.

Something to hang on to and to go towards my slush fund for the new living arrangements I'm about to embark on.

I've just been to see Dan, who owns O'Leary's.

I bought him drinks and I argued with him. I bullied him, blackmailed him, fought with him, until I came out with what I wanted. Which was rather impressive, considering Sophie was single-handedly destroying the bar furniture at the time. After her display at the Stanley Larke gig, I'm amazed she has yet to be officially barred.

Anyhow, successful negotiations are concluded.

A Monday night's residency. Trial period for a month. Starting at the end of October. Just me and a guitar. Plus a drum machine, if I can borrow or hire one for a nominal fee. It'll be tough. Monday night is the graveyard shift. Everyone's skint after the weekend.

But I have complete autonomy. I decide what I play.

It's a golden chance to air some of my songs. I have loads I haven't played live due to the jealous nature of the Blow-ins. I don't need to rehearse much. I can play these songs in my sleep.

I'll have to play a load of covers to begin with. Then I can gradually slip in more and more of my own material.

It'll help fill in the time.

Stop me thinking.

Strange. I don't actually have to clear it with Gina, do I?

18

10.30 a.m. Tuesday. October the something or other. Mid-ish in the month.

I've been busy trying to sort things out.

I've found a flat.

I exaggerate.

I've found a box to live in. Nearly thirty-nine years old and I'm moving into a sodding bedsit.

It's nicely situated, though. Slap-bang in the middle of town, a few doors away from O'Leary's where I'm going to be playing. Big window overlooking the street. Basic furniture and not much of it.

A minimalist's dream residence.

Shit! Who am I kidding? It's so fucking depressing, you'd still want to weep even if the room were filled with laughing gas.

Punishment upon punishment, it seems.

My wife sleeps with another man, and I end up walking away from my children and my beautiful home in the country to exile myself in a cell so small it feels as if I will be residing in quarters that belong in a cattery. My next-door neighbours will probably be called Precious and Tiddles.

I've negotiated a reasonable out-of-season rent, although my landlord informs me he will want me out of here by next May as he can get double the money from some poor, unsuspecting tourist. I haven't got the strength to argue. It's taken me weeks to find this.

Oh, I've got Nicola with me, by the way. She's been teetering around the room, spasmodically managing to fall over. Thankfully there isn't much in the way of furniture for her to collide with or *objects d'art* for her to destroy. I've always thought that any sportsman wishing to become a top-flight goalkeeper should be made to have a child at the earliest opportunity. My reflexes have never been better.

The landlord's given me the key and left me here to make my final decision.

Nicola's fallen over. I've picked her up and I'm giving her a big hug and she's squealing and laughing at me.

I'm a bit frightened, actually.

7.15 p.m.

Nicola's tucked up in her cot. The rest of us are in the lounge. Sophie is standing in front of Gina and me, scratching her head. Mummy and Daddy are at opposite ends of the sofa. Bolt upright. Like oversized bookends.

'Why can't you do your work *here*, Daddy? Like you always do?'

'I have to concentrate really hard, Sophie. If I'm here in the evenings I just won't do it. I'll just flop in front of the television, as usual.'

'But when will you come back, Daddy?'

'Well, in some ways, Sophie, I won't really be going away. I'll be here before Mummy goes to work and won't leave until Mummy gets home. So I'll still spend the days with you and Nicola.'

'But, Dad! When will you see *Mummy*?'

Oh, God! I'd hoped she wouldn't ask that. Why do we adults continually underestimate our children? They are not fools. Their human observation is vastly superior to ours. A child instinctively knows when something is wrong. They sense it.

Surprisingly, I have no desire to lessen her feelings for Gina, either. She's a good mother. Her children adore her. I don't want to be responsible for changing that in any way.

'It's going to be very difficult for Mummy and Daddy, Sophie,' Gina's chipping in. I'm glad. I'm not sure what to say at the moment.

'In fact, it's going to be much harder for us than it is for you. But it probably won't take long. Nobody's saying it will be for ever.'

Oh, really, Gina?

'Just for a little while, Mummy.'

'More than likely.'

'Until Daddy's finished his work?'

'That's the idea.'

'Oh . . .'

Sophie's looking at me with those saucer-shaped eyes.

I can't stand this. It's tearing me apart.

'. . . Okay. I suppose it will be all right. But you'll have to be quick, you know, Dad.'

'I know, Stinks,' I've managed to whisper, brokenly.

'Can I watch a video?'

'I should think so, don't you, Mummy?' I say.

'Yes, go on.'

I've noticed something.

Sophie often wants to watch a video when things are not quite right. When she's been told off, or when she's not well. Or at moments such as this. When she sniffs the wind of change. A child of routine, she likes things just so.

If she's unsettled, she likes to drift off into another world, handed to her on a plate by the screen in the corner of the room.

11.30 p.m.

I'm in my little garret in town. I've been here three days. Well, nights, really.

I haven't settled.

Maybe I *should* move back to London.

No. I can't.

I'd still be a failure, you see. All those bastards, those I-told-you-he'd-never-amount-to-anything gloaters. The people who revel in pleasure as they watch you struggle. Vultures, circling, waiting to swoop for your home, or your wife, or your children.

No. I'd have to be somebody, achieve something big enough to be untouchable, before I moved back.

If I ever move back.

Plus the fact my children are here.

I miss them at night.

I'm still bawling my eyes out pathetically as I go home every evening. Everything feels empty. My days with the kids have 'temporary' stamped all over them. Then I come back here and pace about. I can't get used to not running up and down the stairs to check that the babies are okay.

Then I try to sleep.

Trouble is, I'm soaked in the habit of keeping one ear cocked in case Nicola wakes. Then, having not dropped off until God knows what hour, the alarm goes off at six thirty and I'm immediately catapulted into a state of panic because I haven't heard Baby during the night. I leap out of bed wondering what's wrong with her, before my brain reorientates to my surroundings enough for me to grab a calming cup of coffee.

At least I can smoke something nefarious without a disapproving lecture.

Night shifts. They're going to kill Gina. Still, I suppose that's her problem. I've got to try and stop caring. After all, she's stopped caring about me.

My work isn't really happening either.

I was used to writing in an atmosphere of natural chaos. Interruptions from Sophie or the baby, Gina or the telephone have become part of the creative process. I've spent years thinking how wonderful it would be if I had the time and solitude to concentrate on my compositions and now all this silence is driving me up the fucking wall. I have so much time to think I'm disappearing up my own backside. I'm becoming phobically pernickety, stifling myself either with attempts at perfection or lack of confidence.

Find yourself with an unexpectedly large amount of time to think and you start to brood.

Trust me.

11.45 a.m.

Day four of my part-time exile.

I'm in the car with the children. I'm to have the car during the week. Gina has found another spin to Cork, a woman this time. So, unless she fancies seeing how the other half live, we should be safe from any more scandal.

Not that it matters any more.

Gina gets the car back at weekends. If she needs it in the evening during the week then she'll give me a lift down the hill at knocking-off time.

Day four and the word is definitely out.

Gossip. A major drawback of living in a town this size. Everyone knows your business. Seemingly before you do. I had not been installed in my broom-cupboard five minutes before I was the recipient of sympathetic stares and concerned enquiries. I haven't even been seen out alone at night yet, for crying out loud. The fact that I *am* seen trooping around the town with my children in tow as usual has singularly failed to pull the wool over the eyes of the good people of Ballinkilty.

I have never been so embarrassed.

I'm like an ostrich, frantically trying to find sand in which to bury my head in the middle of a shopping centre.

Today they started treating my kids like the children of Chernobyl – over-friendly, over-concerned, over-the-top.

Sophie's never had so many free lollipops and pound coins pressed into her sweaty paws in all her life. If this keeps up, Gina and I could retire and become her managers. She's completely bemused.

We're driving home. To my *old* home. Sophie is next to me in the front, while Nicola is cooing away in the back. Her hat has fallen over her eyes. Sophie's eyebrows are furrowing in exactly the same way her mother's do.

There's a question coming. I know it.

'Daddy, why does everybody keep talking in that funny way to me? Do they think I'm stupid or something?'

'I don't think so. You're a very clever girl.'

'Why did that woman keep saying, "Are you all right, Sophie?" to me, Daddy?'

'I don't know. I expect she was concerned about you.'

'Why, Daddy?'

'I've no idea.'

'I'm not sick, you know, Dad.'

'No, of course not.'

'Do I look a bit sick, Dad?'

'Not to me.'

A thinking pause.

'Dada, Dada, DADA!'

'Yes, Nicola darling, Daddy's here.'

'Why did that woman call Nicola a big brave girl, Daddy?'

'Search me, Sophie.'

'She's not a brave girl, is she, Daddy?'

'Well, she can be.'

'Yeah, but, Daddy, I mean, she hasn't *rescued* anybody, has she?' She's shaking her head.

'No.'

'Nicola hasn't had an operation or anything, has she, Daddy?'

'No.'

'She's not had any nasty medicine or put a fire out, has she, Daddy?'

'Not that I'm aware.'

'See? So she's not brave, then, is she, Daddy?'

'Look, Sophie . . .'

'Daddy?'

She's put her hand on my leg to help her interject.

'Yes, daughter.'

'What's a "dote", Dad?'

'A "dote"?'

'That's what I said!'

'All right, just checking. "Dote" means sweetheart or poppet or little darling.'

'It doesn't mean you're brave, then?'

'No, Sophie.'

'So when the woman said Nicola was a "dote", she didn't mean hero or something?'

'No.'

She's looking out of the window now.

I'm not convinced the interrogation is over.

'Dad?'

Told yer.

'Yes, Stinks.'

'Dad?'

'Yes?'

'She was funny. Why did she say, "Are you after keeping your spirits up, Sophie?"'

What do I say?

'Did she mean Christmas spirits, Daddy?'

'Yes, probably.'

'But, Dad?'

Don't tell me.

'It's not Christmas yet, is it?'

'No.'

'I know it's not, because Mummy said it was too early for me to write my list to Santa.'

'It is a bit, Sophie.'

'Dad?'

Shit, I wish she'd stop. I can't deal with these questions.

'Er . . . Dad? What does dee-force mean?'

'Sounds like something out of *Star Wars*. I don't know, what does it mean?'

'I don't know, that's why I'm asking you, silly! When I told Richard you were living in Ballinkilty he said Mummy and you were going to buy a dee-force.'

Oh, fuck, fuck, FUCK!

'So you must know what it is if Mummy and you are going to buy one.'

'I don't think we are, Sophie. We probably couldn't afford it anyway. 'Cos guess what?'

'What?'

'We're skint again.'

She's smiling, but she's not buying this.

'Shall we pop into the sweet shop by the supermarket? Then you can spend some of that money you collected.'

'That's a good idea.'

'I thought you'd like it.'

I'm swinging into the car park off the roundabout.

I know I'm avoiding the issue, but I just can't handle this. Maybe that makes me a bad father, but I just can't, I just can't, I just . . . can't.

Not now.

It's too soon.

6.15 p.m.

Gina's home.

'Hi, everyone.'

Sophie's just leapt off my lap to go and hug her.

Nicola's still sat on the floor between my legs, tearing today's newspaper to shreds.

'How've they been?' she's asking me.

'Fine. But I fear word has spread around town,' I say cryptically, above Sophie's head.

'Oh, God.'

'Keep a close eye on madam, from now on,' I'm advising her, gesturing to Sophie, whose face is buried in her mother's skirt. 'Right. I'll get my coat and be off.'

'Yes, okay. Come on, Sophie, get your coat on. We're giving Daddy a lift.'

Of course. It's Friday. Gina has the car.

I'm not looking forward to the weekend.

Gina will have the children to herself on Saturday and most of Sunday too.

We'll just meet up for Sunday lunch, for the kids' sake. Somewhere cheap. It's been agreed.

Long couple of days ahead. I must get down to some work.

It'll help.

19

Monday, I think. December.

Soon be Christmas again. Lord knows what we're going to do about that. The weekends are bad enough. I don't fancy spending Christmas by myself, although it's hard to see how we can be together for much more than a quick present-opening the way things stand at the moment.

I've written some new songs. And what miserable little ditties they are too. Chock full of angst. Lots of lyrics about loss and separation and loneliness and failure. I've achieved the impossible. I've made The Smiths sound positively cheerful by comparison.

Quite good, though, if you like that sort of thing.

I'm feeding Nicola her breakfast as she sits in her high chair shouting, 'MORE!'

This child shows no sign of losing her appetite with age. She's still huge. A career as a supermodel seems increasingly unlikely unless she suddenly and somewhat fashionably develops bulimia.

I arrived to find Gina drinking coffee in her usual state of half-readiness. Towelling robe, bra, tights, knickers, makeup.

Beautiful as ever.

For one brief moment I wanted her again.

Then a mental picture of Connor undressing her and making love to her flashed before my eyes. Here, in the kitchen, just as I had always longed to.

I was immediately overwhelmed by pain and bitterness.

I stopped *wanting* her . . . I didn't say I'd stopped *loving* her. I didn't say that.

Then she went upstairs to finish dressing and to try and stop Sophie stinking in her pit.

'Good morning, Daddy.'

Speak of the devil. Sophie has finally appeared in the kitchen just as

Nicola has regretfully resigned herself to the fact there is no more room in her stomach.

Next shift.

'Morning, Stinks. What do you fancy for breakfast?'

'Honey Nut Loops.'

New favourite.

'Milk?'

'Yuck!' With a face to match I watch her slope off back into the lounge.

No milk on her cereal? Her mother eats the stuff dry too.

Gina's just returned. Fully suited.

'Sophie's complaining of tummy-ache again. Keep an eye on her for me and make sure she eats properly, could you?'

'Of course.'

'She's eating far too many sweets lately.' She says this as she's gathering up her briefcase. There is a hint of accusation in her voice, but because of our situation it's rather restrained.

'If she refuses those, you know she's really sick,' I jest, somewhat pathetically.

'Oh! Nearly forgot. Belly O'Hea was on the phone for you last night.'

'What did he want?'

'Wouldn't say. Just said he had some news for you.'

'Why didn't you send him round to the bedsit?'

She's looking at the floor suddenly.

'I don't know. I didn't know if he knew. I thought if I mentioned the flat he might start asking questions and I might find that ... difficult.'

'I see what you mean.'

I'm well aware that Belly would have found out weeks ago, along with the rest of Ballinkilty. But I'm not going to say anything.

I sit in my bedsit at night, thinking, Why should I be the only one that suffers? Tomorrow I'm going to go into that house and I'm going to be firm. Tell Gina it's all her sodding fault I'm so miserable. Give her arse a metaphorical kicking. Make her pay for her mistakes. Then I get here and I get the feeling I'm not the only one suffering, so I say nothing.

'Anyway, he can catch me at my gig tonight. You thinking of coming along?'

'No. I just feel . . . It's still a bit awkward.' She's looking at the floor again.

Gina hasn't seen any of my Monday-night gigs.

Silence.

A thought's occurred.

'I wonder if he's actually managed to do something with my demo-tapes?'

'Oh, yes. I'd forgotten you'd given him those.'

'So had he, or so I thought.'

'Well, perhaps he's got some good news for you. That would be nice, wouldn't it?'

She's looking at me with the faintest trace of something in her eyes.

What is it?

Hope, possibly?

'I won't raise my expectations. Belly's idea of good news is generally lacking in ambition. I remember him ordering champagne because he'd just swung Mix and Match a season at Butlin's.'

'You never know,' she's saying, her face seeming to fall slightly. 'Take care of my babies . . . sorry, I mean *our* babies. See you later.'

She's gone.

I'm standing at the window watching her walking along the drive. There have been a lot of moments like that. One of us saying something second nature such as 'my children' only to flinch suddenly because it's now open to misinterpretation.

'Daddy! Where are my Honey Nut Loops?'

'Sorry, petal. The bees are just fetching the honey as we speak and I'm busy punching the holes to make the loops.'

'Well, hurry up, I'm starvicating!'

'Yes, ma'am.'

Yep. Her mother's daughter, that one.

'Dad?'

'Yes, Sophie?

'When are you coming home again?'

'I don't know yet, Stinks. Now eat your breakfast.'

10.15 p.m. O'Leary's.

I'm just about to start the second set of my gig and the place is beginning to kick a bit.

The first set went extremely well. People started to drift in from the main bar with every passing number, which is a very healthy sign. I opened with Roy Orbison's 'Pretty Woman', which has that simple but effective guitar riff of an introduction, and progressed from there.

I keep it cheerful. Under the circumstances, it's a bad idea to play 'She's Out Of My Life', 'Love Don't Live Here Anymore', or 'D.I.V.O.R.C.E.' . . . Not that I would ever play *anything* by Tammy Wynette, come to think about it. Not without being paid a vast sum of money.

Up front.

Anyway, suffice to say, I have chosen carefully from my repertoire. Gossip is rife in this town without me adding fuel to the flames.

I have played eight or nine of my own songs so far this evening, all well received.

I met Belly O'Hea as soon as I arrived. He was full of smiles beneath his whiskery face, said he just had to pop out but not to worry he'd be back soon. He returned ten minutes into the first set. Led the applause between numbers and winked mischievously at me every time I looked in his general direction. I got him up to sing a song. Fats Domino's 'Ain't That A Shame' and Belly thanked me over the microphone telling the audience I was a bigger star than I thought I was. Then he winked at me again.

In the interval I caught him at the bar, but he said he couldn't talk because he was just about to pull a German tourist with, quote, 'the biggest pair of knockers you were ever after seeing in all your Godforsaken feckin' life, Andy boy', unquote. He said he'd talk to me after the gig. I watched him go back to his seat and it was true. She did have the biggest knockers I'd ever seen, and thighs like an Argentinian footballer.

So, I'm just about to begin the second set and I'm none the wiser. I still don't know what this 'news' is.

I know one thing, though. Judging by the way Belly's pissing me around, winding me up . . . *he* thinks it's big shakes.

'Right, the next song goes back to the days when these things were the most technically advanced machines you could find in what we used to call amusement arcades.'

I'm now thrashing out the recognisable opening chords of The Who's 'Pinball Wizard' to wake the bastards up for the second half of the show.

*

I'm sat at a table opposite a grinning Belly O'Hea.

He still hasn't said anything, apart from mentioning that the German tourist was obviously frigid, as she had hastily departed.

I'm glad. I want Belly's complete attention, which is inclined to wander at the best of times.

Belly has insisted we wait for our pints to arrive before he imparts his news.

Why is he milking this so much? This is excessive even by his standards.

The barman has very kindly brought our drinks across and Belly has paid him. I'm watching him take a healthy gulp followed by a ritual wiping of his beard. I don't blame him: the head off a pint of stout stuck to his whiskers would make him look like an alcoholic Santa Claus.

'You've had long enough, Belly. Come on, out with it.'

'Ah, don't be so hard, Andy. You know how I like to cherish these moments.'

'What "moments", Belly? What are we talking about? This is shaping up like an over-hyped record. Keep this up much longer and whatever you tell me is bound to be a disappointment.'

'Suspense, Andy. Do you not know that suspense is where all the excitement in life is after coming from?'

'Yes, well, I've had enough drama in my life lately, thank you.'

'Yes, so I'm hearing,' he informs me, as he gollops down at least half his remaining stout.

'Well, before Rumour Control gets hold of *your* news, don't you think you'd better tell me yourself?'

He's putting his glass down. Now he's wiping the edge of the table, his hands going in opposite directions, as if smoothing out an imaginary tablecloth.

'You remember those demo-tapes you gave me?'

'Vividly.'

'The ones that kept getting rejected?'

'Belly . . .'

'The ones neither you nor anyone else could get any joy with?'

'Stop building your part and get to the point, will you?'

'Well, dear old Uncle Belly O' Hea, that washed-up old has-been of a rock-and-roller, the finest blues voice never to make a million –'

'BELLY!'

'– has managed to get a result. Well, to be fair now, half a result.'

Half a result. I knew it. I was certain it was never going to be worth this much of a song and dance.

'Go on.'

'Well, now, I was after sweating blood, breaking my arse for yer, and fair play to yer, you were right. Nobody seemed at all excited by them. Then I realised there was one tape I had shamefully neglected to send out, so I did.'

'Oh, which one?'

'You remember those little ditties you recorded on Michael's eight-track? Three songs you recorded with Bridget singing lead vocals, just before the two of them left your band to form Mix and Match?'

'Oh, yes, I'd almost forgotten about that. I hadn't been here that long. I was wallowing in it all. Going through my Irish-musical-influence stage, if I remember correctly.'

'Yer do. That's right. Yer kept coming out with some bollocks or other about mixing traditional Irish sounds with modern rock. You were after telling everyone that all The Police had done was mix reggae with rock and it made them millions.'

I'm laughing at the memory.

'It's all coming back to me. What was that first song I'd knocked off? You know, the sort of Riverdance-meets-Deff-Leppard track? All thrashing guitars mixed with jiggidy violins, Celtic harps and bloody panpipes. Honestly I can't believe I did that. Probably *the* most awful fucking song I've ever written.'

He's taking another drink.

'I didn't think it was bad, so I didn't.'

'Oh, come on, Belly. That's very kind of you, but what a crock of shit!'

'It was okay, I'm telling yer.'

'What did I call it? Something really naff. Celtic Saxon or something equally pretentious.'

'"When Cultures Clash", actually. I'm telling you it grows on you. After a few plays.'

'It just didn't fuse, Belly. It sounded like three musos locked in a room having a barnstorming argument. Oh, well, you've got to laugh, can't get it right every time. The other two songs were sort of okay, as I remember. Tell you the truth, I haven't really listened to that tape since just after we recorded it. Come to think of it, I don't think I ever sent that out *myself*. I'm surprised I gave it to you.'

Belly's signalled for another round of drinks.

'Well, Andy. God moves in mysterious ways, so he does.'

'Does he now? Care to explain that?'

Why am I suddenly suspicious?

'I decided to try a different tack with this tape. The recording was after being a bit rough, so to speak, so I didn't see the point in sending it to a recording company, no matter how well connected a man like myself may be.'

I'm slugging back the Murphy's now. I've got some catching up to do.

'So what did you do with it, then?'

'I entered it for a competition.'

'Competition? What sort of a competition? Oh, is this that Best Band thing – you know, with all the regional finals and stuff? The thing Mix and Match went in for? Came runner-up in the Cork final, didn't they?'

'No, it would be too late for that. It's been and gone like my youth, Andy. No, this would be . . .'

Why's he pausing?

He's fidgeting too.

'. . . more of a song-writing competition, so it would.'

'Interesting,' I'm saying, having finally finished my first pint. 'I didn't even know there was one.'

'Really, Andy? Now that surprises me a little.'

'So what happens then?'

'Well, in September, songs are submitted from all over the country and –'

'September! And you're only just beginning to tell me about this now.'

'Don't be interrupting when I'm in full flow, now. The songs are gradually whittled down to a small selection of what is after being considered to be the best. Then those chosen few are given an airing on *Kenny Live*.'

'On what, sorry?'

'*Kenny Live*, man! For feck's sake, Andy! How long have you been in the country now and you don't even know what *Kenny Live* is? You be telling me next yer think Gay Byrne is a sexually depraved act, performed by cigar-smoking homosexuals!'

'Oh, it's on the *telly*. Irish telly. RTE and all that jazz. Yes, I have heard of it, of course I have.'

He's rubbing his face with his hands.

'"Heard of it," he says! Do you never watch it?'

'No.'

'Jaysus!'

'It's nothing personal. I'm sure RTE is crammed full of fascinating programming. I just can't get a decent picture. Something to do with the wind that's constantly trying to blow my house down, and a small forest inconveniently positioned in the way of the transmitter, or something. I can't get the BBC on these multi-channel packages either. That's why we had to buy a dish. Consequently I'm an expert on seventies television reruns and bugger all else. It's not my fault.'

'Fair play to yer.'

'So remind me, *Kenny Live* is a bit like *The Gay Byrne Show*, only a bit more trendy. Am I right?'

'Ah, well, it's near enough, I suppose, for the purposes of this discussion.'

'Fine.'

'Anyway, as you've probably guessed by now, unless you have the intelligence of a lemming, I sent in yer tape.'

'And?'

'They liked one of the songs. It's been chosen to enter the final stages and Mix and Match will play it live on the Kenny show, with your permission, o' course.'

I'm staggered.

'You're joking.'

'I am not.'

'Well, who'd have believed it? That's excellent. I think. One of my songs on the telly. Amazing. Thanks, Belly.'

'My pleasure. My fees are minimal.'

'Just a minute. Which song did they like?'

'Ah, now there's the thing. You see . . .'

'Not . . .?'

'"When Cultures Clash". Yes, I'm afraid that was the tune that turned them on.'

Oh, bugger! I finally get a song on national television and it has to be that one.

Now it's my turn to put my head in my hands.

'Don't be after being so hard on yourself. I'm telling you, when you listen to it again after the passing of a bit of time, it is actually a good song.'

'I'll take your word for it. I'm sorry to sound ungrateful.'

I'm now downing the vast majority of my second pint.

'You're probably right. I wonder what made them choose that one, though? I'm sure the other two were better songs. Better performances on the recording too. So why choose "When Cultures Clash"?'

'Well, it suits the competition very well, so it does. The sort of mix of Irish and British. The lyrics helped too, now. All that stuff about us all being cousins and having respect for each other and working together and understanding each other beneath the shite. But fair play to yer. It's very topical, what with the peace process going on, an' all.'

'Really? So what sort of a competition is this? Some kind of Save the Planet sort of thing?'

'In a manner of speaking.'

'Sounds more like Miss World.'

'I wouldn't go as far as saying that, now. Though it's usually fierce overflowing with gorgeous women in outrageous frocks.'

'Well, what is it, then? What do you win? I hope it's cash. I could use a bit of that. Or a recording contract. It's not a recording contract, is it?'

'Well, now, some of the winners of the ultimate final have been given recording contracts, so they have.'

'Ultimate final? Is there another stage after the *Kenny Live* bit, then?'

'Oh, that's when it really hots up.'

'Well, what is it, then? What exactly are we talking about here?'

He's looking at me, thoughtfully.

Why do I get the impression he doesn't *really* want to tell me? He's taken a deep breath.

'It's the Song for Europe, Andy.'

'Song for Europe? Song for Europe?'

'That's right.'

'Song for Europe . . . What's that? . . . Er . . . Euro . . . Euro . . . Euro-ver – something?'

'Good lad. Yer on the right lines.'

'Euro . . .'

'Work away now, you'll get there.'

'Eurovis –'

'In your own time, now. I wouldn't want you worrying about me sitting here growing old while the penny drops, now.'

'Euro . . . Eurovision. That's right, isn't it?'

'It is, son.'

Splash.

'THE FUCKING EUROVISION SONG CONTEST!'

'Ah, come on. Calm down, now, Andy. It's not as bad as all that.'

I'm about to have a seizure.

'The Eurovision Song Contest is the kiss of death to any street cred any artist might have had, Belly. You know that.'

'Fair play, Andy. It didn't do Abba any harm, now, as I recall.'

'Oh, so now you're suggesting we wear platform boots and sequinned skull caps, is that it?'

'Ah, go on. Not at all.'

'I can't do this.'

'Ah, yer must, Andy.'

'Bollocks! Could you see John Lennon entering the Eurovision fucking Song Contest? Ray Davies? David Bowie? Can you see Liam Gallagher singing "Boom-Banga-fucking-Bang"?'

'Yer out of touch, so yer are. The standards have improved enormously, they have.'

'Name me any artist or songwriter that's come out of the Song for Europe with their reputation intact.'

'Abba, now, like I said. I don't know – Sandie Shaw, so?'

'You're struggling now, aren't you? Two, and those only gained respectability in a sort of nostalgic retrospect. What do most people think of when they hear the word Eurovision? Eh? Johnny bloody Logan! Bucks Fizz! Dana! Heaven help us, the Brotherhood of fucking Man!'

No wonder he didn't want to tell me! I cannot believe Belly is sitting here trying to persuade me that it's a cool thing to do.

'Why don't you be the one to change all that, Andy? It's a way in. Use it, for feck's sake. Lord knows, you've been trying to find a door for long enough. Yer can't just slam the first one shut that's been left ajar.'

'Can't I? Watch me. I want out, Belly.'

'Now, you can't be doing that, Andy.'

'Why can't I?'

'Will yer stop being such a selfish bastard for five seconds and listen to me? What about Mix and Match? They're going to be delighted when I tell them. What about sweet little Bridget? Shite, she's gonna be after thinking this is going to make her a star. Yer can't take that away from the girl. Can yer? Now come on, can yer?'

Must everybody in my life take it in turns to emotionally blackmail me? Is there something about my face which says I'm a sucker for it? This has nothing to do with the fact Belly manages Mix and Match, of course.

'Oh, that's unfair, Belly. Why didn't you tell me you were going to do this?'

'I only did it as an afterthought. Jaysus, I was desperate enough, so I was. I didn't think it would get this far.'

'Oh, help!'

'Listen to me now, Andy. Have yer any idea how many hundreds of songs are entered every year for this little shindig? There are two panels, each consisting of ten grand nobs from the music business, an' all those feckers have to like yer song. Even then it only gets down to the last twenty. Next, all the top executives from RTE have to love yer little ditty as well, before it can reach the last eight. And wouldn't yer know it, one o' those last eight has to be in the feckin' Irish language. Those are some odds to have stacked against you. It's a grand achievement, boy. Would yer stop pissing on it from a great height!'

'Belly, my friend, I'm a rock-and-roller! I've spent years looking down on this kind of thing. Everyone will laugh at me.'

'There'll be those that'll take the piss, right enough. But, let me tell you, there's an awful lot of them as have tried to get a song selected themselves and failed, miserably.'

'Oh, like who?'

'I'm not saying. Just keep an eye out for the most condescending and you'll be after figuring it out for yerself. Listen, there's a press launch fer the eight songs that have reached the final. It's in a week's time.'

'*What*?'

'I don't set the timetables. That's just how it is, now. I have to have a decision, Andy. Though heaven knows what kinda shite will hit the fan if we pull out at this stage.'

I have a twinge of pain. I think it's because someone has just grabbed me by the short and curlies.

'I don't know whether to laugh or cry.'

'Do neither. Get yer equipment together and come back to me house. I've a fine bottle of whiskey, just made for drinking while poring over a dilemma like this. Come on, now, let's be having yer.'

What do I do?

I know. Drink the fucking whiskey.

Might as well, I suppose.

I can't see me doing much sleeping tonight.

6.45 a.m., Tuesday. Next day.

I arrived at my old house extra early today. I must look like death. I haven't slept, I haven't shaved, I'm hung over and still partially stoned.

Gina's looking at me now as if her home has just been invaded by an escaped convict.

'You look as if you could use a cup of coffee.'

'If you're making one.'

'Heavy night last night?' she's asking.

'In more one ways than one.'

'How was the gig?'

'Successful. I was quite pleased with how it went, by and large.'

'Good. I'm so pleased, Andy.'

She said that as if she meant it.

'How are things at the magazine?'

'Same as ever. Madness caused by lack of staff. In some ways I'd like to . . .'

'What?'

'Nothing. Here you are.'

She's just handed me a cup of coffee and for a second our hands touched. We both pulled them away simultaneously, like virginal teenagers. Ridiculous!

This is the mother of my two children. We have enjoyed each other's bodies on numerous occasions. Well, not *that* many, considering how long we've been married, but that's another story. How did it get to this stage?

'I finally caught up with Belly O'Hea last night.'

'Oh! That's why you're looking so rough this morning.'

'I don't look that bad, do I?'

'Afraid so.'

'Well, I've found out what all the fuss was about.'

'So? What gives?'

'Are you ready for this?'

'What?' She's smiling.

'One of my songs is to be aired live on RTE1. *Kenny Live* to be precise.'

'That's wonderful, Andy!'

'There's a drawback.'

'Oh?'

'It's competing to be the Irish entry for the Eurovision Song Contest.'

She looks confused.

'But you're English.'

Not exactly the response I was expecting.

'I know. You remember that session I did with Bridget and Michael before they formed Mix and Match? The one where I sort of got carried away with all things Irish?'

'Yes, I do remember.'

'Well, it's one of those songs. The worst one, I think. But, lyrically, it's all about building bridges between the two nations and that's what has appealed. On top of which, they like the fact it's written by an Englishman and performed by Irishmen. It sort of fits the present attempts at *détente*.'

'Fantastic! Congratulations.'

I can't believe it. She's giving me a beaming smile.

'Oh, be serious, Gina.'

'I am.'

'Gina, it's the Eurovision Song Contest. You know, that comedy programme hosted by Terry Wogan back in England. A sort of glorified travel-show advertising whatever country it's held in, interrupted by middle-of-the-road artists singing dreadful songs in foreign languages or pidgin English. It's got sod all to do with rock and roll.'

She's shaking her head, firmly.

'No. I'm sorry, but I think it's brilliant. Hundreds of people try to get their work chosen for this and you just have. "When Cultures Clash". That's the song, isn't it?'

'Yes, it is,' I'm replying, somewhat stunned that she remembered.

'Good song. I always liked it. Weird mix. Works, though. It may well win. Let's face it, Andy, Ireland usually does. In fact, they won last year so they're the host nation yet again.'

'You really like the song?'

'I liked it at the time, if you recall.'

Now I think of it, she did.

'Oh, but, Gina, how can I hold my head up high over this? It's hardly bloody Woodstock, is it?'

'Well, then, don't play with the band on it. Do they want you to?'

'It's going to be talked about, apparently. I played bass and sang backing vocals for Bridget on the demo-tape.'

'Michael could do backing vocals, couldn't he?'

'More than likely.'

'Then don't play. Just be the songwriter. That way you can say you couldn't deny the band their chance. If it all falls flat, you can hold up your hands and plead a certain amount of innocence.'

Gina's good at this. Always has been. Seeing logical options. She did this all the time we were married. We're *still* married, though, aren't we?

'It's an idea, I suppose.'

'Think about it. Although, if it were me, you wouldn't stop me singing my own song. I'd be there with bloody bells on, I promise you.'

'I bet you would.'

'Don't look so fed up, Andy. Darling, this is good news. It's the most exciting thing that's happened to your career for a very long time. Don't throw away the chance for a bit of joy, a bit of excitement at last. Please?'

'I've got to decide soon. There's a press launch next week.'

'Good morning, Daddy. Baby's awake.'

Sophie wades through our conversation, as always.

'Oh, Lord, I'll go,' says Gina, before rushing out of the kitchen.

'Morning, Sophie. Sleep well?'

'I never sleep – remember, Dad?'

'Oh, yes, I forgot. Did you have a nice rest?'

'I never rest either. I stay awake all night, don't I, Daddy?'

'Of course. Silly me. What's for breakfast, then? Honey Nut Loops?'

'Toast and a banana.'

'Coming up.'

Gina has just walked in with a grizzling Nicola in her arms. The baby's cheeks are glowing red. They're hot enough to cook a barbecue on. She's teething. Her Babygro is soaked with dribble. Shit! A bad-tempered baby is not what a man with a hangover and an important decision to make needs in his day.

Gina hands her to me.

'So you think I should let all this go ahead?' I'm asking Gina.

'Definitely. Your daddy's going to be a star, Sophie. Tell her, Andy.'

Gina's disappearing out of the room to get dressed.

'What do you want to tell me, Dad?' she says to me, in that way that sometimes makes me think she was born middle-aged.

'Oh, don't worry, Stinks. It's a bit complicated.'

'Daddy! Stop treating me like a little girl.'

'But you are a little girl, Sophie.'

'Dad,' she says, putting her hand on my arm, 'I'm pretty grown-up, you know, for my age.'

'Okay, I'll keep it simple. Should Daddy let one of his songs be entered for the Eurovision Song Contest?'

'Ooh, yes, Dad. I think you should.'

'Really?'

'Yes, Dad. Now, did that help?'

'Yes, it did, Sophie.'

'See,' arms heavenwards, 'I just told yer and I was right.'

Why not take my daughter's advice? I may as well.

Remember what they say about children's instincts.

3.15 p.m.

Pearse Street, Ballinkilty. Just for a change, it's pissing down.

By the time I managed to put Nicola's buggy together, she was soaking wet. Her mother will kill me. Still, at least I don't have to bother trying to attach the small oxygen tent that's supposed to keep her dry. Hate those things. To me it looks as if you have just kidnapped your child from the nearest hospital casualty department.

I've just emerged from the Credit Union where I've been begging for another loan. Nicola behaved, but Sophie kept sitting in the wastepaper bin, for some reason.

Anyway we've just sneaked back out into the deluge, made an ungainly sprint for the car, and bumped straight into Bridget from Mix and Match.

Dear Bridget.

She's a sort of pocket sex-symbol, really. Very short, yet curvaceous with blonde, spiky hair.

'ANDY!' she's screamed, with her usual youthful subtlety.

'Bridget! How the devil are you?' I say through the torrent, as I park myself and my brood in the doorway of the dry cleaner's.

'Oh, now, I'm so excited by the news, Andy, I cannot begin to tell yer. Isn't it just grand? The boys are all thrilled as well. Michael's trying to pretend he's all cool about it, but he's desperate for the big day.'

Michael and Bridget are an item, as they say. At least, as far as I'm aware.

'Good. Excellent.'

'We've been practising your song. It sounds pretty good, but obviously we need some help and direction from the composer. That's always assuming you don't want to play with us yerself, of course.'

'Just a minute, Bridget. What do you mean you've been practising? I got the impression from Belly that he hadn't even told you yet. I mean, he only told me last night. I hadn't even agreed to let the song be used. In fact, as far as Belly is concerned, I still haven't. What is going on?'

She looks suitably embarrassed at this. To be fair, it's not her fault. It's that bugger, O'Hea's.

'I'm sorry, I had no idea, I swear. You know what Belly's like, Andy.'

'I'm beginning to find out.'

She's running her fingers through her tufts of hair nervously.

'Well, I suppose from his point of view, he's our manager. He was probably after okaying it with us first outa habit.'

'I think I'd better give him a ring. Liberties appear to have been taken.'

'Ah, Andy! You're not going to pull the plug on all of this, are yer? Oh, please don't, Andy. It's such an opportunity for us all, and they don't come along too often in this country, so they don't. Please, Andy?'

I seem to have been presented with the final piece in the *fait accompli*.

'No, you're all right. Of course we'll go ahead. But don't tell Belly that just yet. I want to see him sweat a bit for being a naughty boy.'

'You're wicked, so yer are. Listen, we're rehearsing tomorrow night up at Michael's. Can yer come along?'

'What time?'

'Eightish.'

Translated into Irish time, that means closer to nine.

'Yeah, okay. I'll be there.'

'Thanks.'

She's given me a bear-hug that has taken my breath away.

That's some grip for one so small.

'I've got to run, so I have. I'm supposed to be at my mother's an hour ago. See you tomorrow night.'

She's sprinting down the street.

Not a sight you see often around here. Someone running. Life goes at more of a bimbling sort of pace.

Time to go home and feed Nicola. Again. Then I'll give Mr Belly O'Hea a call.

'Who was that lady, Dad?'

'Don't you remember Bridget? She used to sing in the first band Daddy played in here. She's going to sing my song in the competition I told you about.'

'What competition?'

'The one you said I should allow my song to enter. Remember, wooden-head?'

'I forget things, don't I, Dad?'

'Only when you want to, in my experience, Sophie.'

'She's very pretty, isn't she, Daddy?'

'Is she? Sort of, I suppose.'

'I think she's beautiful.'

'I'll tell her. I'm sure she'll be very pleased to hear it.'

'Do you fancy her, Dad?'

'Where did you pick up an expression like that?'

'Do you, Daddy?'

'No.'

'Are you going to leave Mummy and marry that lady, Dad?'

I'm stunned.

'What makes you think that?'

'At playschool, Richard said that's what his daddy is going to do.'

I'm going to fucking strangle Richard . . . Wait a minute, Richard's daddy? *Norman*?

'Are you sure that's what Richard said, Sophie?'

'Yes. He's going to marry someone called Lisa. Richard says she doesn't eat no meat. Wish I didn't have to eat no meat either.'

Lisa . . . Lisa . . . Oh, Christ! Not *Elisa*, surely? Not Mrs Save the Frigging Whale?

Poor Michelle. Beaten at her own game. I'd never have believed old Norman had it in him. I want to ask Sophie more, but I see she needs reassuring.

'No, I'm not going to marry that lady, I promise you, Sophie.'

'Dad?'

'Yes, darling.'

'Nicola's been sick.'

She has as well. A fair chuck down the front of her anorak.

I'm wiping the residue off Nicola with a baby wipe.

'Dad?'

'Yes, Sophie.'

'I've got a tummy-ache too.'

'That's because you've just watched Nicola throw up. I feel a touch queasy myself.'

'No, it really hurts, Dad.'

'That'll teach you not to eat your meals and scoff sweets all day, won't it? Is it really bad?'

She's nodding.

'Shall we pop to see the doctor?'

'No. It's okay. Come on, Dad, let's go home and watch a video.'

She can't be that bad, then.

20

Midnight. First week of February.

I'm in bed. Thinking. Here in my cheery little cell.

Christmas was dreadful. Pretending to be jolly. I know everybody does that to a certain extent, but this was different. Even alcohol didn't help and, believe me, I tried a variety of concoctions. I just concentrated on the kids until they went to bed. Then went back to the bedsit. Gina offered me the spare room, but I couldn't stay. I couldn't pretend with her.

Since then it's been busy.

Tomorrow we're off to Dublin for the first stage of the competition. This is just to let the public hear the song. A sort of preview. All eight songs are aired on *Kenny Live* at the rate of one a week. Then there's a grand final in early March. That's when the winner is chosen.

Rehearsals with Mix and Match have been long and arduous. We had to rehearse in the daytime today, because the band have a gig in the folk club tonight. One might question the wisdom of gigging the night before, but they insisted it would help steady their collective nerves.

I had the children with me. Sophie Riverdanced continually, whilst Nicola shook her rattle in time with the music and nodded a lot. So the song got their vote.

Apparently Mix and Match have decided to give 'When Cultures Clash' a live airing tonight. I have resisted the temptation to go along and listen. Basically I'd watched them rehearse the bloody song all day and I'm sick of it.

To be honest, I'm a bit jealous. You see, after much thought, I had decided I was *definitely* going to play the song with the band. But when we discussed this it was not difficult to gather that they would be happier if I didn't. Ungrateful gits. If it wasn't for my song they wouldn't have got a sniff of national television. They're only a glorified club band. A good one, admittedly. They can play. But they can't write.

I should have insisted I play. I'm nearly thirty-nine. I may never get the chance again. I love writing, but the buzz of performing, the way the energy soars through your body. That feeling is irreplaceable.

I may just have fucked up. Big-time.

Still, I've quite enjoyed the little bit of local fame that has come my way as a result of the press launch in the national newspapers. Everybody keeps smiling at me and wishing me 'all the luck'. On the other hand, I'm still horrified that a piece of my work is deemed fit for the Eurovision Song Contest and I've hated the almost audible sniggers from the snobbish local musicians I've bumped into in the pubs. Basically, because if it were not my song, I would be chief amongst their number.

The Blow-ins are back in Germany. It will be interesting to hear their response upon their return.

I've mixed feelings about tomorrow. I still think the song is rather weak, but I've rejigged it with the band and it's much more palatable now. And, okay, I admit it, buried secretly in the back of my mind is the thought we may just have a chance of winning the bloody thing.

Belly O'Hea has been organising travel arrangements and generally having a good time playing the big shot with RTE.

I won't be travelling to Dublin until much later than the rest of the troops. They don't really need me for rehearsal purposes any more and all I have to do tomorrow, apparently, is sit in the studio audience and listen. Maybe stand up and take a bow, or something.

Tomorrow is important, but not *that* crucial.

So why can't I sleep?

12.30 a.m.

There's a knock on the door of my *pied à terre*.

Who the hell can it be? Who do I know goes visiting at this time of night?

Still the sound of knuckles rapping on wood. They're not going away.

Well, logic says, if it's an axe-murderer, they're unlikely to knock politely and apologise for disturbing me. I'd better pull on a robe to cover my nakedness and answer the door.

*

12.40 a.m.

A bottle of whiskey has been opened.

I'm sat on the floor, cross-legged in towelling robe and nothing else, like a particularly laid-back disciple of meditation. Bridget is sat on the bed. She's come straight from the gig. Tears were flowing from her eyes when she came in. It seems she has stage-fright. Or telly-fright, if there is such a thing.

'I can't go through with it, Andy. I'm telling you, so. I just can't do it.'

This is just what I needed to hear.

'Why?'

More sobs.

'Look, singing in the back of O'Leary's is one thing. A few tourists, a few friends, a few drunks, that's all who's ever going to hear you if you get it wrong. But this is television, Andy. There's millions after watching this thing. I know I'm going to fuck up under the pressure, I just know it.'

'Don't be daft, Bridget. Of course you won't.'

I'm giving her a big hug. Not an entirely unpleasant experience.

'You'll be fine.'

'I won't, I won't.'

'Listen, Bridget. You're very talented. You have a wonderful voice and you're a fine interpreter of songs. On top of which, you're pretty, full of personality and very sexy. This is a great opportunity. You could go far.'

'Oh, Andy! Do yer really think so, now?'

'I do.'

This time she hugs me. I could get used to this.

'Listen, tomorrow isn't too important. The final in March is when the pressure will be on. Treat this as a dress rehearsal. Then when the final comes along you'll have worked on live television once and you won't be half as nervous about it.'

'Yer right. I hadn't thought of it like that. Thanks, Andy,' she says, releasing me from her grip.

'I'll pour you another whiskey. Just try and calm yourself down.'

'I will, now, I promise,' she assures me, as she flops on to my duvet.

What else was I supposed to do? Tell her she was right, that she's a dead loss and that I would put on a dress and sing the fucking thing myself?

I admit, I'm tempted.

So, I've exaggerated a little. She is talented. But not vastly. In fact, she does have a decent singing voice, probably not shown at its best by the range involved in 'When Cultures Clash'.

Is she sexy, though? Well, let me put it this way. She's sat on my bed in the clothes she wears on stage, which don't amount to much. Short, and I mean *short*, black skirt with matching sheer tights. White top, V-necked, with her ample cleavage struggling to stay enclosed. No bra and the top tied underneath her chest, leaving her midriff bare. A small artificial gemstone is lodged in her belly button.

The thing about Bridget is you always see her as terribly young. Partly because of her pixie-like face and partly because she's never been anywhere or done anything, unless you count a season at Butlin's. She's such an innocent and yet she's mid-twenties at least.

Put it like this . . . you wouldn't kick her out of bed on a cold night.

She's a sort of poor man's Gina, really. With bigger breasts and shorter, chunkier legs. If I were not still besotted with Gina, I would have tried to jump Bridget's bones by now.

There's honest for you.

After all, I am technically single . . .

I'm staring at her now. Gina did it. So why not?

Oh, fucking behave yourself, man! You've got enough trouble sorting out your emotions without clouding the issue any further.

1.30 a.m.

We've been psychoanalysing Bridget's fear whilst drinking heavily. This has meant going back to her terrible childhood and her traumatic teenage years, when apparently she was fat with braces on her teeth.

I've decided against seduction. Now, how can I get shot of her, for crying out loud?

There's another knock on my door.

Hells bells! This is turning into a party!

I'd better answer it.

It's Gina. She's standing in the door holding Sophie in her arms.

'Sorry, Andy. I didn't know what else to do.'

'No, it's fine, come in. Hello, Stinks, what are you doing awake at this hour?'

Sophie's not answering me. She's too busy crying.

'Hello, Bridget. Not interrupting anything, am I?' Gina's asking.

'No, of course not,' I interject. 'What's the matter with Sophie?'

'My tummy, Daddy. It really hurts bad.'

Shit! She's sobbing her little heart out.

'How long has this been going on, Gina?'

Gina is sort of rocking her in her arms. This isn't easy considering Sophie's size.

'She said she didn't feel well just before she went to bed. Then she woke up about an hour and a half ago and she's got steadily worse.'

'Have you been sick, poppet?'

'Yes,' she's replying, between tear-induced gasps.

'She's got a temperature. I've given her Calpol but it's not coming down.'

'Better get her to the doctor.'

'NO, DADDY! I don't want to see the doctor. Please don't make me see the doctor.'

'Ssh, Sophie, it's all right. We've got to get you better. Mummy and I can't magic this one away.'

'NO, DADDY!'

'Come on, Sophie darling. That's what doctors do. They make people better. It's their job. If the car was broken you'd make me take it to the garage, wouldn't you?'

'Yes,' she snivels, before wincing with pain.

'Well, I've got to take you to the *doctor's* to get *you* fixed. Speaking of cars, Gina, how did you get down here?'

'I rang Deirdre from the farm. She gave me a lift. Listen, Andy, will you come to the doctor with us? Sophie wants you.'

'Of course. You try and keep me away.'

I'm picking the car keys off the bedside cabinet and handing them to Gina.

'Car's parked right in front. Get in. I'll be right down.'

'DADDY!'

'Daddy's coming, Sophie. I'll be two minutes.'

Gina's taken her downstairs.

'Sorry, Bridget.'

'Not at all. Is there anything I can do?'

'No . . . Yes. You can warn everybody I might not make it to Dublin tomorrow.'

'Do you think Sophie's that bad?'

'I'm not sure. I'll try ringing Belly's mobile phone and let everyone know what's happening. Make sure he has the bugger switched on, will you?'

'I will, I promise,' she's telling me as she leaves, pausing to give me a supportive hug.

Right.

Clothes and wallet.

I've climbed in the driver's seat. Gina is in the back cuddling Sophie, who appears to have calmed down a little.

'Have you rung the doctor?'

'Yes, she's expecting us.'

A sob of fear mixed with pain from Sophie.

I'm starting the engine and heading off to Rosscarbery, to the surgery.

'Should we stop off for Nicola?' I'm asking Gina.

'No. She's fine with Deirdre.'

'Right, then. We'll just concentrate on our big baby. Okay, Stinks?'

I think she nodded.

'Bridget's a pretty girl, don't you think?' Gina's asking, out of the blue.

'Pardon? I don't know. Sophie said that the other day.'

Now I realise how it must have looked. Past one in the morning and I'm wearing nothing but a robe and a glazed expression and Bridget is on my bed wearing not much more than me. Shit!

'She's petrified.'

'Sorry?' says Gina.

'Bridget. She's got stage-fright about the show tomorrow. She got me out of bed after the band's gig tonight and told me she wasn't going to sing.'

'You're kidding!'

'I wish I was.'

'And you were . . . comforting her, I suppose?'

'Verbally, yes.'

'Not orally.'

'No.'

'Oh, Daddy, my tummy!'

'Nearly there now, sweetheart. We'll soon have you put right. Can we clear up that other matter a little later, please, Gina?'

'Nothing to clear up. I can hardly complain, can I? What's good for the gander and all that,' Gina's replying on a monotone.

'It wasn't – oh, never mind, we'll talk later.'

I wish Sophie would stop crying. I can't stand to see her in pain.

1.45 a.m.

Doctor's surgery in Rosscarbery.

Sophie's screaming in agony.

Gina's in floods of tears.

Why do doctors insist on poking and prodding the area that causes you pain until you feel ten times fucking worse? For people who are supposed to be dedicated to making you well, they seem such a sadistic bunch of bastards.

I must calm down and stop being stupid. It's not the doctor's fault. She's quite a young girl, this one. Not one of the regulars, a locum or something. She's done all the necessary tests, including a finger up poor Sophie's bottom.

'I can't be certain. It could be appendicitis, but on the other hand she could have a virus which is causing the lymph glands in that area to become inflamed. She does have a very high temperature and I think, all things considered, it's best to have her admitted to hospital.'

'NO, DADDY! NO, DADDY! NOT TO HOSPITAL, NOT TO HOSPITAL!'

'Sophie darling, calm down, sweetheart. We've got to get you better. Mummy and I will be with you. You'll be all right, I promise.'

Of course she will. I know she will. I know it. I just know it.

'Do you have VHI?' the doctor's asking.

'Yes.' (It's medical insurance. No National Health Service here, as such.)

'Do you have a preference for any hospital?'

'The Bons Secour,' Gina has replied.

It's where Nicola was born.

'I'll see if they've got a bed.'

It's in Cork City. All the fucking hospitals are in the city. There are none closer. It's at least an hour's drive.

Shit, shit, shit.

'OOH, MY TUMMY! I DON'T WANT TO GO TO HOS-PITAL. MUMMY!'

'It's going to be fine, Sophie. Honest. Mummy wouldn't lie to you.'

Neither of us would.
Intentionally.

We're back in the car and I'm starting the engine.

I've stuffed the letter for the hospital in the glove compartment.

'Damn! Gina, we've got nothing for her. We're going to have to go home first and get some things together.'

'It's all right. I've a bag packed. It's in the boot. My instincts told me we might need it.'

'Oh, Daddy!'

I hope there's not much traffic on the roads. Cork is miles away and the appendix can perforate, can't it? That's dangerous, isn't it? Life-threatening.

I hope it's a clear road.

The way I'll be driving, I won't be taking any prisoners.

It must be about 3.30 a.m. at least, but I'm not sure. I've lost all track of time.

We're at the hospital. Sophie is screaming and crying again.

She's frightened.

I'm fucking terrified.

But I can't let my Sophie see that. Or Gina, who is not handling this well.

Trouble with Sophie is she panics when she's unwell. Fear overwhelms her and she starts to hyperventilate. She also has a low pain threshold, so you're never quite sure whether she's suffering as much as she appears to be or whether her nerves have taken over completely.

They're taking blood. Sophie's on a trolley bed and Gina and I are on either side of her.

'NO! NO! NO! Help, Daddy, HELP! NO!'

I can't calm her down. Neither can Gina. She can't hear us above her own screams.

'OUCH! DADDY, OUCH!'

It's over, thank goodness.

I'm cuddling her.

'Who's Daddy's big brave girl? It's not fair, poppet. Fancy having to go through all this. Poor Sophie.'

'Oh, Daddy, it's terrible.'

'Never mind. Soon be over.'

'We're going to send her for an X-ray, now.'

'NO, DADDY, NO, MUMMY!'

'It's all right, Sophie. It won't hurt, Mummy promises. It's just like having your picture taken, that's all.'

'Yes,' I'm adding, 'except they photograph what's inside you. Yuck, can you imagine what's floating around in your stomach?'

She's giggling. Half-heartedly. Still, that's a relief.

'The Thompsons have a X-ray in the Tintin book, don't they, Daddy?'

'That's right. And they keep looking for the skeleton, don't they? They're too stupid to realise it's their own skeletons. That's right, isn't it?'

'Yes, Daddy, it is. Ouch! My tummy.'

'I know, tuppence.' Keep her talking. Keep her focusing on something else. 'Which book is that in, Sophie? Is it one of the moon books?'

'I think you're right, you know, Dad.'

'We'll wheel her down now, Mr Lawrence.'

'NO, DADDY. I don't want to go on the trolley. *I don't want to go on the trolley!*'

'It's all right, Sophie,' Gina's reassuring her. 'Daddy will carry you. Won't you, Daddy?'

'Oh, if I must. Come on, you great oaf!'

She's in my arms.

'Blimey. I thought you hadn't been eating much lately. You are *such* a lump. You weigh a ton. I hope it's not far. Poor Daddy.'

She's giggling. 'Poor Daddy. Poor Daddy, Mummy.'

'Yes, darling. Poor old Daddy.'

One of the advantages of going to a private hospital in the middle of the night is that there is not the customary four-mile queue to have your insides photographed.

A radiologist, do they call them? A woman in a white coat, anyway. She's appeared as if from nowhere.

'Right, which one of you would like to come in with Sophie?'

We're looking at each other. Gina and I.

'I should mention, Mrs . . .'

She's looking at Sophie's file.

'. . . Lawrence. If there's any chance you may be pregnant, you'd be advised to let Mr Lawrence take Sophie in.'

We're looking at each other again. I realise that for the first time in our relationship I cannot answer that question.

'No. There's absolutely no chance,' she's saying to me, and not the radiologist.

'In which case . . .?'

'Sophie? Shall Mummy or Daddy come in with you?' Gina's asking.

'Daddy.'

Solved.

Gina's not offended. She'd be the first to admit hospitals make her uneasy.

I'm probably the right choice.

Back in the cubicle. X-rays all finished with.

Sophie panicked, yet again. It was only by complaining about how ridiculous I looked in the solid apron I had to wear for protection that I was able to rescue the situation.

My poor Sophie. Daddy's girl, what are they putting you through?

First the doctor in Rosscarbery, then the nurse, and two doctors, including the surgeon, poking and prodding her. Blood tests, X-rays.

She looks exhausted. Drained.

Gina doesn't look much better. This is killing her.

The surgeon has signalled he wants a word with me.

I'm following him out of the cubicle.

'Yes, Doctor?'

'I think we'd like to keep her in over what remains of the night, Mr Lawrence. We'll see how she is and take a decision in the morning about operating, as long as she doesn't take a turn for the worse.'

'Is that likely to happen?'

'Difficult to say. Had she been a bit older I'd have opened her up to take a look tonight, just to be on the safe side. But she's very young and she does appear to have a clogged nose and one or two other signs that could suggest it's a virus, possibly affecting her glands in the pelvic region. However, should anything develop we'll have to move fast. We'll keep a close eye on her, Mr Lawrence. Try not to worry.'

'Can we stay with her?'

'One of you, certainly. Though I'm afraid it won't be very comfortable.'

'That doesn't matter. Thanks for your help, Doctor.'

'Not at all.'

Better go back and break the news.

Shit, Sophie's crying again, I can hear her.

We're in a ward with four beds. No private rooms available. One other occupant. A small boy. His father tells me he should be going home tomorrow. There's a chair next to Sophie's bed for one of us to sleep in.

Sophie's much calmer.

The screaming was due to them attaching connections for a drip into her arm. It looks hideous. Splints covered in bandages with a connecting tube dangling loose. The needle in her vein.

She looks so tiny in that big bed.

So bloody vulnerable.

I've explained we have to be quiet because the other little boy is sleeping.

I'm ferreting through the bag Gina packed.

'Oh, look, Sophie. Mummy's brought the Tintin book we were reading.'

She's taken it from me.

'You try and find the page we were on. I just need to have a quick chat with Mummy.'

I'm leading Gina out into the corridor.

'Listen, Gina, why don't you go home?'

'I can't leave her.'

'I know, but think of Nicola. She needs her mummy too. If she wakes up in the morning and you're not there it might really unsettle her.'

'It's not fair to leave you here alone.'

'Gina, we've two kids and we have to take care of both of them.'

'Oh, Andy. Supposing something goes wrong?'

'I'm sure it won't . . .'

Am I? Am I really?

'. . . It's probably just a virus. She looks better now. She just needs some sleep. So do you. Go home and snatch what you can before Nicola decides it's time to play.'

'You will ring me if . . .'

'As soon as there's any news, I promise.'

'Okay. If you're sure. I suppose it's only fair to Nicola. Andy?'

'Yes?'

'I'm sorry about earlier. About you and Bridget. I didn't mean to imply . . . I mean, I suppose it's none of my business anyway. I couldn't blame you if you did . . . I certainly wouldn't blame her for being attracted . . .'

I'm holding up my hand to stop her.

'Don't worry about it. Quite funny, really. It must have looked dreadful. I just hope she holds her nerve and sings well tomorrow. What am I saying? *Today*. Look, could you phone Belly for me on his mobile? The number's in our address book at home. Tell him I can't make it to Dublin.'

'Oh, Andy, you must!'

'Ssh. My place is with Sophie. Anything else can wait.'

'Andy.'

'Yes?'

'Thanks for being here tonight.'

'You don't have to thank me, Gina. I wanted to be here. Besides, Sophie needed me.'

'*I* needed you. I can't tell you how badly. Goodnight, then. You promise you'll ring?'

'I promise, Gina. Drive carefully. I don't want *you* ending up in Casualty.'

She gives a half-smile. 'I will.'

She's just kissed me lightly on the lips, before departing.

I stand watching her walk down the corridor.

She needed me. Was that what she said?

Was she jealous of Bridget and, if so, what does that mean?

I'd better get back to Sophie.

Being brave for Gina's sake is all very well. Truth is, I'm shit scared.

When I used to tuck Sophie in bed at night, I always promised I'd come running if she had a problem and tonight I wasn't there.

Is it my fault? I'm supposed to be looking after her. She's been complaining of tummy pains for ages and I've half dismissed them as an excuse for wanting chocolate instead of proper meals.

She's going to be fine. Of course she is.

I'm walking into the ward.

Sophie has fallen asleep, thank heavens. She needs some rest.

The Tintin book is over her face. I'd better take it off.

She's half opened her eyes at me.
'Blistering barnacles, Daddy.'
I've smiled at her and she's gone back off.
Time to sort out my sleeping arrangements.

21

It's 9.30 a.m. the following morning.

I've just phoned Gina and I'm walking back to the ward.

Shit. I feel lousy.

No sleep in that bloody chair, which I'm sure had been designed to keep the hospital osteopaths in employment. I ache all over. From top to toe.

After some consultation, Sophie was allowed breakfast, which meant an operation was clearly off the agenda. More consultation from yet another doctor and a virus was pronounced as the most probable reason for her illness.

Something else was also suggested. Something more disturbing. The doctor asked me, rather pointedly, if there had been any trauma in Sophie's life of late. If anything could have upset her emotionally. I was honest with him. After shaking his head he hinted there was a chance Sophie's problem may have been psychosomatic or that the pain had been brought on by stress.

Could Gina and I be responsible for this?

It probably was a virus, but on the other hand the doctor has made me wonder. I must talk to Gina about it.

Anyway, the good news is she can come home after lunch as long as there's no change.

Yippee!

Children really are extraordinary creatures. Their powers of recovery are remarkable. Sophie is a completely different child this morning. What a comeback!

We have to try to keep her quiet as the virus could stay in her system for up to a fortnight or more, apparently.

Gina's on her way up here and Deirdre is looking after Nicola until we get back.

I've just turned into the ward and you won't believe what I'm witnessing.

'Sophie! What are you doing?'

'I'm having a bounce, Daddy.'

'I can see that. Will you stop it? You're not at home now. This is a hospital. I thought you were supposed to be sick.'

'I'm better now, Daddy!'

'Come on. Sit down and finish off that toast.'

'Oh, *Dad*!'

'Come on, monster. We're not out yet. They want to see you eating first. I want to get you home today. So come on, munch.'

I've just jammed the toast between her teeth to the sound of muffled laughter.

2.30 p.m.

We've just got home, just walked through the door.

Correction. Gina and I walked through, Sophie bounded in, happy to be back on her patch.

Deirdre's in the kitchen. Nicola is in her arms.

'My, my, aren't you looking better than the last time I saw you?' Deirdre's smiling at Sophie. 'How are you?'

'Fine, Fine. Dad? Can I watch a cartoon?'

'Yes, and sit on the sofa quietly. No more charging about. You're not as strong as you think you are.'

She's off.

'Seriously, how is she, now?' Deirdre is asking Gina.

'Okay. The doctors think it's a virus. We've got to watch her for a week or two, though.'

'Could have been worse, then.'

'Much.'

'How are you, Andy?' Deirdre gives me a smile as she places Baby in her high chair.

'I'm well. Thanks for asking.'

'Well, I must be off,' Deirdre's saying, perhaps sensing our need to be alone. She's handing Nicola's milk to Gina.

'See you both around.'

''Bye, Deirdre. Thanks ever so much.'

'No problem. 'Bye!'

She closes the door behind her. There's an awkward silence between us. Automatically I go to the kettle and switch it on.

'Something I ought to mention, Gina. The doctor hinted that

244

Sophie's tummy problem may have something to do with the effect you and I breaking up has had on her.'

'Oh, really?' she replies, and looks at the floor. I don't blame her. I know what she's feeling. We don't need to discuss it any further. Just be aware.

'Pop in and see her, Andy. Nicola and I will bring you a cup of tea.'

'Okay.'

I've walked into the lounge and Sophie is sprawled on the sofa watching *The Flintstones*.

'Oh, yes! Good old Barney Rubble. Make room for a small one, Stinks.'

I'm sat on the sofa, giving my daughter a cuddle.

I ache from top to toe.

I'm exhausted from lack of sleep.

My head's a mess because of the state of my marriage.

My career, such as it is, is happening elsewhere in the hands of people I don't altogether trust.

I don't give a flying fuck.

My little girl is all right.

That's all that matters.

It's latish.

I'm too knackered to be precise. We've just watched my song on *Kenny Live*. Mix and Match played very well, a lively performance, and Bridget was fine.

Sophie was allowed to stay up and watch it with us because she was such a brave girl. She wasn't, actually, she was a complete coward. But who can blame her? She's only young and she was in pain.

I'm proud of her.

I like her even more because she said my song was 'Terrific, Daddy.'

Gina squeezed my hand.

'Right, little girl,' I'm saying, as I ruffle Sophie's hair, 'you've had an exhausting twenty-four hours and you need your sleep.'

'I don't sleep, remember, Dad?'

'Whatever, it's time to go to bed. I'll read you a story and then Daddy must be off.'

'NO, DADDY!' She's howling. 'I don't want you to go.'

'Daddy's not going anywhere, are you, Daddy? He's going to stay here and look after his girl.'

Gina.

I'm looking at her.

She's smiling.

'Of course I am. Come on. Kiss your mother goodnight and let's go and read some Tintin.'

It's past midnight.

I'm in the spare room. Gina said she was proud of me, whether or not my song goes on to win in March. Which was nice of her.

Anyway, Sophie will be fine in a few days' and then it's back to my bunker.

Though now I'm back here it has crossed my mind . . .

I don't think so . . . somehow.

9.30 p.m.

Location?

O'Leary's.

Date?

February the sixteenth.

The occasion?

My thirty-ninth birthday.

It's been a funny day. I was really depressed when I woke up. You know, the big Four-O just around the corner and no further on et cetera, until Sophie came storming into the spare room carrying a little fistful of presents. Gina and Nicola followed her in.

I'm still there, in the spare room. It's been over a week now. Sophie's just fine! Thank God.

So we had a little present-opening. Sophie opened them for me, actually. A compact disc from Nicola, a jumper from Sophie and a watch from Gina. Well, they're all from Gina, really.

I admit to being touched by the gesture.

I did kiss her. Chastely, but I did kiss her.

So I decided to banish my usual oh-my-God-I'm-so-old-and-still-a-failure birthday blues and I have had a lovely day. I took the kids out for a drink at lunch-time, then played silly games with them all afternoon. And tonight Gina gave me a spin into town and I'm having a bit of a session in the bar. In fact, it's only, what, a quarter to ten and I'm a bit sloshed. In fact, I can't remember being this sloshed in ages.

I may not be coherent for much longer.

Belly's here, plus Mix and Match in their entirety, including the voluptuous Bridget, who has annoyed me by sticking her tongue down Michael's throat all night. Plus one or two sundry bodies we seem to have picked up along the way.

Belly's going to give me a lift home, which if I was sober would frighten me witless because he's drunk twice as much as I have.

'Hello, Andy. Happy birthday to you.'

I'm trying to focus. Honestly I am.

It's Matt.

Matt from the Blow-ins.

'Matt! Long time no see. Back from conquering Bavaria, then?'

'That's right, boy. And have *you* been busy while we've been away. Eurovision, Andy? I mean, come on, sell-out or what?'

'Oh, I don't know. Might lead to something, if it comes off.'

'Aw! Come on. You'll be offering to write for Julio Iglesias next.'

'I don't know why you're being such a snob, Matt. A little bird told me you've submitted at least two songs for Eurovision and got fuck nowhere.'

I wish someone would photograph Matt's face right now, and frame the picture for me.

'Who told you?'

Bingo!

'Nobody, Matt. I just took a lucky guess. Aren't you going to buy your old mate a drink for his birthday?'

'Sure,' he's muttered at me, before heading for the bar.

Hoots of laughter all around.

'Well done, Andy, yer bastard. Spot on, so you are.' Belly's cackling till he coughs.

Little victories, man. Little victories.

Ssh!

It's late and I'm struggling to get in the house without waking everybody up. I'm trying to go in the back door, the one that leads straight into the kitchen. It's dark out here and I'm so pissed I can't find the ruddy keyhole. If I stopped giggling it might help keep my hand steady.

There we go. Gotcha!

Oh, shit! What was that crash?

Hang on. Where's the light switch?

There.

Damn!

It's one of Gina's best glasses. Crystal.

Nice girl, shame she goes to pieces when you touch her.

Ssh! Stop laughing at your own jokes, Andy.

Right. Where's the door out of here?

Ouch! Ooh, bugger, I've fallen over now.

It didn't hurt, but I bet I don't find it this funny in the morning.

Hello?

That's a pair of feet, isn't it?

Someone's helping me up.

It's Gina.

'HELLO, GINA!'

'*Sssh*! You'll wake the babies.'

She's steering me through the lounge and towards the spare room that lies off it. Thankfully, for both our sakes, we don't have to negotiate the stairs.

She's thrown me on the bed for the first time in all our years of marriage.

'Stop giggling, Andy.'

Hello! She's undressing me.

Off comes the shirt, now the shoes and socks, jeans.

'I don't usually do this on the first date, you know.'

'Be quiet!' But she's laughing.

Boxer-shorts as well, ooh-er, Mrs Lawrence.

Something's just landed on my face.

No need to panic, it's the duvet.

'Go to sleep, you drunken sod.'

Good idea.

Lights out.

Now, focus: the room is not moving . . . it is not moving . . .

Something's happening. I can feel it.

It's not unpleasant.

Familiar.

A sensation.

A nice sensation.

A *lurvely* sensation.

Where am I?

Someone has got my cock in their mouth.

Shit, Michelle!

I've half opened one eye. *No.*

It's Gina.

I don't know what to do.

I'm not talking sexual ignorance here, it's just . . . I'm so confused.

I can't deny it feels . . . seductive.

She's mounting me now . . . moaning . . . whimpering.

Oh, fuck! She's riding me hard.

She's taken my hands and placed them on her breasts.

I'm caressing them instinctively.

Part of me wants to throw her off. This is not mine any more, it's Connor's. Yet I can't help feeling . . . it's home. Can't help feeling desire . . . lust . . . warmth . . .

Love.

This will . . . just . . . confuse things more . . .

What . . . do I . . . do? . . .

I'm alone again.

After we climaxed – and I'm fairly sure we both climaxed – Gina collapsed on top of me. She was breathing hard. Harder than ever before. She slid off me and gave me a long, deep kiss.

Then she left the bedroom.

She never spoke, not a word.

I'm shaking with the shock of it all. Should I go to her? To our bedroom, as was?

I'm replaying it all in my mind. My most lasting impression was the noise of it all. Birdsong, do they call it? In all the years that Gina and I have been making love, I have never heard her cry out like that. Never heard her vocalise pleasure. I've never felt Gina has let go the way she did just now.

And I loved it.

It somehow made it more . . . special, the way she was really giving herself to me.

The trouble is, she gave herself to Connor as well.

I'm just not sure I'm a big enough man to deal with that.

To forgive.

*

UGH!

What time is it? What day is it?

And why does my brain feel as if it has recently haemorrhaged?

I'm giggling now, internally, because speaking of recent strokes, Gina has just entered the spare room.

Oh, God! The morning after the night before.

And what a night!

Gina is wearing her towelling robe, but nothing else. No makeup, no underwear or tights underneath. She has Nicola toddling behind her. Gina sits her on the floor with a few toys. She's eating a biscuit.

'Morning,' I've managed to mutter.

'Just about, sleepy-head.'

'What time is it?'

'About a quarter to twelve.'

'Shit! Sorry.'

She's laughing at me.

'That's all right. I figured you could probably use a lie-in. Have someone else look after the kids for a change.'

'Aren't you going to work?'

'No, not today. I've phoned in and told them I still can't leave Sophie. They can struggle on without me for a day longer. Bugger them. Coffee?'

'Please.'

'I've some filter already made. Back in a sec.'

Nicola's gurgling with pleasure as she eats. I can't see her because I can't actually lift my head off the pillow, yet.

Gina's back.

She's sat on the edge of the bed and handed me my coffee.

I've sat up, gingerly.

'Listen, Andy. About last night.'

'You took advantage of me, Gina.'

'Yes. I know I did. That's what I want to say.'

She's running her hand nervously through her hair. 'Look,' she continues, 'don't worry about it. It was my choice. It was what I wanted. You don't have to respond in any particular way. I know it may never happen again. Probably won't, actually. I don't want you to feel pressurised. I mean ... what I'm trying to say is ... it doesn't matter.'

'Doesn't it?'

250

'YES! Oh, shit, Andy, I'm sorry. I didn't mean it to happen, I just couldn't control myself.' She stands. 'I made a mistake and I know I have to pay for it. But I can't bear being apart from you. I hate it. I love you, Andy, and it was ... other things getting in the way. Not how I felt for you, not really.'

She's pacing backwards and forwards as she speaks, like a fairground duck.

'When we ... look ... What I mean is ... this isn't easy to say ... When we were together at the hospital I realised just how much I needed you. How much I loved you. I knew I wanted you back that night.'

She's stopped pacing and she's staring at me.

'Oh, come on, Andy, help me here. You must have noticed. Sophie's been fine since she first got home, really. I haven't exactly been rushing you out the door, have I? Didn't you guess?'

'Not really, no.'

'Sophie needs you too. She's been so much happier since Daddy came back. Nicola as well, we all have. You're such a kind man, Andy. A good man. I was a bloody fool.'

'Gina, have you thought this –'

'And when I saw you with that bitch, Bridget –'

'Hang on! She's a nice enough girl.'

'She fancies you.'

'Gina, behave!'

'I'm sorry, but she bloody does. I was so jealous. I don't want anyone else to have you. You're mine. The children want you back. I want you back, Andy. I need you. I love you. For all our sakes, please come home.'

She's crying.

I've always hated it when she cries.

'Gina. I'm not sure ...'

'I'll do anything you want. I'll never deny you sex again –'

'Yes, you will!'

'Well, maybe only at the wrong time of the month or something. Oh, Andy, do you still love me?'

'Yes, Gina.'

'Can you forgive me?'

'No.'

'Then you won't come home?'

Decision-time. Now it's my turn to search for the right phrases to explain how I feel.

'I'm not sure how strong I am. I can't promise Connor's face won't leap into my mind and twist it. I can try, Gina. I can't promise any more than that. But I do love you and I do want to see if we can . . . get it back together.'

She's put her arms around me. 'Thank God, thank God,' she's whispering.

We're holding very tight.

Fear? Love? Both?

There's a third pair of arms.

It's Sophie.

'Hi, Daddy. Hi, Mummy.'

'Hi,' we say in unison.

'Why are you being soppy?'

Gina's smiling at me. 'Because Daddy's coming home, Sophie. He's finished his work.'

'Oh, goody!'

Nicola has climbed up from the floor and is joining in the hug. She's giggling at us, as if she was watching a comic turn.

Which she probably is.

22

March 3.

It's the final of the Song for Europe. Tonight is make-your-mind-up-time, folks. In an hour or two we'll know if 'When Cultures Clash' will be representing my adopted homeland in the Eurovision Song Contest.

We're at the RTE studios in Dublin. Gina's with me. We have seats at the front of the audience, along with the other prospective winning composers.

Deirdre and her family have the children up at the farm behind our house.

Right, this is the form then: songs played; break; phone vote.

Ten juries, comprising sixteen people of mixed ages, spread across the country. They've listened to the songs during the day, tonight they watch the show, then phone in their points, live on air. Twelve for the best, down to three points for the song they like least.

I was present at rehearsals this afternoon and they went well.

Bridget has changed out of all recognition. The shy, I-just-can't-do-this girl who sat on my bed has been replaced by an flirtatious *femme fatale*. She's spent the day tarting her way around the studio, making Michael seethe with jealousy at the attention she was giving the producers and the crew. I had to have a word with her. Tell her to calm it down. It was causing friction.

This has, of course, raised doubts about the story I told Gina about my late-night visitation from Bridget. But it doesn't seem to matter. It's added to the myth. Apparently, Gina hadn't realised she was married to such a sex-symbol.

I wish.

Anyway, now I'm here I want to win.

Entering Eurovision may have caused me some internal artistic debate, I confess. However, losing at this stage would want to make me keep a very low profile indeed.

I had a listen to the competition this afternoon – all seven, four of which are a pile of shite, in my humble opinion. The other three are serious threats.

The bad ones? Well, first there's a jinky-jinky, guitar-backed pub song, really. Classic Daniel O'Donnell territory, whatever-happened-to-the-good-old-tunes-they-don't-write-'em-like-that-any-more type of drivel. The sort of song that only sounds good if you're blind drunk and that's because it's easy to remember. It won't win, unless the country's geriatrics leap from behind their Zimmer frames and ring in *en masse*.

Second song: a sort of poor man's Blur. Quite a good song, to be fair, but not a Eurovision winner. The band are trying to retain their street cred by looking and performing like the Sex Pistols.

Third: an out-and-out modern re-creation of a typical Irish folk song. Pushing it a bit far. Lots of talk of bad weather and fair girls and greenery. It rings a bit false. Not a hope, unless the juries have been on the Guinness all day and are feeling sentimental or excessively patriotic.

Fourth: a torch song, in the style of Edith Piaf, sung by a man who looks uncommonly like her.

And the threats?

One rip-roaring ballad, *à la* Johnny Logan. Good, if you like that sort of thing. Sung by the composer. Female, very sophisticated. Evening-gown with plunging neckline. Thinking-man's crumpet territory. More the sort of thing the Italians would usually win with.

Then there's a typical all-girl sexy group. They look good. Very 'pop', very catchy chorus, well-choreographed dance routine showing off their bits and pieces, and very nice bits and pieces they are too. The sort of thing the British usually toss into the Eurovision arena.

Last, but not least, the Irish-language entry. Very simple, very well written, very haunting. If I could understand the lyrics, I'd probably love it.

We've had the warm-up man. The lights are dimming. We're live on air in ten seconds. Gina's squeezing my hand and kisses my left ear, before whispering, 'Good luck.'

Yer man Kenny's come on, and his mere presence has heightened the atmosphere. We have rapturous applause and we're under starter's orders.

Mix and Match are fourth in line to play.

The bottom has fallen out of my stomach.

I just hope the stomach doesn't fall out of my bottom before this evening is out.

All done bar the shouting.

Mix and Match were excellent. First class. Bridget sang infinitely better than I believed her capable of doing.

All the songs have been heard. All the composers have been ushered backstage to see their performers and indulge in a little liquid hospitality. Steady the nerves before the voting.

Someone's tabulating the votes in the interval, whatever that means.

This is nerve-racking.

Why? How can anyone take this seriously?

But you sort of get sucked into the whirlpool of it all.

Imagine what it must be like when it's 'Ireland, *deux points*' territory.

I've hugged them all. Mix and Match, I mean. Even Michael, who's being sullen and moody as usual. Bridget has just leapt at me and wrapped her legs around my waist, squealing. This has got Michael scowling and Gina smiling and shaking her head at me.

'Ah, Andy, didn't it go well? Didn't it?'

'It did, Bridget. Whatever the result, I thought you were all excellent. I couldn't have asked for any more from you.'

'We won't win,' says Michael. 'The girl'll win. They loved her, they did.'

'Keep taking the happy pills, Michael. They're doing a fabulous job,' I mutter.

But I fear he's right.

Except, having listened to them, I have a sneaking suspicion for the jinky-jinky-old-age-pensioners' lament.

Wonder if it's too late to get a bet on?

'Mr Lawrence?' The floor manager's appeared beside me. 'Can you take your seat? They're after collecting the results from the juries.'

A scream from Bridget.

'Okay gang, best of luck.'

Cries of 'You, too,' et cetera, and I'm walking back out into the studio with Gina.

'Do you want to win?' she's asking.

'Of course.'

'You've changed your tune. What happened to rock and roll?'

'I've let it come this far, so now I'm here, why not?'

'I'll still be proud of you, win or lose.'

'Thanks, Gina.'

She doesn't think we're going to win, either.

My face.

Everywhere.

It's all I can see.

On all the monitors around the studio.

Why?

'Stand up! You've won, you daft git.'

Gina's pushing me up out of my seat.

I've suddenly noticed Bridget going absolutely wild on the studio floor.

Well, fuck me sideways!

Who'd have thought?

I was convinced we'd lose.

I can see the scoreboard as I walk on to the studio floor and I wasn't far wrong with my guesswork.

We just pipped jinkity-jinkity-guitar by a whisker.

Not exactly a landslide, but a victory.

Bridget's hugging me.

Yer man Kenny himself is shaking my hand. He's pointing the microphone at me. He's going to want me to speak.

I don't know what I'm going to say.

You see . . .

I'm not used to being a winner.

23

Saturday. April.

Down the pub. About a month or so after the Song for Europe final. I'm a star!

Well, in Ballinkilty, at least. No, cancel that. In Ireland.

Is this, as Mr Warhol once suggested, my fifteen minutes of fame? Possibly. Though if I could stretch it to an hour or two it would be nice.

Am I enjoying it? You bet your fucking life I am!

Who doesn't enjoy a bit of success? I've never understood these dozy twerps who commit suicide because they can't handle being famous. They want their heads testing – well, what's left of their heads after they've fired a bullet through their mouths.

People in this town have been fantastic. An impromptu welcome-home party at the GAA hall. Official dinners, banners in the street, hugs, pats on the back, free drinks, free meals and lots of well-wishing for the grand final.

I've been interviewed by the local and national press, where I've let it be known there's plenty more songs where 'When Cultures Clash' came from. Also that I sing, and play acoustic, electric and bass guitar.

I can drink a pint of beer upside down and wiggle my ears as well, but I've kept those details to myself.

We've recorded the song and it's storming up the Irish charts, with the Song for Europe final performance being used as the promotional video.

I have a replica of the Tom McGrath Perpetual Trophy, sitting on my mantelpiece. It's a nice trophy. A sculpted sheet of music with a solid silver microphone angled across the page.

Plus I'm a thousand pounds richer.

Sophie has been incredibly overexcited. She is acting like my agent. She walks up to complete strangers and tells them, 'My daddy won the Eurovision Song Contest. He's ever so clever.'

I've tried to tell her I haven't yet, but she just says, 'You will, Daddy. Stop going on.'

Nicola is blissfully ignorant. A quick puke down my best shirt and my feet soon touch the ground.

Gina has thoroughly enjoyed it.

Boy, has she enjoyed it!

In the kitchen, in the lounge, in the bed, indoors, outdoors, half dressed, naked, in stockings, in ankle socks . . . (So? I'm kinky) in the morning, in the afternoon, you name it. My success has turned her into a nymphomaniac. She told me many years ago that this would happen if I made it. I didn't believe her. Just goes to show.

I've even had a card from Matt – unbelievable – congratulating me on my success and saying we must meet up for a drink soon, 'old pal'.

Huh!

Still, the world's a wonderful place. My wife's beautiful, my children, whom I'm still looking after, are wonderful and everyone's happy.

I'm on a roll. It seems things are looking up.

No more misery.

Me and my big fucking mouth.

We're back home from the pub. Everyone else is in the lounge. I've just taken a call in the kitchen. I was passing the phone when it rang.

It was Connor. He wants to see me. To explain.

So, I'm off to his house.

It probably isn't a good idea, just when things are going so well.

But I'm going. I have to.

Time to make my excuses.

I pop my head around the lounge door. 'Listen, gang, I'm just going out for a minute. Shan't be long.'

'Where are you off to?' Gina's asking.

'Bit of shopping I want to do.'

'We've just been shopping, Andy.'

'Not *that* kind of shopping.'

'Can I come, Dad?'

'No, Sophie.'

'ᴀʜʜ! Why?'

'It's a secret. Back in a jiff.'

I'm making a hasty exit before more questions are asked.

I'm nearly there.

As I drive all the feelings of hate and anger and betrayal are welling up inside me again. Filling my head, sickening my stomach.

I should turn back, but I can't.

I understand I'm putting it all at risk.

Things are fine now. I've almost exorcised the ghost of Gina's affair. But in a month, a year, five years, it might start to haunt me again. I know myself that well at least. I'll see Connor's face as I undress Gina, just one time, and that will be all it takes for the rage and jealousy to begin again.

So I have to face him.

I've rung the doorbell. I'm shaking with nerves, or anger.

Connor's answered it. He has a half-smile on his face. Parting the lips that parted my wife's, he says, 'Hello, Andy. You'd best be after coming inside.'

I'm following him, I'm right behind him.

We're moving through the hall into the sitting room and he's turned to face me. 'Can I get you a drink at all?'

I've hit him.

Forcefully.

I almost felt my fist passing through his head.

He's fallen back, knocking over the coffee table before landing in a heap on the floor.

He's groaning. The front of his sweater is covered in blood from his nose.

I may have broken it.

I may also have broken my hand.

It's a toss-up which of us is in the most pain.

He's dragging himself to his feet. Wiping some of the blood from his face with his sleeve.

'Right. Now that's over with, I'll open the whiskey,' he's saying.

'Don't bother.' I decide to come straight to the point. 'In the habit of fucking your friends' wives, are you?'

'It was never easy for me, Andy. You mustn't think that. No. You were my friend. A good friend.'

I've hit him a second time. Now I know his nose is broken.

'I never want to see your face again, Connor,' I tell him, as he picks himself off the floor once more. He staggers to a chair and slumps into it.

'You won't. I'll be gone in a fortnight. I'm moving the business to England. I've bought premises and a new house there. That's where I've been these last weeks. I can place the sale of things here in the hands of others. Sure, everything's done by fax and computers today. It doesn't really matter where you live.'

'Why, Connor? Were you following your dick?'

'No, Andy. I'd never have got involved just for the sex. I only wish it hadn't been Gina I fell for. I suppose, in many ways, she reminded me of my own wife. Before the accident. Before I lost her.'

'Oh, please, Connor! It's a bit late in the bloody day to go for sympathy. You lost your wife so that gave you a right to fuck mine, did it?'

'No, of course not. She was just . . . so unhappy, Andy. I started out wanting to help her, as a friend. Put the smile back on her face, make her feel good about herself again. Then I fell in love with Gina, Andy. That, I think you will believe. The house in England? It was to be for the two of us, you see. That was my fruitless ambition. She's a special woman.'

'I know.'

'Being married to one such as she, now, well, that brings its own set of problems, so it does.'

I've opened his front door. He follows me to it, cradling his nose.

'Gina was never really prepared to risk losing you. She's hurt you, Andy, but forgive her. I took advantage of her at a time when she was very vulnerable. And I've hurt you. I'm sorry. Then again, I've paid a heavy price for doing that, I'm assuring you.'

'No less than you deserved.'

'I know.'

'I'd get that nose looked at if I were you.'

I've slammed the door shut behind me.

I chose not to say goodbye.

I need some air.

A chance to think.

Duneen beach, the little cove, remember?

It's bloody freezing. The gusts of wind I'm swallowing are virtually ripping my lungs apart. The rain is splaying across my face as if I was in a gigantic communal shower.

I feel better, though.

My head is clearer. My body becalmed.

I feel cleansed.

Now. What was that about shopping?

I've come home.

I've just walked into the lounge and my family are all here. Nicola is sitting on the floor, playing with an electronic cube with touch-sensitive controls. It says, 'Smile, baby,' and 'I love you, baby,' in a cheery computerised voice. She's really too old for it now.

Sophie and Gina are watching television.

'I'm home. Present for you, Stinks.'

'A Thomas the Tank Engine mag. Thanks, Dad.'

'You're welcome, poppet.'

'Here's yours, fatty.'

I've handed Nicola a squeaky toy. She has dropped the cube and put the toy straight in her mouth.

'Don't I get a prezzie?' Gina's asking.

'Mind the baby for two minutes, could you, Sophie?'

'Oh . . . okay.'

I've dragged Gina into the kitchen.

'What's all this about?'

'There you are, then. That's for you.'

It's a jewellery box.

She's unwrapped it.

Inside is a gold bracelet, antique. I hope she likes it because I've just sent us into an overdraft situation to pay for it.

She's smiling. 'It's beautiful, Andy.'

'You're lucky it's not a chastity belt and a set of manacles. I've just been to see Connor.'

'Oh.' The colour has drained from her face.

'Did you know he was back?'

She's shaking her head.

'But you *do* know he's going to England?'

'I – wasn't sure . . .'

'If he'd still go, alone?'

'Yes.'

'Well, he is. Are you going with him?'

'NO!'

'Do you love him, Gina?'

'No! Andy, I love you. Honestly I do.'

She's crying.

Big breath, Andy.

'Don't ever do that to me again. Please, Gina.'

'Never. Did you hurt him, Andy?'

'I think he was the one who hurt me, wasn't he? Don't worry, he'll live.'

I'm hiding my swollen hand behind my back.

'Are you okay?' she asks.

'Yeah. I'm okay. It's over. Finished with. I never want it mentioned again. Understand? It's you and me and the children from here on in. You and me, Gina. Always.'

She's crossed to me and she's in my arms.

With luck, that's where she'll stay.

24

It's Saturday, 13 May 1997.

Things have been good. There are problems, of course, money, chiefly. As always.

Gina's still at the magazine, we couldn't afford her not to be, but there are a few more staff on board now so the workload isn't so bad. No more late-night crises, fictional or real.

It's been bloody difficult trying to prepare for this competition and look after my gruesome twosome.

Today is the big day!

We're at the Point in Dublin for the final of the Eurovision Song Contest.

When I say we, I mean Mix and Match, Belly O'Hea, Gina, Sophie and even little Nicola.

Noreen, she whom we never really wanted to let go all those months ago, has been roped in to come and help look after the two children whilst we're in Dublin. It wasn't difficult to persuade her.

Everybody is staying at Jury's Hotel in Ballsbridge. We have two rooms next to each other. Gina and I in one, Noreen stuck with the brood in the other. That's the theory, anyway. We'll see how it pans out.

We've already filmed our little tourist-information slot. They call them 'Postcards'. You know, the naff sequences that supposedly introduce the band and the composer but are really one big advert for the host country.

We filmed it around Ballinkilty.

It has taken us to megastardom in our home town. The local townspeople are ecstatic. The local businesses are awash with gratitude.

I'm glad. The place has given quite a bit to me since I've lived here. It's nice to give a little back.

The BBC cottoned on to the fact that an Englishman had written the Irish entry and they sent a film crew across. A short piece for Wogan's Euro preview. Manna from heaven, as far as I was concerned. I was able to talk about myself and my career. Allowed to play several snatches of songs I'm considerably more proud of. To sing and play and generally show off.

So that was nice.

The band and I have been here in Dublin for over a week. It's been wild.

We were met at the airport by our guide, a woman called Mary West, who has basically organised and looked after us all week. There was a welcoming reception in the Royal Hospital, Kilmainham. I don't mean we were drinking and boogieing in Intensive Care: it's now a prestigious conference and banqueting centre. Very posh.

Then what they call 'The Euroclub' moves to different venues around Dublin each night. A variety of meals and piss-ups, culminating in a midnight cabaret on Thursday with Linda Martin, whose special guest was . . . you guessed it, JOHNNY LOGAN!

We even had a line-dancing class, which was a complete hoot. People from all over Europe falling over each other's feet and giggling and cursing in a variety of different languages.

We had a twenty-five-minute rehearsal on Monday. I worked hard with the orchestra and conductor, supplied kindly by RTE, and together we've beefed up the arrangement for the song and drafted in a few specialised Irish musicians to play some of the more indigenous instruments.

For such a crap song, it's sounding pretty good.

After the rehearsal we were taken to the 'review and replay area'. Here you can watch on tape the rehearsal that's just taken place. It's a good idea, and a big help in making last-minute adjustments.

There were two dress rehearsals yesterday, afternoon and evening, the latter in front of an invited audience and recorded as a production standby.

Right now, it's Saturday afternoon and the family are all in the auditorium watching the *final* dress rehearsal before the big event. Very serious. There's even a dummy vote at the end.

I wonder who'll win that.

Mix and Match are a bag of nerves. Bridget is closer to the panic-stricken girl of the midnight visit. There's a lot of talent and an array of female totty around and I think she feels less secure. Even Michael has been seen to sweat.

Competition. That's what I hate about all this. It's sort of false. I mean, songwriting is not exactly an Olympic event.

Still, I suppose you get heard, and three hundred million individuals will certainly hear my shitty song tonight.

I've sat down next to Sophie.

'Dad?'

'Yes, daughter?'

'This is boring, isn't it?'

'Do you think so?'

She's nodding.

'I think it's a bit crap, isn't it, Daddy?'

I'm laughing.

Out of the mouths of babes . . .

'Shall we go back to the hotel and have a drink in the bar with the waterfall, Dad?'

'Soon, Sophie. Soon.'

Mix and Match are on stage now.

This is the last time they play before . . .

8.10 p.m.

It's finally here. We've kicked off.

I'm backstage with the band, watching the opening on one of the many monitors strewn around the room. We've already seen the female presenter and a sickeningly good-looking Irish pop star making all the introductions. The first song is about to be performed.

We're in the green room, a large backstage area filled with circular tables.

Everyone is ready. As ready as they'll ever be.

Makeup is applied, voices are warmed, any alcoholic or illegal substances that were necessary to still the monster nerves that are so large as to be almost tangible have been consumed.

Now we wait. A considerable time, as a matter of fact.

The draw was not especially favourable, but not disastrous. Mix and Match go on about half-way through the running order. Not as beneficial as going on last out of the zillion-and-one entries, one feels, but at least we haven't had to open the ruddy show. That honour has befallen the Greeks, and bloody good luck to them, too.

Their entry would have pleased my mother, were she here. 'Zorba's Dance' on acid.

It's just finished, actually.

'That was a funny song, wasn't it, Daddy? Funny little dance they did as well. I don't think that will win, do you, Daddy?'

'Sssh, Sophie. Keep your voice down.'

'Why?'

'Because all these people in the room with us are in the competition. I've explained that to you.'

'Can't I say what I think, then, Dad?'

'Sssh! Yes, of course you can. But you'll have to whisper in my ear. It'll be our secret. Just you and me. We'll tell each other what we think after each song. But we won't speak too loudly. Then nobody will hear us and we won't upset anyone.'

'All right, Daddy.'

She's putting her mouth next to my ear.

'THAT WAS RUBBISH, WASN'T IT, DADDY?' she's shouted.

'Yes, Sophie,' I'm whispering, as I laugh.

I had to fight to bring Sophie in here with me. It's against the rules. Only those directly involved, musicians, composers, et cetera. Poor old Gina is having to watch from the auditorium with Belly O'Hea for company.

But Sophie wanted to come and ... who am I kidding?

I wanted her here.

To keep me sane.

These little films shown between songs really are the living end.

Swiss bimbettes are taken fishing for mackerel, an Italian stallion is forced to drink Guinness after a trip to the brewery. His speech, in Italian, said it was nectar, such a surprise, the drink of the gods, while his face and stomach were clearly trying to determine who was trying to poison him.

The best 'Postcard' so far?

The French girl, Françoise.

Everything about her screams sophistication: her voice, her face, her body, her dress sense, her demeanour. A class act, sex on legs. So, what do they do with her?

She's French, right?

Bon appétit!

They give her a touch of Irish culinary expertise. Boiled bacon, cabbage and potatoes.

Magic!

There was a wonderful moment when they served her this dish. They slap this slop down in front of her, the smell of salt and cabbage assaulting her cute little nose, which visibly wrinkled in displeasure. She tasted it and grimaced. Covering her hand with her mouth to be spared the embarrassment of spitting it out on camera.

Got to admire her, though. At least she didn't pretend it was delicious, in the name of *détente* – or votes.

I've just watched her song and it was good. The audience loved her.

She's just entered the room and is receiving congratulations from fellow performers as she makes her way to the table allocated to the French.

I'm standing up as she's passing. I'm offering my congratulations. She's saying thank you in French. She has a gloriously deep husky voice and has bent down to talk to Sophie, tickling my daughter's chin as she does so. I'm trying not to look down the front of her dress but it is requiring extraordinary will-power.

She's waving goodbye.

'That lady talks funny, doesn't she, Daddy?'

'Sounded pretty good to me, Sophie.'

'Is she Irish, Dad?'

'French.'

'Is that in South America?'

'What? Don't they teach you geography at playschool?'

'Dad?'

She's beckoning me.

It's time for her verdict.

'I THINK THAT WAS PRETTY COOL, DON'T YOU, DAD?'

My ear is ringing.

I just nod in agreement.

Music should be about notes. As in crotchets and quavers and dotted minims. In other words, in a competition like this, probably melody should be all. Having said that, am I the only one who switches off when a song is sung in Croatian, or Hebrew or Dutch?

Doesn't everybody get up and put the kettle on when someone is warbling in a language you cannot comprehend?

Unless it's being sung by a swarthy, good-looking hunk of a man, or a girl in the briefest of skirts, of course.

How does that affect the voting, I wonder.

We shall see.

They're on, Mix and Match.

I'm cuddling Sophie. She's riveted.

Here goes nothing.

Shit, I feel sick.

I'm disappointed.

They were okay, don't get me wrong, but they've been better.

They weren't as tight musically as they have been, as they were this afternoon. They were scared and the harmonies were a bit off, Bridget's voice a little strained.

These days, so I'm given to understand, the voting panels around Europe are given tapes of all the songs to listen to a little while in advance of the competition. So tonight isn't the be-all and end-all. They will have heard the song before. Which, in our case now, is probably just as well.

Damn!

Oh, well, fuck it! It doesn't matter. We've come this far.

'What did you think, Sophie?'

She's holding on to my ear now. 'I THINK WE WAS PRETTY GOOD, DAD.'

'Really?'

'Yep.'

Oh, well, maybe it wasn't as bad as I thought.

The band have just shuffled back to our table. I have champagne for all.

'Well bloody done! Everyone grab a glass. I thank you. Sophie and I thank you, Ireland thanks you. Everybody did really well. Now, have a few drinks and relax. There's nothing to do now but panic and you might as well be comfortable whilst you do it.'

Hugs all round, Michael included.

'Did it really sound okay, Andy?' Bridget's asking.

'Yes. Absolutely. Would I lie to you?'

Bridget's beaming.

'Well, let's hope we have all the luck, then. Cheers.'

I don't think we have a prayer.

They're about to vote.

For real this time. We won the dummy vote this afternoon. No surprises there. Everyone voted for the host nation out of courtesy.

In the interval an attempt has been made to top Riverdance. I couldn't tell you whether it was good or bad. I was unable to concentrate.

They're calling up the first jury now.

Greece, I think.

Sophie, who has been bored out of her box ever since Mix and Match finished playing, has fallen asleep across two chairs.

Bless her.

She tried to stay awake for the voting – 'That's the exciting bit, isn't it, Daddy?' – but she didn't quite make it.

We've got a six. Not a winning start, but not bad.

At least we won't have the embarrassment of a duck.

The French girl got a whopping ten.

Clearly a male-dominated jury, the Greek panel.

About ten countries have voted.

We've had two tens and a few mid-scores.

The French appear to be romping home at the moment.

Cyprus and Greece have given each other top marks, surprise, surprise. Neither voted for Turkey. The politics involved is unbelievable.

Betcha Turkey gives those two countries zip in return.

YES! YES! YES!

We've just been given our first maximum score. Twelve lovely points from the Swedish jury.

When you get a maximum vote the camera pans your table. Bridget actually just gave a thumbs-up sign.

How bloody naff!

I mean, everyone does that, or waves, or mouths, 'Hello, Mum' – I can't believe someone I know did it.

I've warned everyone that if we get another maximum twelve I'm going to moon.

Ireland have just given the United Kingdom *twelve* points.

I cannot believe it. How bloody ironical. Ireland never give the English any points!

Okay, I confess, I may have watched this a few times. You know, when I've come home from the pub. In fact, when I first arrived in Ireland it was about this time of year. I remember joking about this with someone. Can't remember who . . . yes, I can, it was Michael. I can hear myself saying how annoyed I was that every year, without fail, we'd traditionally give Ireland ten or twelve points and in return the Irish jury gave us bugger-all. 'That's because your songs are crap,' I think he said. 'That's beside the bloody point,' I replied. 'Since when has the voting in the Eurovision Song Contest had anything to do with the songs?'

Judging by what I'm witnessing tonight, I had a point there.

A maximum score has brought the UK right into the reckoning. They're in second place now. It's a good song, I agree. Performed by a band who've been out of the limelight for a few years, a girl singer with a great voice.

I'm superstitiously reticent to mention this, but we're third. Eight points off the lead.

The French are still in front.

I'm getting caught up in all this and I hate myself for it.

It's bloody exciting, though!

We've just scored another maximum.

THANK YOU, NORWAY!

Wonderful country. Won't have a word said against it.

A second little moment to cherish.

The camera panned on to the sleeping Sophie, looking angelic.

Some joke made by the compères out front, I think. I wish I could see into the auditorium, just for Gina's reaction.

Turkey have just voted.

Sod all for Greece and Cyprus. Tit for tat, as they say.

Worse still, they only gave us two points. We've slipped back a bit. But there's still time.

The English have just given us four points!! I ask you! Can you believe it? Four measly, stingy points. The miserable buggers! Now I know why I left. You just can't rely on the Brits any more. Win or lose, I'm going to get shit about this when I'm next in O'Leary's.

Michael's just given me a wry smile. We raised our champagne glasses and smiled until the cameras were off us.

Sophie's woken up.

Probably because of me leaping up and down, shaking my fist and shouting expletives. It got me a few frosty looks from round about as well.

I think some people thought it was not in keeping with the spirit of the competition.

There's just one vote to go and . . .

We're leading!!

My heart is pounding, my blood is racing, my nerves are in sodding tatters.

The French have just had four zeros in a row and it led to a bit of a charge from behind. By my calculations, even allowing for the fact that my grasp of maths is elementary in the extreme, I think we would have to be given less than five points for anyone to catch us. If that happened, then any one of the three or four countries behind us could win.

One vote.

They've gone to the last jury now. I'm hanging on to poor Sophie for dear life. She can't move, poor love. If she does, I might fall over.

One vote.

It'll take three minutes and feel like thirty years.

One point to . . . Bosnia Herzogovina!

For crying out loud, who can remember that song? The jury foreman just wanted to prove he could pronounce it, surely?

Four points to Germany, well, there's proof there's no accounting for taste.

Five to France, looked a winner earlier on – obviously fewer red-blooded males dominating the last juries.

We can't get less than five now.

Six to . . .

Oh, *fuck*!

I can't listen. I can't watch.

I've put my head in my hands.

'Are you all right, Daddy?'

271

'Yes,' I'm reassuring her, if in somewhat muffled tones.

Seven to . . .

I can't believe it.

It's incredible!

Too fantastic to believe.

A duck. A blank, balls-all, zero, zilch, nixie, strike, a big fat nothing!

Who did that? Which jury was it? What bastard gave us nothing?

And you want to know something worse?

The English have won it.

The fucking English!

Can you believe it?

The fucking English have won!

The same joker that gave us nothing gave them twelve.

We've come second, for what it's worth. Which is sod all.

The last jury seemed dedicated to voting for all the lame ducks, with the exception of the fucking English!

Katrina and the Waves.

It's a decent song, fair enough. Well, you have to give the Brits credit. They've been entering the same song for fifteen years or so, since Bucks Fizz won it and the first year they abandon that policy they bloody pull it off.

Can you imagine the reaction!

The Irish entry written by an Englishman loses to his native country.

First Irish entry to lose for donkey's years.

Oh, the bloody shame!

Why couldn't Switzerland have won it?

Bridget is in floods of tears and I don't blame her. We were so fucking close. Michael's hugging her.

'We didn't win, did we, Daddy?'

Sophie's standing in front of me. The look of disappointment on her little face is ten times more painful than losing.

'No, darling, we didn't.'

'Doesn't matter, really, does it, Dad?'

'No.' I'm giving her a cuddle.

It does matter, a lot.

Who remembers who came second in the Eurovision Song Contest? No one rushes a contract under the nose of the runners-up.